COME, THE DARK

The Forever Girl Series Book Two

REBECCA HAMILTON

EVERSCORCH

TRIGGER WARNING

This novel contains strong language, violence, implied incestuous sexual abuse, and scenes that some readers may find disturbing. Intended for mature audiences only. Reader discretion advised. Cordovae's Journey is not intended to indicate the experience of all sexual abuse survivors. If you or someone you know is a victim of sexual abuse, please call the National Sexual Abuse Hotline (1-800-656-HOPE) for support.

CHAPTER 1
AUGUST 1961

NOBODY WANTS TO TALK ABOUT WHAT PA DID TO ME.

Especially not Mama.

We sway on the porch swing, drinking her sun-brewed Tetley iced tea sweetened with cane sugar and chilled with ice from our cracked freezer tray. During our chats, her gaze flits around, never settling on anything for much too long. Especially not my belly. She must not like shutting her eyes, either, as there are always dark circles under them. Maybe the Darkness won't let her sleep anymore.

Does she see those shadow men the same as I do, or have they become a part of her?

"Nice day today," she says.

The words mean to fill the air between us.

Life has stood still since the Darkness came, as though time itself were as lazy as the summer days are long. I watch over the muted and pale sky, the dirt roads and faded grass. Forever in the sun, the dusty, bluish-white paint peels away from the decaying boards of our porch, and the muggy air, dead of a breeze, makes my skin itch.

The weather's just another pressure in my life, suffocating me, and the swell of my uterus against my lungs isn't helping.

If I had a friend to confide in, they might say I should give the baby up, that the baby would be a reminder of all Pa has done. And maybe they would be right. But once upon a time, Mama told me *all* babies are a blessing, and I could use a blessing.

Mama tucks a grayish blonde strand of hair into her sunhat. It's not fancy. Just something she wears to hide her unkempt hair.

"Georgia summer," she says, all breathless-like. "That's why I like it here. I like these Georgia summers."

I do *not* like Georgia summers. They smell like animal piss and wet concrete cooking in the sun. But it's not just the summers. I don't like anything about Georgia. Georgia is a black hole—the home of the Darkness. Home of the shadows that scurry in my periphery. Only the edge of my vision catches the figures gliding past, but they are gone the moment I turn to look.

They are here now, too. Always. Ever since that car accident my Pa and I should have died in all those years ago.

I glimpse a shadow at our window, but when I turn my head, there's nothing there. Nothing but the blinds moving lightly. Another shadow crouches behind Mama's rose bushes on the other side of the porch rails. This shadow-man crowds the edges of my vision, watching me. If I look straight at him, he'll be gone, so instead I watch from the corners of my eyes. Not afraid anymore. Only aware.

When I tire of being stared at, I glance over. All that's there are Mama's strawberry plants, about to be overcome by the vines crawling along our porch, and a few dragonflies humming as they mate in the air above. A praying mantis feasts on a butterfly's cocoon attached to one of the porch spindles beside where an old rope loops around one of the rail posts. In the crawlspace below, animal traps snuff out small and innocent creatures. Sometimes I hear them scratching to get free.

Scratch, scratch, scratch.

Silence.

I wonder if Mama can see my overripe stomach from the

corners of her vision the same as I see the shadow men. If she looked, would it all go away?

It's probably too late for Mama to look now.

As I sip my tea, Mama talks about the cloudless day. But it's not really a cloudless day. If Mama would glance to the horizon, she would see the coal black storm clouds rolling in, casting our sunny day in a dreariness more fitting for our lives.

But clouds are something nice to talk about. Better than talking about the swell of my stomach, or the way even my face and ankles have gotten plump. 'Still a skinny little thing,' Mrs. Kelly says, when she passes our porch on her morning rounds. 'It's in your bones.'

She probably thinks I'm an easy girl, got knocked up six months before my eighteenth birthday in the bed of some young man's pickup truck. No one's going to tell her otherwise. But we can't just ignore what's coming. Today has been a constant reminder, my abdomen so swollen that it crushes my stomach, quelling my appetite completely. Off and on, sharp pains have been stiffening all around my midsection and cramping in my back.

I take a sip of my sweet tea, even though I'm not a bit thirsty, and twist a small emerald birthstone ring on my finger. My swelling has made it fit too snug to remove.

"When the baby—" I start, but Mama's mouth smiles in a silencing way.

She keeps touching her face, the way she always does when she's anxious. So much so that, lately, sores have appeared along her jaw. It's as though she's in there, somewhere, still a mother enough to worry—but part of her mind and soul have been taken. As if her body isn't her own anymore.

I know how she feels.

I close my eyes, wishing myself away from here. One day it will be just me and my baby, Anna. A better life, one day soon. God, please let it be one day soon.

Mama chews at the scabs on her lips and nods to the hills across the street, to the waves of wheatgrass seeded with wildflowers. Closer to the road, poppies grow in bright clusters that make the roadside more vibrant, even in the dull light of our cloudy day.

"You used to play in those fields," Mama says.

I don't say anything. Mama doesn't mind if I'm quiet. I just have to nod along as she tells her stories, as she lives in the past, talking about how Pa used to take me to the carnival and how Pa used to braid my hair and how Pa used to take me to see the horses. I think it makes her feel better.

I'm old enough to know I should be angry with her. Old enough to think she could've stopped him. But I'm not mad, and I don't blame her. It was the Darkness that did this to our family. They took Pa when I was twelve. Made him different, first with his unnerving stares and discomforting touches. Then something more. The Darkness blinded Mama, or trapped her somehow. But the Darkness never took me.

Well, not directly.

Mama and I sip from our glasses and pick at last night's crumbling cornbread until the late afternoon light reddens the porch. A lot of days, when we're sitting out here, she knits, but never anything useful. It's just to keep her hands busy, pearling together doilies or another pair of oven mitts. She has a lot of those.

After much sitting and sipping and pointless conversation, Pa comes home. Mama's smile falls away, and she gets quiet and carries the pitcher of tea inside. I follow her, catching my balance on the doorframe as I step over the threshold into the house. The floorboards seem more uneven today, and queasiness tumbles through me.

Shaky from heat and discomfort, I head to the bathroom to run a tepid bath. The shush of the water is soothing. I lock the door and sit on the bathroom rug, leaning back against the wall. I won't miss this place. When Anna comes, I'll take her away from here. I'll need to get my own pitcher for tea, and some clothes for her, and some diapers and pins. And of course a real crib, not that box I've set up in my room.

At any rate, we'll make do. I'll give her a childhood where fairytales can happen in our backyard. All little girls like fairytales. Even me. And I know I'm having a girl, for sure, because I'm carrying high and craving sweets, and Mrs. Kelly says that's why I look such a mess.

I'll take Anna north to Seaside, with the cookie-cutter cottages right on the beach. Nobody will look for me in Jersey. Jersey is so...unromantic. The kind of place people go only because they have to visit family or take a job. It's exactly what I need.

Exactly what Pa is never going to let happen.

❧

I RAN AWAY ONCE. SNUCK OUT OF THE HOUSE LATE AT NIGHT with a sack of clothes, my old shoes separating at the sole and then smacking back together again with each step. I had on me only what little money I had stolen from Pa's jar in the kitchen. I was going to get away to where he couldn't hurt me—to where the Darkness couldn't make him do things to me.

My bike took me two towns over before the cops picked me up. If not for them, I would have gotten away. I begged them not to return me home; I pleaded, I told them everything. Everything —the things I could bring myself to say and the things I hoped implied what I couldn't.

The cops' mouth tumbled out all the words Pa promised they would:

"We hear this from your type all the time. Kids blaming their parents. You oughtta watch making such claims about your own Pa."

"Learn some responsibility, young lady. Can't go around making up stories to get out of trouble."

Pa had spent years painting me as a problem child, and it worked.

I couldn't shake the reality away. Soon I was home, my Pa apologizing to the officers for all the wrong things. Apologizing on my behalf, as if I was the one who done wrong. Same way he'd convinced the school my missed days were from my playing hooky. As though *I* chose to stay home. As if he weren't keeping me there to hide the bruises.

That night, I lay awake in bed, trying to think up a new way to escape.

The next morning, Pa drug Mama in my room by her hair. Pa had never hurt Mama before, but that day he blocked my doorway and pounded on her until her eyes were black and her mouth bled.

Then he said it: the words that changed everything.

"If you leave, I'll kill her."

It wasn't until Pa knocked me up that I decided I could live with that.

The whole world had already betrayed me. Every single one, except for this baby that never asked to be part of any of it. I was done helping others. Now I was going to focus on Anna and myself. Stop caring what people think. What did I have to lose? The only thing left now was my humanity—and what was the point of having humanity in a world with none?

Yes, I could leave if it meant Pa would never have the chance to hurt my baby, my Anna. Above all else, I was responsible for her. Nothing else mattered anymore. Not even Mama.

I used to think everyone had a right to freedom over their own body. Now I realize that's something you have to fight for. Because if you don't take control over your body, someone else will, and taking ownership back will come with a cost. Perhaps the cost will be Mama's life.

But leaving is my only hope. Since pregnancy has not left me well fit to travel, here I am, waiting for Anna to come so we can escape together. I might not have the money, but I'll find a way. I'll hike down to the train station and go wherever. Anywhere is better than here.

And now that I'm an adult, the cops can't stop me.

I'M TOSSING AND TURNING ON A LUMPY MATTRESS WHEN MY water breaks. I still myself. This can't happen now. Not tonight, not while Pa is home. I'll never be able to get away with the baby then.

The moonlight looks bluish on my walls as I lie here, staring at the paisley wallpaper that's curling away from a fist-sized hole. It was pretty once, cream-colored and soft blues and greens and yellows and pinks. The night is mostly quiet, just the hum of my fan and leaves that rustle outside my window like a hissing rattlesnake.

My eyes sting from lack of sleep, and the room feels impossibly humid. My hair is so damp from sweat that it has darkened to the color of blood against my cream pillowcase. The electric fan on my dresser does little more than push a musky odor around the room.

It seems like ages ago that I found out I was pregnant. Ages since Pa's doctor-friend told us that, if we scraped the funds together, he could scrape the evidence of Pa's abuse from my womb. Rid me of his baby and . . .

My baby.

It was that last part I couldn't move past.

Undoing situations like these...it was legal now. But legal didn't make it right, didn't stop those flutters begging me not to blame Anna for how she came to be.

I didn't care one lick if she was conceived out of abuse; she would be born out of love. She was mine now. Entirely, completely, utterly mine. If Pa wanted her gone, he would damn well have to kill me, and I told him as much. For months, I even thought he might.

I kick off my threadbare quilt, and there's another rush of warm fluid pooling on my sheets beneath me. I want to crawl out of my own skin, away from my body, but I don't move.

Please don't let this be my water broken now. I would rather that I've just pissed myself. If Anna can wait until morning, wait until Pa leaves for work, everything will be okay.

The shadow men whip past my bedroom window, crouch in the corners of my room, hover near the ceiling, outside my window, and in the hall outside my door. They scurry away each time I look, each time I try to catch them in my sights.

Usually I ignore them, but I don't want them here anymore than I want Pa here. I keep looking at them, hoping to make them disappear, but tonight they do not leave. They move, they move, they move, but still they remain, crowding me in darkness.

Somewhere in the distance, glass breaks, and part of me wonders if it's them—if the Darkness can touch things now.

I shift between sleep and consciousness. I keep falling into that place in my mind, the place I always hide when Pa comes into my room. I couldn't let him kill what's left of my soul; I had to escape in some way, save some part of me, the part of me I call Cordovae. Now here, in this place I can only dream of, I spread my arms and lift my head and twirl around, untouched, unharmed. It's my prison and my protection, where only those who know my heart can reach me.

I'm safe here.

But then the pains begin, ripping me from that world. Bringing me back to the unfortunate life I was born into. At first, I feel the way my stomach hardens, the way it squeezes around my little Anna. But as the night drifts deeper, the pain intensifies and spreads through my entire body.

I can't quiet my breathing. I close my eyes and try to envision the cramps disappearing, but I can't think straight. I hum the only lullaby I know, the one Pa always yells at me for humming.

"That ain't no damn song I ever heard," he always says.

But I know the song, and it's as familiar as the sun rising.

The pain shakes my body, and I let out a long, low groan. I don't want to make any noise. I try using a painting I've made for Anna as a focal point. I'd mixed the juice of winterberries with glue and painted the mixture over leaves on paper and pressed sticks and small pebbles into the blue and red and purple swirls, until I'd created our future—a dream of a cottage in the woods where no one would ever find us.

My efforts to embrace a mental escape are crushed as the pains overlap and a pressure builds. I grit my teeth, but another groan forces its way past my lips.

Footsteps rush through the hall. A light flicks on, yellow and brassy, illuminating my bare room in a way that makes it feel colder. Ma's standing here now, her expression fallen. She hurries to my side and holds my hand. I wish she would stop running her fingers through her hair. It makes me nervous.

"Oh, God, Rose. I'm sorry. It's going to be okay, baby, Mama's here now."

I don't respond. Pa stands in the doorway, still dressed in the dark denim pants he put on after his shift at the farm. Sleep marks carve the left cheek of his face, and his short black hair sticks up on one side. My heart skips to near racing. It's so loud in my ears I swear Pa can hear, too.

"Evelyn," he says coolly. "Get the rum and a glass of water."

She keeps staring at me, swallowing, looking at least a decade older than her forty-three years. In this light, her nose looks especially crooked from all the times it's been broken. But my Pa didn't do that to her—no, her own Pa was to blame for that.

She swallows again, and now I'm feeling the urge to swallow, too, but my mouth and throat are too dry. It takes me a moment, but I realize why she's still standing there. She's wants to protect me.

Little late for that.

Pa snaps his dark face toward her. "Go!"

Mama startles, and I startle, too. Everyone startles when Pa yells because his eyes get bigger and darker and his face gets pinker. As Mama darts from the room, my skin gets all shivery.

I close my eyes and wish Mama was back, but when I open them, it's still just Pa and me. I'm shaking so much it makes the pale, painted-yellow headboard of my bed rattle against the wall.

Two of the Dark Ones step closer to Pa. Step right into my direct line of sight. Dark, faceless figures.

I gasp. I've never seen them so directly. But before I can react any further, another contraction crests, wracking my body with a new wave of pain.

A coolness caresses my forehead. "Breathe."

The voice has come from behind me. One of the Darkness. They have never spoken to me before. Why do they care about me now, after having caused me so much pain? Why whisper words of comfort tonight?

Pa steps toward me, but they grab his arms, pinning him in place. He doesn't seem to see them. No one sees them but me.

Pa's brow furrows, and he shakes his head. "Where's your damn Ma?" he asks. He's been drinking, and his whiskey-breath fills the room. "Evelyn!"

Moments later, Mama rushes in with the rum and water. She's also brought fresh towels, which she drops by the end of the bed.

"Is everything okay?" she asks Pa. "You're going to help her, aren't you? You said you'd—"

"No," he says, his face pale. The bead of sweat above his lip trembles. "You deliver the baby."

"Me?" She glances over to me. "I've never—but you—you've delivered some of your siblings…"

Pa came from a family of nine kids, and his Mama didn't believe in hospitals. Not even when some of her babies caught cholera, not even after she lost a few to cot death. So Pa could do this, as Mama says, but I don't want him to. I don't want him to *ever* touch Anna.

"You created this mess," Mama says with a forcefulness that is new and awkward. "You deliver the baby."

Pa turns away. Leaves. The pressure overwhelms my body. I just need to get to a hospital, but I don't think there's time for that now.

"I need to push, Mama."

Mama rushes to my bedside and holds the water to my lips.

She's trembling. Water splashes onto my chin, but I shake my head. My mouth's dry, but even the idea of drinking sounds painful.

"Now," I say. "The baby's coming now."

She sets the glass on the nightstand. "I can't," she says. She backs away, tears filling her eyes. "I—I'm sorry, Rose. I can't."

"You can't leave me!"

She shakes her head and keeps backing away until she reaches the door, tears spilling down her bony cheeks. Then she turns, and all that is left of her is the clomp of her footsteps hurrying down the hall. Hurrying away.

A door shuts. A lock clicks. Mama's shut down again, the way she always does when things are just 'too much to take'.

I shouldn't care. I hadn't wanted them here. But now I'm terrified. I don't know how to—

I grit my teeth against another contraction and cry to myself. Pain rips through me. I must be dying. My body trembles through every limb, and nausea quakes my stomach. I try to get out of bed. Maybe there's still enough time to get to a hospital. I'll take the keys to Pa's truck from the hook by the door and—

Another wave of pain slams through, and I lean back into the bed. The pain is like a fire slicing me in half, and the contractions are right on top of each other now, barely giving me a moment to breathe or even think.

I'm not going anywhere. I can't even get back on the bed. Everything is happening too fast and, at the same time, the pain seems to stretch on for eternity. I just want to have my baby safely —have her and get her far away from this place.

"Mama!" I holler. "Please, Mama!"

Sobs echo from the other room, and I realize I'm crying, too. It's just me now. Me and the Darkness and my baby, my Anna, coming into the horrifying world that doesn't deserve her.

CHAPTER 2

AUGUST OF 1961 TO DECEMBER OF 1691

THAT FIRST MOMENT I SEE HER, MY HEART FREEZES IN MY CHEST. I suck in a quiet breath. The world around me grows still. There is only her.

She looks nothing like Pa. Not her tiny toes, not her delicate wisps of hair. She really *is* all mine, and soon we will be away from this awful place, just her and I.

God, she's beautiful. I guess everyone thinks that about their baby. I purse my lips, considering whether Pa's mama looked down on Pa with this same unconditional love. Did she think he could do no wrong, that he was perfect in every way? If she were still alive today—if she only knew—learning Pa's secrets would kill her.

I should have killed him a long time ago, when he was passed out drunk. The world would be better without him. But I can't let my mind go there—can't let him ruin this moment. He's ruined enough.

I hold Anna to my chest, her cherub cheek pressed close to my beating heart. Her existence is healing. I just smile at her, at everything she does, at everything she isn't doing

I kiss her forehead and whisper, "Don't worry, my sweet Anna. We'll leave this place soon."

As I bathe her over a towel, using just a small sponge and a dish of water, I am awed at every perfect thing about her. Her tiny fingers, her chubby knees, her slender shoulders. And right there, on the back of her left shoulder, is a birthmark to match the one on my wrist—a pale brown misshapen heart.

I know now that heaven exists. It's right here in my arms. And as I watch her sleep, an indescribable feeling of love floods through me, and I know, instantly, that I will do anything to protect her.

❧

I BLINK MY EYES OPEN TO A USED-UP CANDLE AND A GRAY SKY. I shake the sleep from my head. Something's off. Had I fallen asleep while nursing Anna? I can sense her absence even before I check the bassinet I made from a box and old sheets.

I stumble back toward my bed and shuffle through my blood-stained sheets. She's not here.

Anna's not here.

Oh, God.

My heart stutters. How much time has passed? I had been in such a state. I don't even know what time I gave birth, just that it was in the middle of the night. It's past dawn now. I slept too long. Why didn't I wake up? Why didn't I notice that I slept too long without being woken by my baby?

I ignore the aches pulsing in my body and try to remember the last moment I saw her. I can envision the light in Anna's muddy blue eyes. I remember wondering if her eyes would one day be as green as mine. I swaddled her in one of my old shirts, wondering how much she would look like me and how much she would remind me of Pa once we escaped.

Then what? I needed rest to regain my strength. We were going to leave right after Pa left for the farm this morning. But now morning has come, and Anna's gone.

An anchor crashes into the pit of my stomach, and my mind

races. I stumble from my room and dart through the house. She isn't in my parent's room, the living room, the kitchen.

I can't breathe. My lungs hurt from the effort. Where is she? Where's my daughter?

I'm shaking and full of dread and I absolutely can't live if anything bad has happened to her. Please, God, let her be okay. Please!

My sluggish heartbeat turns to a pounding of adrenaline. I rush to the front of the house and burst onto the porch. The first thing I see is the dead raccoon that Pa left beside the house, now swarmed by flies. I spin toward where I know Mama will be sitting.

Beneath the long-ago burnt-out porch light—now a cemetery for moths—Mama sips at her tea. She's cozy, all wrapped in her cotton robe as though nothing is wrong. The glow of morning sun catches the reddish hues of her graying blonde hair.

"Where is she?" I ask, grasping the doorframe to keep my weak body balanced.

Mama jumps. Her tea splashes as she shakily lowers the cup to her lap. "Oh, Rose. Please don't do this."

"Don't do what?"

I'm met with silence. She shifts in the porch swing and lowers her gaze. Her face is all puffy, her eyes red.

I narrow my eyes. "Where's Anna? You know. I can tell you do."

Then I see it—that flash of a smile that is completely devoid of happiness. Her instinctual defense to hide whatever she is really feeling. But this time, even she can't hold that smile in place.

I've lived on the wrong side of secrets long enough to know when someone is hiding something. And that's exactly what Mama is doing.

I step closer, jabbing my finger in her face. "Tell me! I know you know where she is! What did you do to her?"

I'm shaking. My hands clench and my heart pounds in my ears.

Ma stands, the teacup tumbling from her lap. She fumbles for it, then lets it go. She paces, then sits again. Her hands flit around, from her face, to smooth her dress, twisting in her lap. She's coming undone, about to fall apart completely, and I don't care one bit.

"WHERE'S ANNA?"

"Your Pa loves us," she says finally, her words hidden behind her hand as she talks. "He's protecting your reputation."

"*His* reputation?" I say, incredulous.

She smiles weakly. "You'll understand one day."

I won't ever understand. Mama had been good to me once, but ever since the Darkness came, she's someone else. A woman stuck between denial and oblivion.

"Where's Anna?" I ask again, but already I have that sinking feeling in my stomach. The pain of the birth ebbs, replaced by a fresh rush of adrenaline.

"It's for the best." Mama pinches the bridge of her nose. "We can be a family again, the way we're supposed to be. Your Pa's learned his lesson. We all make mistakes, Rose. The Lord implores us to forgive."

Pa's truck crunches over the gravel driveway and starts down the road, tearing away from us. He must have her. I can't even think straight, can't think beyond the thought that my daughter *must* be okay. That she can't be hurt. That Pa can't take her away from me. I'm sick with panic and fearing the worst. I *can't* lose her.

The dusty blue truck kicks up dirt as Pa halts at the end of our road. He's on his way to hide the evidence of what he's done. He can't stand to look at her, to be reminded of the monster that lives inside of him. He already tried to convince me to give her up. I considered it, but only for the sake of protecting her from him. But it wasn't his decision. Anna was never his. She is a product of his abuse, of his drunkenness and Mama's cowardliness.

But she is still *my* child.

I need to get her before it's too late. Before he signs her over to someone who won't give her back.

So I run.

I run without looking back. I run without caring about the after-pains of birth or the possibility of bleeding out or the hot pavement cutting my feet. I run, my body numb, not feeling the ground beneath me. I don't care to know if Mama started after me or if she's stood to watch me flee, staring dumbfounded, or if she's still swaying in her swing, sipping tea, looking at the poppy fields. I don't care about anything anymore—only Anna.

As I run past Mrs. Kelly's she yells, "Where ya off to, Rose?"

She comes off her porch and onto the walk, staring at me with a furrowed brow. "Oh! You had your baby! Rose? Rose?"

She's behind me now, her voice echoing after me. I must look crazy, running like this so shortly after giving birth. But I don't care. No one in this town truly knows me. No one can help me. The only thing that matters right now is getting to Anna, and I don't dare hope anyone would help me with that. There's no time for hope right now.

Pa's truck careens a corner in the distance, and my legs are given a new direction. They carry me mindlessly down a forgotten stretch of pavement that cuts through the fields like an unnatural hairpin valley. Hills on the roadside crest and fall. The road turns to dirt, diverges into a forest.

I don't know which way Pa went, but I have to keep going or I'll lose her forever. If I keep going, there's a chance. There's a chance I can find Pa—find Anna. There's a chance I can save my baby.

I run through the woods, past dried up waterways and dandelion with no fluff. The shadow men rush beside me, and I run harder, the world a blur of tears and movement and shadows. My lungs burn from my effort, but the moist, earthly air sooths my throat and leaves the acrid taste of pine on my lips.

I hear a loud crack and dizziness swarms through my head, and I feel a slam to my core—a shift, a thrust—as though I've stumbled even though I haven't lost my footing. I'm starting to feel faint. My vision darkens, then brightens again.

I stop and look around. I've lost the dirt road that cuts through the forest. I can't smell the rubber of tires from the main road anymore or the piss-stink of Georgia. All I smell is soil, and the hot air has given way to a bitter cold that bites my skin.

The sun, bringing no warmth at all, filters through the rustling leaves of the canopy, creating a confetti of moving light over a snow-frosted ground.

Snow?

Unease creeps over every inch of my body. My sense of time is lost—it was an early summer morning just moments ago, but now I shiver beneath a mid-day winter sun.

What happened? Where am I?

The world spins as I try to look in every direction all at once, try to find where I came from, try to catch sight of Pa's pick-up truck and Anna before it's too late.

But I know I am not in Georgia anymore. I know this as surely as I know it's impossible for me to be anywhere else.

Ahead, the trees part to a clearing filled with rows of small cabins and horse-drawn carts toting cabbage, carrots, and beets. I sneak up, stopping just outside the small village. The people of the town wear drab, old-fashioned clothing. Some kind of Amish settlement?

A dark-skinned woman with her back to me, wearing both an apron and a shawl, gathers herbs from one of the vendors. Her attention dances around, and her face swings in my direction. I'm ready to call to her—Tituba!—but then I realize she's staring toward somewhere deeper in the forest. Her expression sags, and my heart breaks for her. Poor Tituba. My life hasn't been easy, but it would be worse to be the slave of Samuel Parris.

My mind throttles. Who is Samuel Parris? Or Tituba, for that matter? How do I know any of these things, any of these names? My consciousness tumbles around, as though fighting to cling to the reality I am trying to return to.

Where are the fields and the poppies and Pa's pick-up truck? Where's Anna?

There's a tap on my shoulder, and I gasp as I whip around. My head's spinning, and I'm about to fall over sideways, but I steady myself.

A petite woman holding a bundle of wood stares at me with wide, tea-colored eyes. She's wearing a long-sleeved tan dress with a dull green apron. A linen cap covers her long, mousy brown hair.

"Good Lord, Abigail," she says. "I was hoping it wasn't you out here."

"Excuse me?" My voice is shaky and doesn't sound entirely like my own. It's softer. My southern drawl is subdued, fading. This woman has confused me for another woman.

"Well, I couldn't be certain until I got a closer look, but here you are! Oh, poor dear. You look as though you've seen a ghost. What are you doing out in your nightdress?" Her gaze slides down my body. Her mouth falls open and her fingers touch her parted lips. "What happened to you?"

I look down. Small twigs and burrs have caught in my nightdress, and the ruffles are smudged with dirt. No, not my usual nightdress. It is the same cream color, but it's long sleeved and the material is thicker. Blood trickles down one of my pale legs. My feet are dirty and bleeding, but I feel nothing.

"Where am I?" I ask.

"Let's get you home before anyone sees you," the woman says. Her voice is nearly as musical as the water splashing over the mossy stones and roots of a nearby creek. "We'll get you cleaned up and something hot to eat."

"I can't." I attempt to wipe the tears from my face, but instead feel the gritty smear of dirt rubbing from my hands onto my cheeks. I look back toward where the road should be. "I need to find Anna."

"Anna?" A line forms between her eyebrows and she places her hand gently on my arm. "Abigail, we can't stand here like this. If anybody sees you..."

She's too late. A man has already stopped to stare. I narrow my eyes at him, and he shakes his head before continuing on.

I grab her by the shoulders. "I'm *not* Abigail. And I'm not from here. I—I don't know how I got here, but I was looking for my daughter and—"

Realizing how stiff she is in my grasp, I let her go. Her eyes are wide, but she doesn't move. "Oh, Abigail," she says. "Not again."

"I'm not Abigail."

"Really now, enough. Please," she says. Her tone is soothing, encouraging, as though she's trying to placate an injured animal. She's motherly, or the way I imagine a mother should be. "Come, let me make you one of my healing teas."

I step back, shaking my head. "Where are we?"

"Oh, for heaven's sake," the woman mumbles to herself. Then, louder, to me: "Salem Village, 1691. The same place you were when you went to bed last night, and the same place you will be when you wake tomorrow morning. Must we always do this? Now, come with me before you start to raise suspicions again."

"Again?"

"The town already thinks your mind's gone ill," the strange woman says. "But it could be worse, you know, with this talk of witchcraft flitting about."

I glance in every direction for the path that brought me here— looking for answers as though I'll find them in the dark bark of the decaying maple trees or hidden amongst the forest's daytime shadows. But all I see are the shadow men skipping out of sight every time I look where they're standing. I'm catching glimpses of them now, more than I've seen in a lifetime. Faces. Some sinister, some kind. Some confused, others afraid. I always assumed they were all evil. Is that not the case?

"I'm sorry," I say. "I have to...I have to..." My mind stumbles.

I remember two different yesterdays. The yesterday where my womb is full with my child and the yesterday where I am gathering wood with this woman. I look down at her basket once more, recognizing it now. I made that for her.

I know her.

"Verity?" I say, calling her by name, confirming what I know is impossible for me to know.

"Come," she says. "I'll fix you right up. You can tell me all about it."

I can't tell her anything—but I sense she knows this. Sense she understands that I prefer to keep to myself. Further, my memories are slipping away like water on silk. I remember running. I remember chasing Anna, but I can't remember why. I can remember that her skin was smooth and light, and that she held the scent of soap better than anyone else I ever knew.

Anna, my baby.

Verity hooks her elbow with mine and leads me out of the forest and through the town. Every step of the way she peeks around corners and hurries me past anyone that looks our way. I follow, not knowing where else to go and because I do not know who here I can trust but this woman. I don't even know how I know to trust her.

I feel an eternity away from home but, at the same time, I feel that this is exactly where I belong. As Verity leads the way, it's as though I know every turn she will make before it comes to pass.

Memories of this woman flood through me. Of us sitting fireside, knitting for winter. Had that been last winter or had it been just weeks ago? Confusion takes my hand like a long lost friend, and I sense this is not the first time my memory has bled out.

Soon we fall upon a cabin. Inside, everything is familiar: the tiny wooden table by the door, the simple wooden sitting chair by the small fireplace with a hanging metal pot, and the half melted taper candles in brass candleholders scattered about. The room's cluttered with bowls and half-woven wreaths and dried smears of clay.

I know the closed door leads to a bedroom with a cot near a window that overlooks the forest. There will be a spinning wheel with a treadle in the corner, though I cannot remember how to use one.

The room, when I enter it, is just as I 'remember', even as I do not understand how I have such a knowing of this place. This is my home.

Verity helps me sponge off as much as she can. I tell her I'll do the rest. Each time I dip the sponge into the wooden bowl of water, my blood darkens the water like ink. When I'm finished, I sit on a small cot near the window in my room while she warms food over a small fire in the main area. I won't say anything until I know where I am and what's going on.

"Who did this to you?" Verity asks, but I swallow around a knot in my throat and say nothing.

My day up until this point takes on a dream-like haze.

One of the Dark Ones sits at the end of my cot. A woman. I suppose I've assumed they were all men until now. I want to yell at her—Get away!—but I know how that would look to Verity, so I try to ignore the shadow woman.

Another part of me, however, wants to take in every last detail of her. For years I have wondered exactly how they look. Do they all have such angry eyes as this one? Are they all cursed with two sharp teeth protruding past their lips on either side of their mouths?

Verity bustles in with a bowl of herbed broth. My stomach rumbles. The hunger comes out of nowhere but feels as though it's been there for too long.

I lift the bowl to my lips and sip carefully, the steam tingling my face. Whatever it is, it tastes dirty and bitter. I lower it to my lap. The warmth on my thighs makes me feel overheated and flushed and at the same time makes me realize how cold I have been, how near-frostbitten my feet and toes and fingers are. So cold they itch and burn at the same time.

"Thank you," I say.

"Bramble leaves and cedar," she says, as though she's plucked the question straight from my mind. "It's to help you heal. You won't tell anyone, will you?"

I don't see any reason why I would tell anyone, or why it would matter if I did.

Verity looks at me a long moment. "I suppose you won't, especially after I found you in the state I did."

"I won't," I promise her, only because she deserves a response.

"It's freezing in here," Verity says, bustling to an open window. "Why on earth is your window open?"

She stops short, and I glance over. A raven sits perched on my window sill.

"Shoo!" Verity says, swatting at the bird. It takes off, and she pulls the window closed. She stares out the window a bit longer, and her hand lifts to her cheek. "Oh, dear."

"What's wrong?"

She shakes her head. "A bird coming to your window. A bad omen."

For a moment, I'm taken aback, but then my sense of Verity floods through me. She's always been superstitious.

"Nevermind that," she says, sitting on a wooden stool beside my cot. "We'll bring some luck your way. Now, tell me what happened."

It's the same question I'm asking myself.

I don't want to tell her the truth, and I couldn't even if I did. I don't remember what the truth is. This makes it easy for me; now I don't have to lie. "I...I don't know what happened."

She raises her eyebrow. It's something anyone could have done, and yet, it's uniquely something I've seen *her* do before. It's her fine brown eyebrow lifting over her tea-colored eyes and long, dark eyelashes. They are eyes that can only belong to her and an expression she has made all her own, imprinted somewhere in the history of my mind.

"I'd stay with you tonight—to make sure you're okay," she says finally, "but I can't. You know what that could mean for both of us."

I don't know. All I know is that I have four years of memories of living in this place, and I know that I am not from here, that I have another life, and that I have to find my baby. But that life with the baby—it's hazy. I can see her sleeping in my arms, see her tiny hand wrapped around my finger...I feel an overwhelming amount of love for her, and beneath that the feeling that something is wrong. Very wrong.

But what else? Why can't I remember more? Why can't I remember the life she is a part of?

"Maybe you should leave now." I hate the abrasiveness of my words, but I need to be alone.

Verity presses her hands against her knees. "Yes," she says, a note of defeat in her voice, "perhaps I should."

But she doesn't stand to leave.

"Abigail," she says softly, reaching for my hand. I flinch, and she immediately retracts her gesture. She smiles sadly. "If you need anything, you will let me know, won't you?"

I swallow around a lump in my throat. "Be well, Verity."

Be well? Why did I say that?

Verity nods at me as though I'm hopeless. That's probably true. I see her to the door, and she leaves with a wilted posture, her shoulders sinking as though someone has stolen all the air from her lungs. My heart aches after her, the kind woman who offered me her help.

From beneath my bed, I pull out a small wooden box. It's empty, and the emptiness makes me angry. This whole *life* is empty. I don't know what to do, where to go, how to fix this.

I stare at the heart-shaped birthmark on my right hand, right near where the thumb meets the wrist, and I know Anna is out there somewhere, needing me. Needing me even more than I need her.

As the hours pass, more memories of my life, of my Mama and Pa, come and go too quickly for me to hold onto them. When I was six...Where did I live when I was a child? I remember arriving in Salem, at this very settlement, but that was many years ago. Not today. But hadn't it been today, too?

The memory seems awkward, as though the memories can't possibly be mine, and yet they are more real than anything else.

Whatever memories I have been trying to remember blur away like an evaporating dream. The Darkness remains, the only thing that is wholly familiar to me.

I belong to these woods now. What had I wanted to remember? A memory skips through my mind again, and I shiver.

How could I belong to this place from centuries ago? I had only arrived here today, from 1961. Right? Yes. That's it. 1961 feels right. But then Verity's words swim through my mind. No, that's not it. I've got my numbers all mixed up. It's 1691, not 1961. That's what Verity had said.

Another memory pushes in, drowning my thoughts. I arrived here four years ago, in 1687, sixteen years old and orphaned, so yes, indeed that makes today's year 1691. Verity had been the one to find me. She wrapped me in a hug and shooed away all the gawkers and made me a sandwich and some tea, and for two years I lived with her in her small cottage until I was ready to be on my own.

So if I can remember my arrival here in 1687 so clearly, then why does 1961 still feel right? Why do I still remember arriving here today for the first time? How is it that I remember arriving here for the first time...twice?

My head throbs, and I climb into my cot and huddle beneath a thin woolen blanket. This is my home. The pillow fits my head. The straw mattress forms to my body. But this isn't right. I belong here, but I'm not where I'm supposed to be. There is somewhere more important. I was somewhere else just hours ago. I'm certain of it.

I yawn, and my eyelids grow heavy. I just can't keep my eyes open any longer. Even my mind is slowing down, but I hold desperately to my thoughts.

I have to get away from Salem and back to wherever I came from. Where had that been?

I envision a porch. No, not a porch. A boat deck. I came to America on a boat with my family. They left me behind, and I found my way here. I'm forgetting something. Something about today. I just know it. It's there, on the brink of my mind. What was it...?

I can't make sense of anything, and my will to try is quickly evaporating. I fight to hold to the last lingering memory of another life. A life where voices called me Rose. I hold to the one memory I think can bring me back there and force my eyes back open.

Across the room, a table is covered in pigments and canvas and jars of colorful water, and I rush over. There's a paintbrush, and immediately I set to work, painting the one thing I know I can never let myself forget.

Anna.

Yes, I must have had another life before this. As surely as I know that is not possible, I know it is for certain the truth. I will not rest until this memory is preserved. I cannot let sleep steal this last memory away.

I stare at the painting until it has dried, then I set the empty box beneath my bed to a new purpose. A capsule to hold the thing dearest to me—the memory of my daughter.

I have no idea how I will do it, but I must find my way back to her.

CHAPTER 3
DECEMBER 1691

ALL I DO IS CRY. I'M POSITIVELY ILL OVER BEING SEPARATED from my daughter. Pain sears every inch of my body, drowns me in my loss. Without Anna, I only want to die, but the chance she might be out there somewhere, alive, keeps me going. I cling to her memory, keep it crisp in my mind, paint it into pictures and tuck them away in my box so that her memory can never fade.

Verity insists I must take a job, to feign normalcy. She doesn't know I had another life before this. She thinks I've always been Abigail, every damn day of my life. She says I used to work at a bakery, but they asked me to leave two weeks ago. But part of me knows I was not here two weeks ago. That I only arrived yesterday.

My memories, however, are also Abigails, and Abigail knows that no one in Salem will hire her. When I 'remember' this for the first time, it makes me angry. Thankfully, Verity has brought me the things a person would need—food and wood for a fire—and I thank her profusely.

"It's the least I can do," she says. "Besides which, you're always helping me with my laundry."

The comment triggers another thought of Abigail's. A thought from weeks ago, from before I arrived here yesterday. A memory from the last time I hung her linens to dry, I—or rather, Abigail—had noticed a large black circle of a stain on one of Verity's sheets. One of the young women in the town noticed, too. Abigail quickly snatched the sheet back down off the line, but not before the woman glared at her and stomped off, assigning some sort of meaning to the black stain that I could not fathom.

The next day, however, the Good Reverend kneeled outside my home and prayed.

❧

I AM CALLED TO MY CABIN WINDOW, BUT IT IS NOT A VOICE THAT calls. It is a howl, a low groaning of tree boughs. Slowly, it becomes a strange song, a faraway lullaby I've heard before, some long-ago time I can't perfectly remember.

I sense the morning is a long way off, that I have wakened in the dead of night. Outside, smoky wisps of clouds float past the full red moon looming in the dark sky. The folks of Salem call it a witch's moon. Beads from the early night rain blur my window. A breath that's not my own fogs the glass. Lines trace through, spelling my name.

But it is not *Abigail*, the name I keep now. Nor is it *Rose*, the name I left behind. The name in the window is one I gave myself as a child, some lifetime ago. A name I remember and keep as I do all the names that have belonged to me. This is the name of my escape.

Cordovae.

The name is a whisper in my mind and a panic in my chest. A dizziness rushes to my head, but my balance and vision quickly restore. I've felt this way before. When I...when I...I cannot place it. I only know it means something will happen, and I hope it is something that will bring me back to my baby. To Anna.

The fog lifts. My window is nothing more than a splintered

frame for the woods outside, the red moon hanging low in the patchy sky. The music, slow and heavy, sweet but dark, slips through with the draft. The calling is alive in my stomach, pulling me so strongly I feel as though I will surely topple forward if I do not comply.

If I follow this eerie tune, I risk being caught by my town, but I will not know peace until I obey the burning desire to honor the call.

Queasy with the need to run toward the pull, I slip on the fingerless gloves Verity knit for me to hide the birthmark on my wrist—the people of Salem would not take kindly to such markings. Then I grab my shawl and head outside. In the icy night's breeze, my nightdress flutters near my ankles. I can only hope no one catches me stumbling through the darkness, for they already think me lost to the Puritan ways.

Only Verity has shown me any kindness, but after yesterday, she must think me afflicted. The town had found me the same way three years ago: an orphaned young woman in a nightdress and no sense about her. And though I know I cannot afford to let it happen again, my body will not allow me to resist the pull of the calling.

Soon, people will cast their fingers toward me and declare me a witch, as talk of witch hunts has been all the murmur of the town for some time now. With such rumors swirling about the settlement, I have to be careful. Especially now, outside in the night.

I should have stayed inside.

No sooner do I have that thought than the pull intensifies, as though someone has reached into me, grabbed my gut, and yanked me closer.

Candlelight flickers in the window of a nearby home, and I hurry to take cover in the forest. My heart pounds in my chest, and I glance back over my shoulder, trying to look everywhere at once to see if anyone is coming after me.

When I see no one, my fears drift away, carried by the notes that float through the night air. To my right is one of the Dark Ones, and I can't help but look, even though I know he is faster, even though I know he will be gone when I turn my head. All I catch is the last glimpse of his inky shadow as he dips back into the woods.

The bad ones always hide.

The crunch of twigs and rustle of leaves has me glancing over my other shoulder, staring into the swell of darkness for an unwelcome companion. I swear I hear footsteps, but as I strain to locate their origin, I lose the sound completely.

I swallow and try to ground myself in reason: No one from my settlement comes out to the woods any longer, as they fear the town will think they have ventured out to make sacrifices to a dark and false god. That is the real fear in this town—not the wolves or the venomous snakes, but the accusations of our people and what those accusations might mean.

Cordovae.

The music whispers my name. My name is part of a drum beat and a rattlesnake hissing. I tug my shawl tighter around my shoulders and dip under the branches that cut across my path. Perhaps I should return to the cabin, for the dangers of the woods at night are best avoided. My feet shuffle further along the path, not heeding the warning that trembles in my bones.

I blink, trying to adjust my eyes to the darkness, trying to get them to absorb the moonlight shining through the lattice of leaves. Each step is uncertain, my vision limited to the objects closest to me. I keep one hand in front of me, reaching out to ensure I don't walk into anything.

The music lures me along the path parallel to the creek. Even the water runs away from the direction I walk as it marks the air with the tang of wet stone. But now I recognize the song. The song I sang to Anna.

My feet sink into the earth, the soil moist from the melted snow. The dewy leaves of the underbrush dampen my nightdress.

For the past fortnight, the early evening has brought snow or rain, and I'm torn between whether I remember all of those rains or only the rain of the night prior. Even with the rain gone, the air keeps its heavy, murky haze.

Were Verity with me, she would crouch to lift one the dead leaves from the forest floor. She would say, 'They're always here, in the forest. Even in the summer when the trees are full of green, the death of autumn season lingers.' Words she said to me some time ago, some time before yesterday that I remember just the same.

The path makes an abrupt turn, but following it that way won't bring me closer to the music, so I hike into the unkempt forest. As I break from the worn and trusted path into the brambles and forest overgrowth, I pause. I press my hand against a tree for balance, the rough bark digging into my palm and fingertips.

My vision has adjusted, and the moonlight gives a certain guidance on my path. On the tree branch closest to my face a spider is moving. No, not moving. Being eaten. Verity has told me of this before—of the mothers who surrender their bodies to their hatchlings.

I snap my hand away from the tree and step aside. My hand on my stomach does little to quell my nausea. I don't want to go forward; I want to go back. I want to go forever back, back to Georgia, to my daughter.

What if forward is the only way back?

What an odd thing to think, and yet the thought compels me further. Tonight, my body belongs to these woods, the same woods that have stolen me from wherever I've come. My body moves onward despite myself, and the music grows louder. Between the notes, there's a fluttering of wings in the distance and the burble of a creek.

Then I see them. A flock of sparrows. Verity and I used to watch the birds fly. 'Birds are friends that stay together like family,' she said. 'This is a good sign.'

Tonight's cold is mild and the ground is sprinkled with acorns.

All signs of good things to come, as my friend would have me believe. I don't believe in such superstitions, but yet I can't help but feel some small flicker of peace.

A few feet farther and a path starts up again. I have never taken this path before, yet it's as though I've known the way here all my life.

Deeper in the woods, a fire glows orange behind the trees, illuminating my path with an ever increasing brightness. An oddly familiar sensation hums through me. I belong here. I step closer, step around the trees and into the clearing.

The music stops.

A young man pokes at the fire with a large branch. The fire illuminates the clearing, though the night keeps the colors of the world around me muted. The man by the fire is not dressed as most Puritans—no breeches or stockings, no cravat or waistcoat—but his clothing is just as dreary, from the woolen charcoal sweater to his long dark pants.

Most surprising, however, is the golden sheen to his skin. At first I think it's the fire glistening off his pearly white complexion, but the more I stare, the more I realize the sheen is *part* of his skin. But where the darkness of the spirits instills fear, his unique appearance has the opposite effect. It's as though he is radiating a good nature.

"Cordovae," he says, hoarsely.

The name sparks a memory. Rose, hiding in her mind, using that name to bring her comfort. That had been me, and only those I could trust ever called me Cordovae. But those people had never been real...

Yet here is this man, standing right where I can see him, calling me by that very name. How?

His head swivels toward me, shifting earthy-brown hair from his dark eyes. He's a bit older than I'd thought at first. Mid-to-late twenties, would be my guess. But none of this dismisses the most important detail of all: *I do not know this man*. I am not familiar with his red-rimmed eyes, nor his square, shaded jaw or defeated expression.

"You've come."

"It was not so much intentional." I'm surprised by the odd peace that overwhelms me in his presence. It's as though my path has crossed with an old friend instead of a stranger.

"Sorry about that," he says.

I can't fathom why he would be apologizing for my arrival; I sense I am expected here. Shivering cold, I pray silently for the night breeze to die down. But I don't know if that is why I'm shaking or if it's nerves that rattle me.

"Why have you called me Cordovae?"

"It is the name of your spirit."

I feel both safer and more vulnerable that he knows this. Is it really the name of my spirit, though? I do not flee, but I do not move closer to him, either. Though he has done nothing to threaten me, I am at the same time cautious of him.

"What was that music?" I ask.

"A song only you can hear," he says. "Your calling. Ankou, as you are destined to become, are air elementals, and as such ruled by the Earth. We all hear the drums, but only you will hear your music."

"Would not air be ruled by the sky?" I ask, ignoring his senselessness in favor of simply pointing out the holes in his logic.

He grabs a stick and draws a star within a circle. He marks each point clockwise: Spirit, Air, Fire, Earth, Water. He retraces the line from Air to Earth in the star. "See? Air is called by Earth."

It's time to leave. This man cannot be mentally stable. But my feet remain rooted where I stand.

Before I can form a coherent question, a young woman with the same golden skin comes out from the brambles, carrying a large bowl. Behind her, beyond the wall of trees, an ocean crashes against a rocky shore. But once my gaze reaches her eyes, I can't stop staring at her. She stumbles before continuing over, the skirts of her fitted, dark violet dress rustling against the forest floor. Her bell-sleeves are unfamiliar to the style of the Puritans as well, as are the black cords around her waist. After she sets the bowl on the ground beside the man, she assesses me with her sharp, pear-green eyes.

"I thought we were going to wait," she says sharply. Both her voice and appearance indicate she is barely a woman—perhaps not much older than sixteen.

The man shakes his head. "Please, Tess. We've waited long enough."

Tess sits across from him on a twisted log that reminds me of melted wax. I know not what to do but stand there, though I feel horribly awkward doing so. In the bowl, the moon reflects in the slosh of liquid. The man ladles some into three chalices.

Verity would say not to drink that. Never drink anything that reflects the moon. It's bad luck.

He steps a bit closer—close enough that I can smell the ocean on his skin, but not so close as to crowd my space. Not close enough to make me panic. So why are my hands getting moist and my heart fluttering?

His lips fall slightly apart, and he tilts his head, staring at me now as though his vision has finally registered my existence. His eye contact is firm, eyes shining, expression softening. My cheeks grow hot.

"You look flushed," he says, and my heart beats even faster. "The cold will do that to you. Come—sit by the fire."

I'm too stunned to disobey. An odd sensation wracks my body, as though something outside myself commands my actions, yet I still feel in control—I feel I could deny my compulsion if I wanted to.

Why don't I want to?

The warmth of the fire is a welcome relief from the cold, but soon the heat makes me queasy. I scoot back.

The man hands a chalice to Tess who takes a long sip and sets it aside. The other two chalices he leaves on the ground by his feet. There is something about him...something about this night.

Tess pulls her dark hair in front of her shoulders and weaves a long braid. "I suppose it is up to me to explain, as you're draining William."

"Excuse me?"

"William's energy—you're draining it. If you stop resisting, it would make this easier on all of us."

"Resisting?"

"*That's what I said.*" The annoyance is heavy in her sigh if not clear in her tone.

I glance over my shoulder from the direction I came. I know which way to go if I want to leave, yet I cannot see the path from my seat by the fire—not in the way I had been able to see the fire from the path. It's as though I have stepped into a secret world.

"What do you want?" I ask, turning back to them.

Tess laughs. "If you are asking me, nothing. I'd like you to go back to your cabin and your town and forget this ever happened."

William clears his throat.

Tess shifts her gaze to William momentarily. "Unfortunately, this has little to do with what I want. You were brought here yesterday to assist us."

"I wasn't here yesterday."

"Not *here*," she says, pointing to the ground, her teeth clenched together. "*Here*." She widens her arms. "To this settlement. To this century."

"I've lived here for three years." Even as I say it, I know it's a lie. But how else can I explain my memories living this life as Abigail?

"Your voice—does it sound like your own? Do your thoughts sound as you think they should?" Her face contorts in disgust, and she motions at me loosely with her hand. "Do you really think you are *this* woman?"

I press my lips together and narrow my eyes. There is no way she could know these things. No way she could know that I feel trapped, not just here in this town but in my mind as well.

William places his hand on Tess' forearm. "Be patient. You were in her place once before, too."

Tess grits her teeth. "I know that," she says, her voice edgy. She reverts her gaze to me, lifting her chalice closer to her lips but not sipping from it.

"You're a Seer," she says, over the cusp of chalice. "And you've been taken from another time and brought here to serve your purpose."

"A Seer?"

"A human that can see the spirits of elementals. It happens to the human descendants of Ankou."

I laugh and shake my head. I don't know what's come over me.

"Perhaps I best leave," I say. I turn to go, but her next words stop me short:

"If you complete all that is required of you, you can go back."

"Go back?" I ask slowly, turning to her again.

She nods.

"Back where?" I ask, testing her. Could she help me get back to Anna?

Tess swings her arm to one side, some liquid spilling from her chalice. "How the hell should I know?"

William snaps his attention toward her. "Tess!"

"Should we be soft on someone we want to fight at our side?" she asks testily, but she blows a breath through her nose and seems to compose herself. "Cordovae, have you had any fragments yet? A memory not from this lifetime?"

Immediately, my mind goes to Anna, my child. I look to my hands and scratch at the overgrowth of my cuticles. I am not sure I should tell her.

"No," I lie. "I don't think so."

"It's not something you think, it's something you know. And you want to get back to that memory, don't you?" she asks, as though I had admitted to her I did have such memories. "*We* can help you with that. We can get you back to your memories."

I can't believe I'm entertaining any of this—can't believe I have even a modicum of trust for these complete strangers. Tess particularly doesn't seem fond of me, and I have no idea why. Some people are just that way, but it doesn't exactly make me believe she wants to help me.

"I never wanted to leave her in the first place," I say. "I never would have left Anna behind."

She scoffs. "I knew you had fragments. What were they? Tell us."

I shrug, not liking the direction the conversation is going. My memories are personal, and I've already shared more than enough details with her.

"Well, at least you know who or what you are trying to return to. Some of us are stuck here until we figure that out—if we can figure out before it's too late."

"Too late?"

Tess nudges her companion. "You can stop now, William. She's going to stay."

The calling that pulled me here earlier fades, and I sway backwards.

Tess smiles thinly at me—a placating gesture without the placating effect. "You'll have to forgive us. William used his influence to compel you to stay. We won't do that to you again unless we need to."

Why bother stopping then?

For some reason, I'm infuriated more than I think I should be. What right would anyone have to force me to stay anywhere? It is my body and my right.

"If you try to force me to do *anything* again, I will leave."

"Okay, sugar," Tess replies. "Whatever you say."

I admit, though only to myself, that it speaks well of their intent that they didn't hurt me while attempting to hold me under their control. But how were they keeping me here anyway? Had I imagined that pull, or does William really have some way of controlling what I do?

Ultimately, all that matters is that they said they can help me return to Anna.

"Tell me then," I say, "what do I need to do to get back?"

My desire is so strong that I know right then I would try anything—*anything*—for a chance to return to my baby.

CHAPTER 4
DECEMBER 1691

WILLIAM LIFTS A CHALICE AND HANDS IT TO ME. "FIRST, YOU need to drink this."

"I'm not drinking anything." I slant my gaze toward him. Does he really think I would drink some unknown potion in the woods at night?

"It will connect you to us and make you what you need to be to fight this war," he says, as though this will change my opinion.

"There's no war here."

"No?" William asks. He sweeps his arm toward the forest's trees—toward the shadows and the Dark Ones. "I know you've seen them. Your attention drifts to them almost unknowingly. They are mortuss phasmatis, the dead spirits. We call them Morts. There are more here, in these times, than the times you come from. This is because of the elemental war."

Tess smiles in a way I am sure is not meant to be kind. "We're your guides. And you're theirs."

"Excuse me?"

"You have to redirect them," she says. "The ones who are pure of spirit need to be moved to their next lifetime, and the others need to be destroyed before their destructive ways destroy mankind."

"So then...people can be reincarnated?"

"No," William says. "Not *people. Elementals.*"

"Then how did I get here?"

"You've been moved here, temporarily, by the Universe."

I'm in no place to doubt anything. Not after all I've been through. "That doesn't explain why the Morts need to be moved. Why don't they just leave on their own?"

Tess quirks her eyebrow. "Surely you can understand not wanting to leave your past behind?"

"I don't want to help them after what they've done to my family."

"They aren't all evil." Tess' lips twist in a frown. "And those who are were evil in life as well."

"*Why*, though? Why are some evil and some good? Why don't the good ones help?"

"Why is anyone evil?" Tess asks. "Why are some good people afraid to protect those being hurt by awful people? No one knows the answer to these questions, and I imagine no one ever will. All of which is irrelevant."

William nods. "There is no hope your town will survive the Morts without your help, Cord. That's why you need to be like us. Now drink."

The urge to back away surges through my stomach again. My heart palpitates, and my chest tightens. "What's in the cup?"

"We can make you drink it," Tess says.

"Stop, Tess. She must drink it of her own will, with knowledge and understanding of what it will mean."

"We don't have time to convince her!" At her sudden outburst, I glance over. She's tugging at her earlobe and seems frantically distressed. "She won't believe until she sees for herself. Just make her do it."

William hands me the chalice. "It does not taste bad," he says. "It's sweet, like berries. It comes from the Ankou—that is what you are to become to fulfill your purpose."

I would think this is all so crazy, but I can't deny all I have seen. Still, that doesn't mean I should drink some unknown substance, no matter what it tastes like.

While my mind tells me trusting them is not a wise choice, my heart senselessly believes them. But that does not mean I have to blindly accept their direction.

"You'll have to give me more than that," I say. "What is this Ankou you expect me to become?"

"Ankou are the air elementals sent to move the Morts, as you will learn to do," William says. "I fear you will simply have to take our word for it, for the time being."

"I fear you are wrong," I counter. "I don't *have* to do anything."

Tess smirks, crossing her arms. "Still want to leave this up to her?"

William glowers at her, then slides his gaze back to me, pressing his fist against his mouth. He sighs heavily. "We're certainly wasting time arguing. Then tell me, what is it you wish to know?"

"Everything. What are elementals? Why is there a war? Why do you need me? What do I have to do?"

"The questions you ask would take centuries to fully understand, but I will tell you what I can with so little time to spare."

I'm already confused. "How can there be little time to spare when people can be moved through time on the Universe's whim? Wouldn't that make time irrelevant?"

"Do you want to understand this?"

I press my teeth into my bottom lip and nod.

"It started with the Universe's attempt to purge evil from the human race. They created a new life form—the Cruor—who were sent to hunt and kill any humans who had strayed from their intended path."

I stare down at my hands. "Had some omnipotent being really thought that would be the answer to the world's problems?"

When William doesn't respond, I peek up at him. He's cocked an eyebrow that says, 'Are you very well done with interrupting me?' Or maybe it doesn't say that. But seeing as I don't know him much at all, I feel inclined to talk a little less.

"Their intentions were in the right place," he says finally. "But some of the Cruor themselves were evil, and so the Universe sent the Strigoi, with their ability to change form to hunt the corrupt Cruor."

"I'm guessing their troubles didn't end there?" I ask, trying to be a little more agreeable to hearing what he has to say.

"No." William relaxes back, his legs stretching his feet closer to the fire. "That's why the Ankou were sent. Their magic was intended to bring peace among the elemental races, but incidentally this opened gateways for the races to intermingle, which brought with it its own hatred and violence."

I want to be surprised by the negative outcome of something as wonderful as what he has suggested, but I know mankind too much to be shaken by this revelation. "Who did they send after that?"

William shakes his head. "No one, not yet."

"Maybe they thought they did enough damage..."

He chuckles silently, but it's a bitter, humorless laugh. A laugh that hides deep-set anger. "Not quite. A council formed shortly after that. The Maltorim. They were going to oversee the elementals, bring order, but of course they too became corrupt. Power has a way of doing that to people."

When William looks at me next, chills rush along the fine hairs of my pale arms. He's absolutely right. But what does that say about him? Doesn't he have powers of his own? Isn't he suggesting that, if I join him, I will, too?

"Is that all there is to it?" I ask meekly. "The Cruor, the Strigoi, and the Ankou? All fighting. And for what?"

He pulls one knee up and rests his elbow there. "The Chibold came along at some point. Before all that. After. During. I suppose they weren't really considered important at first, not to the reshaping humanity anyway. But they are the only trustworthy connection to the Universe. What's worse is that, through these wars, they are losing the host families they need to survive."

"This sounds like...a mess I just don't want to get involved in. Maybe it would be better if I went back, and the Universe can send someone else."

"You don't understand," he says. "You *can't* go back. Not yet."

"Your 'Universe' has done enough wrong by now that they ought to be a little more open to the idea that they might be wrong about me. Don't you think?"

"It doesn't matter what I think." This time, he looks at me, and I realize the smirk on his face isn't as mocking as it appears on first glance. He's frustrated—not with me, but with *the way things are*. "You see, it is a cycle that cannot break. The evil spirits need to be removed and the good allowed to remain. That is the bottom line, and that is where we come in."

"So none of the Ankou are corrupt?"

"Well, no...some are..." William scratches the back of his head. "It's more complicated than that. But that is why there is a war, and that is why we need you—someone to fight for good, to move the pure spirits and rid the earth of the evil ones."

"I don't know how to do that."

"Not yet, no. But if you were to become Ankou, you would."

It's a lot to take in, and now that he has explained it, I realize he is right. There's no time to help me understand. I don't want to understand. I just want to get back to Anna, and they said they can make that happen. No one in town even knows I have memories I want to get back to, so I have to try my odds with William and Tess. I'll never forgive myself if I don't.

"How does one become Ankou?" I ask finally.

"Either through birthright or through selection," he says. "In your case, selection. But it will not happen until you accept your calling and drink what is in the cup."

There's something about the way he speaks that draws me in. That makes me feel as though I can trust him. Then again, maybe

I only believed him because he was giving me hope to return to Anna.

"And you? Were you stolen from a life, too?" Could he possibly understand my plight?

"In a way, you could say my life was stolen from *me*," he says, his tone dropping to a chill. "But if you mean to ask how I became Ankou, it was my birthright."

I bite my lip and nod. Right. So he *can't* understand. "Do you even know what happens to those who *are* moved? If I'm here, in this body, where is the body I was in before?"

His eyebrows perk up, as though fascinated by my question. "You're...missing."

"Well I know that, but—"

"Not in the way you think," he says, and I stop to let him finish. "It's more like...POOF—" His hands curl into little fists then his fingers pop open. "—gone."

"Like I never existed?" My voice rises in pitch.

His hands relax back at his sides. "People still know you existed," he says tenderly. "They remember you. Maybe put your picture on a milk carton."

My eyebrows knit together. "Put my picture on a milk carton? Why?

He drops his face and chuckles, shaking his head. "Maybe that was after your time. I only meant they would be looking for you."

"But they won't find me."

"No, they won't. The Universe needs to protect their efforts, though, and this is but one step in them doing so. You simply can't be in two places at once."

This, unfortunately, I know too well. "And when I return?"

"If you return, same thing. Poof, you are present again, and maybe people celebrate finding you alive. Or maybe it all undoes and you were never missing at all."

If I return? I narrow my eyes.

"I know it's a lot to take in. Only so much time can pass before it's dangerous to the balance of things for you to return." He places a gentle hand on my shoulder, and peace floods through me. "There's only one way back. You know it, don't you? You *feel* it?"

I do feel it. But is that good enough? I explore the open, honest expression on his face. The imperfections of small scratches on his cheekbone and a dimple on his nose. "*Should* I feel it?"

When he doesn't answer, I tilt the chalice and look inside. The liquid is a blackish-purple, the color of blackberry juice, and smells just as pungently sweet. In that moment, I'm so thirsty I consider it, but just as soon as I do, I feel as though the foolish urge could not have come from me.

It comes from the Ankou, he'd said. What the hell does that even mean? I push the cup back toward him.

"I'm not drinking that," I say, trying to honor my faltering logic.

I stand to leave, but before I reach the edge of the clearing, William darts in front of my path, crossing the clearing in long strides. He grabs my wrists with strong hands, and I no longer feel I can come and go as I please, yet still I do not feel threatened by him. I wonder if something in me has broken to make me this way.

"If you leave now, you will never see her again," he says.

He's not trying to hurt me, not trying to overpower my right to decide. No. I sense he's trying to warn me, to protect me.

His breath is heavy, and I look up at him, trying for anger, but my heart stops. His hands are strong, and he's impossibly tall—my head barely reaches his chest. And I feel...safe here.

Disgusted by my own attraction to him, I intend to pull away or tell him to let me go, but I am too thrown by what he knows. "How do you—"

"It is one of my gifts," he says. "Whatever you knew about your previous life before we first met, the Universe imparted to me as well."

"You know everything I think? Is that what you're saying?"

"No," he says reassuringly. "*Only* what you knew about your previous life before you met me."

"Are you...are you one of the Ankou?"

"Not quite," he says, slowly releasing my wrists, "though not quite not, either."

I don't run as perhaps I should. "And Tess?"

"She is Ankou," he says, his voice rasping.

"And how did you two come together?"

His lips twitch down. "She was sent to me, same as you. I have not failed her yet, and I do not intend to fail you, either."

His body, pressed against mine, warms my stomach and thighs. I'm staring at his lips, but I shift my focus to Tess, who stands near the fire pit with her arms crossed. There's a transparent dome, noticeable only by the film it leaves in the air, arching over the clearing.

William clears his throat and steps back, dark eyes looking up. "It is so your town cannot find us."

Now is when any sane woman would run. What would Verity think? But these people are the closest I've come to answers—the closest I've been to Anna—since I've arrived here. And if anything is worth risking my life for, it's my daughter.

"*Who are you?*" I ask.

"That is of no consequence. Many will die if you do not help us."

"I am not a fool," I say sharply. "How you know of Anna, I don't know, but my helping you will only delay my return to her."

"Cordovae," he says softly. My name from his lips warms my skin. "Your daughter's birth is hundreds of years from now. You have time, I promise you. But the longer you take to join us, the more people who die."

"What do you mean?"

"Some of the Morts—the ones you need to trap—possess humans. They spread pestilence and disease and influence chaos. Through their host bodies, they wreak havoc. They derive enjoyment from destruction, and nothing can stop them but us bringing them to an ultimate end."

"I have no desire to get wrapped up in this mess."

William scoffs. "Do all the people of your time reek of selfishness?"

"Don't you dare. You know nothing of who I am."

"You know nothing of who you are, either!"

Tess stands and brushes off her skirts. "Oh, William," she says, a smile in her voice. "How the tune changes when she's getting on your nerves instead of mine."

After giving Tess a glare, William snaps his scowl back in my direction. "Without your help, many people will die. I understand trusting two strangers in the woods is unappealing, perhaps risky, but this is necessary. These are your ancestors. Without them, there will be no you. The more people who die, the less likely it is your daughter will come to exist. There will be no Anna for you to return to."

The revelation slams into me, and I step back. If I don't help, I may not exist. Anna would not exist. But if I help, I risk my own life by fighting in a war I don't want to be a part of. I would willingly do so if I knew Anna would be safe where she is, but I sense she is in danger.

"Perhaps it would be best for us not to exist," I say. "Sometimes the alternatives are far more...*unappealing*, as you say."

"You need to look beyond yourself and your daughter. Sometimes sacrifice is necessary for a greater good."

I frown. "What greater good is worth sacrificing for that would not allow you your own happiness?" I ask, challenging him. "Show me a world you must sacrifice yourself to rescue, and I will show you a world that is unworthy of being saved."

"You must understand what is at risk here."

I'm not convinced I *must*, but it's only fair to consider. "And you need my help? You truly cannot move forward without me?"

"Yes." He holds out his hand, palm facing upward. "Please, at least come sit while we talk."

I bite my lip, hesitant to join him again. I need time to think. My whole body feels tired, and my mind won't stop pinging around all the possibilities: These people could be lying to me. Or they could be my only way back to Anna. I could die trying to return to her. Or she could never exist if I don't try. I feel hopeless and hopeful at the same time.

It's another fraction of a moment that feels like eternity before I reach out and take his hand. And once I do—once I feel his cool, comforting touch—I sense I'm on the right path. But as he leads me back to the fire, I ignore the tingles in my palm and along my forearms. What if my emotions are getting the best of me?

I sit on a log by the fire. Tess is gone, and panic at her sudden disappearance ravages my chest.

"She...left?" I ask. "Because of me?"

"She'll be back." William offers me the chalice once more.

"Tell me what this is."

"If I tell you, you won't drink it."

I raise my eyebrow. "I won't drink it if I don't know what it is."

His gaze roves over me, and he moistens his lips and takes a deep breath. "Blood," he mumbles. "Ankou blood."

My heart goes into full panic. They want me to drink blood? I shiver and lean back.

"Please, Cordovae. It sounds worse than it is. Trust me this once, and if I am wrong I will never ask you to trust me again."

It only takes once, but something about the softness of his eyes compels me to believe him. Tentatively, I take the Ankou blood, but I do not drink. "What's the story with Tess?"

William laughs. "Oh, you'll grow to love her. She is like a little sister. A dangerous, sword-wielding little sister who is too smart for her own good."

"You're what—a decade her senior?"

"Tess is nearly an adult herself, but surely you can understand the need for family? She has none, nor do I."

"Well, you don't look like brother and sister. That would be a pretty large age gap."

"Larger than you think," he says, grinning. "While I would appear perhaps only a decade older than her, in life I have centuries of experience. Immortality has little to do with appearances."

Immortality? Does being Ankou mean I'll live *forever*?

"Is she always so...hostile?"

His shoulders dip with obvious weight. "It's not personal. In your life here as Abigail, you have someone, don't you? Most of us who arrive have someone outside of other elementals. Tess did not. Until she met me, she was raised by a family who ignored her, with no memories of her life before."

"I just thought maybe you two were...you know...together?"

"Perhaps your mind is better put to *other* thoughts."

Thoughts like whether or not I should trust him. Whether I should take this chance or walk away from what might be my only way back to Anna.

William and I stay up all night talking. The entire time, I feel a pit in my stomach—concern for where Tess has gone and whether she is safe. It seems she has been gone too long. She's quite young to be on her own so long at night. More so, I don't feel entirely comfortable alone with men, though I find myself at ease with William, content with the way his hand feels whenever it brushes mine.

What has come over me? I need to stay focused. I need to get back to Anna.

The sky is growing lighter, threatening sunrise, and William tells me my time is up. It's time to choose. My face warms and my hands tremble, sloshing blood in the chalice.

"What happens if I drink this?" I ask, though it's not as if he hasn't explained it to me three times already. I'm stalling. But William is patient with me.

"If you become one of the Ankou, you will be able to fight with us to capture the Morts and guide them. We will teach you all you need to know."

"Will it hurt?"

William shakes his head. "No, but the sunlight will become

dangerous to your body. Too much time under the sun may cause you to undergo some changes."

"What kind of changes?" I press.

"We've been over this, Cord," he says. "Drink. It's your only way back to Anna."

I believe what this man says from my core, and that terrifies me. There's always been the possibility I would die in this life, never finding a way back. But now I fear, whether I drink this or not, it's a near *certainty* I will. I can't shake the disgust of following through or the terror of what it might mean.

Have I really become so desperate?

I stare at the drink once more.

It's my only hope.

THE NEXT MORNING, I WAKE IN MY OWN HOME, NOT remembering my return or what happened after I drank from the chalice. But I know it happened, feel it in my core. The drink they gave me was Tess' blood, and the magic they performed over the contents of the chalice were meant to make me one of the Ankou as well. I gag as I remember tasting the blood for the first time—feeling how thick it was on my tongue and in my throat. I'd known what I was about to drink, yet it wasn't until then that I'd fully processed what I had done. It had taken a while before I finally stopped fighting it and acceptance took way, allowing the change to occur.

Now I'm here, lighter and more balanced. As I step out of bed, the morning does not feel as cold as the one before. The usual back and neck aches of early morning are absent today. I almost feel numb.

I half-wonder if last night was a dream, but the muslin covering my windows are a reminder of what William had told me. Still, I pull back the curtain to see if it is true. When the dull winter sun spills through my small bedside window, I can't deny the transparent, vein-like wings that flutter behind me like clean linen in the wind. I cringe. My wings stretch down to my ankles, the bottom tips nearly grazing the floor, but I cannot understand their purpose; they are too thin to lift my body from the ground.

William said this would happen. That the wings are both a gift and a curse for the Ankou, though he hadn't explained why.

Stay to the shadows, he had warned. That's what I am to do if I ever find myself without shelter during the day.

I smooth my hand over one of the cool muslin sheets. They offer a privacy I appreciate but that at the same time makes me feel trapped and alone. Perhaps I should have hung them sooner— these old windows tend to distort things. Once, sometime after I arrived here for the first time as Abigail, Verity said I gave her a start when she approached my house and thought she saw two of me inside. That could get a town like ours talking of witchcraft.

Even with the window coverings, the room is still quietly bright, and I smell the wet earth on a breeze that permeates in from outside. It must have rained again, but when? I came home and fell asleep only hours ago, and it hadn't rained all night. The tweeting of birds reminds me of how dark my life has become, and I try to ignore their tune.

Although the muslin sheets block the direct rays of the sun that reveal my wings, they still tingle along my spine. I don't know what I would do without the kindness of natural light. William said the shade of the trees in the forest would be enough to protect me, but I cannot get there without taking the open path, and I cannot risk the dangers of the sun on my flesh.

The sun, over enough years, can shrink the Ankou to the size of the dragonfly.

That's what William had said, and I don't want to be the size of a dragonfly. I won't even try to imagine all the awkward stages I would hit in between.

I should be freezing—there's no fire for warmth, and yet, the temperature feels more like a mild autumn day. Another benefit of the Ankou, perhaps? I wonder if I'm even still myself anymore.

At that thought, I glance to the heart-shaped birthmark on my wrist, gently caressing it with my finger. Did Abigail always have this, or did I bring it with me? I slip on a long dress that covers my arms all the way down past my wrist, hiding the mark.

Does William have such markings? Last night he had seemed so...flawless. Would my skin have that same golden glow in the moonlight now? I felt even more like I could trust him now. Even with his intense gaze, I hadn't felt threatened by him, and my instincts are rarely wrong. But my instincts also told me the beautiful young woman with the pear-green eyes—Tess—wasn't very fond of me, and I still can't understand why.

What if I've made a mistake? If I'm on the wrong path, then I'm getting further from Anna instead of closer. At the same time, where was I before they came along? I was alone in this cabin with no direction, no hope whatsoever. They know a lot more about my situation than anyone else I've spoken to since arriving. Or arriving again?

I bite the inside of my cheek, considering, and the pinch reminds me of a woman. A mother. My mind flashes to a lady with a large sun hat and tendrils of graying hair. Rose's mother. *My* mother. This must be one of those fragments. Mama would certainly chastise me this time. Impulsivity and impatience lead to counterproductive choices, she would say. But something niggles in my stomach, telling me she had no business giving me advice.

A droplet of water plunks my scalp. The ceiling above has a spot of rotted wood and another droplet of water forming. I stick a pan on the floor to catch the water, then inhale deeply.

Where are William and Tess? They had said they would be here when I woke. I close my eyes, trying to remember exactly what was said. They had mentioned it was best I live my days here for now, to avoid people looking for me, but that I should spend my nights with them, training. So that must be it: they would meet with me tonight.

I sigh and turn to the cupboard for the water William had insisted I store. Heaven help me, I can't stop thinking about him. My palms get sweaty and my heart rate picks up just remembering how I felt while talking to him, how I felt every time he touched me, even though I'm certain there were no intimate intentions on his part.

Parched, I swig from the ceramic jug; it's been years since I've had water clean enough to drink, and I wonder how William and Tess have managed to provide me that. New questions fire in my mind. How long will the war last? How long will I be needed here? When I return to Anna, will I still be bound to the night and the shadows?

Perhaps there is another way I can get back to her. Some way faster and less dangerous. In the meantime, this is the only path I can follow—my only hope. I set down the jug of water, then pick it up again and take another swig. I can't seem to shake the nervous energy stirring inside me. I just want to find out what I'm meant to do and be done with it. Tonight cannot come soon enough.

Someone knocks at my door.

"Hello?" I call.

"Abigail!" Verity sings my name, her voice muffled by the wooden door. "Let me in!"

I don't want to let her in. I'm scared of what I've become and scared what Verity would think if she knew. But I know she won't leave well enough alone, so I grab the black hooded cape given me by Tess and tie it on. She says it can help cloak my wings from the vision of humans, though it will do nothing to protect me from the potential effect of the sun's rays.

When I open the door, the blinding brightness of the mid-day sun swells in the doorway. Verity's short, curvy frame hurries past me, the late winter air breezing in behind her. It doesn't chill me as it would have before, but the sunlight creates pressure on my bones.

It seems someone has carved a crucifix on the front of my door. I sigh and close the door quickly, spinning toward my friend with my palms pressed against the wood behind me. "Good day, Verity."

"Good day." Her mousy brown hair is a bit stringy and her eyes look more muddy than tea-colored today. She places a basket with a loaf of bread on the kitchen table and turns toward me with a smile. "Thought you'd be interested in a shared breakfast, though I fear all I have is bread three days past."

"I still have the berries you brought me. Please, sit."

"Still?"

I nod, pointing to them.

She grins, but her skin is grayish and there are bags under her eyes, so the smile seems strained. "You know me," she jokes, "can't see my own hand unless I hold it in front of my face!"

Her smile fades, slowly melting from her face. She's staring at something across the room. In two strides, she's standing in front of a table covered in jars and a mess of paper and brushes. I join her at her side to see what she is examining. It's painting I made the day before William and Tess had called me to the woods.

"That's you," I say, as though it's not obvious by her name painted at the top. "I painted it with winter berries and charcoal. Do you like it?"

She shakes her head, turning slowly to me. After a moment, she gives a half smile. "It's beautiful, Abigail, but please, get rid of this one and make me another."

"You can have this one." I take the painting off the cluttered table and hold it out toward her.

She steps back, her hand jumping to her chest. "You should never write a person's name in red, Abigail. It's terrible luck. Terrible. Please, I'm sorry, please just get rid of this and make something else."

I drop the painting to my side, biting back tears. I nod, but it doesn't feel natural. "I—I didn't know."

Verity takes my hand and smiles upon me warmly. "Oh, no, please don't be hurt. It's beautiful. You didn't know."

"Of course." I shrug, taking a deep breath, and set the painting back down atop some dried wildflowers. "It wasn't my best work anyway."

"Don't be silly," Verity says. She turns around, shuffling through her apron, then spins back toward me and reaches her short arms up to loop something over my head. I look down. She's made me a necklace...with a rabbit's foot on it. I try not to shudder.

"Give it a little rub whenever you need good luck. Perhaps it'll even bring a child your way," she says with a wink.

A child. The words are cold on the air, sharp on every inch of my skin. I already have a child. But Verity doesn't know that, wouldn't understand that.

"Thank you, Verity," I say as sincerely as I can. *Poor rabbit.* I take the necklace off and tuck it in a box on my windowsill. "It'll be safer here, I think."

I hope to never see it again.

Verity frowns, but it's fleeting, and before I know it she's across the room and reaching for the muslin sheets covering my window.

"For heaven's sake, Abigail," she says.

"No!"

Verity snatches her hand back and gives me a long, assessing stare. "Well—" With the back of her long dress sleeves, she pushes some stray strands of hair from her forehead. She looks harried. "Maybe you have the right idea, putting those sheets on your windows. Keeps out the chill."

"You seem a bit...busier than usual," I say, turning toward her. I purse my lips as I look her over. "Are you well?"

The smile Verity offers appears forced. She waves me off.

"What happened?"

"It's nothing, Abigail. You're always concerning yourself with me. What I want to know is how *you* are doing."

I narrow my eyes. She's hiding something. I just feel it, as though I've always been able to sense such things about people. "Did something happen in town?"

"Let's not talk about the town," she says, her voice almost painfully sing-song now. "We can't concern ourselves with them."

I inspect her more closely. She's not wearing her dream catcher necklace. I creep closer, examining her. A thin red mark shows on the sides of her neck, and I step around her to see it continue to the back of her neck, behind her pinned up hair.

"Verity…" I say, but it's more of a concerned breath the way it leaves my mouth.

"Abigail, please, don't worry yourself with this."

I shake my head, nostrils flaring, anger boiling up inside of me. "Who took your necklace?"

She licks her lips quickly—nervously—and offers another of her false smiles. "I can make another one. I shouldn't've worn it outside anyway. It's fine, really."

"No, it's not fine!" I say, dropping my hands to my side. I can't stop myself from the frantic anger swirling in my chest, and it scares me. My hands are balled so tightly that my nails press numbing crescents into my palm. "How is that fine? Someone took that off your body, and clearly it was not with your permission!"

The smile she offers now is one of pity Perhaps I seem unstable, perhaps Verity thinks I have completely gone over the edge. "You are always worried about me, Abigail, but what of you? You shut me out and tell me nothing."

I take a step back, not liking how she is turning this around. It's true, I like to keep to myself. I know it has something to do with my life before, and I wonder if that is where my anger comes from. But that's different. I'm not as though I'm hiding any of *Abigail's* life from her.

Verity's eyebrows are drawn together, and her hands clasp in front of her lap. "Why haven't you been answering your door? Why have you stayed locked away in your home for so long? What is going on with you?"

Locked in my room for so long? All I do is sleep? I just saw her yesterday! She may be crazier than the settlement imagines I am.

"I'm so hungry, Verity. Let's just sit and eat."

She nods and sits at the table, clearing a place for plates. A fresh smile lights her face as though our conversation up until this point never happened. I don't know whether to be thankful or worried. It takes me a few minutes to find the plates; they are hidden behind some pots and a jar of preserves that Verity made for me some time back when Abigail was just Abigail, and not me, too.

I sit across from her, hand her a plate, and watch as she scoops a handful of berries on her dish. The overripe berries mush and stain her palms red. It's not until that moment that I notice the Mort standing in the corner about ten feet away, in my direct line of sight. I hadn't seen it come in with Verity, but I know it wasn't here before she arrived.

This Mort is a woman with coal-black eyes and dark hair. It does not flee from my stare—does not even acknowledge that I see her. The way she peers at Verity with increasing intensity unnerves me. I can see her more clearly than I've seen Morts in the past, but still she appears shadowy, her essence washed out, the colors muted by darkness except for her gleaming black eyes and the ghostly, wolfish-fangs poking against her bottom lip.

William had said this would happen—that becoming Ankou would enhance my Seer abilities.

"What is it?" Verity asks.

I force my attention away from the Mort. "I'm terribly embarrassed," I say. "My home is quite the mess today."

"Oh, I'm not worried about that," Verity says. "But I still worry that I've not seen you in a week. All is well, I hope?"

Shock momentarily holds my tongue, but I harness my confusion. "Verity, were you not just here yesterday?"

Her eyes widen. "Heavens no, Abigail. I hope you do not talk to others as you do with me. There's enough being said about how you showed up out of nowhere all those years ago."

I reach for the bread. "Why would that matter now?"

"Your memory, Abigail. That is what worries me. Reverend Parris' daughters, well, they have not forgotten the day you arrived here, and your appearance has done you no favors."

"My...appearance?"

"Your *hair*, Abigail! As deep a red as Adam's first wife, Lilith. The sign of offspring born of unclean sex. Red, the color of sin, the color of the forbidden fruit. And God forbid you tame those unruly locks—when is the last time you took a brush to your hair? Given all this recent talk of witchcraft...well, perhaps it's best you've been lying low."

The town had thought I was a witch, or does she mean they do *now*? I pull forward a lock of my hair, as red as fresh blood. "But Verity—"

"No, no. None of your excuses today. Just be careful. And for heaven's sake, answer your door when I call on you. A week is far too long to leave an old woman like me to worry."

Had it really been a week since I last saw Verity? I could've sworn it was just yesterday—just last night that I met William and Tess in the woods. I am not sure who is confused—Verity or me?

Unsure what to say, I smile at her thinly. I busy myself preparing my plate. The mold on the bread is not too bad today— it only branches out at one end of the loaf. But as I attempt to rip the spoiled section off, the mold disappears. I hold my hand over the end of the bread and try to distract Verity's attention with a smile, but it's too late.

"How did you—" She shakes her head and reaches for the bread. "May I?"

What else can I say but yes? I swallow and nod.

"Oh, Abigail." She sighs the words as she turns the bread over in her hands. "This is—this is a miracle. How did you...?"

"I didn't do anything," I say quickly, defensively. "Why, what did you think you saw?"

Shaking her head, she breaks the bread and sets some on each of our plates. "I'm not saying anything, so don't you worry."

Verity believes in magic, possibly more than me. She'll probably spend the next few days trying to produce the same results with her herbal mixtures and quiet chants. But that doesn't mean she believes in spirits and time travel and Ankou. She allows me some quiet time while we eat.

I know Verity wouldn't say anything, but something in my stomach tells me Morts don't care about what someone would or wouldn't do. And this Mort, now five feet away and leaning in as if to listen more intently, leers at my dear friend.

My eyes tear and my throat closes up. I avert my gaze and shift in my seat; I don't deserve her kindness. My head throbs with the idea that I need to get back to Anna, but that Verity needs me, too. I can't just leave her, not until I know she's safe. She's one of the few people I've ever been able to count on.

Thanks to William and Tess, I now know what these Morts are capable of. Will the Morts take Verity the same way they took my family, using them to hurt me, or will they simply just feed on her life, slowly destroying her health until she's gone forever?

Her time is running short. My heart beats rapidly and unevenly in my chest, and it's hard to breath. Pulling air into my lungs feels like breathing in needles. I smile, hoping Verity won't notice my trembling hands or pick up on my strained breathing and erratic heartbeat.

I don't want to freak her out, nor spook away her friendship, so I won't tell her what I've seen. That won't help anything. I keep my mouth shut and look at Verity as though there is no Mort looming behind her, though I vow to myself that I *will* find a way to save her.

She'd once told me I remind her of a daughter she lost to typhus many years ago. She's been my only friend, my only companion, and she's always protected me. But now I feel it is my duty to protect *her*.

My mind swirls around visions I can't stomach to repeat. I'm hearing Mama's voice now. Warning me. 'That imagination of yours is a dangerous thing, Rose. It'll distract you—cloud your judgment. You need to just stop it right soon as it starts, that's what you need to do.'

But that's not what I need to do now. I may have an overactive imagination—it might even hurt me at times—but Verity is in danger. And it's right then that I realize how much this woman means to me.

"Now what do I do?" I mumble to myself under my breath.

"Are you all right, Abigail?" Verity asks. "You're so tense."

I clear my throat. I can't think straight to politely end our time together, so I walk toward the door and say, "I'm so glad you stopped by, Verity."

She takes the cue, edging toward the exit. Part of me wants her to stay, so I can try to protect her, but I don't know *how* to. Not yet. William and Tess never made it that far in explaining my abilities as an Ankou. The best I can do is get her out of here so I can figure all of this out. There has to be a way to help her before I return to Anna.

"It was nice to see you," Verity says slowly, stepping out the door. "If you need anything—"

"Thank you, Verity," I say. "I'm just...so tired."

I close the door and lean back against it, hating myself for the way I handled the whole situation. I press a hand to my stomach; I feel woozy. Guilty. Scared.

As soon as the sun sets, I need to seek out William and Tess. I cannot wait for them to come to me. Verity needs my help, and for so long as I am trapped here, I will do everything in my power to protect her.

CHAPTER 6
JANUARY 1692

MY CABIN DOOR RATTLES. "ABIGAIL!"

It's a girl, but I don't recognize the voice.

"Abigail! Show yourself!"

Then I hear the whispering; there's more than one person out there.

I strain to hear what they are saying.

"*I bet she's one,*" whispers one voice. "*I heard she showed up out of nowhere.*"

There's a *thwap*—the unmistakable sound of someone being hit in the back of their head.

"*That doesn't mean anything,*" another girl responds testily.

"*Then why's she hiding?*"

"*Come on, let's go.*"

Footsteps stomp away until they are more of a shuffle. Something clunks against my door—a rock, I presume.

"WITCH!" one of the girls yell.

This voice I recognize. The baker's daughter. One of Abigail's memories float by, hazy and warm. A young, sullen girl peeking beneath cloth to check on the bread. Her father asks her to bring the bread out to me—to Abigail—and when she does, she shoves it into Abigail's hands, then walks away.

Walks away like she and her friends are walking away now.

Finally, they are gone. My heart speeds and won't slow down. Something tells me their implications won't end here.

❧

IT IS DUSK I WILL MISS MOST. THE SUN LOW, LARGE, AND burning orange against the horizon. The sky ochre and violet. Tonight is almost too warm to be winter. Having already let in too much light, I drop the corner of muslin sheet covering my window, and it falls back into place. One day I may forget the feel of this time of day, may forget the cool, earthy smell of these hours.

Even after night has settled, I must stay indoors, waiting until the windows in town go black, until all that remains is the sulfur of snuffed candles. Though my doors and windows are shut, the cool breeze carries through the crack beneath the door, bringing with it the smell of night, the musk of animals in the forest. Each shift of temperature plays over my skin as the dark cools the earth.

I've always felt trapped in Salem—and within myself—but now I am also trapped by the acuteness of my senses.

When the dark has come, I sneak out to the forest trails, ready to make my way back to William and Tess. Tonight, the moon is as bright as the sun, but the world is shadowed in a bluish cool.

The Morts are everywhere, peeking from behind bushes and cluttering the open spaces as though they themselves are the trees that make the forest. An owl screeches in the distance, but it sounds closer, right in my ear. I freeze, looking around. At my feet, a dead bird. I look closer, frowning. Verity would call that bad luck. But I don't have much time to think about Verity, because just as I'm stepping around the poor thing, a pain stabs in my stomach. I brace myself against an old oak, coughing.

What's wrong with me?

Lightning flashes in the sky, but the air is innocent of rain. My legs tremble, and I get a sudden head rush, like thorns prickling my brain. I stumble forward, trying to remember which way to go, which direction I've come from and how far I am from the clearing.

The river is to my right, but I don't remember how far I have gone or where on the path I had turned. If only the music would return...if only it would whisper my name...but there is only silence. There is no calling, no draw—only burning pain, spreading from my stomach up into my throat.

I cough again. This time, I cough up blood that relieves my dry mouth and cracked lips. The nausea and pain drop me to my knees. I scan for the fire, for William or Tess. Unable to make the distance back to my house, I claw my way off the main path. I'm overcome by a thirst and hunger so strong that I cannot tell one from the other. I can't think straight with all this pain. I don't know what to do.

"William?" I say, but my voice only allows a whisper. "Tess?"

I don't know why I would even bother calling their names. I only know I can't do this on my own. Not this, not any of it. Normally I would hate how my helplessness makes me appear weak, but right now I'm in too much pain to care.

One thing does not change: I don't like needing anyone's help, especially not the help of people who can't possibly understand my plight to return to my daughter.

Something creaks behind me. I turn my head, only to catch a glimpse of a man standing at the edge of the forest trail, a lampshade swinging in his grasp.

The diffused candlelight illuminates the face of Reverend Parris.

He can't see me. The light doesn't reach this far along the path.

I roll into the underbrush, grass burrs pricking into my calves, thighs, and the side of my back. A whippoorwill flies out into the forest. All the noise—the rustling of leaves, the flap of wings— grate in my ears. Surely I've drawn Reverend Parris' attention, but when I dare peek again, he is gone. Afraid to move, I curl up in ball and try to quiet my rapid breathing.

My shaking stirs the leaves of the underbrush, but I don't know if I'm shaking from the pain and nausea or from the fear. The world blurs and darkens.

"HOLY FUCK."

Tess' voice is the first thing I hear as I'm returning to semi-consciousness. I know it's her because her voice has been imprinted in my mind since the first time I heard her speak. Even for all the anger and vulgarity of her tone, there's always that innocence behind it that makes me wonder about her.

Trying to bring my vision back, I blink, but everything is dark. I'm lifted. An arm under my neck and another under my knees. My sense of space spins and tilts with each heavy step. When the scent of an ocean breeze washes over me, I imagine William is carrying me. His breathing is steady and masculine, and his hands are rough and worn. I'm certain it's him. When I am set down, his voice confirms.

"Drink quickly," he says.

Still I cannot see. Something cold with a metal tang is thrust to my lips, and a sweet fluid rushes into my mouth, the ache cooling first in my throat and then in my stomach. Strong hands ease me to lie back onto something soft.

Slowly, my vision returns. The room is a haze. It's not much different than my own home—Abigail's home—except there's no door for a bedroom. No tables, no chairs. I'm lying on an unmade cot, and there's a small basin on the dirt floor beneath the window. A sword leans against the wall nearest a door made of warped boards.

"Where—where are we?"

Tess flops Indian style on ground beside the bed. "At the corner of *you're an idiot* and *we're saving your life*."

Grateful, I look to William, but as soon as his eyes meet mine, my warming cheeks alert me to turn away.

"Thank you," I say quietly.

Silence. I'm forced to look at him again. His jaw clenches, and his eyebrows pull lower over his eyes. He walks over to the window and grips the windowsill hard with his hands. Tess puts her hand on my forearm, drawing my attention and giving me a quieting stare.

What did I say to upset him? As I sit up, I get another bout of dizziness. I put one hand to my head, trying to stabilize my vision. "What happened?"

William spins toward me, his fist pressed to his mouth. He drops it away again. "Did you stop to think of someone other than yourself? Did you think, for even a second, that maybe you ought to wait for us to call on you, as we said we would?"

Of course I had thought of someone other than myself. I was thinking of Verity.

I open my mouth to speak, but William stalks toward me, not stopping until he reaches the end of the bed. "You could have gotten yourself killed, or worse, exposed our kind."

"Nice to know your priorities," I choke out.

"You want to help your daughter? Do us all a favor—use your head."

He stops there, his stance wilting. I swallow. The silence is loud in my ears. I want to be anywhere but here, but I don't want to move, don't want to draw attention to myself.

William sinks into the edge of the bed, leans forward, and rests his elbows on his knees. He drops his head into his hands, then looks at me, his eyes softer now. "I'm sorry. But Cordovae—what were you thinking?"

"I had to talk to you."

"Next time, wait. We were coming for you. We will always come for you if you just *wait*." He reaches over and places his hand on mine. I want it to stay there forever, but I can't even look at him when he's touching me without feeling an attraction I should not feel.

I'm immediately overcome by anger with myself. I shouldn't be thinking of him in that way. I barely know this man. I'll be leaving soon. We both have more important things to worry about, and I have no reason to think the attraction is mutual.

"Sorry to get cross with you," he says when I don't respond, then he stands and strolls a few feet away again.

"Where are we?" I ask.

"Tess' home. Miles from the settlement. It took most of my energy to get us here in time to save you. If you hadn't drank the nightshade in time..."

"Nightshade?" I repeat, unable to hide the panic in my voice.

My mind flashes back to the Pa of my childhood. Camping. Warnings about what plants to eat and which to avoid. Nightshade could kill me. How can I reverse this before it's too late? Before I'm dead? My lungs constrict. I'm too panicked to breathe.

"Why on earth would you give me nightshade?" My words come out all wobbly from fear.

"That is what the Ankou eat," William says. "The plants and berries poisonous to humans sustain the Ankou's life and abilities. These things are not harmful to you now."

If the Nightshade doesn't kill me, I'll believe him. In the meantime, I'm still hesitant to eat or drink anything else they give me. I push my apprehensions aside, knowing there is no time to waste.

Tess heads for the fireplace, her dark braid swaying near the small of her back. There's something different about her tonight, but I can't place it. "We must work fast. Cord needs to return by morning," she says. "We can't risk their suspicion over her missing."

Now I have a nickname, apparently, but I hardly care. In fact, it makes me feel a little more at home.

"What if she goes into another collapse?" William asks. "She can't possibly have completed the first one."

Tess shrugs. "So they might think she is ill and no one will want to go near her. If she keeps her curtain up and her cape on, it should be fine. What is important is that they are not out looking for her."

Something about the way she says this draws attention to her mouth. Her bottom lip is fuller than the top, like she is perpetually pouting. I've figured out what's different about her tonight: her lips are stained red. Maybe from that radish on the counter...but why would she do that? It makes her look old, and this is not a world where a young woman should be in a rush to look older.

William swallows and gives a single nod. "Warm something for her to eat."

"Something human," I clarify. "Or is that not allowed?"

William chuckles. "That's fine, Cord."

I sit up, the moment sudden and cold on my skin. I feel...better. "What happened to me back there?"

Tess pours some dark liquid and cubes of meat into the iron pot over the fire. "When you awake for the first time after a collapse, you need to get the right herbs into your system immediately. I didn't sense you'd awakened until it was too late."

"I've been awake all day."

Tess shrugs. "Guess we're lucky you made it as long as you did, then."

"That's it?" I ask, irritated. "You guess we're lucky?"

Perhaps I am thinking too poorly of Tess, but part of me wonders if she really didn't sense I'd awakened until just now, seeing as how it sounds like they are supposed to be able to sense such things.

William places his hand on my outstretched leg. The touch creates a flutter in my stomach. "Tess is new to this, too. Don't let her fool you. When we did finally get to you, we had to wait for the man who followed you to leave. We can't risk anyone seeing us."

But apparently they can risk me dying.

These are the people I'm fighting for? Well, if that's what it takes to get back to Anna, so be it, but they won't get any more from me than I'm obligated to give.

"If you want my help," I say, "then you're going to have to answer some questions."

I think I've been pretty easy-going up until now, but as my shock and confusion erode, I find myself getting angry.

William's brow furrows. "What kind of questions?"

"For one, it's bright as day outside right now. In the middle of the night."

"Our kind are able to see at night as though it were daylight," William says. "It is to help us hunt."

"Should I suppose it's also normal for our kind to touch a molding loaf of bread, and it...it..."

"Heal?" Tess supplies.

"Yes," I say. "A friend of mine witnessed me doing so this morning."

William shakes his head. "Healing things, especially things made from the earth, is one of the gifts of the Ankou as well. But you absolutely *cannot* let people see you do it."

"It's not as though I did it on purpose," I say. "Perhaps you two should tell me what to expect. I can't hide things if I don't know what to hide."

"It's sounds as though you aren't worried your friend will say anything," Tess says, but it's more of a question.

"She won't. But a Mort followed her when she came into my house and again when she left. In the short time of our visit, it seemed to be drawing closer to her. I came looking for you both to ask what to do."

Tess stares off into space as she uses a large wooden ladle to stir the food in the pot. The salty aroma of beef and the sweet smell of wine waft toward me, but the stirring in my belly tells me the liquid is not wine.

After a moment, her focus returns to me. "I wouldn't feel good about it, either," she says. She's tugging her earlobe again. "Especially if that woman knows what you are capable of. If the Mort overtakes her, it could mean death for you both. And the Mort won't stop there."

Her answer isn't comforting, and I shrug, unsure of what to say and feeling a little defensive.

William closes his eyes and shakes his head. "We need more time, Tess."

"Time for what?" I ask.

Tess sighs heavily. "More time to train you before you start moving spirits. But," she says, "we don't *have* time. We can teach you what you need to know to help your friend, but you might not learn quickly enough. That could cause problems for us, but we can't exactly run off to fix this for you now."

"Why not?"

Williams frowns. "Tess is right. It will draw too much attention if we enter your town now, especially if we are moving Morts while we are there. We can't risk our lives for that—we need to make sure we survive long enough to handle all the Mort population, not just one. That requires time and strategy. As for your friend, you might be able to save her discreetly on your own, once you know how, but you haven't had any training yet."

"Right," Tess says, "and we're supposed to wait until two weeks after a collapse before we start, but if this woman knows your secret and there is a Mort seeking to possess her..." She freezes when her eyes meet William's. "We can't wait."

Good. I don't have time to wait, and Verity doesn't have time for me to wait, either.

"What about this 'collapse'?" I ask.

"It's like hibernation for the Ankou," Tess says. "It happens every time you sleep. You—"

I narrow my eyes at her. "That's going to happen *every* time I sleep?"

William chuckles and removes his hand from my shin. "You'll only sleep once a decade. The collapse can last anywhere from a fortnight to a month, and when you awake, you'll need to feed immediately."

"Why didn't you tell me this before?" I ask.

Tess sashays over with a wooden bowl filled with a burgundy liquid and meat. "Here," she says. She sits beside me again with her own bowl of food. "When a human is turned Ankou, they always have a collapse their first night. I thought we'd be able to get to you before you awoke, but you only slept a week."

Only a week? I thought it was only one *night*. "Well, that's just...lovely."

She rolls her eyes and takes a few bites of the stew then passes the rest to William. She points to my food. "Eat," she says. "Gain your strength. We have much to do tonight."

CHAPTER 7
JANUARY 1692

WE'RE STANDING IN A FIELD THAT STRETCHES TOWARD CLOUDS hovering like smoke on the horizon. Standing as prey though we aim to be the hunters. I'm noticing for the first time the way my skin sheens gold in the moonlight. It almost makes up for those ugly veined wings that plague me in the light of day. It's strange that I can still feel my wings, even when they are not visible. They make me feel ugly, even though no one can see them now—not even me.

This I can handle, though. It's William that makes me woozy.

The golden sheen on *his* skin affects me differently, more mesmerizing. Or maybe it's the way his lightweight clothes drape on broad shoulders or fall to bare feet. His attire is ideal for combat, but consequently also ideal for showing off his perfect physical condition. I have to stop my mind from wandering; he looks so heavenly that I can barely think straight.

What would Verity make of tonight? Clear skies, she says, signal good luck. The lack of birds, however, would be unsettling. I sigh deeply, trying to push thoughts of my dear friend away. I can't worry about her tonight.

In the distance, beyond the cold, whitewashed field, a deer

faces me before leaping into the darkness, into the forest, into the safety of trees that obscure her from view.

William approaches me in that way of his—that open body posture that makes me feel instantly comfortable around him, and the steady eye contact that makes me feel both uncomfortable and trusting at the same time. The sword strapped to his back—the hilt peeking over his shoulder—makes him look even stronger, even more capable of keeping me safe until I return to Anna.

I catch my breath just as he reaches me and hands me a small pouch.

"Open it," he says.

So I do.

Inside are three small wind chimes. He's wearing the same ones on a cord around his neck. My heart skips a beat, thinking at first it's a romantic gesture, but then Tess' chimes clink as they dangle at the end of her silky black braid.

"Don't get them wet," William says simply.

"They won't work when they're wet?"

He grins, stretching, and takes an easy breath. His gaze falls back to me. "Just don't get them wet, all right?"

"I'll take that to mean I don't want to know...So what's it for?"

"We wear them when we hunt," Tess says. "It calls out the Morts."

The twinkle of the chimes reminds me of home—of the place where Anna waits for me. For a moment, I imagine the field flooded with red poppies. They're turning black. They crumble like dust and disappear from my mind. There's a cradle in the distance, a baby crying, and then it's all gone, and it's just me standing here with Tess and William. The vision had seemed so real, so unlike my usual daydreams, that I'm startled.

"Something's wrong," I say.

Tess takes my hand and gives it a gentle squeeze. "You will overcome these feelings. Stay strong."

William steps in front of us, his broad shoulders blocking my vision of the field beyond. "Seers who join the Ankou are more sensitive to the influence of Cruor spirits. They will play tricks on your mind, but you must fight. You must separate your past from your current reality."

"Just the Cruor spirits? What about the spirits of other elementals?"

"When a Cruor meets their ultimate death, they are the least willing of any immortal to cross over. They use their power of influence to save themselves, to inhabit a new life. When that happens, it's too late. We can't move the Mort then, not without risking the human's life."

"Possession?" I whisper, chills prickling the tiny hairs on my arms.

Before William can respond, a blue pickup truck screeches to a halt just a few feet ahead of us. It revs, circling us, moving faster and faster, ripping the earth beneath its tires, polluting the air with the pungent taste of gasoline and upturned soil.

I shouldn't know what the strange machine is, but in my heart I know, and I feel closer to Anna. I feel close to home, and I don't want to separate from it, though fear picks up in my chest as the truck whips past. I can feel the way the truck displaces the air, my clothing shifting against my body and hair lifting.

Pa's truck.

Pa's the one who endangers Anna. He can't be left alone with her.

"I'm going back," I say. "I can feel it—I'm going back to Anna!"

William grasps my wrist. "It's not real, Cordovae. You need to focus. I promise you will get back to her."

"She needs me *now*," I say.

"Trust me, Cord, please. You need to fight this."

I narrow my eyes. "Trust you?"

My hand goes cold; Tess is gone from my side. Across the field, she stands by a dark figure—one of the fanged Morts. She digs her nails into the figure's scalp, and their collective form vibrates, their edges blur. The Mort explodes into black particles that fall like charcoal snowflakes to the shadows between the roots of grass. The truck circling us fades.

Tess returns to our side, panting, eyes shining and alert. "See?" She sucks in a breath. "Illusion."

Mama warned me about letting my overactive imagination cloud my judgment—but I don't think this is what she had in mind.

I just stare into the space where the truck had just been, shaking my head. "It seemed...so real...I guess I'll believe anything these days."

"It happens to everyone in the beginning," William says. "You will become stronger."

"How long?" I ask. I need to know. "How long until I get back to Anna?"

"As long as it takes," Tess says sharply. "You will be here until the numbers are manageable. Believe me, we are all working as quickly as we can. None of us want to be trapped here."

"Trapped here?"

William gives Tess a sidelong glare. It's a moment too long before his attention returns to me. "If we do not move the spirits quickly enough, they will prolong the war. And the longer you are here, the higher the probability that you become stuck."

I step back. My heart might as well have stopped in my chest. "You never told me that."

Tess sighs, but it is not her usual irritated sigh. Tonight, her sigh sounds sympathetic and thoughtful. "It protects the balance. The longer we are here, the more influence we have on this time. If we try to return after influencing this time for too long, we can throw the newly-created paths off balance. And imbalance is the breeding ground for evil. It's part of what created this mess in the first place."

"How so?" I ask.

Tess looks to William, then back to me. "You can't get all the answers you want in one night, or we'll never finish. You need to focus. Tonight will bring you one step closer to your daughter. Just keep that in mind."

Closer? What does that even mean? Days? Years?

As much as they try to pacify me—to tell me not to worry—it is impossible. Part of me doesn't want to believe them, but as much as my heart begs for a reason to distrust them, my soul knows everything they have told me is true.

There's nothing I can do now. My ancestors are among these people; if they are killed, I will not exist.

Anna will not exist.

New determination takes root, and anger burns toward the Morts for giving me false hope with their illusions. I take the wind chimes William has given me and tie them around my waist, making a thin rope belt that clinks when I move.

Yes, this is war.

Morts weave through shadows, creep across the horizon, and crowd together at the edge of the forest. I will kill them and anyone else who stands in my way.

I exhale through my noise and tilt my face slightly toward William. "Just tell me how this works."

"First step is learning defense," Tess says. "Watch."

She runs to the far side of the field and spins before kneeling to the ground. The wind chimes in her hair draw a Mort from between the trees. Tess stays still as the Mort approaches her. Panic rises in my chest.

"What's she doing?" I ask William. "Is she hurt?"

"Shhh," he says. "Watch."

My whole body is shaking. The Mort isn't more than a foot away from her, and she hasn't done anything. His sights are set on her.

"The chimes call them out," he whispers, "but they are afraid of us. They won't stay long once they see us."

As though to illustrate William's point, the Mort turns quickly. He glances in every direction. He backs away, looking everywhere, then turns and runs back into the shadows between the trees.

Tess stands and walks back over to us.

"Are you okay?" I ask.

She laughs. "Of course."

"What happened? Why did he just walk away?"

"He saw you and William."

"But not you?" I ask.

"Our wings can shield us—make us invisible to them. It helps when outnumbered by the Morts. They don't fear us as much then. It can also be used to trick them into coming closer."

"But our wings aren't visible at night," I say.

"Exactly." Tess' grin is so wide it brightens her whole face, and I think how I like her better this way. "While others cannot see our wings at night, what they offer us against the Morts is something greater. They cannot see what our wings protect. You have to learn to feel them and be one with them."

William's hand comes to my elbow. "But they won't cloak you from anyone but the Morts. So be careful with it. And you'll have to get a better sense of your wings before you'll be able to accomplish this effectively. There's a learning curve—you won't know if you've done it wrong until it's too late."

"So perhaps it's more important you teach me to fight."

"Of course," William says.

He steps behind me, his stomach pressing against the top of my back, reminding me how unbelievably tall he is. If he were anyone else, I would feel vulnerable with him so close. But it's different with William. With William, I just feel...safe.

He sweeps my hair over my shoulder, and it spills in a river of red past my right breast. My center of balance falters, and I sway a little, but he holds me up.

"Easy, there, Mimosa," he says.

"Mimosa?"

He chuckles. "You smell like the yellow flowers of a silk tree."

I hope that's a good thing, though I shouldn't care one way or another. I'm not here for handsome men to tell me I smell nice.

"I'm just nervous," I admit.

"I'm not going to hurt you."

And I know it's true. I hold my breath as he rests his hand on my shoulder and his other hand grazes my side as it comes around my body to rest on my stomach.

"God, your shoulders are tense. The Morts are going to smell the fear on you before you get anywhere near them if you don't get it under control."

I can't help but laugh. "Fear isn't exactly a choice."

"Sure it is," he says. Then he leans in closer to my ear and whispers, "Close your eyes."

I do as he says, swallowing around the lump in my throat, hoping my trembling is not so obvious to him as it is to me. Uneven and shaky breaths tumble past my lips.

"Relax. Breathe."

"I am breathing," I mumble.

"Focus on what is. There is nothing else." His breath is warm on my ear, the feel of his deep voice reaching down to my stomach where his hand rests. "Here," he says, pressing a little firmer, effectively pulling my body closer to his. "This is your energy. When you find the Mort, you will feel everything here."

I think he is trying to help me calm down, but his body so close to mine does anything but. I open my eyes and look down at his hand, noticing for the first time the scars across his knuckles and wondering where he got them. His hands seem so large resting on my stomach.

"Feel what?" I ask. Surely he isn't referencing the desire spreading through my body, this odd attraction I feel whenever he stands too close. But at the same time, it's an uncomfortable feeling—a feeling I'm not ready for.

"You will know what to do," he says.

"How will I know when I know?" I ask. "How will I know what to look for?"

His thumb caresses my abdomen. "You'll know."

Tess lets out an irritated huff. "I think she gets the point, William."

The moment I turn toward her, she flicks her gaze skywards, arms crossed. I look to William, hoping his response will decode her reaction.

He steps back, his expression darkened. "She didn't come to me with the training you did."

"Oh, that's part of the training now?" She smirks. "The person who trained me before you must not have gotten notice. You realize we only have five hours until sunrise, and more than five hours of work to do."

I furrow my brow. "Why does it matter how much we do?"

Tess closes her eyes. "We need to move the spirits faster than they repopulate, or we'll never finish."

Never finish . . .

Her words halt me at my core. I need to get back to Anna. I can't be trapped here forever.

"How long have you been here?" I ask her.

"Nearly two decades."

My hope deflates. If there was a way back, wouldn't someone have found it by now?

"There will always be more elementals dying, more Morts entering this space." I slouch where I stand. "We'll never get rid of them, will we?"

Tess' expression is cold and unmoving. "Not if we stand around talking all night."

My eyes implore her for something more than a catty remark, and, for a moment, her expression softens.

"We do what we can." She points to my scrawny arms and adds, "Let's just hope you're stronger than you look."

I have to admit, she is far more muscular than I am.

Then, just as fast as her compassion has come, it's gone. Her face grows serious. "Time to work."

CHAPTER 8
JANUARY 1692

TESS TELLS ME TO RUN. RUN, AND THINK ABOUT WHERE I WANT to be. That's how I got here. That's how I get where I'm going.

But it's *not* how I got here. I never wanted to be here. I just wanted to be with Anna.

"Run, now! Go, go, go! This is it!"

I know Tess means for me to run toward the Morts, but I try running back to Anna. I don't know where that is—I can't picture the place—but I keep running, feet pushing off the ground, thighs burning, weeds thwapping my shins. I run until my belly gets the feeling of being suspended in air. I run until I burst through the forest and into this same field. Again and again.

On one of my passes across the field, I see my old room. I see the peeling paisley wallpaper and the dull yellow headboard and my threadbare quilt and Mama brushing my hair. I push myself hard, want it with every fiber of my being. But still I pop out on the wrong side.

This side.

Sweat trickles between my shoulder blades, my lungs burn desperately for oxygen, and my damp, apple-red hair sticks to my scalp. The sweat keeps me cool and makes me feel alive. Alive, but weak. I thought being Ankou was supposed to make me stronger?

How can it be that I have more power now but feel just as powerless as before?

I'm meant to save humanity, but it's humanity who endangers my daughter while I am trapped here, unable to protect her.

Panting hard, I turn back to look in the direction of the open field I just ran through. I'd run straight across, from the north end to the south, and popped right out the north end again. A loop.

"Stop," Tess says. "That's not going to work. We don't have time for this."

"Why"—I suck in a breath—"not?"

Tess tugs at her earlobe. "I don't get you, Cord. You knew your daughter for what—all of an hour? Why do you care so much?"

Her words struck a nerve. I loved Anna before I ever even met her, even more so when I first laid eyes on her. But I couldn't expect Tess to understand that. "What more reason do I need than that she is my child? Any mother would do the same."

Tess' arms tightened across her chest. "Yeah. So they say."

Maybe she was right. Mama had given up on me. But that was different. "Most mothers, then," I added. "Most mothers love their child instantly and intensely."

"Must be nice," Tess mumbles. "But it's still selfish of you. If you leave, what will happen to Verity? Or do you not care anymore?"

If Verity knew, I'm certain she would rather I save my daughter, but that's not to say I don't care about the woman.

"I don't understand why you need me anyway," I spit back. "I'm just getting in your way. You could get more done if you weren't busy training me. You can handle the Morts without me. The Universe could find someone else to help you. There—"

"I've heard enough," Tess says sharply. "If you don't focus, you're going to put us all in danger. That means no future for you *or* your daughter."

I rock back, my head spinning and my breaths bursting, finally understanding this situation. This isn't *a* way back to Anna. It's the *only* way back to her. If I return now, there will be no Anna to return to.

William trots over. He's been running all night, too, but his runs have been more productive than mine; he's taken at least a dozen Morts by surprise. His shirt, soaked in sweat, is thrown over one of his strong shoulders. His body is perfect—lean, firm, smooth skin...

His beauty is terrifying.

I can't make sense of my feelings, of how attracted I am to him and yet how uncomfortable seeing him makes me feel. Staring at him makes me wonder if the golden sheen of my skin in the moonlight is as stunning as his or as elegant as Tess', or if, to them, I'm just another person. To them, has the terrifying beauty of the Ankou lost its magic? I could never have dreamed of something so stunning. It's walking, living, breathing art.

William places his hand on my shoulder. "It's not just about where you want to be. It can be about where you don't want to be. Wishing you were anywhere but where you were."

Offended, I pull away. "I did *not* wish to be taken away from family. I am not *you*."

I don't know if I've insinuated accurately, but I must believe I have. His eyes search mine, and I know there is a hurt there, a hurt his expression cannot hide, though his anger is building around his jaw line. He's keeping something from me. Hiding something.

"Am I wrong?" I ask. I can't control myself. All my pent-up hurt throttles straight at him, as though he is to blame for all of this. Perhaps he is. "Maybe you just don't care if we get back because you're already stuck here! Come on, William, tell me—how long *have* you been here?"

"What does it matter?" he shoots back. "Not everyone wants to run away from the opportunity to help others. Maybe some of us *want* to stay here. *Belong* here."

I shrug, wishing I could just erase the entire conversation. I hate him and admire him at the same time. I force my mask of anger to stay frozen in an attempt to seem unaffected by his anger.

"We have a plan, Cord," William says. "And you need to honor it."

"I understand—"

"*Do* you?" He narrows his eyes. "Because I'm starting to wonder if you're capable of having a plan, or if you are completely run by your impatience, impulsivity, and selfishness. You're all over the map, and we can't afford for you to get us killed!"

For William, life is about saving Salem. For me, it's about saving my daughter. One singular person in a sea of many. Perhaps that does make me selfish. Or perhaps it just makes me human. I don't expect him to understand that.

I hate when William's mad. Tess' anger I can handle—she's always angry, even when she's not. But when William's upset, I start to think it's my fault.

Tears blur my vision, and I hate that I'm crying, that my weakness is so apparent. "I didn't ask to be brought here! Stop blaming me! Blame your god or whoever created this mess!"

"Yeah, well, it does make me wonder." He shakes his head and sighs. "You are capable, you know. You were chosen for a reason, even if none of us can see it yet."

"Thanks," I mumble. "I think."

"I know it's difficult, Cord, but try to focus," William says. He's softened now, and I wonder if it's because he feels bad or just finds me too pathetic to scold anymore. "We'll try it again, all right? Focus on the Mort and run, thinking of them, until you lock."

"Fine," I say, residual anger still bubbling in my gut.

Tess has already moved three Morts and, while William was talking, locked onto a fourth. I spin away from him and take off.

"Fine," I say again, under my breath. "Fine, fine, fine."

But my frustration and fear don't make me want to fight harder as much as they make me want to find a way around this situation. I can't risk getting stuck here. I need to get back to Anna. *Now.*

I break through space—through time and distance, through the blur of grays and blacks and green—and collide into one of the

Morts, knocking him down onto the crisp grass. His face is inhuman; his nose more of snout. Had he been a Strigoi once?

My abdomen tingles, and the energy rushes through my body and out my fingertips. I dig my nails into his head as I've seen Tess do. My fingers go cold, but he steps away. He pauses, his grin like a jack-o-lantern before he runs off.

This is it. This is what my life has become.

Either I stay and fight or keep trying to go back. What if Tess is right? What if every time I try to go back, I'm just wasting time? What if I waste so much time I lose Anna altogether?

I glance around until I've spotted another. If I'm stuck here because of these Morts, then I have no choice but to get rid of them. I focus on making all the motions one—making contact with the Mort and locking my fingers into its skull. This time, a static shock snaps me into place.

This one—a child with shadowy wings, perhaps born Ankou—makes no effort to escape. It's almost as though she has been waiting for me. A white light glows from her body, and there's a shift inside my stomach. She's meant to live again. Her intended future surrounds me. I'm not in the field anymore. I'm with a weeping woman—another Ankou—in a small nursery, my hands on her head, though she is unaware of my presence. She clutches a small blue bear to her stomach and leans forward, her mournful wails echoing through the room and in my ears.

I look up, taking in the cream-colored walls and the red and blue sailboats painted in a border along the ceiling. The powdery, soft scent overpowers the air in the room, and it feels as though my lungs are constricting. A patchwork quilt hangs over the rail of a crib.

An empty crib.

There is a knowing in my stomach that hits me as hard as though it is my own child missing from that crib, and I try to step back, but I'm stuck. The woman's grief flows through me, or perhaps the grief is my own.

Once the Mort spirit has taken life in her womb, I am back in the field, tears streaming my cheeks. She's lost her first child, and nothing can heal that. But now there is a new spirit—a new life—growing inside of her. A new life meant to replace the old. But hearts just don't work that way. I wish I could take comfort in knowing not all Morts are evil, but even that knowledge cannot fix the brokenness inside of me.

I rub the tears away roughly and lean forward, resting my hands on my knees. My stomach empties into the grass. Tess and William jog over and each puts a hand on my back.

"You okay?" Tess asks.

I nod, straightening, and then walk away as I wipe my mouth with the back of my hand. *That's* traveling? It felt as unnatural as it is, falling through time and space like that to move a spirit where it belongs. And yet, at the same time, once I had done it I felt as though it was something I had done every day of my life. It was as easy as breathing, only much more unsettling.

William's heavy steps follow, but I sense him stop a couple feet away. "I know it's hard."

I don't say anything.

"Your body will get used to the traveling," he says. "You did good."

But I haven't. I'm not like him. I'm not completely selfless, completely devoted to saving the lives of total strangers. My admiration for him certainly fuels me when I'm feeling weak, but in the end, I'll never be as strong as him. For Anna, though, I will try.

I take off again, to a Mort far off toward the open horizon but near the south edge of the forest. This Mort resists. She tries to push her way into me. My fingertips ache with an icy burn, but I feel the flickering, the spark. I feel this Mort and me between time and space. It tries to show me another host to move into, but I know. I know just as William said I would. Through the hazy film of their projection, I see the field. I see the darkness radiating from their core.

They're staying here, and they will die tonight by my hands.

Heat stirs inside of me, but I feel the cold of the Mort spirit still trying to push its way into my body. Then I see it, I am watching it happen to me. I'm outside my body, and my body is trying to pull me back, but the Mort is pushing me away. My hand outstretches toward my spirit, but I see the Mort's claw-like fingers trying to take form around my heart.

My strength fades. I see myself—my body—holding Anna. I don't know if it's my dreams of holding her or my fear of her being in someone else's arms, but I'm filled with anger.

The Mort is trying to influence me! Trying to get me to give up my body so it can take me over...trying to trick me into thinking I'm with Anna now.

There's a jolt, and my spirit snaps back into my body. The energy at my core rockets through me and into the Mort, and, just as I witnessed Tess do earlier, we convulse. My power, driven by hatred, terrifies me, as though it is I who is evil. But I don't stop. I don't let go until I take this Mort from a spirit to a pile of black particles.

I killed it.

I shove the thought away. I'm not a murderer. They were already dead. And if I hadn't moved them, they would have killed somebody else.

These are the things I will tell myself from now on—the things that will make me believe I am not actually a killer. That I'm not as evil as I feel.

The silence is sudden. The calm in the field around me only serves to magnify the panic in my chest.

"Now what?" I ask, looking up.

The field is empty. Even the trees seem horrified, large knots twisted into their bark like melting faces.

"Tess? William?"

They aren't in any direction. The tar-black particles seep into the ground and dissolve. I lean forward to take a closer look.

Something whiffs past my ear. An arrow hits the ground in front of me. I jump to my feet and spin around. Nobody's there.

Where did that arrow come from?

A stinging pain starts in my shoulder, followed by a wet trickle. My dress is torn at the shoulder, as is the flesh beneath, pale white split open to dark red.

I dart off, ignoring the pain, thinking of Tess and William. I'm completely off balance, but I stay focused until I stumble through space and come out on a path in the forest. It's darker here than it had been in the field, but my Ankou vision grants me clear vision. Two unfamiliar figures—large men without shirts—pin William and Tess to the ground.

They are not Morts.

I am staring but not focusing, one hand holding my arrow wound to try to slow the bleeding. The events unfolding before me —William and Tess hadn't warned me about anything like this, about any possibility of being attacked or dealing with anything other than the Morts. A cold wave rolls through my stomach, and a weight sinks in my chest. The moment feels more real than life itself, and at the same time, feels as though it's happening a million miles away. A dream, a nightmare.

No one seems aware of my presence. I could walk away. I would be safe—I would live—but would I be able to return to Anna? Could I forgive myself for abandoning such noble people? William and Tess don't deserve to die.

The cold night air chills the blood between my fingertips, and my hands feel sticky, and I know I am going to need some help patching up this arrow wound. Help that William and Tess would give me.

Help that I would give them.

Without William and Tess, I will never make it through the trials of my calling. I'll never move the Morts fast enough to return to my own time and place.

If I die, though, I definitely won't make it back to Anna.

The skin of William's attacker glistens alabaster-white in the bright shine of the moon, his blond hair cropped short and a shadow darkening his jaw. Thick, inky lines mark the side of his neck with something reminiscent of the letter 'F', but the lines that should be horizontal slant down, and the 'F' faces the wrong direction. The attacker tries to grab William by his throat, but he's determined and fierce and claws at the man's face.

Tess struggles against a man with dark tanned skin and long black hair that's tied back with a thin strip of cloth. He has the same marking on his neck as William's attacker. He has her on her back, all of his weight on her, his knees digging into her forearms beneath him. Bile rises into my throat. The unease comes from somewhere deeper than fear; it comes from an inexplicable hurt and anger—a familiar feeling, though I can't place it exactly.

How am I supposed to decide who to help—William, Tess, or myself? William wouldn't even have to think twice. He would never leave someone else to die just to save himself. But I'm not him. I'll never be anything like him. But Tess is practically still a child. Would she try to save me if the situation were reversed? I honestly don't know, and yet, at the same time, it doesn't matter. It would kill me to see her die.

Tess manages to free one of her hands and punch the man in his temple. He tumbles to her side, and she pounces on him, her dark braid whipping into her face and then falling in front of her shoulder. She digs her fingernails into his cheekbones, right below his eyes, and tar-like fluid seeps out of the wounds on his flesh. Right now, everything about her looks strong. Even her fingers. The look of determination in her eyes is enough to kill, but she doesn't count on that. She reaches back beneath her cloak and pulls out a wooden camping stake.

My gaze darts back to William. I should do something, but I'm every bit as selfish as William said. I can't risk death to save them.

The attacker lands a punch to William's gut, and William's head lolls to the side. Blackish-purple blood seeps from his nose and over his lips. Something tugs at my heart and in my stomach. I shake my head, feeling the apology on my lips but unable to speak. He's going to die if I don't do something, but if I risk my life to help him, I'm risking Anna's life as well. I can't let my inexplicable connection with him get in the way.

William shakes his head as though warding me off from even considering it. He doesn't want my help. He wouldn't hold it against me, in life or death, if I did nothing to save him right now. But if he dies, his death will be on my conscience forever.

William's attacker brandishes a silver dagger from his boot and starts to dig it into William's side. Where William's shirt has ripped open, I see purple-black vein-like lines spreading over his skin, away from the dagger's wound. I can't just stand here any longer. I cannot live in this vulnerable place, I can't go through this alone.

I rush forward and tackle the shirtless man. I swing my fists at him, but I can't feel the impact of any of my blows. I swing at him unseeingly, furious that his presence has forced me to this. Furious that he is standing in the way of my returning to Anna.

The back of his hand hits my cheek with a force that creates an instant numbing sensation. I try to crawl away, but he grabs my leg and pulls me back, the forest ground cutting my knees, shins, stomach, and the side of my head.

I claw at the dirt, my fingernails scraping over stones. They catch a large rock, and I cling to it until it lifts from the ground. I grasp it with both hands, twist onto my back, and sit up, holding the rock over my head and then slamming it down into my attacker's scalp. There's a crack, and the attacker stumbles. William, standing behind him, whips the blade of a large sword across his neck, decapitating him and covering me in a spray of black blood.

I'm not as disgusted as I would have expected. Instead, the bloodshed has ignited both a physical and mental hunger in me.

Tess is sitting with knees tucked to her chest beside a dead man and a blood-stained wooden stake. Her blood-soaked clothes hang from her body—stretched, ripped, dirty. I can't move or speak—only stare dumbly at the scene before me, the dead men lying there. They don't dissolve away like the Morts do or like the Cruor would.

I tell myself I only saved William and Tess for their help in getting back to my daughter. It cannot have been for any other reason. Yet I know this is a lie.

My focus unwittingly shifts back to William. Though his face carries the dirt and bloodstains of a warrior, his expression is gentle, perhaps even regretful. I want to run to him and wrap my arms around him and bury myself in his chest. But I don't move. I've acted foolishly to risk my life tonight. I can't allow myself to care about anyone, to get torn between worlds. I need to protect myself for the world I belong in. My world. Anna's world.

"What happened?" I ask.

William drops the sword and it clangs against the rocks embedded in the forest terrain. "Cordovae," he whispers. "You're bleeding."

He touches my cheek, and I wince. When he pulls his hand back, there is blood on his fingertips.

"Are you okay?" he asks. His attention drops to my wounded shoulder and then away. "There was another attacker?"

I nod. "He ran off. I didn't see him."

Tess' face snaps up, eyes wide. "There's only one reason he would run off."

William hisses, shaking his head and cutting her off. He leans against a tree, hand cupping the wound on his side. The vein-like marks are spreading, but all I can do is step back, step away.

"Iron-poisoning," he says. "We need to get back to the cabin." He levels his gaze at Tess. "They've come."

CHAPTER 9
JANUARY 1692

Back at Tess' cabin, I sit on the edge of a cot, clutching a woolen blanket around my shoulders. Though we are away from our attackers, I am still sick with fear, as if at any minute they might barge in.

"Take off your chimes," William demands. Tess and I hand ours to him, and he shuts them in a drawer. "We don't need to draw any attention to ourselves right now."

After that, he sits by the fire, silent. No one says a word, and neither Tess nor William seem as though they want to hear a word, either. But I have questions. Lots of questions. If we're not trying to attract and destroy Morts, does that mean our mission is on hold? If so, for how long? What does that mean for me?

The fire casts a golden glow that makes the room's otherwise unnerving darkness more bearable, and the warm, musty air and scent of burning wood is almost comforting. Closest to the cabin's front window, a cobwebbed spinning wheel crushes a second pea-shuck mattress on the floor. The linens are scuffed with dirt. I doubt anyone sleeps there.

I've just finished a large drink made of nightshade and monkshood, a perfect blend of poison to help an Ankou recoup.

Tess' boots peek out at me from under her medieval dress as she stitches my wound.

Her unique scent of lemon and lavender soothes me. She's been gentle enough, though each pass with the needle pinches. Perhaps adrenaline numbs the pain, or maybe it's the horror of William healing himself. Though watching makes me queasy, I can't help but stare as he cuts away his infected flesh and cauterizes the wound with the red-hot fireplace poker.

The stench of burning skin makes my stomach churn harder, yet I'm helplessly fixated on his otherwise perfect, unmarred body. My eyes remain pinned on the fine but dark hairs on his chest that tangle together and run a line down his stomach. It scares me that the thought of him keeps distracting me from Anna, and guilt pangs deep in my gut that anything or anyone could have that effect on me. But when I'm with William and Tess, I don't feel nearly as lost in this world. I don't feel nearly as far from my child.

Impossibly soon, William's skin has regenerated.

"He's part Cruor," Tess whispers, which I suppose is an explanation intended to help me understand the rapid healing he experiences that Tess and I do not. But I don't fully understand what Cruor are. I never bothered to ask—never saw how it was of any relevance before now.

"Why doesn't he just drink some nightshade?"

Tess chews her lip. "He's allergic. May be part of being a dual breed."

I swallow, but my throat is so tight that I'm suffocating. It takes some effort, but I find my voice. I don't ask the question I want to ask—the question about William being part Cruor, or what being a dual breed means—because it doesn't feel like the most important question right now. "Who were the people who attacked us back there?"

Tess inhales through her nose. "You saw their markings?" she asks, indicating the clear skin on her own neck where theirs had been branded. "That was the Ansuz, reversed. It's a rune that represents misunderstanding and the power of delusion. Those that carry the mark are known for their manipulation magic. They are a prideful kind of Strigoi who have pledged their allegiance to the Maltorim. Do not underestimate them. They have offered their servitude to their natural enemy, and only those with grandiose delusions would ever do such a thing."

People who had betrayed their own kind? I don't ask why anyone would do that. Mankind does it all the time. I've always considered it a sign of weakness or fear, though right now I find it hard to see the men who attacked us as driven by anything other than blind fury.

"And the one that ran off?"

Tess frowns. "To alert the Maltorim of our location, I'm sure."

"Tell me more about the Strigoi and the Maltorim then."

Over the course of the next hour, Tess explains to me in detail about the Strigoi. They are the elemental race of water with an ability to change their essence from a human appearance to animal. Most are good, here to hunt the Cruor, which I come to learn are, in majority, bloodsucking monsters—earth elementals originally meant to purge the evil from mankind. So much for that idea. William is one of the few exceptions, but he is also part Ankou, and perhaps that is what sets him apart.

As Tess describes the Maltorim, her tone is dark and heady. They are a preternatural council comprised mostly of Cruor, thought by some to be messengers of the Universe. But rumor is they are not the true messengers—they are imposters with self-serving agendas who have brainwashed the masses of elemental races.

The rest of what Tess says sweeps by me, unabsorbed. I know all I need to know to get by, to do what I need to do and get out of here. Remembering the specifics are better served to people who plan to stick around. Like William.

The silence that falls on the room makes my skin itch. I drum my fingers on a nightstand. Then I pick up the little wooden box that's sitting there and examine it. I wind a small metal piece at the bottom.

"What's this?" I ask Tess. I've never seen anything like it before, not in this lifetime, though I seem to know the word for it: *music box*. I open the lid, and sure enough, a song begins. The first few notes are almost familiar.

Tess snatches the music box from my hands and snaps the lid closed. "Don't touch that."

"Sorry." I frown. "Where did it come from?"

She tucks it in a drawer. "I made it. It doesn't even exist yet; just pretend you never saw it."

Something tells me she shouldn't have made it. This is the kind of thing that gets us trapped here. Making too many changes outside of what we have been sent to do, altering history further than we are allowed.

Before I can say another word, William calls us over to where he sits by the fire, his fist pressed to his mouth. He still wears no shirt, and it's impossible not to take in his muscular chest and broad shoulders. I'm thinking of him more than I should allow. I pull myself together and lift my gaze to his face to see his eyes are already on me. My face heats. My heart is silenced by his intensity.

"The Maltorim have sent their warriors," he says. "The Mort community is larger than we anticipated, or growing too rapidly. Why else would the Marked Ones be here?"

I take it the 'Marked Ones' are the Strigoi marked with the Ansuz runic letter. I don't answer William's question, though. The question is clearly intended for Tess.

"The Maltorim should be working *with* us," she says. "Not that they ever do."

"Unless they are here to deal with my kind," William replies solemnly.

I shake my head. "Your *kind?*"

He turns to me. "It wouldn't be the first time the Maltorim were more concerned with the dual-natured than the Morts."

Tess cuts in before I can ask what he's talking about. "But why protect the Morts? The last time the Maltorim did that..."

Their eyes meet in a knowing I cannot share, but I feel it's nothing good.

"Another army?" William asks. His eyebrows cut lower over his eyes. "It would risk too much to do that here, to do that now."

Tess' expression is apologetic and, for the first time, I see her as vulnerable. I wish I were strong enough to be her rock, though I'm sure she would just turn me away.

William's sorrowful eyes aren't directed toward me, although my stomach still sinks when I see his expression. He devotes his attention to Tess and rakes his hand through his hair.

"If they are trying to stop us from moving the Morts, that means the Maltorim *want* the Morts here," he says. "Which means those Strigoi that attacked us tonight have the resources and strength in numbers that we do not."

I wait for someone to look at me so I can respond, but when that doesn't happen, I interrupt. "Then we have to fight the Morts and these Strigoi—these Marked Ones."

Tess lets out a bark of laughter. "You say it like it's nothing."

This time, I'm not offended by her biting sarcasm. I've noticed the way she's tugging on her earlobe, which I'm starting to think is a sign she's distressed. She's scared and defensive.

"I didn't mean—"

"You don't know what you are doing or what you are up against," she says. "We aren't prepared for this. It is one thing to fight the Morts but another entirely to fight the Maltorim."

That's not what I want to hear. "If it's hopeless, it should mean nothing if I leave."

"No," William says. "Tess is right: we aren't prepared for this. We don't walk away, though. Whatever we do, we fight. Any elemental would tell you that is your only chance for survival."

Tess folds her arms across her chest. "We don't have time for pep talks, William."

She crosses the room and grabs a large, leather-bound book from a shelf beside the door, then returns to sit beside me. She opens to the first page and gently traces her hand over a symbol much like a star within a circle, but she quickly stops and flips through to a later page.

"Cord, this war has been going on for some time. It's not just our war against the Morts. It's the war among the races that create the Morts in the first place. We're just cleaning up the mess. Unfortunately, there is more to learn than we have time to teach."

I swallow, not sure I want to know anymore, not sure I can take any more. I just want to go back to the life I belong in. But I manage a nod and stare at the displayed pages.

Tess continues with the details I don't care to hear. "The Cruor should have eradicated the evil in humans, but instead became evil themselves. They sustain their immortal life by drinking the blood of humans."

"And your creator sent them?"

"You could say that," she says. "We are told the tale of the Universe, of an entity that has always been and always will be, the ones who oversee our planet, who create but cannot destroy. When the creation of Cruor went wrong, the Strigoi were sent to stop them."

William lowers his head and pinches the bridge of his nose. "The war started first among them. That is when the others came."

"The Ankou?" I ask.

"Us," she confirms. Her tone and patience right now reveal an almost sentimental air about her, and I wonder if I'd been too quick to let her usual attitude fool me. "We were supposed to bring peace with our magic and were also intended to do as we do today—reap the spirits of immortals who have met a final death. Remember how I told you that when the Ankou arrived, they brought with them the ability for other elementals to cross-breed?"

She says this with such gravity that confusion sweeps through me. "Yes?"

"There is a reason the Maltorim doesn't like that. Dual breeds have less pronounced weaknesses and a wider range of abilities, which make them a threat," she explains. "And also an asset to the humans. They are the most capable of actually protecting humans against the darker elementals."

Tess spends the next hour showing me these things in her book, as though I need to be convinced. What is there to convince me of? I do not bother to doubt things any more than I dare to trust them. I just listen, only wanting to learn enough to get by.

She flips back to the front of the book and shows me the star within the circle once more. "This pentagram indicates creation is not done," she says. She touches the east point. "Air. This is us, the Ankou." She touches the bottom points of the star and names them each. "Fire, for the Chibold, and Earth for the Cruor." She continues around to the west point. "Water, for the Strigoi." Finally, she touches the point at the top. "This is the spirit."

"The Morts?" I ask.

"No," Tess says gravely. "Our world does not yet have an elemental for the spirit. Morts are merely the spirits of the elementals that have already existed."

For all the answers Tess and William have, there are still things that even they do not know about this world. It's hopeless.

Tess closes the book and returns it to the shelf. I expect her to talk some more, to explain and define and everything else she has done, to drone on in her somber tone with words and ideas that hold no meaning for me. But instead, Tess grabs her coat, her boots thud across the ground, and she walks outside, the door creaking closed behind her and shutting with a quiet *puff*

CHAPTER 10
JANUARY 1692

I'M ALONE WITH WILLIAM. MY HEARTBEAT RATCHETS UP. I'M suddenly so alert I think I'll never sleep again, and I don't know if it's because I'm worried about Tess or excited to be alone with William.

My attention darts to him. "Is she okay?"

"She'll be back."

I pull the blanket Tess gave me tighter around my shoulders. "I wish I could go back." I swallow around a lump in my throat. "I can't get stuck here, like you guys said." I look up to him pleading. "I can't."

A long silence stretches between us. He crosses the room and slides a large leather pouch from beneath the cot. Crouching beside it, he pulls out some clothes, then freezes, a crumpled shirt in hand, and slants his gaze toward me.

"Sorry," I say, and quickly look away, thinking perhaps he wants some privacy.

I hear more shuffling. Then his footsteps crossing the room. The fire casts his shadow over me, and he sits on the floor right beside me.

"Cord..."

When I look up, he's holding a small doll, staring down at it in his hands.

"My mom thought I was going to be a girl," he says. He chuckles, but there's another emotion behind that. Sadness. A lingering sadness.

"You okay, William?"

He nods, swallowing, then pushes his arm toward me, holding out the doll. "Here," he says. "For when you return to your daughter."

"I—I—" I'm on the verge of tears. "I couldn't take that from you. Your mom gave it to you."

"Not exactly," he says. "But come on...I don't need it. Your little girl, she needs it."

I hold the blanket around my shoulders with one hand and reach out to take the doll with my other. I hold the doll in my lap. It's made of rags. Strings of fabric make a mop of brown hair, and holes are worn in the skirt of the doll's blue dress. There's a smudge of dirt on her face and a rip in the arm.

"It's perfect," I whisper, staring in awe.

"You're going to get back to her, Cordovae," he says in a low, hoarse voice. "It'll all work out. You'll see."

I press my lips together and nod. "Thank you."

I set the doll aside. I won't be able to bring it with me back to my cabin in Salem—they're all a little off kilter there these days, thinking dolls are voodoo. But I will bring it back to Anna. William has given me hope of that.

In that moment, my feelings for William shift. I can trust him. Why do I feel as though he's the only man I've ever been able to say that about? William hasn't just given me a doll. Hasn't just given me hope. He's given me this idea...this idea that I could love a man. And that scares the hell out of me.

I glance up, catching his soft gaze. An urge to kiss him flits through me, but I tamp it down.

"Thanks again," I say.

"It's nothing. Come, now. We better check that arrow wound

for an infection." He moves to my side and slides the blanket away from my shoulder to check my wound. As he does, he chuckles. "I don't think I've ever seen so many freckles."

I smile, thankful for his light tone during such a stressful time, but my heart is racing and my mouth is dry, so when I finally speak, my voice comes out shaky and nervous.

"Verity says it's the curse of having fair skin."

"No, absolutely not a curse. That red hair of yours however..." he starts, and playfully I slap his arm. He grins and raises his eyebrows at me.

It feels good to be this close to him. Like a warm, buzzing feeling that makes me lightheaded and induces fear in me that I'll become addicted to being around him. Suddenly, the fire in the cabin seems to combat the winter chill too easily. The sudden heat makes my stomach dip and flutter. I need to shift the focus, before I really lose my head over him.

"Does the wound look all right?" I ask.

He peels back the bandage Tess placed earlier and assesses the wound. "It's superficial. You should heal quickly."

"I should?"

His canines elongate, and he bites into his arm. He holds his wound out toward me. "Drink. My blood will heal you faster than the herbs."

I stumble beneath his firm eye contact and swallow around the tightness in my throat. "Because you are, uh." I can't even think straight with him looking at me. "I—uh—you're also—you're a Cruor."

"Do you think of me as a monster now?"

Isn't that what Cruor are?

"N-no," I answer. It takes me a moment to realize I'm answering truthfully. William is different.

His own wound has almost healed completely. I feel guilty that he hurt himself for no reason, but I am not willing to drink his blood. I'll wait for the herbs I've consumed to do their job.

William drops his arm to his side and raises his eyebrows. His expression wavers, and the shakiness in my chest melts away a little. "I know you want to get back to your past. That you want to remember."

"Of course."

"Suppose remembering were a curse?"

"What do you mean? Do you know something else about my past?" I can't hide the hope in my voice.

"I'm sorry, Cordovae, but I know nothing of your past that you didn't know when you first encountered me. However, I remember my own. Sometimes it's better not to remember. Sometimes it's better not to go back."

I shrug, dismissing his sentiment entirely. "What do you know, anyway?" I ask, suddenly defensive. "You couldn't possibly understand."

"No," he says sternly. "*You* couldn't possibly understand."

There it is. That look in his eyes that tells me he's hiding something. If it's not something about me, though, then it's something about *him*.

"Try me," I say, challenging him.

"You'll hate me," he says. His anger has already dissolved, and it's not hard to see the emotion it was meant to mask: sadness.

"There's nothing that could be so horrible," I say, "not as horrible as what I've lived through."

My words freeze on my lips. What *have* I lived through? What did I even mean by saying that? Something in my mind tries to break free, to answer my questions, but instead I just feel uncomfortable. Uneasy. Disturbed.

William raises an eyebrow.

I shake my head. "I'll hate you more if you don't tell me."

He exhales slowly and sits back, resting his arms on his knees.

"I was not born a dual-breed," he begins. "This is why I cannot walk in the sun and why I can no longer consume the poisonous plants that keep most Ankou alive. Had I been born of equal parts, my dual nature would have been a gift. A dangerous gift to possess, perhaps, but a gift nonetheless."

I feel all the muscles in my face tense. "Why would I hate you for that?"

"Because of what I did when I was turned."

A silent moment stretches between us. He's staring at his hands. Finally, he speaks. "I had been born Ankou. But late one night, while out gathering food for my family, I was attacked by a Cruor. I awoke to a bloodlust so unbearable I could not control it. My maker and my coterie thrilled in their own innate nature and wanted the same for me. 'Why should we fight what we are?' they said. 'Why ought we fight mother nature?'"

His voice filled with contempt, he continues, "They enjoyed my bloodlust as a newborn Cruor. They cheered me on as I hunted one human after the next, blinded by thirst. They chained me in silver and starved me for months. Then..." William's head tilts, his expression almost daring. "Then they brought me home."

His jaw tightens, and his eyes glisten. The pain in his voice is too raw to have no effect; I am wounded and unnerved by it. "*Home*, Cordovae, to my family. Home to where my hunger so overtook me that I slaughtered everyone I had ever loved. It was not until my hunger was sated and I was standing there among the carnage, among my coterie's laughter and cheers, that the weight crushed into my chest over what I had done."

I can't look at him while he tells me these things. It doesn't seem right. It feels like he shouldn't tell me this. Or perhaps I just don't want to absorb the point he is making.

"You see, Cord? I *am* a monster."

I don't know what to say. It would be insensitive to tell him that my past is not so dark. Insensitive for me to tell him that, if I remembered, it would not be such things. I am not like him. I'm not Cruor, and I do not have any kind of rage or bloodlust or anything he has experienced. Though my heart breaks for him, though I understand why he would not want to go back to the way his life was before, his story has no impact on my own desires.

"I'm sorry," is all I can say.

"But you still want to go back," he says, defeat winding though his words.

"I'm sorry," I repeat, for a different reason this time. "But you...But I wouldn't...We're not the same."

"You fail to understand, Cordovae. You can't trust yourself to love anymore. An elemental's heart is never strong enough to overcome instinct. Not strong enough to honor love above all else," he says. "If you want to survive, Cordovae, you must step away from your heart as well."

He speaks of the rules that govern his own heart. Clearly he doesn't trust himself to love, but I am not him, and he cannot possibly comprehend the love I have for Anna. It's different.

"Cordovae, if you wish to return, I hope that is one day possible for you, but right now you need to focus on surviving. Anna can wait."

In that moment, my resolve bursts like a pin-pricked balloon. My nails grate against the dirt floor beneath me as I try to repress my boiling anger. "If I had all the time in the world, it would still not be enough. And I do not even have that much. I do not know how much longer I have before I am trapped here for eternity! Anna is, and always will be, my priority."

"And neutralizing the Morts' presence will always be mine," William shoots back. "If we don't, the Morts will possess others. Every day they remain able to walk freely is one day closer to irreparable damage. You can believe they aren't sitting about fantasizing of alternate lifetimes. They're working quickly to achieve their goals before we have the chance to take them out. The situation is already leaning in their favor as they appear to have the Maltorim's support. We do not need to make their job easier with your weakness!"

As furious as I am, I admire that William is devoted to his beliefs in the same way I am devoted to my daughter. He and I aren't so different after all.

"Don't yell at me," I say, too tired to put any energy into my demand. I close my eyes and shift my weight. An ache trembles through my body, but I try not to wince. When the pain ebbs and a calm returns, I open my eyes and focus on him. "I must be as honest with you as you've been with me. I am only doing all this for Anna. This is not my fight."

"Then my breath is wasted on you" he says, scowling. The shadows in the room make him look angrier than I would have thought possible.

My own anger, however, has washed away. I merely feel defeated. But pushing these emotions away is the only way I know how to cope. Still, I had secretly hoped that he would open up to me. And then I had gone and completely rejected everything he said. He'll probably never open up with me again. Moments ago, I thought we were growing closer and now I feel as though he and I are a million miles apart.

Maybe it's for the best, but a part of me doesn't want to feel so alone in this world, even if I'm only here for a short time.

William moves away from me and sits closer to the fire, where he sharpens a small knife with stone. A long minute passes before he speaks to me again. "If only you would use that strength for what is needed right now."

I give up on explaining to him the danger I sense she is in, how she needs me now. How perhaps it is better she die with me by her side than endure what she may endure without me there.

Which is what? I don't know. I just sense it's horrible.

Instead of saying these things, I play to his logic. "Tell me, William, how did I exist before this? How did I exist before I came back in time, if I could not exist in the future without being here now?"

"I don't know," he snaps. "Perhaps the last time your spirit was here she was a little less self-centered."

"And yet clearly did not accomplish whatever it is that is expected of me now?"

William's scowl deepens. He won't look at me. I jump to my feet.

"Damn it, William! Do you even know?" I lean closer to him,

my voice rising. "It doesn't make any sense!" My throat tightens, my eyes sting, and I know the outpouring is coming if I don't reign it in. "I just want to go *home!*"

In an instant, William is on his feet, too. The stone thuds to the floor and the knife clatters by his feet. I don't feel so strong now, but he's not trying to intimidate me. I'm shaking for entirely different reasons. I bury my face in my hands and shake my head.

"These timelines must exist," William says, and his hand comes down softly to rest between my shoulder blades. "Until we get it right."

"For what?" I say, and the next words that tumble out of my mouth don't come from the psyche of Cordovae or Abigail. "For *World Peace? For a dream?*"

Suddenly, my Pa's voice is in my head; just hearing it is enough to know it's him.

Fucking dreaming again. Always with your fucking dreams.

That night, during his drunken rant, he smashed a glass against the wall by my head, and some of the shards from the glass bounced off my arm, and his whiskey splashed against my side and my back.

I can't be here for you forever, but God help me, I will fucking teach you what life is about.

God hadn't helped him.

When I come out of my daze, I am sobbing and shaking, and William is holding me against his chest.

I want to forget. That part, that man, I can forget forever. I try to find Anna somewhere in that memory, but she isn't there, and I let it fade. I don't fight to keep the memories of my previous life this time, for those memories harbor nothing but darkness.

"William?" I whisper.

He smoothes hair from my face and looks down into my eyes. "Are you all right?"

I nod, wiping away tears with the back of my wrist. I am as all right as I can be, and William is a part of that. He is the one man I don't fear—the one man I know would never hurt me.

"Explain something to me," I say. "I remember parts of my life as Rose. I remember parts of my life as Abigail. I remember every memory created since I've arrived here. But I don't have any memories of Cordovae, and yet that is who I am called here to be."

He stares toward the fire. There are wrinkles on his face I hadn't noticed before—on his forehead, around his eyes, even some small ones by his lips. He raises both eyebrows as his gaze returns to mine.

"Well, at first, we thought people like you were the Universe's first attempts at making spirit elementals—our missing link. But there is a distinction, and perhaps that may help you understand."

"But no one really can know, can they, if spirit elementals do not yet exist?"

William shakes a finger at me. "You catch on quickly. Yes, these are only rumors. But let's just say our source is fairly reputable."

"And what does your source tell you?"

"Well, it's believed the Forever Girls will be killed before their time, but their spirits will stay with their lineage. Reincarnation."

"But I *was* reincarnated."

William frowns. "We *thought* people like you had been reincarnated, but your previous life did not end. You aren't really here, not completely. One day, you will go back. You can become one with other spirits or you can separate from them or you can take their place for a short time. But in the end, you're just...visiting." He shifts beside me, and I sense a new distance budding—not physical, but perhaps mental or emotional. "Because your ancestor was an Ankou, you were a Seer. When we needed more Ankou, the most effective solution was to initiate Seers, because they are already familiar with Seeing. You weren't born an elemental, you see? You were chosen for this."

"And a Forever Girl is not a Seer or Ankou?"

"Let me put it this way: you can join *with* the spirit of your ancestors," he says. "A Forever Girl, however, is the *same* spirit. It moves only when the body dies. If they ever did join with a spirit, they would all become one. They can only go forward, through their lineage. They don't *move* like you; they only reincarnate."

"Why Cordovae?" I ask. "Why her spirit?"

"Because she is the one who has brought the ability to See into your ancestry. She must have been an Ankou who bred with a human sometime before her death. Seeing is just a gift you inherited."

"Do you at least know where she's from?"

William shakes his head "By her name, I would guess maybe she was around during the Spanish Inquisition. Cordovae is a very old Spanish name."

"But it's not my name. So why were you told to call on me by this name?"

"Does it feel right to you?"

"Yes...I suppose..."

"And did it effectively help you see that we could be trusted?"

"Somewhat."

"Would you prefer I call you something else?"

"No, but—"

"Then stop worrying about these things. Embrace who you are right now and what you are meant to do. The reality is, you will always be joined with her," he says. "Or connected in some way."

"What about the Morts?" I ask. "Don't they reincarnate, too?"

"Yes," he says. "Or, rather, we reincarnate them. Morts and Forever Girls can both reincarnate, but it's hardly the same. Forever Girls come from a mortal existence and are made immortal *through* reincarnation, while Morts were immortal *before* they died. But you—you are special." He smiles. "You still own your life."

I'm not sure I own my life, considering, but I understand what he means. When Rose dies, I'll be separated from Cordovae. Cordovae's spirit will live on with another ancestor, where I will just...end. Completely. I am not sure how that is more desirable than the immortality the Forever Girls achieve through reincarnation.

"If my ancestor was an Ankou before she died, then why didn't she become a Mort?"

William's eyebrows pull together. "She did. That's how she joins with you now, how she joins with and visits her descendants when she needs to. No honorable Ankou would move a Mort that the Universe doesn't intend to be moved."

I'm not sure I'll ever understand this all. The way Cord is part of me and yet who I have become at the same time. But there's still other questions I have—questions that are more important to get answers to.

"If I'm Ankou, then I'm immortal, right?"

"Right."

"So then how do I get back?" It always comes down to that question. The question of returning.

William's lip rubs against his teeth. "I know this is a hard world to understand. Do you think any world is easy?"

I shake my head. "But that doesn't mean I don't want to understand it."

"Right," he says, giving a single nod. "Your life right now, even though you are here, is your life as Rose. You are just visiting. Abigail is the life you visit, and her life will become her own again once you leave. Cordovae, however, is the ancestral spirit that ties you both together. She is the one who has granted you the ability to See. Abigail is the one who has become Ankou, for this is her body. Not yours."

I sway back. I didn't think of that, and now guilt wrenches my gut. I have taken over her body and made decisions about it that were not mine to make. William must read the alarm on my face, because he pulls me back in and runs his fingertips down my spine.

"She would have done the same thing," he whispers, but there's a strain in his voice. Does he feel as badly as I do? Who is he trying to convince?

I close my eyes. I'm too tired to make sense of it all, and Cordovae's consciousness is a welcoming shadow that hides the life I once led. But through the tears and heartache that yet remain over a memory I can't recall, I am aware I've remembered something. I have hope. Hope that I can find a way to remember Anna and get back to her. Hope that I will remember the right things next time, remember my way back.

What do I do now? Do I stick around with the odds of death being higher now that the Marked Ones and the Maltorim are after us? Or do I run even though now, more than ever, I'm needed to protect the future...which by default means protecting Anna? If I fail, there will be no Anna to return to. I'll never get to see her again, not even one last time.

I still don't know how to get back, but I know that I will not let myself fail my daughter again. As much as it kills me inside, I will stay. I will fight.

There's no turning back now.

But the question that yet remains is...*how*? With the Maltorim working against us, and little resources to overcome them, where will we go from here?

Emotionally exhausted, I bury my face against William's chest, hiding the saltwater tears that slide down to my lips. I hate that he is part of the world that keeps me from my Anna, and I hate him for his kindness that makes my tears come all too easily.

But most of all, I hate that I need him right now.

CHAPTER 11
JANUARY 1692

THE CABIN DOOR SLAMS CLOSED, AND CANDLES RATTLE ON THE tabletop nearby. I startle, turning slowly to see that Tess has returned, and she is not alone. I step back at the appearance of a dark, attractive man with long, finely woven hair who stands well over a foot taller than her. William's Adam's apple bobs, and he quickly distances himself from me. The moment between him and me is like a spell that has been broken, a sudden sobriety from the time we just shared.

I look back to Tess' companion. The room has gotten colder and darker since the moment he stepped in. The warm golden glow that had been in the room just moments before is replaced by a pale gray aura.

I stare at the fire and, seeing it's dying now, I chastise myself for my silly thoughts. I worry at my lip, trying to take the man in without judgment. He's dressed in a sleeveless cotton shirt that reveals his toned biceps and the same relaxed cotton pants William wears. It's as though elementals have their own dress code that the rest of the world is unaware even exists. How do they travel unnoticed?

My gaze drifts down, and when I see his hand resting at the small of Tess' back, something puffs up within me. I don't like this guy, or the way he looks at me as though my existence is confusing or offensive. He stares at me as though he's seen a ghost, but I see ghosts every day, and it's nothing to dwell on.

But Tess seems comfortable with him, smiling in a way she doesn't smile when she's just around William and me. Her medieval dress floats more when she walks, and her boots glide more than clomp. Soft, dark brown strands of hair escape her long braid, framing her face, and her raddish-stained lips have softened in color. Her cheeks are flushed an even, pale pink, and her whole demeanor has brightened, turned into this weightless presence in the room.

This girl, this young woman who has hardened herself against the world and seems to avoid emotional connection, is in love. And she doesn't know it.

I eye the man warily but say nothing.

William tips his head toward the man and gives a curt, "Adrian," as though the name alone is a greeting.

"William," the man says with the same clipped tone.

Tess turns to me. "Cord, this is Adrian," she says, in case I am too stupid to have gathered that much. "He is the only person who can help us right now. He knows more about the Maltorim than any other rogue out there."

"Rogue?" I ask.

"A Cruor who has no affiliation with the Maltorim. We are very lucky to have him here. He helped us the last time we were in trouble, though admittedly the circumstances weren't quite as dire as they are now."

I'm not prepared to put my trust in yet another stranger. I look to William for some kind of feedback, any non-verbal tick to clue me in on how I should respond right now. But William is absorbed with sharpening his already-sharp knife again. No knife could ever be sharp enough to cut the tension in the room right now.

Adrian clasps his hands in front of him, and I feel better now that his hand is off Tess. I hate to judge him, to let my overactive senses distract me, but I know when someone is hiding something. And Adrian's secrets burn deep.

He strolls farther into the cabin, bringing with him the distinct smell of coal.

"Nice to meet you, Adrian," I mumble finally, though I feel uncomfortable being the one to break the awkward silence.

"As it is to meet you," he says. He reaches out to shake my hand, and I repress a shudder at his icy touch. His hands are so cold it's unnerving. "We have little time to resolve the mess you've created—"

"The mess *we* created? You mean the mess *they* created!" William says testily, but Adrian continues as though William hasn't said a word.

"—so we will commence discussing the plan immediately. Please keep in mind I can make no promises. I can only take your hopeless situation and give you hope."

Is he serious?

"Tess and William will distract the Maltorim soldiers by addressing the Mort population on the surrounding lands, drawing the Marked Ones away from the settlement," Adrian begins. "Meanwhile, the Maltorim know nothing of Cordovae, making her the perfect ghost. She is to return to her settlement and remain under her human guise. At night, she will exterminate the local Morts undetected, while the Marked Ones are distracted with William and Tess. Any questions?"

I don't like this guy. He's bossy, talks like he knows it all, and comes across as rude. I don't like the rushed feeling he gives off, as though I'm not supposed to think about the things he's said before committing to his plan.

"Yes, I have a question," I say.

He frowns, then says, "Hmm?"

"A Mort is after one of my friends. I've seen it following her around during the day. It follows her everywhere—how am I supposed to get rid of it without being seen?"

"If the Mort overtakes your friend, it can use your friend to turn the town against you. You must get rid of that Mort first, before all else. You absolutely cannot, at any cost, allow that Mort to overtake your friend. I hope you understand my urgency. You will return immediately to your settlement to resolve this. Whatever you do, be certain no one sees you doing this as that could sacrifice both your life and the goals of you and your comrades altogether."

Did he listen to a word I said? I just asked *how* not to be seen. I already knew I couldn't let anyone see me. "I understand that, but—"

"No buts." He claps his hands together, and it's like thunder in the room, silencing me. "Anything else?"

"*Yes*," I say, a little annoyed by him rushing such an important discussion. "Why is the Maltorim doing this?"

"I can't say for sure," Adrian offers dejectedly, "but it is not up to us to determine their reasons or analyze what they are up to. It is up to us to mediate the problem at hand as quickly and cleanly as we can. Now, let's get to work."

A pit grows in my stomach. Something is off about this guy. Why is he avoiding discussion? We can't be in that much of a rush . . .

Can we?

Just as I'm thinking this man cannot be trusted, a dizzy spell rushes my head, and I'm thrust into an unwelcomed fragment.

I'm in my room. My Pa hovers over of me. The blanket seems like it's weighing him down, holding him there, like he'll never move, never take himself off of me. I used to fight it, but he would just pin my arms over my head and clamp his dirty farm-hand over my mouth so hard that my lips crushed against my teeth. My arm is still broken from the last time I fought him.

Mama passes the room, her eyes full of tears, peeking through the cracked-open door. She swallows and looks away quickly, then disappears down the hall. I keep staring at that crack in the door, willing her to come back, to stop him, to save me, but even my own Mama has betrayed me since the Darkness came. I'm black inside. I'll never be whole again. And I'm dead. Just a lifeless doll, waiting to be tossed away, to finally have this misery end.

When I come back from my fragment, I'm outside, vomiting in frostbitten grass beneath the cover of a cloudy night sky. *Pa is Anna's father.* Bitter acid burns the back of my throat. I'm so shaky I feel the trembling will never go away. There's a crunch of dry snow behind me, then William is standing at my side. I can hear his voice but not what he's saying. Then it starts to get louder, clearer.

"Cord? I asked if you're all right. What happened?"

I spit on the ground, wipe my mouth with my wrist, and shake my head. "Nothing."

My birthmark peeks out from my dress, and I quickly pull my sleeve back down to cover my wrist. The birthmark reminds me of Anna, as it always has, and now my dread has doubled. She is alone with that man, and the danger he poses to her is worse than I had remembered.

"Talk to me, Cord. You don't look well."

I push past William and hurry back into Tess' cabin, not saying a word. I don't want to see him right now. Inside, I grab the fingerless gloves Verity made me from the end of the cot, slip them on my hands, and sit by myself.

I'm lightheaded and woozy, and it's enough to send Tess over to me with a herbal mix she insists I drink. Though food is the last thing on my mind, I drink, hoping it will help the aches I still have from running earlier and the blisters on my feet.

Adrian continues on with all of his planning as though nothing has happened. William checks on me one more time before joining them. He's leaning over a table, chanting something in another language as he draws mark after mark on a large map.

I don't concern myself with whatever they're doing, and no one seems to care. I just stare at them, all working together. Adrian smiles and makes some remark that has Tess smiling, too. Her hand goes to his forearm, grazing a scar I wouldn't have noticed otherwise. He's leaning on the table also, watching William work.

I sit here, feeling as though I'm watching art move, watching a painting in motion as I question everything. They work well together. I'm supposed to trust Adrian, as they do, but I don't. This man wants me to fight alone, and I don't sense it's because he has great confidence in my abilities. Before tonight, I didn't even know exactly what I was called here to do. I'm still not entirely sure. But either I try what he suggests, or we're stuck in the same situation we're in now.

What choice do I have but to take the risk? The risk of doing nothing is worse—it's certain death. If William and Tess trust Adrian, and I trust them, that should count for something. Even if I can't place my finger on why I trust them in the first place.

William rolls up a map and hands it to Adrian. "I'll meet you by the mountains," he says.

Adrian nods. "Let's move."

As he turns, he replaces his hand on the small of Tess' back, then ushers her outside.

I spin toward William. "Who the hell is that guy?"

He swivels his face toward me, expression glum. "Our only hope."

❦

Daylight has expired, making it safe for us to walk outdoors without risk of harm from sunlight. William suggests we head back to the settlement. He can guide me there, but he can't stay with me—there's no way to explain the strange appearance of a new man in the village, especially one staying in my home, but I am grateful for his company on the way back. Besides, Tess will need him to help distract the Maltorim and Marked Ones.

This is all moving too fast. Even for me. How could anyone be in more of a rush to end all this than I am? We haven't even considered any other options.

At least it's just me and William now. A certain happiness overcomes me when I'm with him, even though being alone with him always makes me nervous. I can't eat, I can think straight, I can't sleep—and that's okay, because I don't have the luxury of any of those things right now anyway. I just have to do what Adrian told me, unless I can come up with a better plan in the time it takes to get from Tess' cabin to the settlement. Thankfully, Adrian suggested we walk as humans, so as not to draw attention to ourselves from any nearby Morts, Cruor, or Marked Strigoi.

"We could move them during the day," I suggest. "With the speed we move, no one would see us at all, let alone our wings."

"We would still be exposing ourselves to the sun," William counters. He walks so assuredly, with strong posture and long strides.

"But you aren't pure Ankou. Can't you…"

"Burst into flames?" He grins. "The Cruor can't go in the sun, either, Cord."

"I hate this," I mumble.

"It could be worse."

I raise my eyebrow. "How so?"

William stares into the distance and breathes heavily through his nose. He rubs his thumb across the stubble on his jaw, then glances sideways at me. "Before the year 1000 A.C., the Ankou had been *completely* trapped. Then, it had been the moonlight that revealed their wings, but the sun still caused their bodies to shrink."

"That sounds awful. What changed?"

"At the turn of every millennium, the magic to the Universe opens. It's the only time the rules of a species can change, at least to some degree. The Ankou used that opportunity to change one thing. They chose to make the daylight their only weakness, by making their wings only visible to the sun during the day. This way they were free to live and hunt at night, where only other elementals can detect us by the glow of our skin. For the Ankou, the decision meant at least a thousand years of some sense of freedom."

Some idea of freedom. But it's good to know that my skin can't be detected by humans at night.

"Why do you say 'at least'? Why would they want to change it back to the way it was, if it was so awful before?"

"They don't," he says. "But *other* people would prefer the Ankou be trapped. Each millennium is the battle of the species. A battle that determines whose magic is stronger, who gets their desires."

"Sounds stressful."

William places his arm around my shoulders and playfully tugs me against him, so that my shoulder falls against his ribs. "It's nothing you have to worry about, right?"

I look up to him and our eyes lock and the whole world seems to freeze and my heart does that fluttery thing. My mouth goes dry, and the humor melts under the desire I have for him. The irises of his maple-syrup eyes are encircled with a midnight blue I've never noticed before, and I can't break the stare, can't stop staring at the way his oaky-brown hair falls against his pearly-white skin. The golden sheen of the Ankou looks so much more...*magical*...on him than it does on me. He has the beauty of an angel.

I feel warmth with him. Feel safe. I've never felt safe around men before, and thanks to my fragment earlier, I now know why. But William is different—I trust him. Even if I can't explain it or understand why. At the same time, I can't help but wince when his hand slides a little lower on my arm. The closeness makes me uncomfortable. I know William would never hurt me, but his intimate touch still reminds me of those who have. Will I ever be comfortable with intimacy, even with a man I trust?

It doesn't matter anyway. Only Anna matters. Although I sense I will miss William, there's a comfort in knowing that soon it will just be Anna and me.

William clears his throat and drops his hand away. He stares straight ahead, and I rub my hands over my arms against the biting chill of winter that seems suddenly crueler.

"Anyway," he says. "We'll get you back to Anna soon enough.

You'll never have to deal with our millennium changes."

"You really think so?" I ask.

"Yeah," he says. He sounds so sure—so sure it almost feels like a promise—and that makes my heart soar. "But only if we all stay focused..." He glares at me. "Just don't let your capacity for love become a weakness."

"What do you mean?"

"Nothing," he mumbles. "I don't want you to end up like...me. Just follow Adrian's directions. We're all counting on you."

He stops, and I turn toward him. His hands hesitate near the back of his neck, and it takes me a moment to realize what he's doing: removing a necklace. He thrusts it toward me, not looking at me. "Here."

I take it gently and inspect it—a large, round, wooden chip with a tree engraved on the front. "What is it?"

"It's good luck," he says. "It's always kept me safe."

I can't help but smile. Verity would approve. I clasp the charm tightly in my palm. "How will I know where to find you afterward? Or when?"

He pulls his map from his pocket and points to a mountainside I don't think I'll ever be able to find. "If we aren't at Tess' cabin, you'll find us here."

I point to the marks on the map. "What are these?"

He stops walking and crouches down, pulling me down beside him. He flattens the map as best he can against the forest path's rocky terrain. "Each mark is a spirit or cluster. My father taught me how to map them as a kid, using a kind of magic. See, he was dying and I was the one nursing him back to health, but he was afraid he wouldn't make it. He wanted me to protect my mother, and the best way to do that was to always know where the Morts were—to find them before I could even see them. This is important in the event they possess any humans, because at that point they become more of a danger to us than we are to them."

"Can you teach me?" I ask.

"Only if you have a lifetime to learn. It takes a lot of practice."

He rolls up the map and helps me back to my feet. "It never served me until now, you know. I was supposed to use it to protect my family, but then..."

I get the feeling he doesn't open up with people often, and it makes me feel as though we are connected in some way—a way that's not just in my head but that he feels, too.

"Go on," I say.

William shakes his head. "How would you feel if the boy that saved your life grew up to be the man who took your life?"

"I...well...I don't know." I hadn't expected the conversation to take this turn.

"Of course you don't." He shoves the map in his pocket. "My father hadn't even fought back. He just let me kill him."

"You're different now. He would be proud of the man you've become."

"Right."

I sense our 'sharing time' has ended. I slip the necklace he gave me into the deep pocket of my dress. The dress has been torn in a few places to allow for better movement while fighting, and I can't help but wonder what the people of the settlement will make of it. Hopefully they won't notice me at all.

"All right, Cord. You know what to do." He looks down the path, and I follow his gaze to where it ends—to where the settlement begins.

I know this place. As Abigail, I once rescued a young boy from a snake bite, right here where I stand now. His mother saw me, and she'd thrown a stone that hit me in the back of my head. But I didn't stop until I removed all the poison. Once she realized what I'd been doing, she apologized, but the apology was rushed and given beneath a skeptical glare before she hurried her son away from me.

Abigail and I are nothing alike. Abigail believes humanity is worth saving. I'm just doing this for Anna.

William places a heavy hand on my shoulder. "You're on your own from here."

CHAPTER 12
JANUARY 1692

I ENTER THE SETTLEMENT IN A DAZE. ENERGY RETURNS TO MY body as my aches ebb. My whole body tingles. My heart thuds in my chest. I feel eerily balanced, senses so sharp it's nauseating. I don't want to be here. Even the wind is harsh—cold and unrelenting.

The sun has tucked in for the night. The sky is still light enough to lend a clear quality to the world around me but dark enough that I can walk without my Ankou wings being visible to the townsfolk. I wish I could use my wings to make me invisible not only to the Morts but to the people of my town as well. But they can see me, and I fear that, somehow, they will be able to tell something about me has changed.

Some of them stare at me with coal-black eyes and graying skin. The arm of a young man has begun to decay. He licks his yellowing teeth, and I shudder, ducking my head and looking away. The Morts must have gotten to some of the people of Salem.

I bustle by the hushed whispers that spread like wildfire—talk of the afflicted, talk of witches—and try to ignore the disproving glares, the indicating fingers. I try to be invisible, but it's not as if I can blend in here—not with my fiery-red hair and startling pale face. The healing bruises from earlier look like grass stains on my skin, and I curse myself for bruising so easily. What will they make of it? I cover them up as best I can.

The aroma of the town overpowers my senses. Human sweat. Horse manure. The welding of hot metal. I intend to go straight home, but as I'm walking past the blacksmith shop, Verity pays the nearby vendor for some winter squash. She looks right at me.

Right at me. It's as if she can see me from this distance, even with poor vision. And yet, at the same time, it's as though she doesn't know who I am. As though she is looking right through me.

I walk around the woman pulling up her night's water from the well. I try to get closer to Verity, but a small boy runs into my path. The mother grabs her son in time to save him from getting trampled by a horse and cart. The loud clatter of hooves thunders in my head, but the whole while I do not take my focus off of Verity. I grow more and more anxious the nearer I get to her without her acknowledging me.

Closer and closer, until I can confirm what I feared most.

Verity has been taken.

Her tea-colored eyes are now two black coals. Her smile is not her own. Her hair is limp and her skin is graying. I swallow around a lump in my throat. When she turns, I realize the Mort has not fully overtaken her—its back still protrudes, and its feet have not stepped into Verity's shoes.

My spark of hope.

But with the whole town out and about, saving her now would expose me. Just the same, if the Mort completely overtakes her, it can expose me as well, using her as a witness against me. I chew my lip, debating what to do.

I need to get her away from here.

"Verity!" I say, waving, forcing a smile as though I have no idea of the truth. As she dips her head and starts to walk by me, I fall in line beside her. "I've been looking for you! Come with me, I have something to show you."

I tug at her arm in as friendly a way as I can, but the Mort resists. Its left foot steps into hers. Its back protrudes a little less as its form melts into her. It's clear I won't be able to get her alone in time.

I can't take this. I can't handle her being forced into this, her body becoming not her own. It reminds me of Pa—I shake the image away. I can't think about my old life right now. I can't even think of my life as Abigail. Right now, I need to honor my spirit. I need to be Cordovae.

I can't let myself be exposed, but I must act now. Either I stand back and do nothing, or I try to save her. One option *might* risk exposing who I am, but the other *definitely* will.

Something rips in my chest—an emotional turmoil over this Mort taking my friend. If I'm going to be exposed one way or another, the least I can do is save my friend.

Maybe if I move fast enough, I can get through this without the town noticing.

The back of the Mort nearly absorbs into Verity. It's now or never. If it possesses her completely, it'll be too late.

I step behind Verity and sift my hands into her hair. My Ankou nails snap out, piercing her skull. They are like ghost fingers, though, unable to harm her physically. It is the Mort I attack now. I glance around, confirming my elemental abilities have allowed me to move fast enough to go unseen. My speed may just be what helps me pull this off.

The Mort screeches, and the sound pierces my ears. In the nearby blacksmith shop, a hammer pounds hot metal. It sounds so much slower now, as though five minutes pass between one clang and the next.

The Mort separates slightly from Verity. I'm close. But I hear the chatter of the town dying down, which means I'm not moving fast enough. Slowly, they are turning toward us, gathering. I was warned against doing this around other people, despite our ability for speed, and now I am seeing why. But what choice did I have? I'm still limited in that I cannot move Verity —only Ankou with advanced gifts can *travel* with a human without killing them. I'm stuck here, and I need to finish before it's too late.

Vibrations shudder through me. It's almost done. Just a few more...seconds...and...Christ, this Mort is strong—much stronger than the ones I fought in the field.

My teeth shift, all turning to sharp points, and I accidentally bite the inside of my cheek. The sweet, berry-like taste of my own blood fills my mouth.

Instinctually, I know my last hope is to bite Verity. William was right—I always know what to do, as though all this knowledge came when I was transformed. The way a newborn baby knows to drink its mother's milk. Biting Verity will release a high dose of my poison that no Mort can withstand.

When I bite her, the bite mark steams, and the Mort explodes into black particles.

Immediately, I set to run, knowing I need to get away before the town can get me. But my movement is restricted. The world slows. Everything comes to a halt. Something restrains me, but I still don't understand how. I am stronger and faster than these people.

"Did you see that?" a voice shouts.

My arms are bound painfully behind my back. My wrists are burning.

Iron. It must be.

How could they know to bind me with iron? Or was this mere coincidence?

A young man comes into my line of sight and kneels in front me. He touches a red splotch on the ground that I know is my blood. It must have fallen from my mouth. It's healed the dead winter-grass it landed on.

Slowly, he looks up at me. "*What are you?*"

An older man points to the revived grass stained with my blood. "Her blood is cursed! It brings the dead back to life! It will curse us all!"

I struggle to escape, but the iron has completely shut down my ability to move through time and space. My teeth at least have returned to normal, but blood still dribbles from my mouth. My attention slides over to Verity. Her tea-colored irises are filled with sadness and sympathy.

She shakes her head. She's already saved me once from this town, when I first arrived as Abigail, and I know that was only because she saw me like a daughter, having lost her own child to cholera around the same time she discovered me in the woods as a young teen.

But she can't save me this time.

No one can.

"Abigail, you shouldn't have," she says.

With that, I know she knows that I saved her. Wishes that I hadn't.

I have to get out of this, though I can't imagine how. I'm stuck. I just want this all to end.

"Look at the bite on Verity's shoulder!" a young woman yells.

"A demon bite!" hollers another.

Quickly, Verity adjusts her dress, covering her shoulder where I bit her. Covering the perfectly circular wound created by my razor-edged teeth. Good luck, she would have called it, a perfect circle like that. But her luck is a death sentence for me.

Two large men seize Verity by her arms. "We'll put her in quarantine for now. Bring Abigail to *the cell*."

The cell? Why did they say it like that? As though it means something more than their words alone imply?

I look around for some further clue, some indication, but my vision is clouded by a sea of horrified and fascinated faces.

And then, I'm yanked away.

CHAPTER 13
JANUARY 1692

I'm in *the cell*.

I understand why they said it that way now. They took me past the cells more frequently used and down into the jail's basement. I hadn't even known the jail had a basement. Although I appreciate the darkness here that conceals my wings from impending daylight, being underground makes me panicky, especially here where I fear the dirt walls might cave in and bury us alive.

I can't breathe.

I can't breathe. I'm going to die in here.

"Pa, please, let me out!"

I rattle the closet door. The padlock knocks against the wood. The slats of the closet doors do little to let in any light.

Why did I tell the neighbors what he did to me? They weren't going to believe me anyway.

Pa says I am ungrateful. I don't appreciate the life he provides. Food. Shelter. Love. But there's never any of those things.

"You think you don't get those things?" he shouted when I said that. "Then perhaps you need to see how it is to live without."

It's days before the door opens, before light stings my eyes.

Days before my Pa needs me again.

I WIPE AWAY THE TEARS AND TRY TO FOCUS ON ANYTHING OTHER than the fragment from my past. I look around for someone to talk to, someone to occupy my mind. Something to keep me in the present time, where I need to be. I'm not alone, but I can't see my company as well as I can smell them.

Urine. Feces. Dirt. Sweat. Decay. Rot.

Each scent brings a fresh rise of vomit to my throat, and the sweet herbs I drank earlier taste bitter as they come back up. I've tried to determine how many people are here by the number of moans and whimpers, the different locations from which the rattle and clang of bars originates, from the rustle of hay sliding along the ground.

There's no source of light except for the soft glow of a lamp set on the ground at the end of the hall. I see the shadows of at least a dozen people. I wish my Ankou sight was working. I wish I knew why it wasn't. Even without the iron shackles, I do not feel the way I know I should. I need a way to escape without getting killed, but I am not able to travel out of the cell, as I should be. What will William and Tess think when they don't hear from me? They have no way of knowing what happened.

I nudge the person beside me. "Hey."

They don't move. I nudge them again. Whisper a little louder. "*Hey.*"

This time I nudge harder, but before I can open my mouth to say something, the body slumps over. A scream burns the back of my throat, but I cover my mouth and scoot away.

They're dead.

"Dead," says the person I've consequently scooted closer to. It's a young woman. "His name was Robert. Robert Zimmermann. Z-I-M-M-E-R-M-A-N-N. That's two N's, now. Nice man."

She says this as though completely unaffected that this 'nice man' now lies dead two feet away.

I swallow and nod. "Anything I need to know in here?"

"The guilty hang at sunrise," she says. "You won't escape. No one escapes."

Her lifeless voice gives me the chills, but I write off her claims as insanity. Salem hasn't hanged anyone, and I can't give up hope as she has. I need to talk to someone else, but I'm too terrified to move or draw attention to myself. I hear the troubled cough of an older man toward the corner. I notice the bony ankle of the woman I was just speaking to. And I realize she's probably right in her own way.

This is where people are brought to die.

A small sliver of light filters through a window the size of a brick, and I crawl quietly around the woman then scoot my way closer to the small window. Outside, a cluster of large rocks blocks most of my view, but here I feel a little closer to the outside world. A little safer. The first thing I need to find out is how this cell is stopping me from using my Ankou abilities. But who is going to have the answer to that question?

William and Tess might, but they're not here.

My throat gets painfully tight as I fight the tears. In my previous life, I loved being alone. I felt safest when no one was around. What has come over me, that now, without William and Tess, I feel so lost? Feel like pieces of me are missing. And not just Anna.

My touch moves to the birthmark on the back of my hand, near my wrist. I caress it through my sleeveless gloves, keeping it hidden, allowing it to let me feel a little less alone. A little closer to my Anna, my baby who shared the same mark.

I can only hope it is the only thing we share.

She needs me.

Damnit, Cord!

This is what William had feared. My impulses getting in the way. My impatience causing trouble. William would have walked away. He would have turned his back on a friend if it meant serving a greater good, would have risked the Mort ratting him out long after he was gone. William—he was unbiased. Not me. No, I was the one who justified my foolish actions as though I had no real choice in the matter.

If I were more like him, I wouldn't be in this mess. But at the same time, I like him a little less when I think of him that way—think of him as someone who cares more about his duty to humanity than he does about humans themselves.

And yet, I *do* care about him. Here I am, thinking about him now, when I certainly have more important things to think about.

Why?

He'd made me go to him in the woods. Made me become something I didn't want to be, even if he let me do it on my own terms. And yet, none of that is *really* his fault. Is it? He hasn't used his influence on me since then.

I shake away my thoughts of William. I would be better served thinking about Tess. Because she, despite her frequent hostility, is easier to understand. She's opportunistic, like me. Adventurous. She acts on her instincts, and even if that's not quite the same as the way I act on my impulses, it's at least something within my reach. One day, perhaps, she and I will have more in common. I just have to figure out that line between acting on instincts and acting on impulses. Then I won't leave so much damage in my wake.

I sigh, unable to get her out of my mind. Unable to forget her dark pendulum braid and radish-stained lips. I care about her, too. Not in the way I do about William, but in the way that makes me feel like I'm a terrible person for letting her down, even though I know she'll be fine. Perhaps even happy that I'm gone. She'll probably just boast to William that it's for the best, that I was just getting in the way, and now the Universe will be forced to send them someone more competent.

Because that's Tess' way.

And yet, somehow, she still seems more vulnerable than William.

I catch myself spiraling down, too far down into my thoughts, staring into space, probably looking crazier and guiltier than I need to while trapped in this place. I try to run my fingers through the tangles in my hair, but the knots are so thickly matted that I can't get them out. This will probably only add to the court thinking I have a pact with the devil, if I am ever even given the opportunity to stand trial.

I shake my head. I can't think this way. I won't be here long. I won't die here. I won't have to wait for a trial. I will get out of here. I keep repeating these thoughts to myself, trying to believe them.

I tuck my knees to my chest and close my eyes, trying to figure out my next move. I'm too cold and too terrified to come up with a coherent thought. The gritty, moist ground unsettles me. Hay pokes sharply into my thighs. The bumpy stone behind me crushes into my spine and skull as I lean back again the wall, but I'm too tired to sit upright or do anything about it. My arms and shoulders still hurt from when they seized me in the courtyard. I feel the tender ache of a bruise on my elbow and the drip of blood from a scrape on my hand—both wounds I received as I was thrown into the cell.

But the greatest pain of all is my heartache. This is a hopeless place.

The guard—a chubby man with pants too short and sideburns too long—keeps dozing off. His head falls forward, then he jolts awake again. If he falls asleep, that could make it easier for me to escape. I need to formulate a plan so I can be ready if that happens. But I know he won't be my only concern. We passed dozens of guards on our way in here.

My mouth is so dry that my lips crack and bleed. Early hunger pains jab through me with my need for herbs. With each moment that passes, I feel hungrier just thinking of how long I might go without the life source I need.

As my eyes adjust to the darkness, I look around. Just past the dead body on my other side, a man keeps touching and exposing himself in his sleep. My skin crawls and my stomach churns. I quickly turn away.

The guard stands and nods to a middle-aged man holding a lantern that fills the cell with so much light I soon find myself wishing for darkness again. "Good evening, Thornhart."

"Good evening," the man says. "You are excused."

The guard leaves, and we are left alone with this man with a thin pointy nose and long, gray, stiff hair that looks as though it's been smoothed with spit.

He turns to us. His eyes are black, just like Verity's had been. He must be possessed by a Mort as well, though with my Ankou abilities disabled, I cannot confirm.

One thing I know for certain: there will be no convincing him to let me go.

"Witchcraft is an evil thing," Thornhart begins. "An enemy to light! An ally to the powers of darkness, destruction, and decay."

My mind swims with why he would be telling us this. Why do the Morts act as though it is others who are evil? Why act this out here, where no one is watching the charade? He's speaking so loudly I can only imagine the display is for the guards out in the hall who might overhear him. The ones who aren't yet possessed by Morts themselves.

I tune him out, focusing instead on the details of my surroundings. Any way I can get out of here. I wonder if the book Thornhart holds might have some answers. The *Malleus Maleficarum*. I don't know what it means, but just looking at it gives me an ominous feeling.

If I can't use my abilities to escape, then I must find another way. Fighting these guards as a human seems futile, but I can't just wait around to die. I can't act rashly, either. Not again. Though time is not a privilege I have, I need to learn more about this place before I try to escape.

CHAPTER 14
FEBRUARY 1692

NIGHTS IN THE JAIL ARE FILLED WITH THE RUSTLING AND stomping of guards and the clinking of keys and creaking of doors and hushed whispers of prisoners. Insects scamper across the ground, looking for a warm place to burrow away from the moist cold. A few feet away, a mouse nibbles on a crumb. I pick at small stones embedded in the dirt floor, watching the guards in the narrow hall outside the cell, trying to learn their patterns or find weakness in their actions or opportunity for escape.

But there's nothing. Not that I can see in this dim, almost non-existent light.

There's just enough glow outside the window to watch the rain dripping, turning into icy spots on the ground between patches of lingering snow. My wrists always hurt when it's cold and wet out, the result of old injuries—phantom pains from the broken bones of another life. Scars branch out on my shins, and my stomach churns. As soon as they've appeared, they dissolve, and I know I'm going crazy in this place, unable to maintain sanity while trapped in this small room.

It's been several weeks now, and that hope I told myself to keep is rapidly wilting. If it weren't for Anna, I would have given up by now. But even as my brain clouds every time I think, still I try. Still

I attempt to formulate a plan of escape. Each time, my mind draws a blank.

My mouth, throat, and stomach burn with thirst and hunger, and that's the only thing that makes me think I'm still Ankou—this need is much different than a human need for nourishment.

I try not to, but I miss William and Tess. Before arriving in this cell, I'd spent the last weeks—aside from a few moments of weakness—wishing to get away from them and back to Anna. But right now all I want is to see William's handsome face and know that Tess is safe. She reminds me of myself, and I wish someone had looked out for me.

I need to get out of here. I remember what William told me...'*Next time, wait. We will always come for you.*'

But he'd also told me to meet with them. They have no way of knowing I'm trapped here, and they *aren't* coming for me. Not this time.

Sitting here with nothing to do but fail to think up a plan for escape, I've had a lot of time to think. Time to get to know myself better—the me I'm supposed to be and not the one I've become. I remember sitting on the edge of Mama's yellow floral bed right after Grandma had passed away.

I'm eight. Mama is sitting at her vanity, brushing her hair, making eye contact with me through the reflection in the mirror. My heart feels as though it has burst, and my face is red and blotchy and streaked white with tears. Mama sets her brush down, moves to sit beside me on the bed.

"It's a process, Rose," she says. "However long you care for someone, it takes half that time to stop caring for them. Your world might be crumbling now, but it will get easier. Give it few years, and you'll see."

I always thought the clock for that would start at the moment of separation, but that's not the case now. I am nowhere near getting over Anna, and I had only spent a few hours with her. And I can't stop thinking of William, even though we'd only known each other a few weeks before my capture.

Now I understand, though: the clock doesn't start until you are *ready* to stop caring. But I'm not ready, and I never will be.

I've thought about why that's the case with William and have finally come to understand why I am so drawn to him—why I forgive him for playing such a large role in dragging me into this life. Because although he led me here, he did not force me to drink, even though he could have. He is *not* the kind of person to take away a person's right over their own body, and I think that, although he hides behind his duties, his role in the Universe takes a toll on him.

Knowing him has been...healing. It's given me a chance to reclaim power over myself, taught me that I choose how I'm connected with another person. That I can let the right person in, if I want to, and I don't have to let the things Pa has done leave me running forever.

If I ever see William again, I'm going to embrace these new realizations of mine, even if for no other reason than to prove to myself that I am *not* broken. I am *not* ruined. I am capable of loving not only my daughter, but a man as well.

But none of this matters unless I find a way to travel out of or otherwise escape this cell. What if I've somehow lost my abilities completely? What could cause that? William and Tess never warned me that anything like *this* could happen.

It's hard to fall asleep in this place, but my attempts to leave haven't gotten me anywhere, and I'll need more energy to give it another try. Several times as I'm trying to fall asleep, I catch myself grinding or clenching my teeth, every muscle in my body tense. One time, I accidentally bite the inside of my cheek, and a small pool of blood puddles beside my gums. I take a deep breath. If I close my eyes and imagine a perfect world, sleep will come.

I don't mean for my perfect world to include William, but it does.

After spending the first half of the night chastising myself for thinking of William that way, I give in, because it's the only way I can fall asleep.

I DON'T KNOW IF I SLEEP FOR HOURS OR DAYS, BUT I IMAGINE IT can't have been long. When the sun rises the next morning, I'm determined to escape and to learn as much as I can about where I am and what is going on.

Immediately, as I do every morning, I move away from any sunlight, remembering what Tess and William told me about staying to the shadows. It's my only hope of concealing what I am —or at the least, hiding that I'm not entirely human. Perhaps the dark is better for me anyway, even if I were entirely human. It hides my freckles and makes my hair look more like tree bark than blood.

I glance around, not finding many inspiring options of people to talk to aside from the two new arrivals. One is a petite young woman with long, curly blonde hair, pretty teeth, and a soft chin. The other is a heavily pregnant woman with high cheekbones. The blonde woman smells like honey and flowers, and this is perceptible even over the piss stink of the cell and the decay of the dead body that still hasn't been cleared out.

Everything about her calls me to her. Although a little unsteady and dizzy from lack of fresh air and food, I inch my way over, unsure what to say when I get close enough to talk to her. But that doesn't stop me.

No, something else stops me.

About two feet away now, my skin is buzzing with energy. The caretaking woman seems to have a glow about her. The closer I get to her, the more my body warms. My thirst and hunger ease, and at the same time, the woman's countenance seems to wither. When her light honey-brown eyes lock on mine, images flash through my brain.

In an instant, I see what appears to be this woman's future. Hanged as a witch, body burned by a lover, and then living again in a world that looks more like the one in my previous life. Just as quickly as the images flashed, they are gone. The woman isn't even looking at me anymore. How long was I staring at her? It feels like moments and lifetimes all at once.

For a brief moment, the craziest idea tingles the edges of my mind.

She's a spirit elemental.

The idea is so far-fetched that I nearly laugh. Is this place stripping my sanity? Am I delirious from lack of nourishment? I'm reading more into this woman than is actually there because I want so badly for someone to be able to help me get out of here.

I don't let my brewing insanity stop me from getting answers, though. I swallow around the knot in my throat and continue over.

Without even looking at me, she hands me a tin with some water, and I gratefully take a swig.

"Thank you," I mumble.

She nods. "It's worse out there, you know. The town is...they aren't themselves. Something is going on."

My heart sinks to my stomach. Morts. That's what's going on. Which means I need to get out there. Now. The longer I'm in here, the more my chances slim of ever stopping them in time to return to Anna.

"This woman needs to get out of here." She indicates the pregnant woman she is caring for, but the woman waves her off. "*Far* away from here."

"We all do," the pregnant woman says, but her voice sounds so weak I wonder how she would be able to move if the opportunity arose.

I introduce myself and soon come to know the pregnant woman as Vanessa and the fair-haired woman as Elizabeth. Elizabeth, it turns out, has been arrested on the charge of witchcraft. Am I here because they think I'm a witch, too?

Still, I almost find myself entertaining the idea. *Is* Elizabeth a witch? She is subtly different, though nothing sinister. If I get out of here—*when* I get out of here—I should mention her to William and Tess. They might be able to tell me what she is.

Sadness pangs in my heart as I remember what I saw about this woman. About her being hanged. I can't tell her this, though the remembrance is making it harder for me to look her in the eye. At the same time, I half wonder if she already knows. It certainly wasn't my abilities that showed me her future—that is not one of my gifts, and none of my gifts work in this Godforsaken place anyway. She is magical, and by the curious way she looks at me, I can tell she senses something about me, too. Perhaps her own gifts have caused her future to be played in my vision this way.

Whoever this woman is, she is here and might be able to help me. "So how do you suggest we go about escaping?"

"I might be able to help," she replies quietly. She steals a peek toward the guard. He's snoring. "There's no escaping here—not without something *more* on your side."

My hopes lift. She does have some kind of magic. She must. She's guarded about it, but I sense her desire to help will override whatever she holds back.

"Then we can all get out of here," I say.

She smiles sadly. "I won't leave here, no. But you will take Vanessa with you, won't you?"

"Of course," I promise. Now I'm almost certain Elizabeth already knows she is destined to die, but if that is so, then why wouldn't she fight it? "Are you a . . ." I lower my voice. "*Are* you a witch?"

A shuffling outside the cell steals my attention. The guard's shoe, sliding across the dirt. I study his face, confirm his eyes are still closed, that his chest is rising and falling in the true shallow breaths of slumber. He snorts, his body shifts, he sucks in a deeper chunk of air. But he's asleep. I slide my focus back to Vanessa, and I can tell she's holding her breath as I have been.

"Well, are you?" I ask. I sense we don't have much time before the beast awakes.

"I'm not what they think I am," she says. She's not looking at me, though. She's staring at the guard still. "I'm not what they think witches are."

Well, that's evasive. How can she help me if she's not honest with me? There are too many lives at stake to hold back now. Hers included, if the vision I had holds any truth.

At the same time, I haven't exactly offered anything up to her about my abilities—or the ones I had before I arrived here. I consider opening up first, in hopes it will bring her around, but I can't risk the guards or other prisoners finding out the truth about me. In the end, I settle for this shared *knowing* we seem to have. I might not know who she is, and she might not know who I am, but I sense she trusts me as much as I trust her, and that we both *know* the other has something preternatural about them.

Besides, there is no time for building trust. We need to escape *right away*. I've already been in here too long.

Before I can say anything, she grasps my hand and gazes into my eyes. "Who is Anna? Who is William?"

I snatch my hand back. "I thought we were trying to get out of here."

"Sorry." She takes my hand again, and I let her. "Please try to keep your mind clear."

Suddenly it's as though I can't stop thinking, and I *feel* her in my head, but she doesn't say anything this time. Energy passes from her hands into mine, and a cooling sensation runs through my veins and spreads through my body.

The energy jolts—it's a snap that has broken the connection. Elizabeth releases my hand, shakes her head, then grasps my hand again. The flow of energy returns, building again, a little stronger this time. My heart beats so hard I worry the guards will somehow hear. The connection, however strong, feels fragile at the same time. As though we're only connected by a thread instead of a rope, and it can snap at any moment.

"Relax," Elizabeth says easily. Like this is the most natural thing in the world, what we are doing right now.

I try to push my apprehensions aside. She seems to at least know what to do, and perhaps it's best we don't talk aloud about what we are doing. I have to trust that I'll know what to do when the time comes. William would be proud.

The connection between Elizabeth and me solidifies, and my patience is renewed. The way she gently squeezes my hand is now somehow comforting. A golden glow blooms between our palms, but so far nothing has happened that I can see helping us. If anything, this shimmering light between us will only expose what we are doing. We are running out of time. If something is going to happen, it needs to happen soon.

My breath rushes from my lungs. I'm terrified and awed by the energy between us. This could be it. I'm desperate yet hopeful. We're almost there. I can feel it.

And just like that, my strength returns. I almost feel like *me* again—like my Ankou abilities are back. My body jolts through time and space, the way William and Tess taught me, as though any moment now I will pop out right beside them.

"Abigail!" Elizabeth yells behind me.

I crash into the cell bars. They're like fire on my flesh.

I wasn't trying to leave her behind. It was instinct. I wouldn't have left without her or the young woman, or I would have gone back for them. I know this, and I hope she does, too. But there's something more concerning right now.

I *don't* have my abilities back.

It had felt like I had, and it terrifies me that I could be so wrong. Whatever I had felt, it must have been the start of something different. But now it's too late.

Before I suck in another breath, a lanky, blond guard appears at the front of the cell. I see the black in his eyes, a Mort controlling him.

If only I could move the Mort. The guard would still be a guard, but he might appreciate being freed from the possession enough to help us. Suddenly, destroying the Mort overshadows any other goals I have. I'm not sure if it's instinct or impulse.

I step toward the edge of the cell, but hesitate as a shred of reason prods into my skull. If I try to remove this Mort, I will expose my magic. That could make escape even harder. Maybe it's best I stick to my original plan.

The one that doesn't exist.

I frown. I have to try *something*, but I've never moved a Mort that has already possessed someone before; even Verity had not been possessed completely. And it'd been a risk—a huge risk. She could have died.

I steel myself against my doubts. If the Morts are this deeply involved, we'll never escape unless I get rid of them. And this guard is as good as dead if the Mort possesses him anyway. I need to act. Now.

I lunge forward and reach through the bars, ignoring the searing on my shoulders and face as I dig my fingernails into the guard's head, hoping that at least my hands will work once outside this cell. But it's no use, and I can't handle much more of the burning iron cell bars.

The guard grabs my wrists and pushes back. The iron has weakened me, and I can't hold on. With another hard shove, he knocks me to the floor. He thrusts the cell door open and stalks toward me, lifting me by my neck and pushing me back against the wall.

I grasp his hands with my fingers, try to pry myself free. My face burns, and I cough, choking. I muster any resolve I have left to move my hands to his scalp once more, allowing my body to dangle from his grasp around my neck. I visualize moving the Mort from the human vessel, but my energy is sapped and the pain is debilitating, and it's undeniably true—my Ankou abilities are *gone*. My hands and fingers are so weak they've gone numb.

Through the haze of my pain, I see another guard in the cell. He's nearly as tall as William but his muscles hide beneath a fatty bulk. He grabs Elizabeth by her arms and drags her from the cell. The cell door is open, and it seems the perfect opportunity to run. If only I wasn't incapacitated by this Mort-Guard.

Through the blur, I see another prisoner try to escape, only to be kicked in the face by another shorter guard that has run up to us. Finally, the black-eyed guard tilts his head, grinning, and drops me to a heap on the floor. I tumble against the wall, the stone whacking the back of my head.

My hands and face burn. My skin bubbles, and pus oozes from

the wounds on my hand. The fire rips through my body, replacing the cool from Elizabeth's touch earlier. My stomach twists in pain. I shudder.

Iron poisoning.

A lot of it this time. Worse than the shackles they used. It's in my body now. Killing me. Blacking out the world around me and blurring the people in the room as the cell gate clangs shut once more.

My only hope—Elizabeth—is gone.

CHAPTER 15
LATE FEBRUARY, 1692

IT'S BEEN RAINING ALL NIGHT, THE SKY WEEPING FAT RAINDROPS on the ground outside the cell window. The water dribbling in, sliding down the stone walls. Splashing in muddy puddles and up against my ankles.

When the hours are too long, my thoughts drift to William and Tess. Are they looking for me? Is William pressing his fist to his mouth, pacing through Tess' cabin? Is Tess pulling at her earlobe, tossing off indifferent remarks that everyone can tell are just a mask for how she really feels?

I sigh deeply. Do they even know where I am? Or, for that matter, *care*?

Maybe I hope more than I should, but I imagine they do care. William would anyway, if only because he cares about helping those in need. Tess, on the other hand...would she feel justice served, that I am paying for my foolishness? Or would her anger over one of her own being imprisoned override that, change where her sense of justice lies?

I need to see them again. When all this is done, I'm going to find a way for us to be together. All of us, including Anna.

The slivers of moonlight that weave in through the cell window touch on the freckles of my shoulder, now exposed by a huge rip in my clothing. In the gentle light, I use my fingernail to draw William and Tess and Anna and I in the dirt floor of my prison. I miss them, and that scares me. I never thought I would miss anyone but Anna.

I close my eyes, envisioning them, holding on to them the same way I hold on to my lost daughter. In my mind, I see William, his long strides as he steps through the tall dead grass of the forest, and the way Tess whips between the trees as easily as she would through an open field. I can almost hear the jingle of their chimes, teasing the Morts, calling them out as she runs.

And then a fragment cuts me off from the world I'm in now.

I'm running along an embankment of the Chattahoochee River. Pa watches from afar, laughing. I feel safe. It was before the Shadow Men came. I'm wearing a yellow sundress, and my hair trails like ruby ribbons behind me on the breeze. Mama wears a big sun hat, and she's smiling, too, and her lips are stained red and she has pale skin like me and twice as many freckles on her shoulders. She's drinking lemonade.

Then, my vision tumbles. It's not beautiful anymore. It's muddy and rippled. I'm outside of myself, looking down, and Mama is screaming and Pa is running down the hill of the bank. There's blood in the water. He wades in, closer, and I realize it's not blood. It's my hair, soaking wet. I'm floating face down, and my pale skin is clammy.

Pa yanks me from the water.

"Rose!"

He sounds so far away.

"Rose, come on. Hang in there. Hang in there Rose. Please."

Pa carries me back to the embankment. The ground thuds under my shoulders and back, and then he's shaking me, saying my name over and over again. Mama is crying. I cough up some water and my eyes shoot open and now they are saying my name with more joy and less fear, but Pa's eyes are still sad.

Mama hugs me tight. "Oh, Rose. Rose, Rose." She shakes her head, mumbling everything and anything with my name in it, rocking me in her arms. "Thank God you're okay."

Pa presses the pads of his fingers into his eyes and exhales sharply, shaking his head. He paces a few steps, then sits beside us and stares out over the river, his wet pants rising to reveal the hair on his ankles.

"I don't know what I'd do if anything bad ever happened to you," he whispers. His jaw clenches and he wipes the moisture away from his eyes, then stands again and puts his hand out to me. "Come on," he says. "Let's get you home."

I force the memory away. It makes me angry to remember that side of him. I can't reconcile it with who he became—who the Morts made him into. I can't forgive him for not fighting it. I can't forgive him because it was *his* hands that hurt me and *his* face that stared down at me with such hatred. It was him, and it wasn't him, because he was stolen from me, and I can't bear to try to make sense of it.

Why him? Why my family? We were nothings. Nobodies.

I liked it that way.

Now I'm the one who needs to fight. The one who needs to honor her daughter and not let anyone stand in her way.

I'm freezing and sweating at the same time, and the hot flashes from the iron poisoning churn my stomach. My only solace is the night. The corners of dark sky outside the cell window bring me peace, where daytime leaves me feeling twice as trapped, threatening to reveal my nature.

My inmates, however, do not feel the same. As the darkness of the night deepens, they become more and more distressed.

Come to think of it, they've been this way every night I've been here, but I'm only noticing the pattern now. I cannot relate to their fear. Night is my only comfort—the only time of day I know without question. The darkness soothes me, calls to me. I welcome it. I wait for it, always, to come to my rescue.

I hate myself for thinking it, but I want to get away from my fellow inmates as much as I want to get away from the guards, the jail, this entire place. I try to ignore everyone—all but Vanessa, the young woman I promised Elizabeth I would look after. She is the only one who sleeps, her head on my shoulder, her back against the wall beside me, and her body curled toward mine. Her stomach swells between us. She must be due any day now.

I shift my weight to get comfortable, but a sharp piece of hay pokes into my side, and my skin itches. Pain trembles through my body, and a wave of nausea rolls through me. It feels as though the iron in my system is destroying my blood, as though somehow I can feel the death of each drop that flows through my veins. I feel woozy. If I'm to escape, I need to recoup, but I'm not sure how I can do so without the herbs my body requires.

If there was any hope of escaping, wouldn't I have escaped by now?

I try not to dwell on such thoughts, but I can't prevent them from popping into my mind. Tonight is the night. Vanessa said we couldn't wait for opportunity to come to us. We've been here too long. She's right. So tonight, when they open the cell to feed us, I will rush the guards, and Vanessa will run to the end of the hall ahead of me so I can protect her during their inevitable pursuit.

I can't stop trembling just thinking about it, so I try to focus on other things. Try to pretend I'm not about to risk my life. We have to do this. We have to take the dive.

The low ceiling above us shakes, and loose dirt between the wooden support beams sifts down. I glance at the roots that protrude from above, still quivering from the movement overhead. Outside the cell, shoes squeak against stone. The aroma of wet grass accosts my nostrils.

As the guards' footsteps slosh down the hall, I can just imagine the splatter of mud all over their boots. I'm ready to rouse Vanessa and tell her to get ready, but as they draw closer, I distinctly smell blood and moist earth, and I know these are not Morts or guards coming down the hall.

Five men stop at our cell, accompanied by one of the guards. They stand with hands clasped in front of them, their eyes sinister and alarming. They're all refined, handsome men—but there is nothing welcoming about their appearance. One of them smiles, and his canine teeth snap down to press against his pale bottom lip. He's white as death, and immediately I realize what these men are.

Cruor.

The sight of them puts a metallic taste in my mouth. I swallow the sense of defeat. I can't let fear of the unknown get in my way. Not now.

I pull Vanessa closer and wrap my arms around her, my attention never leaving the men. A sense of certain doom flutters in my lungs. I try to breathe quietly, as though somehow that will make me invisible, though I know that is not the case.

One of the men reaches in his pocket and retrieves a small pouch. He holds it out to the guard, his attention never shifting away from the cell. The guard—a stout man with the face of a hungry swine—opens the pouch. Gold peeks from inside. He pours some into his palm, but the Cruor who handed him the money growls.

"It's all there," he says, his tone colder than he looks.

The guard fumbles with the coins and pouch and hurries down the hall. The basement door thuds shut, and the cell door clangs open. The smallest of the Cruor runs his hands along the bars, looking over each cowering inmate one by one.

"Yes," he hisses.

And in a blur, the Cruor press inmates to the stone wall, their faces buried in their necks, blood leaking in rivulets to the floor. Bones crunch. The cries of agony are deafening.

Vanessa stirs, panic in her wide eyes as she sits up straight. Inmates cower further into their dark corners, blocking their heads as though not seeing these men will make them disappear. Other inmates dash for the open cell gate, only to be yanked back so hard they fly across the cell and crack against the wall before slumping to the floor, dead on impact.

It occurs to me that they bought these people as food. Now it all makes sense: the Cruor advised the use of iron bars. Does that mean they expected some of the captives here would be their elemental enemies? This isn't just dinner to them. That's the perk to something bigger. My mind spins trying to find the connection between what is happening in Salem and what I know I am up against as an Ankou, but I can't piece it together.

The pain from the iron poisoning nearly cripples me, but I can't sit here and wait to die. I grab Vanessa's arm and start to pull her toward the cell gate. It's our only hope.

We don't make it far before an auburn-haired Cruor appears in our path. He looks down at Vanessa, and a slow grin slithers onto his face.

"Look what we got here," he says, and he laughs. "An Ankou trying to help a Strigoi!"

The other Cruor stop in their tracks, dropping nearly dead bodies to encircle Vanessa and me. Can they smell and sense our nature the way I had with them? They seem particularly interested in Vanessa and, for a brief moment, I entertain the idea of using her as a diversion to get myself out of here. William and Tess need me. Anna needs me. What good is it to die alongside this woman? Trying to save her will only draw attention to myself.

But my body doesn't move. I can't leave her side. I feel compelled to help her, as though saving her would somehow mean saving myself.

That only leaves us with two options: Outsmart these men, or fight.

Whatever you do, fight.

William's voice echoes in my head as though he's right by my side, and a strong sense of pride rushes through me. He's right. There's no honor in going down without a fight, and a fight is inevitable. Even if we run, it will only put our backs to them.

I need to keep it together. Let them think they are in control and make a move when they least expect it—or at least when an opportunity presents itself. Which it hasn't yet. If all else fails, plow through them. Whatever I do, I will do *something*.

The fight in me is rising, but my strength of spirit is no match for my weakened body. I frantically look around, as though a solution is going to present itself any moment. The lead Cruor standing in front of us grins, and suddenly Vanessa is shaking beside me.

No, not shaking.

Convulsing.

The auburn-haired Cruor crouches in front of her and stares into her eyes. Everything about him is imposing, from his square jaw to his dark eyes and the deep lines across his forehead. His teeth have grayed and give off a sickly pinkish hue in the moonlight, and his fangs are so large his smile looks more like a snarl.

Vanessa's eyes grow distant. As I reach to take her hand, the Cruor's hand shoots out and catches the wall between my head and Vanessa's. I startle. Vanessa whimpers and squirms, but her eyes seem locked with his, and she doesn't move.

Her skin ripples and tears form in her eyes. Hair sprouts from her ears and face. I grab her arm, trying to get her to look away, but it's as though she is frozen inside her body. Vanessa's jaw elongates and her thin pink lips stretch. Her ears perk into sharp points. I can't help but flinch until I see the tears sliding down her cheeks. Her hands curl into tight fists, and her face begins to shift back. I need to reach her somehow.

"Vanessa," I whisper. "Stay with me."

The auburn-haired Cruor growls, but he doesn't make a move for me. No one does. They're all hyper-focused on Vanessa.

"Stay with me!" I say, louder this time. More frantic.

"Stop!" she screams. Her desperate voice pangs my heart. "PLEASE, STOP!"

Her voice turns to a growl, and her pleas turn into something inhuman. Her face is more animal now. Her hands melt into paws as her spine curls and pops and lengthens. As she's forced to shift, I see her fighting it, see her wolfish nails dig into the ground, see the color of her eyes flicker from normal to a glowing orange. Her stomach contracts as she transforms, no longer able to resist.

Then I smell it.

Blood.

The auburn-haired Cruor throws his head back, his sinister laughter shaking his shoulders. I follow his gaze to the space between Vanessa's legs.

A child, not yet ready to be born, has expelled from Vanessa's body, and I can tell its bones are broken. I squeeze my eyes shut and pull Vanessa's wolf-face into my shoulder, shielding her from seeing this, but knowing I cannot shield her from her loss. Knowing from her howls that she is already broken. Knowing I am broken now, too.

No sane person in this room will ever be the same.

My heart crumbles, my body completely crippled by the sight. I fight the bile rising in my throat while Cruor laugh and jaunt and cheer. And then, I don't think I'm really there anymore. The Cruor are a faraway haze, their voices fading.

I force myself to look, to take in what is left of the little boy's angelic face, the small fingers on his hands and the tiny toes of precious feet that will never learn to walk. I commit the vision to memory so that I can never forget just how evil the Cruor are. So that I will never feel an ounce of compassion for the monsters who stole his life.

The anger inside me is all consuming. The preternatural world has taken everything from me. My family. My daughter. My life. And now they are trying to do the same to this woman, and I'm sitting here doing nothing?

He did this to her—that auburn haired Cruor. That *monster*. His influence forced her to shift, knowing it would abort her unborn child.

I leap from the ground and tackle him. He's caught off balance and tumbles to the floor, me on top of him, my mouth crashing into the ground above his shoulder. I don't know if the loud crack was his head or my jaw; my whole body still hurts from the iron poisoning.

Dirt rubs against my teeth, lips, and tongue, and hay pokes at my gums. I push myself up, spitting the dirt and hay from my mouth, and dig my nails into his face. It's like ice under my fingernails, but I don't care. Even in the state I'm in, he struggles beneath me, and for a moment I feel strong.

He backhands me and sends me flying into the wall. Vanessa, now in her human form once again, is wailing, but I do not have the strength to avenge her child. I don't even have the strength to save myself.

The Cruor sneers at me from across the room.

The pig-faced guard comes in and rattles the bars. "All right, 'nough for one night."

My attacker is back on his feet now. On his way to the cell gate, he crouches beside me. "Next time," he says, "I promise to give you my complete and undivided attention."

It takes every ounce of strength I have left to spit in his face, but I do it. He just laughs, wiping my saliva away, and joins his coterie. The guards quickly file them out of the cell.

I try to stand, but instead I wobble and stumble back against the wall. I slide down to the ground and rest back, my head throbbing and my heart completely wrenched. I sidle closer to Vanessa and hold her while she weeps, all the while I'm wishing, praying, willing myself able to heal her, to undo what the Cruor have done, for my abilities as an Ankou to return.

But it's useless.

I'm useless.

Tonight presses new questions into my mind. What had the Morts wanted with my family in my old life? What did the Cruor want tonight more than to feed? Why would they make this woman suffer, only to leave her, and why didn't they kill me while they had the chance?

I won't get these answers here, but each night that passes makes me feel more and more helpless to escape.

CHAPTER 16
LATE FEBRUARY, 1692

WHEN THE CRUOR ARE GONE, I AM ALONE IN A ROOM FULL OF loss. The loss of lives, be it through death or imprisonment, and the loss of a child who never got a chance to live. And worst of all is the loss of my own daughter creeping in. The memory I need to have but cannot bear to remember.

Tess told me she'd never experienced a fragment. She doesn't realize how much of a blessing that curse might be. It's knowing what you lost that hurts the most. I wish I had the strength to be there for Vanessa, who needs someone right now to hold her up while she falls apart. But I can't be that person.

Why haven't Tess or William come to help me? Have they left me for dead? I suppose I shouldn't expect them to risk their lives to save me. They have the 'greater good' to concern themselves with.

My anger and bitterness toward them drown in emotions I would sooner deny. As tough as Tess acts, I know deep down she's just a hurting girl who feels abandoned. Does she feel I abandoned her by getting myself caught? She would have preferred I allow the Mort to take Verity, I'm sure. William, too. I could have let the Mort take her and fled the town. If I had, I would be closer to returning to Anna by now.

What would William tell me if he were here? To fight? To stop feeling sorry for myself and *do* something? But what? What *can* I do? Perhaps he would just wrap his arms around me—then everything would seem all right, even if it wasn't.

❧

I AM LOST IN THE HAY.

I sit in a corner, weaving together the bits of dirty hay beneath me, trying to piece together all that has been shattered. The night I brought Anna into this world plays so clearly in my mind it's as though I'm reliving it all over again. After I bathed her, I tucked her in a small blanket, I nursed her, and I held her close. She smelled like rain. Her toes were tiny and perfect, her small hands grasped at mine when I touched her palm.

Then Pa snatched her up and took her away, and I hadn't saved her. Within hours of her birth, I had failed as her mother. Now I might never get back to her. Certainly not as long as I am trapped in this cell. The muddy quality of the air and the dust floating around cloud my vision.

Every now and then, feet shuffle beyond the door at the end of the hall, a reminder that there is a world outside of this hole. Water drips from somewhere in the cell, one of the men nearby keeps wheezing, and several of the prisoners sob, though none as deeply as Vanessa.

After I've finished the straw doll, I hand it to her. We don't exchange words; her eyes on mine have crippled my ability to form words. There are no words for the loss she has endured. Inwardly, I cringe at my own selfishness.

At least I can hope my daughter is alive. Vanessa doesn't have hope. She has nothing. The Morts took everything from her the way they took everything from me. They stole everything beautiful about the life I had before and turned it black, and they will do the same to me in this life if I don't stop them. They need to be eliminated, and then I will return to my daughter and rebuild what the Morts have destroyed.

I won't make it much longer in this prison. Even my sense of smell has gone numb. I can feel the grit of dirt in my mouth but can't taste it. My dry, chapped lips and ache in my gut demand me to eat, but there is nothing here. My injuries fight just as strongly for my attention, but I can't concern myself with them now. Morning is coming, even the darkness has lightened. I have few hours left if I'm to escape tonight as Vanessa and I had planned.

Glancing around the room, I take in the haunted faces of those who have survived the horrors of this night. One woman in particular catches my eye. It's almost as though I haven't seen her at all before now. It's almost as though *no one* has seen her. Surely even the Cruor overlooked her, to leave her so untouched in this room.

Her deeply tanned skin looks grayish in the dark, and her long, raven black hair tumbles in knots over her shoulders and down to her small breasts. Her hand moves by one of the folds in her dress. An alarming, nervous energy—like a vibration in the air—sweeps through me. When a guard approaches our cell, however, my trance is broken. He's clearly being controlled by a Mort, and I groan. He grabs the iron bars and shakes them, hissing at us. A few of the prisoners startle, but Vanessa just sits limply with a dead glare in her eyes.

The raven-haired woman is whispering something, but she's not whispering at me. I can't make out what she's saying, only that she's speaking very quietly and very fast. Her tone seems to repeat a pattern. A chant of some sort. And as she chants, the guard's grip on the cell bars loosens.

The woman's eyes glint. She emanates a soft, pale glow, and I glance around, wondering who else has noticed, but it's as though the other prisoners still can't see her. Is it because I'm Ankou that I can see her? If that were true, wouldn't I have noticed her sooner? Or not at all, since my abilities here have been so limited? Was she brought in at some point tonight without my noticing?

Her whispers grow fiercer. Somewhere behind those whispers is unsettling music. Chimes, mostly, and a distant beating drum. The music is not beautiful. It's discordant, disturbing, and full of magical energy. Sweat soaks my scalp and drips down my spine. It chills on the night air, and I shiver.

My attention shifts between the woman and the guard who is now backing away from the cell. The intensity of the energy in the room builds. She's doing something, I know it, and it has to do with whatever she is hiding in the folds of her dress.

The guard turns and leaves. This woman is controlling the Mort inside of him. This world is more magical than I ever imagined, and I can't let this opportunity slip through my fingers. I inch closer to her, wincing at the pain shuddering through my body, more noticeable now that my adrenaline has worn off.

"What did you do?" I ask her, perhaps more roughly than I intended.

"Nothing," she mumbles.

I sidle close to her and drop my voice to a whisper.

"I'll tell them." I hate to threaten her, but at this point getting out of here is more important.

"That wouldn't do you any good," she says, and I know it's true.

"You could have stopped the Cruor." My words sound exactly as accusing as they are.

"I couldn't. I could only shield myself. But I saw you help that woman." Her whole body grows eerily still, and her gaze levels with mine. "You're...different."

"Couldn't you have helped her? You controlled that Mort," I whisper.

"Cruor are different from the spirits."

"Why not compel him to release us, then?"

"I am not strong enough," she says, her voice cutting out. "I need more time."

"Let me help you," I say, holding out my hand. "Show me what you have."

She pulls away. "No."

"Come on," I say. "I'm the only one who noticed you. There must be a reason for that."

"Forget that you saw me," she says. "You only saw me because I allowed you to."

"Why, then? Why allow it and then turn me away?"

She waves her hand in front of my face, practically staring through me. "Forget it. It was a mistake."

I'm starting to understand Tess' approach to life. She's unbiased, even if it hurts good relations with other people. Now I know why. It's about survival, in every sense of the word.

I grab the woman's wrist. "What are you afraid of? You aren't strong enough. Fine. But we might be strong enough together."

She sighs, almost as if conceding with me. "Yes, yes. We might be strong enough together," she says, though it sounds more like she is trying to convince herself than agreeing with me. Her sad face stares into mine. "We might."

I nod encouragingly. She bites her lip, staring at me for a long moment. Then something changes in her expression. Apprehension turns to determination. To urgency.

"We need to hurry," she says, pushing my hand back down into my lap. Before I can react, she reaches up and yanks out a small chunk of my hair.

"Ouch," I hiss. "Why did you do that?"

She looks at me in a silencing way. "We don't have much time before the guards return."

I open my mouth to speak again, but she presses her hand to my mouth and shakes her head. Then she closes her eyes, rolling my hair into a rope between her fingers.

"A knot is not a useless thing," she whispers, tying a knot in the hair she's ripped from my scalp. I am about to respond when she shakes her head, as though even with her eyes closed she knows she needs to silence me. "It keeps in place with rope and string."

The tone of her voice settles over me. Her words are rushed, but I realize this is some kind of spell.

"Not all kept is hard or soft. Knots can keep wishes, hopes, and thoughts." She ties a second knot in the cord she's made of my hair. "Held by magic knots we make, for life and love not to forsake."

Now a third knot is tied. Her words seem even more rushed now than before. "And this ladder be imbued, with the Mother Goddess to end this feud."

A fourth knot.

"Give this woman the third sight, and grant her the magic to make things right."

After the woman ties the fifth knot, she pushes it into my palm. "It's a witch's ladder."

"Now what?" I ask.

"That's up to you."

"But—"

"Shh!" She nods toward the creaking door at the end of the hall. "Just use it."

After that, she disengages. It's almost as though she is going out of her way not to look at me, not to make eye contact with me, and all I have is a burning spot on my scalp from where she ripped my hair and something she calls a witch's ladder that I don't know how to use.

Somehow, though, it's supposed to help me control these Morts, and I intend to use it to get out of here. Perhaps this woman was not strong enough, but if I can figure this out, I will be.

I have to be.

A guard throws open the cell gate. Two more stand behind him. I glance behind them to the empty hall, then back at Vanessa. I could come back for her . . .

The first guard walks past me and grabs the woman who made the witch's ladder by the arm. I can't save her now, and I can't risk that her gift to me will be useless. I brace myself, take a deep breath, and dart for the space between the two guards waiting outside the cell.

Without moving from where they stand, they hook me around

the waist and toss me back into the cell. Wind rushes from my lungs, and I ache everywhere from my chest to my stomach. The room dims. I try to suck in some air, but nothing comes. I'm suffocating.

Through the blur of my vision, I see the woman who helped me being dragged away and the cell gate closing. A guard locking it. She let the protection of her magic down for such a short time, and now they're taking her away. How long have they been overlooking her, and what's to become of her now?

Two of the guards escort the woman away, while the third sits on a crate and stares at me. He grins, his teeth yellow, a few missing. But, most importantly, he's human. At least there's that. But with him watching me, it's a matter of time before they drag me off next. Using magic risks drawing more attention to myself, but I'm in a race against time and I don't know when my time will be up. There's no room for trepidation anymore. No more room for caution.

I've made it this far, I've survived this long, but that's not enough anymore. I need to use the witch's ladder, but the only thing I know to do is hold it while I chant something. Chant what, though? I try writing one in my head. How hard can it be? Just something that sounds good and intends to get the Morts to do what I want. There are three in the room that I can see and perhaps more hiding in the shadows.

Place me in the head of those in control of the dead.

I think the chant, but nothing happens. I whisper it as quietly as I can. Still nothing, although now the guard is smirking, surely amused by my apparent insanity.

My palm and fingertips itch where the witch's ladder, hidden at my side, touches my skin. I rub my thumb over the knots, chanting quietly to myself over and over, waiting for something, even just some small spark to let me know this damned thing works and the lady wasn't just a lucky, crazy old woman. I fail in my efforts to still my shaking hands, but I don't give up. I repeat the chant again.

Please, let this thing help me. What do I do? Tell me what to do.

Then I hear it—a voice that's not my own.

. . . realize it is not strength in numbers we need. Competence. That is all it takes. A few strong warriors . . .

They aren't talking to me, I don't think. I'm not incompetent. Everyone has to learn. What I need right now is help getting out of here, though, and I hope listening to this voice will help me figure out how.

Who are you?

The voice is demanding, but there's an edge of fear there that makes me think they weren't expecting my company. I admit, I didn't expect them to hear *my* thoughts. And this person clearly isn't a Mort.

Of course I'm not a Mort!

It's another Ankou! One much older than I, or even William or Tess. I sense it in the same way William said I would just know how to handle Morts.

Get out of my head.

I need answers first.

Answers to what? You have come uninvited.

I wasn't trying to, but—

Then leave!

I don't know how, and I wouldn't even if I did. Where are you? Can you help me? I'm trapped in a prison in Salem and I need to get out of here but the guards are possessed by Morts.

That has nothing to do with me. Go away.

I'm not going anywhere until I get out of this cell. You don't get anywhere in life by giving up, right? The Morts certainly aren't going to give up and neither are the Cruor.

That's not my problem.

Isn't it, though? Just tell me what to do, and I'll leave you alone.

The older Ankou growls. *I shouldn't have to explain this to you, but if it will make you go away...it's quite obvious. Move the good Morts into the guards.*

I'd forgotten there is such a thing. How am I supposed to do that when I'm trapped in an iron cell, though?

With compulsion magic.

Oh, right. Of course! Why didn't I think of that? Compulsion magic...What on earth is compulsion magic?

You get into my head but can't figure out compulsion magic? Get in the Mort's *head, visualize them moving into the guard, that's it.*

I was trying to get into the Mort's head when I ended up here.

Well, you messed up. Try again. It's easier to get a Mort in a host than to get one out.

Thank you.

I try to leave their head, but instead the connection lingers while I try to figure out how to sever our ties. Finally, I let go of the witch's ladder. That does it. Now I know that thing isn't worthless, but figuring out how to use it the way I need to...that's another story.

What if the advice that Ankou gave me was inaccurate, or worse, intentionally harmful? I hadn't even considered that their advice might not work or might get me into more trouble. Right now, it's all I have. Trying couldn't possibly make things worse.

Could it?

I don't have time to think about that. It won't be long now before the guards catch on to what I'm trying to accomplish.

CHAPTER 17
LATE FEBRUARY, 1692

I SPEND SEVERAL HOURS OBSERVING THE MORTS, TRYING TO determine the good from the bad. While I know they aren't all bad, it's hard to see them as anything else—hard to let go of reservations that they all, deep down, might be evil. It's all part of my new role in life, though, and now, more than ever, I need to refine my skills as an Ankou.

The chanting didn't so much work out for me, so now I'm holding the witch's ladder and just trying to envision what I would do if I weren't trapped in this iron prison. Somehow I need to utilize my magic without physical contact. And all I really have is this witch's ladder right now, because my Ankou abilities are disabled. At least I know it's possible, though. If that raven-haired woman could do it, so can I.

Unfortunately, most of the Morts here are undoubtedly evil. Each time I connect with one, cold dread swims beneath my skin, and my mind is flooded with the memories of their lives before their spirit separated from the preternatural bodies. Strigoi that once ripped the entrails from an Ankou; Cruor that have drained small, innocent children. I can only witness so much rape, torture, and murder before I break. Perhaps they have stories of redemption beyond that, but I disconnect from them before I finding out. If the things they did can be redeemed, I don't want to know. I don't want to see any more.

And then I see her. A Mort I immediately trust before a connection is even made. The spirit of a young Strigoi that died before she grew old enough to shift. A child, really, maybe eight or ten years of age, with mouse-like features. My heart aches that she has somehow ended up trapped here, and it pains me that I won't be able to help move her spirit, that this time I need *her* to save *me*.

At least it will get her out of this place.

I look at the yellow-toothed guard I plan for her to possess, and guilt squeezes my stomach. He's just doing his job. It violates the right over his own body to put a Mort there against his wishes. At the same time, how many times has this guy forced his will on someone else? Mama always said two wrongs don't make things right. But this time—just this time—maybe it makes things even.

I wrap both my hands around the witch's ladder and rest my head against my fisted hands, sending my energy out to her. I feel this new ability struggling to break free, and I know this iron jail has made me weaker in more ways than one, but I can't let that stop me. I envision my fingers prodding gently on her scalp, my nails piercing into her skull...

There's no cold. Instead, flutters rush through my veins and spark in my mind. I urge her into the guard sitting on the crate nearby. My abilities feel more otherworldly now—not part of me. Borrowed. And I wonder how far gone my Ankou abilities are, if they play a role now or if they only lend me knowledge of what to do with this new magic I have acquired.

The Mort girl's fear rumbles through me, but I send a calming energy to her. It's amazing how natural this process feels, as though I've done it a million times before.

I move energy around the room as naturally as my human form breathes air. The witch's ladder seems to be my only allowance to use magic in this place, and I say a silent prayer for the woman who gave it to me, the woman who I will not be able to save. She sacrificed herself for me. Maybe William was right. Maybe it is worth sacrificing ourselves to save this world.

Compelled by me, the Mort girl enters the guard. Her panicked form trembles, and guilt stabs through my lungs, and I know then that my escape will not be so easy because I cannot leave this girl behind.

I rouse Vanessa from her troubled sleep and help her to her feet. Her brows pull together and she looks around frantically.

"It's all right," I whisper, squeezing her hand gently. "We're leaving."

Her body has already healed; perhaps the iron cell has no effect on the Strigoi; it wasn't put there to slow them down the way it was intended to slow down the Ankou, because Strigoi can't kill Morts and they can't travel through time and space. The prison alone is enough.

Right now, Vanesa is stronger than I am physically but weaker than I am emotionally. Or maybe I'm just numb. Either way, I'm counting on Vanessa to carry her own weight in this escape. It's hard to see her as a strong woman, though, when her body—now returned to its human form—is so pale and her dress is soaked in blood. I try not to look at the stains and try not to remember where they came from. I hope she can manage the same, or that remembering can drive her the way it drives me.

The young Mort has already grabbed the keys from a hook at the end of the hall and is hurrying back toward us. I subtly raise my hands to her, urging her to slow down. We can't give ourselves away. This needs to be done carefully and quietly.

The Mort girl, inside the body of this bulky, filthy guard, shuffles down the hallway. I hold my breath, wishing she would just move at a normal pace. I slowly exhale as she approaches and fumbles with the lock. Something creaks at the end of the hall, and I hear the banter of at least two other guards.

The sky outside the cell window is lightening, but the sun must still be tucked away as no beams of light are breaking into the room just yet. We really needed the night, but daylight can only be minutes away now.

I swallow around the knot in my throat, staring intently at the keys, willing the process to speed along, until finally the lock pops open. She eases the cell gate open. Half of the inmates are still sleeping, but those that aren't look at us with wide, fear-stricken eyes. I expect them to follow, but instead they cower away.

I bite my lip as I step out of the cell with Vanessa, stealing another glance back, trying to will these people to get up and fight for their freedom. To try to save themselves while they have the chance. But I can't save us all, and I don't have time to persuade these men and women.

Vanessa and I creep down the hall with the Mort that possesses the guard close behind us. When we reach the end of the narrow hallway, I peek through the barred window of the exit, trying to determine where we will go from here. The other guards aren't far off. The hall outside this door stretches in both directions. We either have to wait for those guards to leave or try to outrun them. But if we wait it out, and they come in our hall instead of leaving, we could get trapped in here all over again.

"Vanessa," I whisper, "do you know which way we need to go?"

She shakes her head.

I clench my teeth and peer out the small window again, trying to decide which way we should run. My instincts tell me to veer right, but my mind screams at me to go the other way, because if we go right, we'll run into the guards. That doesn't give us much chance to make any ground before they start after us.

A fragment strikes me, and I try to fight it. I don't have time for it, but the fragment won't let up. Soon, I am in the woods with Pa, camping, sometime before the Morts ruined our lives. Sometime back when Pa was still Pa.

We hiked too far. Pa doesn't remember the way back. We hadn't marked our trail. For over an hour, we walk around hopelessly. I slide on steep ground. My shin bleeds and my ankle won't support my weight to walk. Pa scoops me up.

"It's going to be okay," he soothes.

He sweeps stray hairs away from my face. I'm crying, but I don't let out a sound. It's getting dark, and Pa always said you have to stay quiet at night or you will attract the wrong kind of wildlife. I press my lips together, trying not to let the trembling whimper escape my lips.

"Come on, buttercup," he says, "You know the way home, don't you? Tell me which way to go."

"I don't know." I bury my face in his shoulder, wetting his shirt with my tears.

"Sure you do. Just tell me what feels right."

"I—I—don't know." I simper, then shake my head. I've always worked well under pressure. "Maybe that way."

I point toward the small creek, and he starts hiking that way.

"I hope you're right, buttercup. I hope you're right."

And I am. We find our path twenty minutes later. Pa rushes us home and the doctor comes to bandage my sprained ankle.

"We saved each other, huh, buttercup?" he asks, and I smile up at him.

Now the guards have strolled a couple feet closer to the prison door. We need to move, now. And, as much as I dread it, we need to go right. Knowing which way to go...it's always been a sixth sense of mine—even now, even while completely disoriented.

"Follow me and move fast," I whisper.

I push the door, gently at first, but the wood creaks, and the guards shift their focus in our direction. With a deep breath, I throw the door open and run with everything I have in me toward the guards. Once we're through the door, my strength begins building from my core. These halls are not protected by iron the way our cell was, but recovery won't be instant.

We are past them before they can react. There's lots of shouting. Their footsteps clamber behind us, but I don't look back. I've always been a weak and slow runner, probably because of my wiry arms and thin legs, so with my Ankou abilities being suppressed by this jail, I'm relying on Vanessa's speed to carry me along. I run my hardest on shaky limbs and ignore the pain shooting through my body as I push my way through the shortness of breath.

The walls are crowded with Morts, and I'm reminded of running through the woods, the only other time I've ever run so fast. Hadn't it been running that landed me here, away from my daughter? But I had been running toward her, to save her. Both physically and emotionally I had wanted to be *closer* to her. I would certainly never run away from her, not even to get away from Pa.

Vanessa yanks my arm and points with her other hand at another door at the end of the hall. That door is the only thing that exists right now. We're a bit faster than the guards and reach the door first, but it's locked. The young Mort girl tries one of the keys without success. As she tries another, one of the guards grabs me by the hair and yanks me back.

I twist toward him, swing with everything I have, and connect my fist with his ear. The large man stumbles back, now half his height as he hunches over—but just as soon, another guard lumbers at me with his bloody knuckles. He misses. I duck out of his way, consequently into the path of a third guard whose stomach is bigger than his chest. He wraps his arms around me, but before he can get a good hold, I elbow him swiftly to the gut, then again in his face. The blows perhaps hurt me more than him, but it gets him off of me.

The Mort girl is out of keys and one of the guards is lunging toward her now. Vanessa grabs the door and digs her fingertips into the space between the door and the wall. My attention is ripped away from her when the first guard that attacked me grabs my arm.

I spin around and kick him in his shin, just below the knee. Something cracks. I'm frozen, stunned by my own strength, though I know I am still not restored to my Ankou abilities or we would be out of here by now.

Vanessa rips the door open as more guards approach. Another two wait on the other side of the door. We're surrounded. She tackles them, letting out a war cry. I know he won't last long in her hands, but we'll never win this battle with so many guards outnumbering us.

Still, we will fight. We'll fight even when it seems hopeless, because this is our only chance. If we don't escape now, they will kill us for trying, just as I will kill them if I must—if that's what it takes to survive.

One of the guards clips me in my mouth, and the metallic taste of blood pools along my gums. I stumble back, but the icy air against my fevered skin delivers a stronger impact than my opponent. It revives me, and I charge toward the guard, knocking him back into the hall's cold stone walls. His head cracks on impact, and his blood trails along the rough stones, but the injury only disorients him. He stomps toward me again. I swing at him, but he blocks and grabs me by the throat.

Out of the corner of my eye, I spot a Mort I can use to my advantage, but I can barely breathe and struggle to concentrate long enough to move him. The guard squeezes tighter. I kick at him, but he doesn't so much as flinch. My arms flail at him uselessly. My vision darkens, and my head buzzes as I fight to hold on to consciousness. I can't let go. I can't let things end here.

I thrust every last bit of my energy into moving the Mort, but by the time I've succeeded, I don't have the strength to compel him to my will.

The young Mort girl I compelled earlier uses the strength of her stocky male host body to push my attacker off of me. I flop to the ground but waste no time working my way back to my feet, trying once more to compel the Mort I moved into my attacker. It's useless. He's still moving after me, and I realize my ability is not fail-proof.

Frantically, I search for more Morts I can move, but none stand out to me. But then I see it. Two Morts staring at one another with a murderous glint in their eyes. They communicate in grunts. The threatening vibe they give off peg them as enemies, and I waste no time moving their spirits into two of the guards.

Immediately they lunge for one another, which not only

eliminates two guards from our concern but also distracts the other guards, who try to break it up. They receive a few blows in their efforts and soon have joined in the brawl. They're diverted enough to get us through the second door, and we pound our way up the wooden steps beyond. Only one of the guards tries to follow, but he's unable to work past the fight that clutters the narrow hall.

At the top of the steps is an empty courtroom. I stop dead. This is definitely the way out, but only if we want to draw attention to ourselves. I press the door at the top of the steps closed and Vanessa helps me barricade it with a bench that I doubt will hold for long. Then I lead Vanessa and the Mort girl in the guard's body toward the back of the courtroom, looking for an exit that won't deposit us into the middle of the town. All I can find is a small window.

Light pours in. Outside, the daylight is fresh. Bright. Clean. It's like lemonade and fresh linens. I wish more than anything that peaceful, cotton-white light was safe for me, but in reality, daytime is the worst time for escape, for more reasons than one.

The door to the cellar rattles forcefully. I open the window and help Vanessa out onto the frosted ground. The Mort girl, in the guard's body, struggles to fit, but I push and Vanessa pulls until she is through. The cellar door bursts open and three guards, bloody and already bruising, stumble out, falling on top of one another but scrambling to their feet. I climb out the window and take off.

We're out. Free. And yet, I don't feel any better. Nothing will be the same. The things we have left behind...they cannot be replaced.

Still, I do the only thing I can do.

I run into the daylight.

CHAPTER 18
LATE FEBRUARY, 1692

WE NEED TO GET TO THE SHADE WITHOUT BEING SEEN. I RUN AS fast as humanly possible, because that is still all I am capable of. The iron poisoning most likely won't cure completely until I get my hands on some nightshade, and now is not the time to hunt down plants. I have to reserve what little spotty magic I have left to move the Mort girl out of this guard's body.

Our escape will most certainly attract some attention from the other townsfolk, but they wouldn't have seen us yet. The forest is just ahead—shade, shelter, safety. Something to hide the hideous, amniotic wings that flutter behind me.

"Hey!" a man's voice shouts behind us.

He's too late. We're in the woods now and a good enough distance away to get ourselves lost here. By the time they assemble a search team, we could be anywhere. I know that won't stop them from trying, but I breathe a little easier.

Ahead of me, Vanessa navigates between the trees as though it's home. I am practically dragging the Mort girl behind me, the body she possesses sloppy and weak. We run until my sides ache, until my legs stop burning and go numb. We run until my body threatens to collapse, until my lungs feel as though they are bleeding, and until my heart stabs in my chest. I'm nearly delirious, and then we run more.

Vanessa stops by a cluster of trees, and I slow to meet her. I give her a long look, then turn to the guard's body.

"Thank you," I say to the girl inside. "But you know you can't stay here, don't you?"

The guard's Adam's apple bobs, and his head nods. I can almost see the young girl trembling inside of him. Moving the girl does risk the life of the body she possesses. That's what William had said. If we move a Mort that has possessed a human, the body may die. But this Mort deserves a future more than a man who would turn a blind eye when Salem's people are mistreated.

"It won't be bad," I promise. "May I?"

The guard's head nods again, and I step forward, placing my fingertips on the scalp. His chest freezes—the Mort girl is holding her breath, bracing herself for the part that is unfairly cruel right now. My nails slice into the scalp—she can't feel it, but she will know the true end is near. The air around us vibrates.

Please let this work.

I can feel my powers fizzing in and out. I'm still weakened by the iron, but my Ankou abilities are there, somewhere.

It takes all of my energy to conjure the ability to do what must be done. I close my eyes and let my core guide me through some unknown space, some space I'll never understand, a tunnel that is dark yet comforting.

The Mort girl doesn't fight. That weird thing that happened with my teeth when I tried to save Verity doesn't happen.

"We're almost there," I whisper, although I'm not sure if she can hear me in this place.

We arrive on the embankment of a water hole. Elephants wade lazily through the water. A young woman with elegant bones, a kind face, and dark skin carries a basket at her hip. A small girl carrying sticks teeters behind her.

What I know that this gentle mother does not is that her child's heart is about to fail. And when that happens, her human spirit will be plucked from this world. But the life of that child is not over. Within moments, the time has come, and the Mort girl at my side is given a new home and a new life. It is a miracle no one will ever know or hear about. And as they walk away, I realize I never learned the girl's name. I don't know a thing about the girl who saved my life.

Then I'm back at Vanessa's side. I vomit in a bush and fall to the ground. The move took more out of me than I had. At my side, the guard is still on the ground, and I don't know when he will wake. Or *if* he will wake. I don't check for a pulse—don't care to know if I've killed him, because I can't handle the guilt if I have.

An annoying tingle in my stomach and throat turn to outright pain. I feel as though I have been ripped inside out. I curl in a ball and squeeze my eyes shut. Vanessa crouches beside me and rubs my arm.

"Abigail? Abigail, what's wrong?"

She doesn't know me as Cordovae, but she certainly knows by now that I'm different. That I'm like her, but not like her. An elemental, but a different race. If it hadn't been evident by the hideous wings that the sunlight reveals, it must have been by my disappearance just now as I delivered the Mort girl to her new life.

"Abigail!" She's more frantic now.

"Nightshade," I say through trembling lips. God, please let that be enough.

"Nightshade?" Her voice sounds far away. "Nightshade! Right. Hang in there."

It feels as though minutes pass before she actually leaves, but perhaps it was only moments. She hesitates, but once she leaves, she moves with urgency.

I just hope she makes it back to me before the settlement's men find me first.

I'M FALLING INTO BLACKNESS, BUT THIS TIME, THE DARK DOES not comfort me. This is a cold, ominous dark that will end with more darkness instead of new light. I want to apologize to William for failing him. I want to apologize to Tess for not getting to know her better, for thinking of her as mean instead of seeing her hurt. I want to forgive my parents that they weren't stronger somehow, for their bodies hurting and neglecting me, but I can't separate them from the Morts. I can't stop blaming them. Most of all, I want to be whole, but I am broken, and a huge piece of me is missing—Anna. Nothing in this world can be good if she's not safe.

A woman's voice rattles outside of me. "Abigail."

I moan.

Someone—I hope it's Vanessa—grabs me by my arm and pushes me onto my back. "Come on, wake up."

She shakes me. She presses something against my chest—her ear, I think, because her hair tickles my arm. She tugs my chin, opening my mouth, and presses something inside. My mind stirs. Nightshade.

She did it.

Vanessa.

I'm not yet strong enough for words.

"You're going to be fine," she says, placing more nightshade into my mouth.

It's sweet but tart. I can taste again. The nectar of the flower bites my tongue but soothes the ache of my mouth and throat. A small vibration—the feeling of life—buzzes through me. I blink my eyes open and attempt to sit up, but fall back. Vanessa catches me.

"I'm sorry," I manage to say, awash with guilt that she has to care for me right now when I know she has to be more broken than I am.

And yet, I don't know that it's just her I'm apologizing to. It's everyone.

"Don't be sorry," she says. "You saved me. And you will save many more. I know it."

She's wrong, though. How can I save anyone if I can't save myself?

⚜

THOUGH I FEEL MORE STABLE NOW THAT I HAVE EATEN, MY energy and strength have not returned enough to use my Ankou abilities to travel beyond what I have already done. Moving that Mort girl took everything out of me. I nudge the body of the guard. He's still alive, but barely.

"We need to go," I say to Vanessa. "Before he wakes up."

We trudge by foot. It's probably for the best. I need to keep careful not to trigger their attention as much as possible. I can't help but hurry my step toward Tess' cabin. They need to hear what happened. They'll know what to do next. I won't feel safe until I find them.

I grab a hiking stick to help guide our path, to check for traps and wild animals and snakes as we travel. My instincts tell me where to go, and yet something else in my gut tells me not to go any further. To stay away. But I can't. I need to get back to Tess and William. They need to know what I've seen, and they need to help me finish what I am called to do so I can get out of here. I don't belong here. Surely they will see that now.

I stay to the shade as much as I can, but there are times I must traverse through sunlight. I move quickly. Passing through the sun is painful. Not in a scorching way, as it must be for the Cruor before the sun consumes them completely. Instead, the sun hurts me through unbearable pressure, cutting through the chill of winter on my skin.

Vanessa never looks at my wings, and I wonder if it is because she finds them too grotesque, or if it's because she cannot see them. I try to remember what William and Tess told me, but I'm too tired to think straight. I know humans can see my wings, but what about other elementals? I suppose it doesn't matter now.

Vanessa already knows the truth about me, and she's just as inhuman as I am.

I hear voices, and I freeze. Vanessa's eyes meet mine. She must hear them, too. They are on the other side of this wall of trees, and when I peek through, my stomach lurches, and I cover my mouth so to suppress a gasp.

Vanessa takes a look, then shakes her head sadly.

"What is it?" I whisper.

"*Ankou.*"

I shake my head vigorously. They are too hideous to be Ankou. The Ankou still look human. These things...they're gray with enlarged skulls and razor teeth.

Anxiety sinks into the pit of my stomach. My teeth had gotten like that once. I wasn't going to...to turn into them...was I?

"How?" I ask finally.

"Come," she says, "you need shelter."

She grabs my arm and hurries me away from the supposed Ankou's campsite. When we're a few yards away, she whispers, "They were exposed to too much sun and tried to reverse the effects by drinking Strigoi blood."

"How can you be sure?" I ask.

She levels her gaze at me in a way that imparts the mindlessness of my question.

"*Oh...*"

"Right," she says, nodding. "As Strigoi, we are raised on what to look out for. In this world, everyone is a predator, and everyone is prey. Survival means knowing who would kill you to live themselves."

I shiver and squeeze my own arms. I wish William and Tess were here. I always feel safer with them. As much as I appreciate Vanessa's wisdom, I don't see her as capable of helping much if we are attacked.

"We should pick up the pace," I say, just wanting to get back to Tess' cabin as quickly as possible.

"Of course," she says, and we hike on with a little more urgency than before.

***

WIND HOWLS AROUND THE TRUNKS OF TREES AND DISTURBS THE crunchy leaves of the forest path. Winter birds squawk their protest in the soughing winds. Vanessa, however, is silent. I don't know what to say to her, and I don't think she wants to say anything more to me. Talking right now, it hurts. It hurts the heart, the soul. I try not to look at her because I'm not sure what I might see in her eyes, and I worry what she might read on my face. Would she resent my pity?

William and Tess were right. Whatever you do in this world, you have to fight. I had waited too long, and because of that, Vanessa's baby is dead. This isn't a world where you wait for opportunity. This is a life where you keep moving, keep trying, keep *fighting*. I'll never forgive myself, but somehow, Vanessa forgave me enough to save my life. She could have kept going and left me for the men of the settlement to find.

"I'm sorry," I say. "For not getting you out of there sooner. For not..."

"You can't do that," she says.

I freeze and glance back at her, immediately regretting it when I see the tears in her eyes.

"*They* did this to me. Not you."

A stinging knot lumps in my throat, and my eyes water. I try to pinch back the tears. My voice will crack if I try to speak.

"Please," she says, taking my hand. "Don't let my son's death be for nothing."

I can't look at her anymore. I turn away, letting my hand drop from hers. "The cabin is just ahead," I say, my voice cracking and uneven. "I'll make you something to eat, if you want."

I don't disillusion myself into thinking she missed my emotion, but as it stands, she likely already thinks I'm mentally unwell. How many times has she seen me in the trance-like state of having a fragment?

When we reach a small creek, I spot the familiar makeshift bridge constructed of stones and thick branches and old planks of wood, and we cross to where there's a break in the trees that I also recognize. We're close.

I veer from our path through the small space and tread over thin, wiry branches and vines that have knotted together on the forest floor. We climb a hill, and I see Tess' cabin a short ways off. I look in every direction, but see no one. Vanessa and I hike over. It's too quiet. Shouldn't I hear them? Has it always been this silent here?

Anxiety creeps in. What if they aren't here? Does that mean they went to the location William told me to travel to if I didn't find them here? I can't bear to think about sitting around an empty cabin, waiting for the darkness so that I can hike even farther to find them. I've sat around waiting for too long. I need to see them.

I hurry my step, until soon I am running, my heart pounding erratically in my chest. The closer I get to Tess' cabin, the more unsettled I am. I need to talk to them. I need them now.

I burst through the door. The quiet is painful, but it's not the worst of what I find.

The table is overturned. Tess' cooking pot is on its side across the room. The mattress is sliced open. Cabinets are emptied, the contents strewn across the floor. A plate of stew has tumbled from the table, spilling herbed water and chunks of meat onto the dirt.

The doll William gave me for Anna lays in the middle of the floor, limbs bent in unnatural ways. Tossed aside. Discarded. Unimportant to whoever destroyed this place. William and Tess are nowhere to be seen.

I lift the doll from the ground, comb out her hair with my fingers, and straighten her dress.

I can't give up now.

I can't give up ever.

CHAPTER 19
LATE FEBRUARY, 1692

DON'T PANIC.

We can't just stand here, doing nothing. We need to get the hell away before whoever destroyed this place returns.

I can't make assumptions. The cabin could have been ransacked *after* they left. I visualize the location in the mountains William had shown me on his map before leading me to the town. Do I go there, or have our efforts been compromised entirely?

Trying to find them could get me captured again, or worse, murdered. I've already witnessed the Cruor cause a young woman unbearable suffering—perhaps death would have been a kindness. Why didn't they kill us while they had chance?

Focus, Cord.

Do I risk what little time I have in search of William and Tess, or do I continue my journey alone?

The doll in my hand gives me my answer. My hope comes from them. I toss the doll into a sack lying on the floor nearby and sling the sack over my shoulder. I can't do this alone, and I need to know if Tess and William are safe. I shake away the deeper thought trying to poke through—that I shouldn't care about them. That I am the worst mother ever to let my feelings for them get in the way of returning to my daughter. I can't let my feelings for them determine my decisions. Not now, not *ever*.

Vanessa places a hand on my forearm. "Abigail…"

I snap my attention toward her, blinking back the moisture in my eyes.

Her eyes are full of sorrow, her face long and lips downturned.

"What is it?" I ask.

She bites her lip, then her gaze dips behind me. Slowly, I turn my head to follow.

A piece of William's shirt.

Blood.

I stumble back, catching myself against the cabin wall. "We need to get out of here."

"I know a place not far off. Let's take refuge first, then we'll figure this out."

What's there to figure out? The crushing pain in my chest reminds me of losing my daughter all over again. Vanessa's haunted eyes tell me she knows my pain, but it just makes me angry. She shouldn't pity me. She lost her child. There is still hope for mine. My daughter is alive.

And William…Tess…We don't know enough yet for me to get upset, and I resent Vanessa acting as though we do. And I hate myself for being angry with her. And I hate her for staying calm all this time, for being patient with me when I'm falling apart when she's the one who has lost everything.

I am so full of hate that I'm disgusted with myself.

"Lead the way," I mumble, and I follow her back into the forest, hating myself most of all.

⊷❧⊶

As I trudge behind Vanessa, the silence only angers me more, so finally I say what has been bothering me most of all. "How are you okay right now?"

She pauses, then continues walking.

"Okay?" she asks. "Is that what you think?"

"It's as though you don't care. As though none of this fazes you."

"Not everyone is so easy to read, Abigail."

I yank her arm, and she spins toward me. "You lost your son."

Her brow furrows. "Yes," she says through her teeth. "And I've lost two of his sisters as well. And many of my siblings also never made it to this world. This is part of my reality. Perhaps you should be a little more grateful and respect that everyone grieves in their own way."

She pulls away from me, and I feel the muscles in my face drooping. Why did I say anything? Was I really so offended by her acceptance of her situation that I would be so insensitive? Who have I become; what has this life turned me into?

I should leave her now. I've done enough damage. But I don't know this area or where to go, and she at least deserves my apology before we part ways.

"You're afflicted," Vanessa says, her calm tone returning. It's as though she has already given me the forgiveness I haven't yet asked for and certainly don't deserve. "You're on the run from both the mortal and immortal world, and you've been separated from people you love."

She doesn't know about Anna. I don't think. She must be talking about William and Tess. "I don't love—"

"Sometimes our mind won't accept what our heart knows, and that is how we survive."

I shrug one of my shoulders and try to push away the thought she's put in my mind. I bite my lip and pick at my fingernails, scraping the dirt from underneath them. It seems I can never get rid of it all.

"Are we far?" I ask.

"No," she says lightly. My anger at her dissipates a little more each time she speaks in that soft-spoken way of hers. "Another few miles."

There's a rustling between the trees, and I pull Vanessa back and hold a finger to my lips. She nods.

I creep slowly to where the trees break and peek through to the path on the other side. A young woman is weeping over a dead body.

A body I recognize.

My stomach seizes, and I squeeze my eyes shut, trying to will away the truth. But I can't unsee what I've seen.

Elizabeth is dead.

She was a good person. A good soul. And now I am almost certain of what I could only surmise before. She was a spirit elemental. I sense this because her spirit is visible to me unlike any other Mort I've seen before. She's not a shadow. In fact, she's glowing. She stands beside the sobbing woman, rubbing her back, but the woman is unaware of her presence.

"Hang on," I whisper to Vanessa.

"Oh my." She gasps, a hand going to her mouth. She shakes her head. "Is that . . ."

I tug her arm, spinning her away from the sight of Elizabeth's dead body. "Wait here."

I scan the bushes, looking for something to give me a boost of energy. There's no nightshade anywhere. I move as quickly as I can without making too much noise, but I don't see any poisonous plants anywhere. Vanessa had only brought such a small amount of nightshade, and admittedly, I'm not sure what I'm looking for. Only what William and Tess have given me previously.

There are some red and black berries on the ground, but they're dead. I close my eyes, thinking. I can heal them, but if they aren't what I need, it will be wasted energy I can't afford right now. I wave Vanessa over.

"What are these?" I whisper. "Do you know?

"Rosary peas."

"Are they poisonous?"

"To me, yes. The nightshade didn't help?"

"I need more," I mumble, not wasting time to explain.

I pick them off the ground, and they heal at my touch. Then I pop them in my mouth. I eat two whole handfuls, hoping, praying, that these are strong enough to give my spotty abilities a boost.

I walk back toward the scene, watching silently as the weeping woman buries the body and runs away. I wish I could run away from this place, too.

When I am sure the woman is gone, I climb between the breaks in the trees and walk right up to Elizabeth's spirit. She doesn't run. She just turns toward me, staring at me with sorrowful eyes. I reach out my hand in offering, and gently she takes it, and although I know I shouldn't travel again so soon, I do. I take her to a place many years from now, to the Province of Georgia, so that one day soon she can be reborn as Mary Parsons. Because I know the world needs her, or one of her incarnations, and though she might not have survived this lifetime, it wasn't her time to meet a final end.

When I return, Vanessa simply says, "We ought to move quickly."

We are so far from where I need to be. I refocus on the here and now: Who went after William and Tess? How did they find them, and are they looking for me, too? If William and Tess escaped, will these people find them again?

I reach in the pocket of my dress and thumb the witch's ladder I've held on to. I take a deep, slow breath, thinking of William, trying for find some connection to him. I've connected with an Ankou before, now if I can just focus on one in particular . . .

My fingertips warm, and my palm crackles with sparks. Come on, William. Come on, where are you?

The sparks fizzle. Nothing.

I know this magic works, because I've done it before, but at the same time I fear it may be hopeless. I hadn't been trying to get in touch with anyone specifically the first time. In fact, I hadn't been trying to get in touch with anyone at all. What if it'd just been a lucky accident?

The ground beneath us gets rockier. Running water roars

louder. The sun hits her peak in the sky, then sinks behind the trees. The moon frowns at us as he climbs up behind the night clouds. Finally I do not need the shade of the trees, and the pressure of the sun releases me. My wings are hidden from view now, and that brings me peace. I hate those things, hate that they mark me as being different.

As the day disappears for good, complete peace and silence claim the forest—eerily quiet, as though even void of wildlife. But I still cannot connect with William. I cannot hear even a whisper of his voice.

Verity would call the lack of birds an omen. A bad omen. God, I hope she's safe now.

We climb between large boulders and through a narrow trail of overgrown underbrush until we reach a small clearing. There are pinecones—so many that it's impossible to walk without stepping on them. My center of balance jolts as one rolls beneath my foot.

On the other side of the clearing, trees grow so close together they nearly create a solid wall, but Vanessa squeezes through a small opening and waves for me to follow. On the other side, she pushes aside the branches of a large bush, revealing a small opening to what appears to be a cave hidden beneath moss and wild vines.

Only little slivers of moonlight illuminate the inside of the dark cave. The air is damp, metallic, and reeks of wet pine.

I sit on the gritty stone floor to rest, but Vanessa keeps moving about. She lights a small lantern, reaches her hand into her apron, and drops a pile of herbs and berries into a wooden bowl that was stored toward the back of the cave.

She passes me the bowl. "I thought you might still need more to eat."

It's not just nightshade this time. It's a variety of poisonous plants she must have gathered as we travelled. "We never talked about..."

"I'm probably more familiar with your nature than you are,"

she says. "Your kind has helped many against the Maltorim, against the Morts, and against the corrupt Cruor that plague this world."

"I'm sorry about earlier," I blurt out. I don't know what else to say. Obviously not all Ankou are noble. At least I'm not.

"Don't worry." She sweeps her hair away from her face, then points at the witch's ladder I'm still fumbling with in my hands. "You couldn't reach your friend?"

I shake my head.

"He might still be okay."

"You don't really think that," I say, trying to measure her reaction. Her lips tremble, and I take it that my accusation was true.

"You said there were two people supposed to be at the cabin," she says. "Did you try the other one?"

"Tess," I say, more to myself than to Vanessa. "No. No, I haven't."

What would be the point? If anything, I'm less connected to Tess than to William.

"You ought to try. Otherwise, I can bring you to the Chibold. They might be of help."

I only vaguely remember William and Tess telling me about the Chibold. That they are the only accurate way to communicate with the Universe.

"Thanks," I mumble quietly.

Vanessa smiles. "I need to hunt for my own food now," she says. "I'll be back in a while."

Is she hunting or just trying to give me some privacy? She's been by my side since we've escaped, trying to help. Doesn't she have someone *she* needs to reunite with?

After Vanessa heads out, I try again with the witch's ladder to connect with William. When that fails, I cave and try Tess.

The speed of my connection with her unnerves me, but I heave a sigh of relief to have made contact.

Cord?

Tess, it's me. I don't have time to explain. Are you and William safe?

Yes. Where are you?

I am going to come to you two, if you are where William said you would be.

We are...We've been trying to think of a way to get to you. How did you get in my head?

A witch's ladder?

That's unusual for an Ankou...How did you escape?

My magic wasn't working there. Iron. I had to fight my way out.

The effects should wear off soon, but you have to keep low. Don't use your abilities. We can't risk you drawing attention to yourself.

Okay, I won't use them anymore. What else do I need to know?

Cordovae! You didn't!

I can't change what's done! Just tell me what to do now.

Head west toward the mountains. But I have to warn you first: There will be many Morts and Cruor around the edges of the forest. Avoid those areas if you can. And don't trust anyone. No one, or you might lead the wrong people to us. You MUST come alone. We'd come to you if we could, but it's more likely you can get to us unnoticed since we've already been spotted. In the meantime, I have to go stop William. He's on his way to try to get arrested in your town.

No! Why would he do that?

I tried to stop him. Just hurry here. Maybe he'll listen to me now.

Please stop him. I'll be there soon.

I drop the connection. There's still so much I need to talk to Tess about: Elizabeth—the woman I sensed might be a spirit elemental—and what happened to me while I saved Verity...how my teeth had turned to sharp points. And why was it unusual that I contacted her with a witch's ladder? I push those thoughts away. Right now, Tess needs to focus on stopping William. The rest of my questions can wait.

As soon as Vanessa returns, I need to leave. Without her. Or I could leave now, but...no, she deserves an explanation. I only hope that the traveling I did earlier has not already put us all at risk.

Anxiety creeps over me, almost as itchy as the bitter cold of this late winter night. I don't know the area or much about the elemental world. Vanessa would have been a helpful guide. Regardless what Tess thinks, I can trust her, but perhaps it's best I leave her behind for other reasons. The less people with me as I travel, the less likely I am to be spotted.

As I lean my head back against the cave wall to rest before the journey ahead, a fragment tingles at the corners of my mind, and for once I am glad to give in to it, to be carried away by the worries that are behind me—the worries I cannot change and no longer stress about.

I'm playing in a creek with a small blonde girl. We're catching tadpoles. They're almost too fast for us, and when they're not, they're so surprisingly slimy that we squeal and let them go before we can get a good hold on them.

I can't remember the girl's name because when she introduced herself I was distracted, thinking about how she probably has a perfect life with a normal family. Not a father who recently started visiting her room every night. I'm too shy to ask her again what her name is, so when I want her attention, I just say, "Hey!"

All summer we hang out together. One day we even catch a frog and don't freak out or let it go. We keep it in a shoebox with holes poked in top, but it escapes when we open the lid to take a peek.

One night, I'm helping Mama shell peas and telling her about our day when Pa walks into the kitchen from the living room.

'I don't want you hanging 'round with that girl no more,' he says. 'Catching frogs? That's what you two have been doing all summer?'

'But Pa—'

'No buts. She's not a very lady-like influence on you, and you can bet girls like that use people like you. Before you know it, she'll have boys joining you to play kissing games and offering you up to any guy that's interested. That's how girls become whores, having friends like that.'

'We're not seeing boys! Pa, you're not making any sense! We're just—'

'That's my final word, Rose. Don't test me.'

I don't have it in me to fight for her friendship. I can't talk freely to Pa anymore. Not since the darkness came.

As the fragment fades, I wish more than anything I could have a friend. Someone I could confide in and would never have to leave behind. Perhaps I'm not meant to have friends. I've left Verity behind, and now I'll have to leave Vanessa behind as well.

But I can live without friends if the Universe would grant me just one person in my life—the one person I will always fight for.

Anna.

It always comes back to Anna.

❧

A LIGHT TRICKLING OF WATER DRAWS MY ATTENTION DEEPER into the cave. A small stream runs along the back wall, and I use the water to wash up. The water has pooled a bit and gives off a stagnant smell, but my touch purifies every drop. Realizing it won't be so easy to hide what I am during my travels, I frown. I'll need to go completely unseen. But I make the most of it and scoop some of the water into a tall jug, thinking Vanessa will need some clean water to drink in her travels as well. I'll miss having her with me.

While she's gone, I weave together some twigs with red berries that were rotting in the cave but renewed at my touch. At first it is just to pass the time, but soon I realize I'm making a hair wreath for Vanessa.

Something stomps overhead, shaking the cave and sending dirt cascading into my hair. I drop the wreath, my hand giving favor to cover my mouth and stifle a gasp. More thumping, like thunder cracking against the ground in quick succession—but there is no storm tonight. Horses, I realize, right before I hear the lighter thud, then voices that I can't make out.

People. Good people or bad people, it's still bad news for me. Minutes later, wisps of smoke float into the cave. Thank God it's not cedar. The last thing I need now is an allergic reaction. They must have set up camp just above the cave. I keep my breathing as quiet and shallow as I can, though I'm certain they aren't aware of me beneath them as I am of them above.

Hours later, Vanessa creeps back into the cave. She's worse for wear, twigs tangled in her hair and dirtier than she was when she left. If that's even possible.

"Don't worry," she whispers. "They can't see us from where they are, and even if they knew we were here, they would never figure out how to get here."

I press my lips together and nod. "But I do need to leave soon."

"Of course."

"Alone," I say apologetically. "I didn't want to leave without saying goodbye, though. Will you be all right?"

"Absolutely," she says, patting my knee. "You've done enough for me."

"And you for me," I offer.

The night air is so cold that even Vanessa—with all the warmth the Strigoi are known to have—is shivering. It strikes me it's not just the cold that makes her body tremble, though. It's the loss of her child.

"Are you sure you're going to be all right?" I ask again.

"I've spent the last eight months living as a mortal. So I wouldn't...well . . ." She chokes up. "You know we can't shift when we're pregnant, or—"

"I understand," I say, so she doesn't have to say it. I don't think she wants to, and I don't want to hear it, to be haunted any further than I already am by the image of her stillborn child.

"Those months have made me weaker," she says, "but you see how fast I have recovered already. In a few days, I'll be fit to leave here."

I hope I will recover as easily. My pain has ebbed, but I'm still not myself. The aches coursing through every limb in my body are nauseating. But I can't let that slow me down; I need to make some ground tonight.

"You'll do great," she adds. "You were made for this."

I sigh my doubts. "I'm not sure."

"You made it this far."

"With your help," I point out.

"You may not have needed my help if you hadn't been trying to save me. I'll never forget you, Abigail."

"Cordovae," I say. "My name, in my heart and in your world, is Cordovae."

Sharing this with her makes me feel as though we're closer. As though we can keep a connection even if we never see each other again.

"Well, then, Cordovae—thank you. For everything."

I nod and, before I realize what I've done, my arms are wrapped around her. I release her and bend to lift the wreath I made her from the ground. I place it on her head like a halo. She smiles, and I return the gesture. But the soft moment withers as anxiety creeps through my veins.

"Stay safe," I say sharply, as though it's a command. I grab her for another hug, then turn away, not pausing to look in her the eye. If I look at her again, I will cry.

I have to leave.

So I head out of the cave alone, into the night of a world that wants me dead.

CHAPTER 20

LAST DAY OF FEBRUARY, 1592

THE SHARP NIGHT AIR IS LIKE ICE MELTING ON MY SKIN, EASING away my pain, stirring an energy in me that slowly renews my strength. A strange calm washes through me, though my heart does not steady. Determination takes hold in my core, thumping within me, and all over again it's like the first night I met Tess and William. As though the earth is a beating drum.

The air is soiled by the pungently sweet scent of rotten fruit and the musk of a skunk. I lift some overripe winter berries from the ground. The bumpy, crinkled skin of the fruit turns smooth as my touch heals them to a fresher state. I pop them in my mouth. They roll over my tongue, velvety and cool. A few Daphne berries are all it takes to kill a small child, but to me, they are a lifeline. Eating them has the same warming effect as drinking alcohol, and my whole body relaxes and reenergizes.

Time stretches ahead of me, though I feel the urgency of needing to travel such a great distance before sunrise. Normally my senses lead the way, but with my mind racing with fear that I'll waste time heading in the wrong direction, I have to stop to think.

Tess said to go west. I study the land around me, the trees, the stones. Moss grows on the north. From that, I determine my westerly path and trek steadily in what I hope is the right direction.

Nighttime casts a whitish blue ambience over my world, and the towering trees with their knobby bark send the flutters of a fragment through my mind.

I'm a child peeking over my freckled shoulder at Ma's smiling face. She reaches past me and brushes a new stroke of color onto a small canvas.

The trees in the woods tonight have the same clumpy appearance as Ma's painting. She was the one who taught me about art. And when the Morts stole my parents, it was the art that made me feel safe. I can remember the night the Morts came.

Ma stays home to do her pottery while Pa takes me to see the horses. We're on our way back from the farm when he loses control of the car.

As I float in and out of consciousness, dark figures dangle in the corners of my vision. The Shadow Men. One of the times I wake, I startle with a gasp, roll to my side, and check on Pa. He isn't breathing. I grab his wrist to check his pulse. It's fading. Fading...

I slip back into sleep.

An ambulance never comes.

Then, as though it was all a dream, I wake, and Pa is driving us home. Quiet. Eyes focused on the road. But it hadn't been a dream. A wound at his temple is still bleeding. My body still aches, and my shoulder and hips are bruised from the seatbelt. A new kind of darkness surrounded us, shadows whipping by the windows as Pa drives.

Suddenly, I feel helplessly alone.

I keep saying, "Pa, are you okay? Pa? Please talk to me, Pa."

But he doesn't say a word.

When we arrive home, Ma's pottery sits unfinished. She lies on the couch, her hands muted and pale from the clay.

The Shadow Men never left, and my parents never returned.

Now, tonight, the woods are plagued by such Morts as those—Morts that watch me from between the trees. They are the shadows left behind by the shells they once inhabited—some good, many bad—but each of them instinctively wary of what I might do to them. None of them knowing what kind of future would await them if they come in contact with an Ankou. But although my Ankou abilities have finally returned—finally tingle for my acknowledgment from deep within—tonight is not the night I will determine their fate. Tonight I will not allow them to unsettle me. Tonight, they can watch...but they can't hurt me.

There were many like them who had destroyed me in my life as Rose, but now I know there were some who had tried to protect me as well.

Movement in the underbrush rustles the leaves, and I gasp. I hold my breath, frozen, until a small raccoon scurries past. How am I to handle the Morts and Cruor and Marked Strigoi if I am so easily taken off guard by a small nocturnal animal? I shake my head, scolding myself to toughen up and keep going. I need to get through this for Anna.

I step over a fallen tree and cross an abandoned campfire. Ashes and debris stir in a pit surrounded by stones, and I recognize a piece of torn fabric dangling from a low lying branch of a nearby oak. Tess and William must have come through this way. That means I'm on the right path, but it also means that the Morts and Cruor in this area will be on high alert if they know this is where Tess and William passed by undetected.

As I near the edge of the forest, I suck in the icy night air, preparing myself for the worst.

But there's nothing.

Relief doesn't swoop in to comfort me. Instead, panic rises in my chest.

It's *eerily* empty.

I want to push myself forward, but I step back. I must be missing something. I look as far as I can see, but all I see is a cold, low-lying fog rolling in the open land beyond the edges of the forest and wisping between the trees.

You can do this, Cord. You have *to.*

I creep out of the forest, into the open now. The next step is harder. Every step after that is taking me farther from the cover of the woods.

Here, I am the deer in the field.

I am the prey.

With my apple-red hair and dark dress, and the golden sheen of my skin in the moonlight, I am a fire burning in the middle of this world of gray and brown, crunching footprints across a field dusted in white. I caress the birthmark on my wrist. It makes me feel closer to Anna and reminds me why I'm doing this.

I pull my invisible wings around me, hoping I have done so correctly, the way Tess had shown me all those weeks ago. It won't hide me completely, but it will make me unseen to the Morts, and that means one less elemental race to deal with.

My breathing drowns out the sounds of the forest, until I realize I've been holding my breath all this time. I freeze a moment longer, taking this realization in. I'm not breathing. But someone else *is*.

I dart away, not sure where I'm running or what lies ahead. At this point, I'm sure every preternatural being can hear me, see me, notice me. Footsteps snap in the snow behind me. Several loud thumps startle me, and I can't help it—I look back.

A tall, dark-haired Cruor, fangs snapped out, is charging at me, and three more have just cracked down beside him. At least a dozen more are breaking out from the forest I've just escaped. I can't fight them all, I can't outrun them. I have no choice but to *travel*. Tess warned me not to, told me of the risks, but if I don't, I will certainly either die or lead them where I am heading. I have to choose between a hopeless choice and risky one.

Within moments, I break away. I'm in a tunnel of dark. When I snap out, I crash into something.

My lungs ache as I gasp for air and force my eyes open. A man with shoulder length knotted blond hair and broad shoulders stares at me with extended fangs. He wastes no time reaching out to grab my hair. When I try to pull back, he sweeps my legs, knocking me down and landing on top of me, pinning me down.

He's sitting on my chest and his hands are pressing my shoulders into the ground. If I could breathe, he would only be marginally stronger than me, but right now my body betrays me.

I freeze, unsure what to do until he lifts his hand to strike. I have only a few moments to act, and I need to use his uneven balance to my advantage. I grab the wrist of the hand that's still pinning me down and, with my other hand, I push his shoulder on the same arm. At the same time, I pull up my opposite knee and turn my hips.

He flips to the side, and I roll on top of him, landing between his legs. He's struggling beneath me, and I'm not sure how long I can keep him here. My hands slip to catch my balance on the ground, and before I can react, he pummels hard against my chest and sends me flying back. I crash into the snow. The aches pounding through my body drain me. I try to lift myself, but my arms offer little support after the blows I took to my chest.

The Cruor stalks toward me. I don't have the strength to travel, especially not so soon after my last. I can't run from this. I have to fight. And I have to win.

It takes everything in me to pick myself off the ground. This only incites the Cruor to laughter, but I waste no time—I lunge forward and tackle him to the ground, following immediately with a blow to his head. Then another, and another. His nose dribbles blood, but heals just as quickly. With no stake, no sword, and no fire, I am not equipped to kill a Cruor. Any damage I inflict won't last long.

He pushes me away again, but this time with less force. I roll away and slip back to my feet. We crouch opposite of one another, walking a slow, circular dance, as though a large animal paces between us. I should travel again, but I can't find a window of opportunity. Faster than I can blink, he's grabbing me by the throat and slamming me to the ground.

I clasp his wrist and pull it to my chest, hook my leg around the back of his neck, and then lock my feet together at my ankles. He's stuck now, choking against his own arm, but it doesn't stop him.

He just stands up, lifting his arm, and slams me back to the ground. Pain thuds through me, pulsing, spreading. I try to breathe, but air won't come in. My whole body is radiating with pain, but I have to force my way through it. Finally, I suck in a huge gasp of air and force my way through the pain to twist out from beneath him. When I'm free, I kick him in the ankles, then pounce on him, sending us back into a rolling battle across the snow.

He lands hits to the side of my face and multiple blows to my upper body. My sides are on fire with pain, and my face numbs from the swelling in my cheek. My hands ache. My lungs feel even tighter than before.

I manage to roll him beneath me once more, then jump to my feet and run as far and fast as I can. New forest juts against the night sky in the distance and, just beyond that, the mountains roll along the horizon. He's right behind me when we hit the forest wall. If I can create a little more distance from him, I can travel without worry of him stopping me. For now, I run alongside the woods, looking for something I can use as a weapon.

How many times has William told me? Whatever you do, fight. Yet I'm running. What else am I supposed to do when a fight can't be won?

There must be a loose piece of wood that could be used as a stake somewhere, but with him so close behind me, I'm not sure if I would be able to grab a weapon fast enough even if I found one. Instead, I start willing as many Morts out from between the trees as I can, sending them all back for the Cruor.

I stop to watch for the payoff, but they pass right through him, like the ghosts that they are. But then, in the blink of an eye, he drops, his own decapitated head at his side. I'm too stunned to react.

"Morts can't possess an immortal," a voice says calmly behind me.

Not my attacker, though. The voice is female.

I look back—a woman with silky black hair tied in a long pony tail stands behind me, the tip of a bloodied sword poking into the pink-splattered snow beneath her. I step away, creating distance between us as I try to take it all in.

A few feet back in the other direction lays the beheaded body of the Cruor, the Morts having cleared way to return to the forest. The warm wind of early spring blows away his existence, his body slowly flaking away until nothing is left.

"They call me Grace," the woman says, drawing my attention back to her. She extends her hand.

I take in her gleaming violet eyes, porcelain skin with the same golden shimmer as my own, and easy smile. She's petite—frail—with round eyes, a small nose, and thin lips. She is nearly dwarfed by the sword she carries, yet she took down the Cruor chasing me and hadn't even broken a sweat.

"This is where you introduce yourself," she instructs, the same cheery smile still brightening her face. I don't shake her hand, and she drops it back to her side. "A person in your shoes might even say thank you, you know, for me saving them."

"Thank...you," I manage, still stunned. "I'm Cordovae."

That wasn't my best idea. Why would I tell her that name, the name that means the most to who and what I am? I shouldn't trust her, can't trust her, even if I wanted to, even if she saved my life. For all I know, she only wants to keep my alive so I can lead her to William and Tess.

"Nice to meet you, Cordovae," Grace says. "You really shouldn't travel alone around here, you know. Where you off to?"

"Uh..."

"That's fine," she says too easily. "You don't need to tell me. But us Ankou, we ought to stick together."

That would explain her speed—quick enough to make the kill without being seen, only to pop up behind me when she was done. But...Tess said I shouldn't trust anyone. I should assume that means even people who come to my rescue. Part of me feels so strongly I can trust this woman, but my better sense reminds me that I've already defied Tess' advice by traveling, and that didn't work out so well.

Grace's gaze slides over me, and she purses her lips. "Did you come from Salem? I heard about Sarah Good and Tituba being accused of witchcraft today. Is that why you're on the run?"

I try to put faces to names. Sarah Good. I don't know her. I think I remember Tituba, if she was the Indian servant I'd seen around town a few times. Talk of these accusations has me even further on guard, though. Were they accused because I escaped? Would Grace try to bring me back to Salem if she knew?

"Not the talking type?" she asks. "That's all right. I'm used to doing the talking." Grace grabs my arm and pulling me into the woods, the sword in her other hand dragging a trail through the snow behind her. "Let's take a look at your wounds, shall we?"

As she leads me away from the open land, I can't stop looking back, at the dead Cruor wasting away, carelessly left behind.

I shouldn't go anywhere with this woman.

❧

GRACE BRINGS ME TO HER CAMP, REVITALIZING ME WITH MORE herbs, and applies some directly to my wounds to speed my healing. I should be thinking how kind she is—and that thought does pass through my mind—but more so I am considering how to get away from her.

Here is this kind woman who put her life on the line for me, and I can't seem to get away from her fast enough. As though she is who I needed to escape from, when in reality I would likely benefit from her help.

Still, I can't take any chances.

It's the same old battle. My mind tells me that my heart cannot be trusted. Tess has planted a seed of distrust in my mind to only further compact my doubt about my instincts.

Maybe there is a way for me learn if she's someone I can trust. As she brews a fresh batch of herbal tea, I ponder ways I might accomplish testing her, but no idea brings me peace. I've always struggled to trust people—that is, until I met William and Tess, who I've managed to trust beyond reason. And now I just can't bear the idea of finding out someone I want to trust cannot be trusted.

If I leave now, the possibility that Grace can be trusted will remain open, and that is exactly the kind of hope I need right now.

In the end, it's not about whether I can trust Grace. It's about whether I can trust myself—my instincts. And I can't. How can I trust the person who failed my daughter?

After I have recouped, we hike a while longer, deeper into the forest. She tells me about her efforts as an Ankou. She, too, she says, is fighting the good fight. Eliminating Morts and Cruor alike to make the world a safer place for everyone. I want to believe her.

The dirt gives way to spongy moss, and pine needles catch in the hem of my skirt, poking at my ankles. We stop a few times near the rushing waterfalls, where the water is so loud we can barely hear the world around us. I am on high alert, fearful of who might be watching us, following us. But I need to recoup, and the fresh spring water washes the bitter taste of anxiety from my tongue and gives me the energy to carry on.

Water splashes onto my dress, and my sleeves are soaked from plunging my hands in the stream, but despite the cold, it's surprisingly refreshing. Part of me wishes I never had to leave here, that I didn't have to worry about who might be following, that I could have Anna here with me, safe, and that together we could watch the frothing waterfalls and squish our toes in the moss. But that is not my life, and our trek must continue.

The land inclines, and I am taken aback by the amount of dandelion that grows here. It covers the mountainside like a blanket. Large slates of unyielding stone jut from the ground, and wild onions sprout from the soil. Wolves howl in the distance, and rabbits peek from bushes.

"Where is the dandelion coming from? I've never seen dandelion grow this early."

"Magic," Grace says, grinning. "This is what the Ankou do, remember?" She climbs up a small plateau then turns to pull me up with her. "Where are you going, anyway?"

I don't know how to answer.

"Do you have family this way? Are they expecting you?"

"Something like that..."

"You seem so purposeful, you know? Family can motivate us like that. Don't you think so?"

She's probably just being nice, trying to fill the otherwise empty air between us, but what if her exceeding interest in where I'm going and who I'm meeting stems from something other than concern?

"Family can motivate some people," I say, trying to disconnect myself from the question.

"So how much farther until we get there?" she asks.

"I don't know," I say, and I'm a little relieved that finally I was able to give her an honest answer.

The sky has hit its darkest moment and is already beginning to get lighter once more. If I am to lose her, it's now or never. I feign exhaustion and collapse against a tree. I sink to the floor and cradle my face in the nook of my arm.

"Grace, I really need to rest," I lie.

If anyone here can't be trusted, it'll be me.

I peek up at her, hoping to convey weariness with my eyes. "Do you think we could set up camp here and continue tomorrow night? Morning isn't far off, and we need time to secure shelter."

She nods. "You're right. We should see if there is a natural shelter nearby, otherwise we'll need this time to gather supplies to build something."

I wobble back to my feet, then catch myself on the tree again. "I just need a minute."

Grace rushes over and helps me settle back down. "No, Cordovae. You stay here and rest. I won't be far. Call out if you need anything, otherwise, I will return after I've found shelter."

I swallow around the lump in my throat and grasp her wrist. "Thank you," I whisper. "Sorry."

"It's nothing," she says, but she doesn't know why I'm apologizing.

When I am certain she is far enough off, I sneak off to continue my journey alone.

CHAPTER 21
MARCH 1692

Early spring morning is still dark, still cold, but it's also hopeful. It's warm enough to melt the dusting of snow, and only a few patches evidencing winter remain.

At first I creep through the mountain forest, building distance between myself and the woman who saved me from certain death. Animals howl and the wind whistles along the slopes. Small cliffs and crags force me into an indirect path, but soon the shale gives way to soil and early spring grass that fills the air with the hopeful aroma of life instead of destruction.

Certain I've made enough ground to go unheard by Grace, I pick up my pace, and soon I'm running. My knees and ankles ache as my feet thud against the hard, uneven terrain of the mountainside. Whenever I misstep, I use the trees to catch my balance.

I wipe the sweat from my neck and face. My skin and lips are chapped from the weeks of dry cold, and my throat feels raw from the thin air, but the night is warmer than weeks past. I stop by a stream to recoup. The water is soothing but chilling all at once. My body craves the heat of a fire. The sooner I reach Tess and William, the sooner I can rest.

The next field I cross is covered with dandelions—I wonder if these, too, have grown by way of magic, or if spring is finally calling. Tess and William's haven won't be far and should be secure, but still I need to be prepared in the event I have misjudged how much farther I need to travel. I won't have anyone to fight alongside me or rescue me should I be forced to face another Cruor, so I grab a large branch and sharp rock to carve a stake.

I'm done needing others to fight my battles. If I am to return to my past and save my daughter, I need to save myself.

From now on, I rely on no one.

I rip the sleeves from my dress and use one sleeve to tie my hair away from my face. I kneel onto one knee and use my second sleeve to strap the stake to my opposite calf. The only thing covering the birthmark on my wrist now is the fingerless glove Verity gave me. I hope she's okay back in Salem.

I pause a moment, looking out into the distance. Out into this huge world that goes on for as far as the eye can see. But I don't feel small today. I feel determined.

Don't worry, Anna. I'm coming.

I carve a second stake, this one much longer so that I can also use it as a hiking stick. Nothing will get in my way. I am stronger than ever.

As I pass another waterfall, shouts echo over the roar of the rushing water. I crouch behind a cluster of trees and train my attention on where the noise is coming from. I creep a few more yards to the west, then follow the voices north from there. Ahead of me, just beyond the trees, stretches a clearing, and it's here the noise originates.

Wedged between two trees and obscured by the underbrush, I peek out and scan the area. To the far northeast side of the clearing, bodies move in a blur and swords cut through air and flesh. It takes moments for my vision to adjust to their speed, but soon things slow to a near stop.

Cruor.

This wasn't part of the plan, and I don't have time to come up with a new one. Nothing is happening the way it should. This place is supposed to be safe. And it's not. Cruor should not be so close to our shelter and safety.

Tess hadn't prepared me for this.

A young man, at least a good foot and a half taller than myself, fights a losing battle with more than a few Cruor. Outnumbered, bleeding from the gut and stumbling, he swings his sword and falls to his knees as an elbow lands sharply to the back of his head. In the moonlight, his skin sheens golden—one of the Ankou. One of our own.

The young man looks up, dark, maple-syrup brown eyes locking on mine, his square, shaded jaw covered in rivulets of blood.

My heart stops.

William.

His name leaves my soul like a dying breath. Before I can think, my feet pound across the field and a sound not quite human comes from my mouth.

Gone is the doubt that plagued me the last time I saw him in battle. We need each other. There is no way to do this alone. We are each valuable, and no one can be left behind. Hadn't that been why William was on his way to save me?

Several of the Cruor turn their heads in my direction, but before they can react, my stake is already through one of their hearts. I yank it out, black blood splattering on my face and clothes as I spin toward the next monster.

This one falls as quickly as the first. I dart into the center of the commotion, knocking Cruor off of William long enough to pull him to his feet. I spin back to my opponents, three of them with their attention on me now that my sudden appearance has resonated with their group. There must be at least a dozen of them still standing.

I lean my back into William's and brace myself with his body to jump and kick two of the Cruor in one fell swoop. They stumble back, and I drop to my feet to shoot for the legs of one of the other Cruor. But as I do, another one lands a kick to my hip.

I go with the force, swiveling to the side, but all I feel is pressure. My body is numb. I *will* kill this monster I've taken down. I plunge the stake into his chest, then duck as another one tries to grab me. I roll back and onto my feet and plant myself firmly on the ground.

Another of my opponents comes up behind me and hooks his arm around my neck. I thrust my hands up between my throat and his forearm before he can tighten the grip. With a good hold on him, I bend forward and push toward the ground. He flies over my shoulder, but before I can finish him off, there's another Cruor rushing up beside me.

In one quick motion, my stake is in and out of his heart and plunging for the Cruor who is already picking himself up off the ground. A head rolls on the floor by my feet, and I glance up to see William has decapitated five of the men on his own.

Something stabs into my side, and my hand instinctively grabs the wound. When I pull my hand away, it's covered in blood. The cut burns as though on fire, and the fire spreads outward, into my hip and between my ribs, around to my back and stomach. Nausea rips through me. The bloody blade swings toward me again, but I stumble back before it hits, falling to the ground and catching myself with my hands.

A tall Cruor, eyes black, hovers over me, pointing the sword at my chest. I grab the sword, the blade cutting into my palms and burning them with iron poison, then I roll away, forcing myself to my feet despite the pain threatening to shut down my body.

I lunge for the man anyway, taking another slash to my side as my stake rips through his heart. When I turn to find my next opponent, the remaining two Cruor are already across the field and disappearing into the trees.

Cowards.

The sun perks up in the sky, and I know time is running short. We need to get out of here. Our translucent veined wings capture the sunlight like a spider web catches drops of rain. Hideous and almost-beautiful all at once.

Once they are out of sight, William keels over on the ground. I reach into my pouch and grab a fistful of rosary peas. They won't do William any good, and I can't help him in the state I'm in. I shove the poisonous peas into my mouth and close my eyes, willing them to work. It takes a moment, but they give me the strength I need.

I heave William up. Taking his arm across my shoulder, I feel more than just the weight of his body. I feel the sun's rays like a pressure on my bones. Something bubbles against the back of my neck.

Oh God. It's his skin, scorching in the daylight. I nearly forgot he's part Cruor. That's how he'd been able to influence me when we'd first met. He hasn't done it since, and I'd almost forget he was able.

My heart rate ratchets into a panic. "Which way to camp, William? We have to hurry!"

Wearily, he nods his head to the west, blood dripping from his mouth and nose and scalp, and we use what is left of our strength to make our way to a small shelter, where we collapse in each other's arms.

❧

THIS ISN'T OUR FINAL DESTINATION, I KNOW, BECAUSE TESS isn't here, nor is there any sign she ever has been. We can't stay here long. The Cruor will surely return. We need to recoup and make ground before they return or we'll never have the clearance to make our way back to Tess.

The shelter is stocked with nightshade, Daphne berries, and oleander.

He really was coming for me. Why else would he have all these herbs, these herbs he can't use for himself? With my adrenaline wearing off, it takes every last ounce of my strength to feed myself, to chew, to swallow, but once I do, I slowly start to recover. It makes eating easier, and now I am able to feed William as well. I shuffle around the cabin looking for something that will help him, but I don't see anything.

"There," he rasps, nodding to a basket in the corner.

There's a half-dead raccoon and a knife. No food.

"There's nothing here."

I think he shakes his head, but the movement is too weak to say for sure.

"Animal blood," he whispers.

I frown. He's too injured to heal on his own, and we don't have much time. I pick up the animal, trying not to think about what he's going to do, and place it in his hands. His fangs snap down, but they're broken. He waves toward the knife, and I hand it to him. He struggles to cut the animal. I can't look at it anymore. Both the raccoon and the man are struggling more than necessary.

I kneel at William's side, swallow hard, and take the animal and knife from him. I slice the animal across the neck and hold the wound to William's mouth as it streams blood onto his lips and tongue. His mouth barely moves to eat.

"Eat!" I order him. "Come on!"

He breaks away.

"Sorry," he mumbles. "You shouldn't...see—"

"Don't dare worry about me," I say, and I push the animal back to his mouth.

Watching the effort it takes him breaks my heart, and watching the life leave the animal's eyes kills me inside. I want to save them both, but I can't.

You're going to have to choose.

I know this is only a test. It's not the raccoon and William that is the choice I have to make. It's this life and the one before. It's him, and it's Anna. He doesn't have a chance—*we* don't have a chance.

But I can't think about that right now. I fight back tears as I wait for him to finish. When he is able to feed himself, I wash my wounds in a basin and make a healing ointment from the Daphne berries and Oleander. I apply the paste and rub it into a deep gash on my side, wincing, but within moments, my wounds, like his, are already mending themselves closed, the edges turning to bright pink scars.

"Not exactly keeping a low profile, were you?" I ask lightly, trying to smile.

"You're all right," he whispers. "You're here."

"Of course I am," I say, trying to keep my voice steady. "I can take care of myself."

William grins, or winces. Maybe both. "But how—"

"Shhh..." I press my finger to his lips. "You need to rest."

His skin is pearl white now that we're out of the moonlight, and his earthy brown hair sticks to his forehead. He is even more stunning than I remember. My finger lingers on his lips a moment too long, his gaze burning into mine, and my cheeks flash hot. I drop my hand away and rub my temples.

I need to forget about this man, but how can I when every inch of my body reminds me of that need to forget? My palms sweat. My heart races. My mouth is dry. All I can think is that I want my hands on him, my heart by his, to drink him in. Looking at him is like a drug in my system. I want more, and at the same time, I want the desire to go away, forever, to never return, to never distract me ever again.

William props himself up on one arm and turns toward me. The wound on his opposite shoulder is still bleeding, so I turn away to grab the rag to clean it. Is the animal blood not enough? When I turn back, he seems suddenly closer, his face inches from my own. Slowly, I reach for his wound, but when I do, his arm reaches up around me, his fingers slip into the hair at the nape of my neck, and his lips move for mine.

My breath disappears from my lungs. His lips press into mine, and my heart rattles in my chest. I'm frozen and at the same time wanting to throw myself into this moment. I'm still weak from the iron poisoning, and I rationalize to myself that that is the reason I am slowly falling forward, falling into him.

Falling for him.

I close my eyes and give in to the kiss. He tastes like bergamot, and I breathe him in like a cool ocean breeze. His strong hands caress my arms, his touch as cool and smooth and comforting as bed-sheets in an air-conditioned room mid-summer. A fragment tries to push through, to remind me how I know of air-conditioners, but his kiss melts those thoughts away, and I'm only here with him, here in this moment.

God, I care about this man. I care about him, but I shouldn't. I don't have time to care about anything right now, only Anna, and I don't have time to be with him. When this war is over, I still won't care about him enough for it to matter. It will never be enough to forget Anna.

I try to push my feelings aside, to tell myself my body is betraying me, my mind hungry for connection. This feeling can't be real or important.

But still, it's there, even after I chastise myself for feeling this way.

His tongue slides across my lips, tickles against my own, and this moment feels so safe. He's the only man I trust. But as his hand creeps up my side and caresses the underside of my breast, my emotions swirl with confusion. Fragments from my life as Rose —fragments of my only other experiences of "intimacy" try to push through, and my heart and my body know this is different, but suddenly I am not sure if this is what I want or if I am just trying to prove something to myself.

I put my hand over his and slide it back down to my hip, pulling away slowly, smiling apologetically.

"William…there's something I need you to know."

He raises his brow. "Anything, Cord."

"Anna…" I shake my head. "Anna is my father's baby."

"Your sister?" he asks, his brow furrowing.

What would he think if he knew the truth? Would he be disgusted? Would he think less of me? I can only stare at him, and soon, his eyes widen with realization.

"You didn't want that," he says.

"But I want her."

He pulls me to his chest. "I know you do," he says, pressing his mouth against my scalp. "I can't think of any woman stronger of heart and mind than you, no one any more likely to make the return. You'll get back to her. You will."

I shake my head. "I'm...sorry."

"No, Cordovae," he whispers, sweeping a loose strand of hair behind my ear. "You have nothing to be sorry about."

Those words cement my feelings for William. I can trust him. I can love him. He's safe for me, in every way but one: that eventually, I have to leave him behind.

He lays back and gently pulls me against his side, and just being near him sends a new energy zinging through me. I'm more alert than I've been in days. I'm even...happy...and I can't deal with the guilt of being happy right now, not without Anna here.

I rest my head between his shoulder and chest and close my eyes, and we are floating in everything unspoken.

WE LIE THERE UNTIL OUR HEALTH RETURNS. THE KISS HANGS IN
the air between us; I'd stopped things before we got carried away.
I'm not ready for this. I don't think I ever will be. As eager as I am
to be connected to William, I need to escape the intimacy.

And yet, at the same time, as much as I hate to admit it, I need
him. I need to know for myself that love with a man can be pure.
William is the only man who can heal this broken part of me. The
only one who could erase the things I want to forget and help me
get back to the things I want to remember. In a way, being with
him is reclaiming myself.

But I'm still not ready, and he belongs to the wrong world. Or
maybe it's me that does.

"We're lucky there weren't more of them, aren't we?" I ask.

William turns his face toward mine. "Cruor?"

I nod.

"It's the dandelion," he says. "That's why we chose this
location. It repels them; it is like poison to them the way iron is to
us. Some always get by though with magic of some kind or
another."

I remember the field I passed before I found him and wonder

why Tess and William hadn't set up their safe-haven there. "So Tess isn't far from here, then?"

"It's close," he says, and it seems as though our bond has shattered. All that exists in the few inches between us is miles of cold.

William slowly disentangles himself, reaffirming what I sense, and changes into fresh clothes with his back to me. There is a new tension in the air, and awkwardness between us, an iciness that radiates from him, and I need him to look at me so I can tell myself I am imagining it all, that I'm irrationally swept up in emotions that I will blame entirely on weakness caused by injury and stress.

But he won't make eye contact with me. He hands me a fresh change of clothes.

"I brought these for you," he says, then he turns his attention to packing a small pouch with food and filling a canteen with what's left of our fresh water.

"So you really were coming after me?" I ask.

"We need you to fight this war with us." His tone is distant.

"Is that all?" I ask quietly.

William turns to me slowly, and everything I feared I would see in his eyes is there: regret most of all. "That is all you are meant for here."

He's right. And I knew this, planned this.

I look at the dress he's handed me. It's one of Tess', made of velvet, with long bell sleeves. I'll have to keep my fingerless gloves to hide the birthmark on my wrist.

It strikes me that I don't need to hide my birthmark here as I had needed to in Salem, but I've revealed enough of myself. I've made myself more vulnerable than I ever should have allowed. I am better off not sharing anything about myself anymore.

I take off my dress and go to crumple it up, but feel something round and hard. I check the pockets. Deep in one of them is the necklace William gave me with the large, round, wooden chip and engraved tree. I bite my lip, staring down at it. I know he cares, in his own way. I slip the necklace around my neck and quickly get changed.

"Tess was supposed to stop you," I say slowly. "Wasn't she?"

"She may have tried," he says, shuffling quickly through the cabin to throw some last minute items in his pouch. "I haven't seen her. The borders are locked up. I couldn't get through. I was on my way back to get her, to bring her to help."

I scoff. "She wouldn't have."

He shakes his head. "You don't know that."

"Right," I say. "Well, I don't really know much of anything."

His focus slides down, centers on the necklace he gave me. Then he lifts his gaze back to my eyes, and his expression grows serious. Steady. "I wouldn't have taken no for an answer."

"You know better, William. Neither you nor Tess can risk yourselves."

William busies himself preparing his own traveling pack. "All we ever do is risk ourselves, Cord. I wasn't going to fail you, the way I've failed others."

"You said our lives are too important to make sacrifices. That we have to stay focused on what we are meant to do."

"I can't be a coward in my efforts to be a hero," he says. "Perhaps I am meant to sacrifice myself this time. You've shown me what it truly means to fight for what we believe in. And I believe in...I . . ."

Say it. Say you believe in us.

I narrow my eyes, lips pressed together, wondering if he can be as brave with his feelings for me as he is with risking his life.

William shakes his head. "Nothing I have done has hurt our goals. We need you to help us fight this war."

"That's not what you were going to say!"

"Damn it, Cord! What do you want from me?"

"The truth."

"You didn't like the truth so much the last time you asked for it."

I tilt my chin up, though really I feel like storming out of this place.

"I know you're after some fairytale," he says. "You think I can love you the way you need me to? Well, I can't. I can *never* love *anyone* the way they deserve. Not so long as I am a slave to my nature."

"But you aren't a slave to your nature. That was *decades* ago, and I'm not your father."

"Jesus Christ, Cordovae, you aren't my shrink, either."

Shrink. I press my lips together. He's travelled to other times before, outside of this one. Could he travel with me to mine?

"You keep making this about me," I say. "But it's not. You're afraid."

"You should be, too," he mumbles. "Now drop it."

Why won't he just admit he cares about me? He must, to have taken these risks and to have made these mistakes. I can't be imagining it. We may have no future together, but I want to see it hurt him as much as it hurts me. I can never truly embrace how I feel about him until I've seen him just as torn, and at the same time, that is what tears me up inside as it is.

Why do I care? Is it possible my emotions for him could compromise me returning to Anna? I can't forget what is really important here. The lives that could be lost if he chooses me over his duty, or the repercussions if I let my feelings for him get in the way of my own goals.

There's nothing good to be gained. And yet, being with him...it's healing. It heals me in all the ways the earth cannot. William and I are not meant to be, but my feelings for him keep spiraling like a rogue leaf caught on the wind. I can't control what's happening, and I'm terrified of what happens when I hit the ground.

Do I love him? Is this why they call it falling in love?

And, most importantly, what happens to the fallen?

I don't want to know. I need to escape before I find out.

"Clearly I don't know enough to be any help here," I say, spreading my hands.

William frowns. "You knew enough to save yourself."

"Only with help."

"Help?" His eyebrows dig deeper over his eyes, and he steps closer. "What do you mean? Who helped you, Cord?"

I scowl, holding my ground. "Some woman I met. If it weren't for her—"

"What if she followed you, Cord? Did you think about that? That maybe she helped you live so she could follow you here?"

"Yes," I hiss. "I *did* think of that. She didn't follow me, all right? And this location of yours obviously wasn't as secure as you thought. I won't let you blame that on me."

William exhales slowly, his expression softening, tension leaving his shoulders and his posture relaxing. "I apologize. Try to understand that it's not only myself I'm worried about here."

I want to ask him who else he worries about. Me? Would he admit it if he did? Would it even matter?

I grab up a pouch of supplies and pull aside the flap of our tent, staring out into the eerily still mountainside forest. "It'll be getting light again soon," I say. "We better go."

WE TRAVEL IN SILENCE. TRUDGE THROUGH DARKNESS. I thought the dandelion field I crossed earlier would have been the best location...until we reach our destination. The ground outside the small, tucked-away cabin is completely blanketed in sweet yellow blooms. It's as though winter hasn't touched this place at all. The air is pungent and the floral aroma stings my nose. It almost feels wrong to walk on the land here, each step crushing dozens of innocent flowers.

When we arrive at the cabin, I see Tess through the window, her long, brunette braid tumbling down her back. She's standing by the fire with a man, her petite fingers wrapped around his dark hand and her head leaning against his shoulder. *Adrian.* When we open the door, letting in a gust of cold air, her gothic dress flutters over her boots. Tess snaps her hand from Adrian and hurries to the kitchen, where she busies herself with a bowl of fresh herbs.

William places his hand at the small of my back and sweeps his arm toward Tess' fellow. "You remember Adrian. Adrian, Cord."

The man turns toward me. His large hands clasp behind his back, and he lifts his chin. "Pleasure to see you again, Cordovae."

I smile, trying to disguise my discomfort. I would prefer some time alone with Tess and William. "Are you and Tess—"

"Friends?" he asks, the thin braids of his cocoa brown hair quivering in some undeterminable emotion. "For a long time now, we have been allies through this tragic division of our species."

Friends. Right. I can't shake the bad feeling I get about this guy. Seeing a Cruor right now is the last thing I want, ally or not. I feel oddly protective over Tess as well.

I step further into the cabin and set down my pouch. "So you'll be here—"

"Fighting along your side 'til the end," he says. His lips curl into what I imagine is meant to be a smile. "Though my presence is entirely welcomed here by at least some, I assure you."

I glance back to William, and he nods.

"Well, if you don't mind—"

"You wish to speak with Tess and William in private?"

I press my lips together, attempting to hold my tongue. It doesn't do much good. "Yes. Although, you could let me finish—"

"And yet it saves much valuable time to cut to the chase." He takes a small bow, his chocolately eyes never leaving my own as he takes leave from the cabin.

I spin toward William, and he looks at me, warmth coming from behind his thick lashes. "I'm not entirely fond of him, either," he says, "but we need him."

"Isn't he affected by the dandelion here?" I ask.

William frowns. "It is not entirely impossible for a Cruor with the right connections to have some tolerance for it. We have given him some help, though I imagine he's still not comfortable."

That makes two of us.

Tess bustles into the room, and I drop the conversation. Whoever that man is, he is clearly the 'someone' William once told me Tess keeps company with. As it is, we have more pressing matters to discuss.

Now that we are all together, I notice none of us are wearing our chime necklaces. Me, because I'd left mine behind before heading back into the town. I imagine they have theirs put away because, for now, we *don't* want to attract any Morts.

Tess hands us each a steaming cup of steeped herbs. "I returned here when I couldn't find William."

He wasn't far.

"No matter," I say. "I found him. But I don't think we are really safe to stay here much longer."

Tess' pear-green eyes settle on mine, and I see something there I've never seen before; I'm not sure if she's happy to see me or if seeing me has just renewed her hope. "Glad to see you safe."

I feel the shift in dynamic between us, or perhaps there's only been a change in myself. "I'm still not sure how I survived long enough to make it this far," I say. "The Cruor had several opportunities to kill me before my escape."

William sets aside his cup and sits on a nearby crate. "They probably wanted to do worse than kill you."

"Just me then?" I ask. "There was another woman—a Strigoi—who got away, too. They killed her unborn child by making her shift, but left *her* alive."

"You'll only drive yourself mad trying to understand them," Tess says. "They don't like the way Strigoi taste, and they don't often kill unless they must—either to feed or to protect themselves. They get more enjoyment out of making people suffer. But you got away, that's what matters."

"Is it?" I sigh heavily. "Two other women have been accused."

"Sarah Good and Tituba?" Tess asks. "They're arrested now. And Sarah Osborne, too."

"You know them?" I ask, incredulous.

Tess shakes her head. "We received word. Did you know them?"

"No...but..."

"But what?" Tess asks. "Now they are too busy with them to worry about you."

I open my mouth to defend how unjust that is, but something tells me Tess already knows. There aren't many who care about justice as much as she.

William runs the blade of his knife against a stone, sharpening it. "You never told me how you got caught in the first place. Didn't heed our warnings would be my guess."

I narrow my eyes. "I did what I had to do. I though you of all people would understand."

He shrugs. I drink the rest of the herbal mixture. It's gone cold.

Tess takes the cup from my hand and sets it next to Williams, then takes my fingers in hers and leads me over to the fire. "What happened between *you* two?"

I stare over at him, trying to ignore the anger and attraction and heartache.

"Nothing," I mumble.

Tess squats beside me, one hand on my knee and the other resting on my shoulder. "Don't mind him anyway. We all have our days."

I make an effort to relax my neck and shoulders. "Right. Well, I suppose we just don't always see eye to eye."

"No one does," she says. She's so close I can smell the lemon and lavender on the soft golden glow of her skin. "I have not been so easy on you, either, but I hope you can understand why. This really isn't the time to train new Ankou."

"I can handle myself, if only you two would tell me what to expect." My tone is harsher than I intend.

Tess pulls back. "I think we did a fair job preparing you. It's a lot to take in."

"You did not tell me the monster I would become."

"Monster?"

I scowl at her, then point to my mouth. "When I tried to save my friend, I ended up biting her. Like the Cruor, but worse. It worked, but my teeth got me caught."

"Your teeth?" Tess asks, her eyebrows rising. "Did they all turn to sharp points?"

"What else?" I ask.

Her whole face lights up. "How rare! I never would have thought to prepare you for that. But it doesn't make you a monster.

This is…it's…*wonderful!*" She squeezes my leg and turns toward William. "Did you know she's a Ferrum?"

I close my eyes briefly. William makes some snorting sound. "Of course," he says sarcastically. "She would be, wouldn't she?"

He sounds bitter about it.

"I thought you would appreciate that," Tess said. "Wasn't your—"

"*Tess*," he says sharply, and she stops.

"I just thought it might come in handy is all."

William scowls. "If she knew how to control it, maybe."

Tess settles beside me. "He's just grumpy because…well, you know how he can get."

"What's a Ferra?" I ask.

"*Ferrum*. Really not so different from the Ankou," she says. "They're just more evolved. They can save a human that has already been possessed without the risks."

"I've done it without my teeth, too."

Tess shakes her head. "To a *willing* Mort?"

I nod.

Tess nods, too. "That's different. We can all do that."

"I've also used compulsion magic to get them to possess on my order."

"Very good! Did you learn that while imprisoned? Just keep in mind that helps only with possession. You can't use compulsion magic to undo the possession—that's where Ankou nature comes from."

"Oh?" I'm trying to absorb these new details that will dictate not only my life, but the lives of many.

"The Ferrum have a unique purpose, too," Tess continues. "You can get the Mort *out* of a human, against the Mort's will. Your bite will poison's the host body with a substance that only affects Morts. They won't stay in the host body after that. You can end the possession without risk of killing the body!"

"Can we use that for anything other than getting ourselves caught?" I ask.

Tess' grin brightens even more. She's...excitable. "So, did you learn anything else while locked away?"

"I think there was a spirit elemental there, but they took her away."

"There are no spirit elementals yet," Tess assures me, but after I explain the events, she purses her lips together and stares at the fire for a long time. "She would have to die first, before her time, to become one."

"How so?" I ask.

"It hasn't been proven, but there is a rumor that some Chibold claim the Universe said Forever Girls will be those reborn by our magic."

"Then it might not be long," I say solemnly. "I couldn't save her. The cell was encased in iron; I couldn't travel or use most of my abilities for that matter. Once I escaped, I saw a woman weeping over her body during our escape, and I moved her."

"You *what?*" Tess' smile turns to glowering. "Now is not the time to be traveling, Cord!"

"I had to!" I ball my fists at my side. "It's done now, and it was the right thing to do."

"I hope you're right." She shakes her head. "You still haven't told us how you escaped."

"The compulsion magic. I was able to control one of the Morts long enough to escape."

"Thank goodness," she says.

"This is bigger than I thought." When Tess doesn't respond, I add, "The Cruor are killing humans that are awaiting trial at the settlement."

Tess' shoulders sag, and she walks to the cabin window, looking out toward where Adrian sits in the lingering darkness, his back against one of the trees that obscure our location. She's distressed —the way she tugs her earlobe gives her away.

"We're aware," she says. "You aren't the only one who has been controlling the Morts. There are others...with the Maltorim."

"Others?"

Tess still doesn't look at me. "They are controlling the evilest of the Morts, using them to possess some of the humans in order to lure others. But that's not all."

"Hmmm?"

I think she must not hear me, because moments pass without a response.

"What's not all, Tess?"

"Cord—" Her voice cracks. Slowly her gaze sweeps toward me, haunted. For the first time, I think I'm seeing Tess afraid.

"Please, just tell me."

She takes a long shuddering sigh. "The Maltorim are using a form of...necromancy. They're not just making the Morts possess the living, Cord. They're also making them possess the dead."

CHAPTER 24
MARCH 1692

I ROCK BACK ON MY FEET. THE MALTORIM ARE USING necromancy to compel the Morts to possess the dead? "How, Tess? Is that even possible? The Maltorim can't do that! I thought they were mostly Cruor? Is it anything like what I did in the cell? The compulsion magic, maybe?"

She twists her lips. "No, it can't be that. Possessing the dead is very different from a spirit sharing a body with a living host. If they are performing this kind of magic, they must have help from an Ankou. That's the only explanation. Cruor simply were never designed to perform such magic."

"Why would the Ankou help the Maltorim do that? It goes completely against our calling!"

Tess scoffs. "Can't you see, Cord? What is it humans say when they make mistakes? *'I'm only human.'*" She says this mockingly. "Well, if that's true, we're all only human."

I cross the room and grab Tess by her shoulders. "We're *not* human."

Her big green eyes look up at me, and the weight of her words settle into my chest. "There is no perfect race, Cord. The Morts— there are good and bad. The Strigoi—there are good and bad. The

Cruor—there are good and bad. Do you think all Ankou are good? Do you think we're *all* good guys?"

I drop my hands to my side. "I guess—"

"Please, Cord. Don't guess." Tess grabs my shoulders this time. "Just give us something useful. Anything useful. Think hard—what happened when you were in that cell? What can we use to fix this?"

The desperation in her plea tugs at my heart. I reflect on my time in captivity, trying to figure out how it might all tie together. All I can see is Thornhart reading from that evil book. Why would Thornhart be involved in this? Some of the men had clearly been taken over by the Morts, but not all of them.

"What can you tell me about the Malleus Maleficarum?" I ask.

"Written by the Maltorim over two centuries ago, delivered through a possessed man—Heinrich Kramer—and a comrade of his. Why? Where did you see it?"

"Thornhart had a copy. He read from it to us."

"If that's true," Tess says, "then they have been planning these events for long time. Much longer than we could have imagined."

"Then some of these people are possessed, and others are being led by the possessed, and more yet have simply been influenced by the times—by a *book*?"

Tess frowns. "It's all being blamed on witchcraft, and the possessions have helped make witchcraft a believable plague. It explains the unexplainable, gives them a solution to their fears. The Malleus Maleficarum is clearly just one piece in their puzzle, one more thing that can reinforce the ideas being pushed on your settlement."

My settlement. Not really. Abigail's settlement, sure. Aren't I, in a way, possessing Abigail? Whose life has Tess taken over? William is the only one of us here who was born Ankou. Are we no better than the spirits we hunt?

Tess continues on, unaware of my inner conflicts. "This whole charade is meant to give the Cruor an easy blood-life source. It weeds out the lives people are willing to sacrifice—then the Cruor can feed. Unfortunately, even those who are not possessed have become caught up in the witch hunts. The settlement will destroy themselves, and then the Cruor will move on to find new life to feed from."

"Well...are we doing anything about that?"

Tess turns back to me. She stares at me a long time, as though studying me. "Do you want to?"

IT'S NOT JUST GETTING BACK TO ANNA THAT MOTIVATES ME, AND I am not sure if I should feel guilty to admit that. There was a time where she was all that mattered. Somehow, I've come to see this world as worth saving. People have the right to their own bodies. Tess says those involved need to be brought to justice, but I know her idea of justice isn't quite the same as mine. William, though, is the only of us who is driven by pure nobility. All he wants to do is help these people because these people need help.

It would be nice if my motivations were as simple as that.

When Adrian joins us inside, he at least proves more useful than I expected.

"The Maltorim have built an army of possessed," he explains. "They have found the only known living spirit elemental and are forcing her to use her abilities to control the Morts."

Tess shoves him hard in the shoulder. "Damn it, Adrian! You should have told us sooner."

"I didn't have a chance," he says sharply. "I only found out on my last trip back to the Maltorim, and I only got as far as to tell you that they were possessing the dead using necromancy when Cord arrived."

I lean back. My alarm bells are going off. "Adrian is with the Maltorim?"

William waves me off. "Not really. It's for appearances. He's our 'in'. He grew up there. We can't choose what families we are born into, can we?"

"I guess..."

William nudges Tess in the shoulder. "Don't be so hard on him. It's better he tell us together anyway, all at once."

I roll my eyes. Because God forbid Adrian repeats himself. I huff, shaking my head. "Tess said there are no spirit elementals. And spirit elementals are not the only ones who can control the Morts. Anyone who knows compulsion magic can do the same."

Tess clears her throat. "There is no proof of any spirit elementals in existence," she says. "I'm afraid Adrian and I are not in agreement on this."

Adrian turns to her. "The girl is a spirit elemental, I assure you. There is no other way they could possess the *dead*. Compulsion magic alone wouldn't be enough for that. They have Ankou working for the Maltorim and need her blood to perform the necromancy."

"There's no evidence," Tess shoots back. "I just find it odd that a spirit elemental would turn up now. That would make two, if Cord is right about the girl she met in the cell. How could it be they have been here without us knowing?"

"Yet you don't find it odd that these events have not taken place before now?"

I put my hands up. "Enough. So this woman may or may not be a spirit elemental, but she is controlling the Morts. That is what is important, correct?"

William bends up a knee and rests his elbow there. "More so that they are using her blood to do it against her will."

"What does this mean for us?" I ask, trying to get William and Adrian refocused. From the corner of my eye, I see William smile, and I feel a smile within myself, too, hidden in my heart where no one can see it. For once in my life, I feel...in control.

"I'm not sure what the end goal is," Adrian says, "but they are using Morts in human bodies to carry out their wishes during the day—to hunt the Ankou."

"The Maltorim has the *Morts* hunting *us*? Why?"

"Because," he explains, "the blood of the Ankou allows the Cruor to walk in the sun."

The hunters, it seems, have become the hunted.

⚜

As it turns out, some Ankou are cowards that will sell out their own kind to protect themselves.

The windows are quickly covered before daylight arrives, though every now and then the sheets will catch a draft and flutter, and a few rays of light will squeeze by, revealing our veined wings, a reminder of how inhuman we really are.

We're insects. Very *large* insects.

Adrian, however, manages to always stay to the shadows, even when indoors, perhaps because the sunlight would be far more damaging to him.

I sit on the splintered wood floor, wrapped in a scratchy blanket but thankful for the warmth against the draft. A stew Tess has prepared gurgles in a pot over the fire, and she serves us bowls of rough meat and bitter wild onions. We cannot build our fire larger than required to cook our meals, for fear of drawing attention to ourselves.

I hadn't realized how famished I was until I smelled the food, and although the meat does not taste fresh nor the onions sweet, I greedily consume every drop in my bowl.

The day passes uneasily, my stomach twisted in knots of fear over whether we will be discovered and how much longer we are safe here. But we cannot travel into daylight; we are prisoners of our own nature. By midday, it's evident spring is coming a little early this year. The cold is gone. I would almost say the day is warm.

How long have I been trapped in this life? If spring has just begun, then no more than a season. The fire adds a smoky haze and yellow glow to the room that seems more alive than my daytime vision.

Not nearly soon enough, night arrives. As our location is compromised due to the Maltorim soldiers we battled earlier—

and, Tess says, because of my traveling—we set out immediately at sundown. Adrian leads the way.

"We need to find a find a good location to travel through," he says, his gaze steady on Tess. His expression is somber, perhaps even sad. "Do you know of a good place?"

Tess tips her chin. "Not far ahead, still surrounded by the dandelion. I haven't seen any Morts or Cruor in the area."

"We'll need transport to Damascus. Once we arrive, we'll need to break in to rescue the girl," he says. "It's important we stay together."

Tess picks up the pace, leading the way. "Do you know any Chibold in that area, or must we bring her back here?"

The question is clearly directed at Adrian, but William cuts in. "We'll bring her to the Chibold here," he says. "We know them best."

"So be it." Tess cuts her attention to him. "They'll be able to tell us if she's a spirit elemental and protect her if needed."

"Protect her?" I ask. "Shouldn't we want her to help us?"

Some trees block our path. Tess squeezes through, and Adrian puts his hand on my shoulder to push me onward as well. "Perhaps, if she's capable of helping," he says. "But if she's not, she will only get in the way, risk her recapture, and put us back where we started."

"Where we are *now*," William says. He cuts between Adrian and I, placing his hand at the small of my back but devoting his attention to Adrian. "We're getting ahead of ourselves. We haven't even attempted the rescue yet, and we need to discuss the risks. Is this really our best course of action?"

Adrian stops walking, as does William. Adrian raises an eyebrow. I try to continue walking, to catch up with Tess, but William's hand slips to mine, and he holds me steady at his side. His touch is cold, his presence colder, but my whole body is heating up. Tess' footsteps come to silence, then shuffle closer.

"Everything all right?" she asks.

Adrian's expression softens, and he turns to Tess. "William was just expressing some... concerns."

"We're not simply going to waltz in the Maltorim asylum," William says. "There are risks."

All at once, the situation comes rushing at me, and I'm woozy. I lean my head against William's shoulder. I can feel him turning his neck, to look at me, and I imagine the annoyed expression that must be on his face right now, but I can't pull away. I just need a moment.

When I look up, however, his expression is not one of annoyance. He seems...worried, but restrained. What is he trying to protect? His heart...or mine?

William frowns and turns to Adrian, staring him down, his pale skin almost ominous against his oak-brown hair. dark eyes, and shaded jaw. Tess glares at William, as though doing so can somehow get William to back off.

The tension is unsettling. Adrian has the connections necessary to pull this off, and Tess trusts him. Which to me says a lot. The Maltorim are stronger and more powerful than us four, and none of us know the extent of what we are up against. Attempting to save this girl will expose us and further put us at risk. We can't be weakened by lack of unity.

We need to pull together.

William faces me again. "What do you think, Cord?"

"Me?" Now they are *all* looking at me. How should I know? "If we try to save her, we might be captured ourselves?"

"Correct," William says.

"But if we don't save her, they will continue to grow their army, who will hunt us, which could also lead to our death or capture."

Tess nods.

If we are to overcome the Morts in time for me to return to Anna, we will have to first stop them from hunting *us* during the day. Which means we need to stop the Maltorim from creating these possessions.

Indeed, it's my thoughts of Anna—not the wellbeing of this

world or my comrades—that finalize my decision. Perhaps I haven't changed so much as I would like to think.

"Well, then," I say, still uncertain, "it seems obvious that we need to save her."

And so it is decided.

I'VE NEVER SEEN ANYTHING LIKE THIS.

A world of gray. Stone stacked on stone. Dry dirt that lives on every surface, that claims even the air, drowning the world in hues of worn gold beneath a midnight-blue sky.

So this is Damascus. This is where the great, mighty, powerful, and corrupt Maltorim call home.

"Where do we go from here?" I ask, staring out over a humble cemetery that stretches on acres of land.

Adrian points to a large building in the distance, but even that looks like a grave. It goes against my instincts to approach such a destination, to enter a final resting place with hopes of saving a life. But if we don't save this woman, the Maltorim will continue to build their army, and we'll never overcome the Morts.

And if we never overcome the Morts, I'll never return to Anna.

William frowns. "That's it? It looks a little small for an asylum built for so many Cruor."

Adrian laughs. It's an easy, relaxed laugh, and it doesn't suit him and doesn't suit the moment. It's unnerving. "It's beneath the mausoleum. Truly, it does take up most of this land, right below our feet. But you will never get inside."

Tess' brow furrows, and I feel mine do the same. We all turn toward him.

"Then why did we come here?" Tess asks.

The smile falls from his face, and he looks at her with sad eyes. "I'm sorry, Thessaly."

Before any of us can make sense of the exchange, a dozen large men approach us from the distance.

Cruor, each one. Some short, some tall, some thick, some thin. The only thing they have in common are their navy blue and scarlet-red uniforms with large brass buttons that glare at me as though they themselves are the poison that can end my life.

Anger rips through me, but I can't pull my focus from Tess; she looks more anguished than angry. Tears have already glazed her eyes and her face is bright red and she's shaking. Just looking at how hurt she is cripples me.

"How *could* you?" She lunges toward Adrian, but we don't have time for shattered trust.

I hold her back, reach down, grab a stake from her ankle, and thrust it into her grasp.

The Cruors' waltz toward us turns into a blur, and before I can retrieve my own stake, one kicks me in the shoulder, knocking me back. I grasp the stake tighter and pull it up just as he pounces, and the stake tears through him, demolishing him into ash that seems to belong all too well to this dreadful place.

Adrian neither defends nor attacks us, but his attention never leaves Tess. Two guards have grabbed her by each of her arms, but she throws her head back, hitting one of them in the face. The guard seems unfazed, despite a bleeding nose that quickly heals.

William stakes one of them, and Tess twists enough to kick the other in the chest. She removes a sword from the hilt at her side and decapitates him.

I know each of us moves with a speed that would go unseen to the human eye, but it's as though the events are rolling out like honey. These Cruor are not the best trained, and I know it's a matter of time before more competent minions of the Maltorim are sent out for us.

Now we either run, or we fight. William and Tess told me we always fight. And, eventually, we will have to. But there is fighting smart and there is fighting because you have no choice, and this is neither.

This is not the fight we need to wage.

We need to get out of here and come up with a plan. A plan we build without the man we cannot trust. Without Adrian.

"We need to get out here," I yell to William.

As I start to run, Adrian blocks my path. Tess turns to him, sword in hand, anger burning in her eyes. But she doesn't do anything.

I don't blame her. I wouldn't be able to kill him, either. Just like I hadn't been able to kill my father. Because I'd loved him once, and love can be a crippling thing.

But not anymore.

If I ever get back to where I came, I will do whatever it takes to save Anna.

The tip of Tess' blade falls to the ground, and her dress slips from her shoulder. Her eyes are shooting daggers at Adrian as she grabs the sleeve of her dress and yanks it back up to cover her skin.

All I can do is stand there, unsure what either of them will do next, all the while trying to find my path away from here and a way to bring Tess and William with me.

But Tess only has eyes for Adrian, tears swelling on her lower eyelids. Her hand is shaking, gripping the hilt of the sword so tightly that her knuckles lose her skin's golden glow. Adrian stares at her regretfully, and his hands fall to his sides.

This is my chance. I dart past him, successfully this time, and William grabs Tess by her wrist. But before he can pull her from the fray, another Cruor rushes from the shadows in a blur and grabs her around the neck. With Tess against his chest and another Cruor standing behind him, there's no clear angle to stake him from.

Adrian finally moves from his spot. Gone is his calm and restraint. He hurdles across the field, a deep, animalistic war-cry wrenching from his mouth, and he tackles the Cruor.

"Not Tess!" he growls.

Apparently he was fine with leading William and I to our capture, but not if it meant Tess would go down with us.

William grabs her hand, and we run as fast as we can until we are gone, traveling into the black where they can't get us.

We tumble out from space into a sparse forest of dark tree trunks, clumps of bushes, and tall shadowed pines that stretch up like arrows into the sky. My mind struggles to process what transpired, but my desire to stay alive won't let my thoughts linger. I can only think of escape.

I have no real sense of which direction we came from or which direction we are running in now, but it is still night, evidenced by the moonlight cascading through the lattice of branches overhead and the odd night-vision glow of the world around me. Darkness and shadows stretch around us, as though the night wishes to consume us.

Wind slips through the trees, stinging my face with cold, and I've never been more aware that I am running than I am right now. Every breath is shouting in my ears. A fox yips in the distance. Fallen branches crack beneath my feet. Tree trunks creak, weeds slide against my legs, and thorns catch my clothing, ripping fabric and flesh alike.

We're in and out of the black. Traveling and not. Our skip through locations should serve to lose the Maltorim from our trail.

When finally we stop running, Tess and William vomit into bushes, and my own stomach churns. For a moment, I think it will pass, but soon I am getting sick in the underbrush as well.

Once I'm recovered, I turn to them. "Are you guys okay?"

Tess is still hunched over, grasping her stomach, and William is resting with his hands on his knees. He straightens slowly.

"Too much traveling," he says, eyes on the ground as he wipes the blood residue from his mouth with the back of his wrist. "Our bodies can only handle so much at a time, and we've pushed it this month. Much more, and we might not make it."

Then it's true. We really *can't* run forever.

Over the metallic scent of their blood, an earthy fungus aroma carries on the wind. The air is a bit moister than I remember.

Tess sucks in a huge gulp of air, catches her breath, and stands upright. William spins slowly, then nods for us to follow him. We creep around the underbrush, animal eyes glowing from their depths, and duck beneath the cobwebs until we reach a path lined with flower blooms that are shut tight against the darkness.

At the end of the path, there is life. A small town spattered with cabins.

William leads us a few houses down and quietly raps on the door, looking in every direction as he awaits a response.

A squat woman with clear skin and large, kind blue eyes open the door. "Come in, come in!"

William shuffles Tess and me inside.

The woman rubs her hands over her apron, then swings her arms out. "My son! You've come! You've brought company!"

Son?

She hugs us as though she's known us for ages, saving the biggest, tightest hug for William. He stares into the distance somewhere behind her. I want to make sense of everything that just happened, but I still don't know what's happening right now. Maybe William feels the same. Maybe that's why he seems to avoid looking at anybody.

Pa's words flash through my mind, back from when his sentiments were useful instead of hurtful: *Don't worry about the past when you're running through the present.*

And yet, a fragment is trying to force its way through. I squeeze my eyes shut, willing it away, and when the dizziness subsides from my effort, I open them again.

"You all right, dear?" the woman asks. She's released William from her embrace.

"Not really," I say, but one look at Tess tells me I'm not the one anyone should be worried about right now. "Sorry, I haven't introduced myself. I'm Cordovae. And I take it you're William's mother?"

"Heaven's no!" she says. "I'm too young to be a mother!"

The woman is at least fifty, but I force a smile. Young at heart, where it matters.

"Madelina," William says, "I don't mean to be rude, but we need a place to stay and a little time to settle down."

"Of course," she says. She turns from him, facing me again. She smiles brightly as she bustles past. "I'll prepare the guest room immediately."

"Madelina." When William says her name this time, his voice conveys the impending doom more befitting our situation. "We need something a little more...out of the way."

Her hands bunch in front of her, and she turns back to us, frowning. "I see."

"If you can't, please say so. I would hate—"

"Nonsense. You'll stay here."

"You understand what that may mean for you?" William's chest heaves with a deep breath.

An older man hobbles into the room. "What have we here?"

"Some friends stopped by for a visit, John," Madelina says. "Now be nice..."

"Who, me? I'm always nice!" He pokes his cane at William. His hair is impossibly white. "I know you. Imagine you didn't stop by for tea and biscuits, then?"

"No, sir," William says, staring down at his feet. "But we will be out of here as soon as we can, if it's all right we stay."

Madelina solemnly takes the man's wrinkled hand, and he presses his lips together, nodding.

"They'll have to get through us first," the man says. His large eyes grow wider, and I can't help but notice how exaggerated everything is about this man—from his large protruding ears and bulbous nose to the knotted cane he pokes around with. "Go on,

Madelina. Show them to their quarters. I'll stay here in case any more unexpected company shows up."

Through this all, Tess is silent. Her eyes glaze over, her face a stony, unreadable mask, and yet I can read what story her expression tells all too well. I grasp her hand, and even though she doesn't grasp back, I don't let go.

Madelina leads us through the dining room, where flour dusts the table and meat lies half-chopped on a wooden block. Pots and pans scatter beside each other, and wooden chairs adorn the wooden table. A vase of dried flowers and a pot of herbs rest next to the sack of flour.

The kitchen, attached to the dining room, is not much bigger than a closet with a stove and some cabinets. Steam whistles from the kettle, and the laughter of children echoes from upstairs. So much for her being too young to be a mother, I suppose.

The aroma of potatoes, onions, carrots, savory meat, and fresh bread waft from the small room. This place feels like home—or like how I imagine a home *should* feel. I can hardly remember anymore.

I want to trust them. To believe they won't lure us to our demise, the way Adrian had. Can we trust anyone?

In the corner of the dining room, Madelina shoves some pans out of a small, doorless pantry, then moves aside.

"Through there," she says, pointing to a space below the shelf.

William crouches inside the pantry and shuffles on his hands and knees, beneath the lowest shelf. He's nearly too tall. His back lifts the wooden slat. But he drops to his belly and wiggles the rest of the way through the small opening. I let Tess go ahead of me, whisper my thanks to Madelina, and follow them through.

Once on the other side, I pull a thin piece of twine to shut the small door closed behind us. The clank of pots being thrown back into the closet echoes through the thin wood that blocks the entrance to the small room we've just entered.

The room is wide enough for us to all lie down and tall enough for us to sit up comfortably, perhaps even tall enough for Tess or me to stand. The main area has been swept clean, but along the edges are feces of small animals—rats?—and spider webs in the dusty corners. From somewhere in the walls, something scratches its claws against the wood.

I stare at my hands. My fists and arms are bruised. I've always bruised easily. My father would laugh and tell anyone who asked, *'Kids, huh? They're always bumping into things.'*

I swallow hard. Not today. I won't remember that man today.

Now that I'm Ankou, my body heals much faster, and already my bruises are turning a greenish-yellow. I take some nightshade from a pouch at my hip and chew it quickly, wanting the evidence of everything that just occurred and the reminder of everything in the past to disappear as quickly as possible.

When finally I can handle the silence of the room no longer, I gaze over at William. "What...happened?"

His own wounds have healed easily from his second nature alone.

"We were set up," he says plainly. He still won't even look at me.

"He *betrayed* us," Tess spits. "Betrayed *me*."

I frown. "Tess—"

"I don't want to hear it," she snaps. "You don't know what it's like to lose the one person you should be able to trust."

Ouch.

I most certainly do, but now isn't the time for opening up with her. She's dealing with her own fresh emotional wounds.

"What about the girl the Maltorim captured?" I ask instead. "Are we going to get her? Did we risk all that for nothing?"

"At this point, we don't know that there was any girl," William says. "So, yes, we risked all that for nothing. We couldn't go back there now anyway. For now, we'll stay here. It's the only place I know we can hide. They'll be looking for us now. This sets back *everything*. It's the exact opposite of what we needed."

"So what *are* we doing to do?"

"Focus on where to go next. We must move soon." Finally his

pained expression reaches me, but only for a moment before he winces and looks to the small passage behind me that leads back into the kitchen. "If they find us, it can't be here. Madelina and John are good people. We can't bring them into this."

I bite my lip, shifting my weight on the gritty floor. "Haven't we already?"

THE WIND BATTERS THE ROOF OVERHEAD, AND THE NOISE KEEPS me on edge. The Maltorim will come barreling in at any moment. My body aches from the tension. No one is talking. No one will even look at one another.

I poke at the vegetables in the stew Madelina has slid into our small room. The soggy vegetables and undercooked potatoes have gone cold, and anxiety fills the void that was once my appetite, but I force down the stew and nibble on the bowl of fresh berries because there's nothing else to do.

Tess had said my Ferrum nature might be able to help us, if I can learn to control it. So I practice on the stew. I press my teeth to a chunk of meat. Nothing happens. I envision my teeth turning to sharp points. Still nothing. I try to *feel* something in my core. I remember the time William stood behind me, his hand on my stomach, telling me I would *know*. That things would just happen. The memory stirs so many emotions in me, and for a moment my teeth tingle, but the sensation fizzles out, and instead I find myself staring at William.

He must sense it, because his gaze shifts up, and I quickly look up at the ceiling and sort of trail my attention around as though I was just checking out the room. Things are so weird between us now.

I don't think I can handle staying here much longer. It's too much like being in jail all over again. I can hardly breathe in here. The mold and mildew and rot of damp wood is overpowering. I carefully lift a drop cloth from the floor that is cluttering our space. I fold it carefully, trying to keep from kicking up the dust, but the stale air still catches in my lungs, and I cough.

I watch William as he presses another bite of bread into his mouth, followed by a chunk of raw meat, and I'm reminded that he is allergic to the very herbs that sustain my life.

I wonder if God exists—if he is part of the Universe, or separate. If the Universe created Him or He created it.

Maybe William has these answers.

"Do you ever pray?" I ask.

Tess must know I was speaking to William, because she doesn't even look up. She just keeps twisting the small pieces of hair that stick out at the bottom of her long, dark braid.

William pauses, dropping a bite of food away from his mouth. "In my own way, I guess."

"To whom do you pray? If the Universe has created us, doesn't that make all known religions inherently wrong?"

He shrugs. "Or it makes them all right. I suppose it depends how you look at it."

I frown and slump lower against the wall.

"I'm not sure how to look at it," I mumble.

"I wouldn't worry about it," he says. "Religion divides people, when otherwise they are unified. It didn't always, but there it is. People take sides when it doesn't really matter what anyone believes. We all believe we exist, and we all believe the world once wasn't and now is. That something made it be so."

"You all say 'the Universe'. That the Universe is the creator. What does that say about God?"

William chews a piece of meat and swallows before speaking

again. "There's a saying. *A rose by any other name would smell just as sweet*."

How fitting. I suppose it's true. I am me, whether called Rose or Abigail or Cordovae.

William nudges my foot with his own, and when I look up, he grins. "Just because we have another name for something, does not mean by another name it does not exist. No one is ever wrong for their beliefs. Faith, hope, trust—these are the good things in our world. Why question it?"

I shrug one shoulder. How can I *not* question it? After everything that has happened to me in my life before and my life now, how can I not want to know the truth?

Tess clears her throat, and when we look up, she says, "Will you two be ready to leave in a few hours?"

"Maybe we should go now," I say quietly.

William lifts his eyes, his glaring annoyance at my suggestion drenching his expression. "It's daylight, Cord."

"How are we supposed to make any ground at night with Cruor after us?"

"We *need* to leave at night," William presses, "so should we encounter the Cruor we will at least have the strength to fight. That is all we can do. That is all anyone can ever do."

Except that's not entirely true. Nothing is ever entirely true.

"I know that. But daylight won't kill us. You could drink some of Tess or I's blood, right? Then you would be fine for a few hours. It would give us a head start on the Cruor."

"Brilliant idea," Tess says, as though it's the least brilliant idea she's ever heard. "Gee, why didn't I think of that?"

"I just thought—"

"Who cares if the daylight can reduce us to the size of insects?" Tess is nearly maniacal now, smiling and angry at the same time, a crazy look in her eyes. "At least it'll give us a head start in escaping the inevitable."

I scowl. "I don't hear any better ideas from either of you."

William closes his eyes and pinches the bridge of his nose. "I know you mean well, Cord, but please, now is not the time. We will leave at nightfall to speak with the Oracle. She will know what to do."

I hope he's right. And I hope we make it that far, because I have a bad feeling about all of this.

❧

I'M FALLING IN AND OUT OF DREAMS ABOUT A WOMAN I'VE never met. Who is the Oracle? What can she tell us? William spoke of her like some omnipotent being, but even he said she's not the Universe—just the woman who carries its secrets...the oldest living fire elemental, the first Chibold ever to walk this earth. Will she be mischievous or serious? Kind or cold?

A knock at the entrance to the small opening of our hidden room rattles me from sleep. It's dark. Cracks in the exposed wooden beams let through only the smallest slivers of moonlight, but they are equally as powerful as daylight to me now that I am Ankou. The shadows, however, still remain the one true darkness.

Across from me, William jostles Tess from her sleep. "It's time."

I hear the crinkle of her dress against the dirty floor as she shifts around.

A loud crash shakes the house, and I brace myself against the wall. "What was that?"

Before Tess or William can answer, screams shatter from the other room.

"Where are they?" booms a deep voice.

My heart leaps to my throat, and my lungs contract. Lord help us, no matter where we go, they will find us. I hold my breath and stare at the small passageway door back to the kitchen, then back to my companions.

Tess nods toward a large wooden wheel in the corner. Slowly, she tilts it to the side, revealing a small tunnel, but my attention drifts back toward the door. I shuffle close enough to peer through a crack in the wood.

"We know they're here," bellows the same deep voice. It's more of a growl. I can see the back of his bulky shoulders and, on the other side of him, pressed against the wall by her neck, is Madelina. "You know what will happen if you don't cooperate."

"They left hours ago," she chokes out. "We didn't know you were looking for them or we would have called."

John stands a few feet away, his path blocked by Adrian and another Cruor—a large albino man—who stand in the corner by a large crate barrel. "Leave her alone! She ain't done nothin' wrong here!"

The albino Cruor alongside Adrian holds John back in the least committed way. There's fear in Adrian's eyes...but fear of what? It's us who should be—and are—afraid of them.

Tess tugs my dress, and when I look back, she nods again toward the passage. I shake my head. I'm trembling and sweat is dripping down my spine and I can hardly breathe, but fear can't rule my next move, and we can't leave. Not like this.

I peer through the crack again. The large man turns away from Madelina and sweeps everything from the dining room table, bowls cracking and flour exploding like a dust storm in the room. He opens cabinet after cabinet in the small kitchen, pulling out anything he finds and sticking his head in as though at any moment he will find us there instead of a bag of rice or an iron pan.

Adrian raises his eyebrows at Madelina and gently grasps her hand, but she shudders.

"Please, Miss," he says. "No need for any harm to come to you. We are not after your comrades, after all, just the woman they have with them. Tell us what we need to know so we can be on our way. I can assure you that, if they cooperate with us, they will not be harmed."

Madelina shakes her head. The large man is out of sight now, but the slam of cabinets is getting closer. It won't be long before he reaches the pantry.

Two more Cruor stomp into the room. The larger of the two—a dark-eyed man with tanned skin—holds a girl in his grasp, and his smaller counterpart, the one with the weasel-nose and drawn in cheeks, holds a young boy. Tears streak the faces of the children. They're shaking. Unceremoniously, the dark-eyed Cruor stabs the boy in the chest, then drops him to the ground. My nails dig into my palms and tears pinch in my throat. The beast then points the knife at the girl, who is now kicking and screaming. Madelina's cries screech over the noise.

She *was* a mother. Whatever she said, whether she birthed that child or not, she was every bit the mother, because that was the scream of a mother's heart breaking.

I can't sit here any longer. I look back at William, shaking my head. Fighting for these people is fighting for Anna; turning my back on them is turning my back on her. I have to do something.

I grab Tess' sword and bolt for the door. I charge through on hands and knees, breaking through the shelf that blocks the top half of the door. As I climb to my feet, I nearly trip over the contents that have fallen to the floor, but I keep moving, arcing the sword around me to decapitate the auburn-haired Cruor who was checking the cabinets.

The Cruor that killed the boy and the Cruor still holding the girl step toward us. They release the girl, and she runs out of the room and up the stairs. I wish I could go to her, but I can't right now. No one can. Today, she is forced to grow up faster than any child ever should, and my heart aches with the pain of understanding exactly what that feels like.

I wrap my grip tighter around the handle of the sword. I feel Tess and William standing behind me now. I glance over to Adrian, narrowing my eyes. How could he come here after helping Tess escape—does he want to help her or *not*? Adrian's comrade, a tall young man with teal eyes, dark lashes, and tangled hair, stares at me with a strange intensity. He's hiding something. I know, the way I have always known. But it's not *us* he is hiding something from.

The other two Cruor charge at us, but since Adrian and his comrade do not join them, we have them outnumbered. Madelina breaks away from Adrian, and Tess tosses her a stake. The albino Cruor stops blocking John to go after her, but as he tackles her, she drives the stake into his chest, obliterating him. John's form trembles, and the house shakes. Before I know it, there's a large wolf in the room and several more Cruor.

"Come on, Charles!" yells a tall, sinewy, golden-haired Cruor as he tosses a sword to Adrian's comrade in the corner of the room. "Don't just stand there!"

Charles tenses his jaw and nods, but he holds the sword in front of him as though unsure what do with it. After a moment, his body begins to tremble also, and I see his face twist into something animalistic. I would swear I'd seen fangs on him not moments before, but he must be Strigoi. But he's not marked . . .

"There's a dual breed in there!" someone shouts from the other room, but by time they reach us, the young man looks normal again.

John, in his wolf form, takes an aggressive stance against the tanned Cruor and weasel-nosed Cruor that killed the boy and tormented the little girl, but they don't back down. The two monsters have John and Madelina backed up against a wall.

"Which one is it?" asks a dark-haired, husky-voiced Cruor that has just joined us in the room. The Cruor coming in the room behind him points his bony finger over his shoulder—points right at Adrian and his comrade.

John tears into the tanned Cruor, and the flesh he rips from its calf smokes and turns to ash. Madelina stakes weasel-nose, and William and Tess take on the new Cruor filing into the room. Of the newcomers, a man with a large, veiny scar along his jaw that demands all the attention on his face, squares off with me.

I need to focus on this beast, but even as he kicks me in the stomach and sends me flying back into the wall, I'm staring at

Adrian and the young man he's brought with him. Beyond the blur of my vision, I see one of the Maltorim guards hold a sword to Adrian's neck.

"Abomination," the Cruor grunts.

I should be terrified or shocked, but instead I'm stuck somewhere between compassion and indifference. It hurts to have someone on your side turn against you, but I can't think of anyone more deserving of such treatment as Adrian.

The Cruor coming after me lifts me from the ground by my neck, but I press my shoulders back against the wall and kick him as hard as I can in the chest, knocking him off of me. I jump to my feet and decapitate him as well, but instead of watching the light fade from his eyes, my attention is back on what will become of Adrian.

Sweat trickles down his temple, and he shakes his head. "It's not me."

Charles steps forward, his face transforming right before everyone's eyes.

"Wrong guy," he growls, slaying the Cruor.

He lifts the crate barrel from behind him and throws it across the room, setting back the remaining Maltorim guards while he reaches his hand down to Adrian and helps him to his feet. Adrian swallows, and for a moment, they stare at each other.

Charles tenses his jaw. "We're in this together. Right?"

Adrian nods and draws his own sword, and the two turn to face the rest of the room.

Someone wraps their arm around my neck from behind me, cutting off my oxygen. Instinctively, my hand rushes to grab their arm and try to pull it off, but they're too strong. So badly I want to suck in a breath of air, but I can't. My face and ears are aching with the pressure.

I grip my sword the best I can and stab it into my attacker's foot. It's just enough to loosen his grip, and I drop my sword and shoot my arms up between his forearm and my neck to break away.

I immediately kneel to the ground to recoup my sword, but another Cruor kicks it away.

Then, to my surprise, Adrian decapitates the man. His comrade takes out two more. William and Tess have already cut down several of our attackers, and now there are none left standing. John is lying on the ground, still in wolf form, and one of his hind legs is bleeding. Madelina kneels beside him and crumbles on top of him in a heap, crying against his fur.

I'm too stunned to move.

William moves to my side, and Tess jumps in front of us, a small knife pointed at Adrian. "You'll have to kill me to get to them."

Adrian gives an almost unnoticeable shake of his head. "I do not intend to harm you, Thessaly."

She shifts her weight and tightens her grip on her knife's handle.

Adrian places his own sword on the ground, and turns his back to her to face his warrior friend. "You're a dual breed, then."

Charles crosses his arms across his chest and tilts his chin up. "Yes."

"You could have let them kill me," Adrian says. "They wouldn't have known any better."

"But I would have."

Adrian nods slowly. "This forces me to reconsider my alliances."

"For what is right, I would hope," Charles says.

Adrian nods once more, then turns to Tess. "I didn't know, Thessaly. They promised me you wouldn't get hurt. Please, forgive me."

For a long moment, she stares at him blankly, then she tosses her knife at his feet, takes her sword back from me, wipes the blood on the skirt of her dress, and returns it to her hilt.

"Take care of these fine people," she says, and she walks out the front door.

William and I follow. The windows of the surrounding cabins are empty, but I know the houses are not. Our enemy is gone for now, but not gone for good, and the sacrifices made tonight never should have been made.

William grabs Tess by the arm, spinning her toward him. "What was that, Tess? An act of mercy? You're going to let him walk away? What ever happened to bringing these people to justice?"

Tess' face pinches in, and she yanks her arm away from him. "He let us walk out, didn't he?"

William scowls, his hand dropping to his side. "I can't believe you."

Tess grabs her sword and shoves the handle to his chest. "Fine. Kill him, if you want him dead so badly."

"No." He grabs the hilt of the sword and pushes it back toward her. "You need to do it. You *need* to, Tess."

I step beside them, lowering William's hand until the tip of the sword's blade presses into the dirt. "I don't like him, but I have to agree with Tess. He helped us, didn't he?"

William rolls back on his heels and scoffs. "After nearly killing us!" He closes his eyes and pinches the bridge of his nose. "If he comes near us again—"

I grasp his other hand, and his words fall dead on the air. Upon looking at me, his expression softens, and he lets out a sigh.

"Now what?" I ask, staring out into the dark night of the trembling village.

"Now," William says, wrapping his hand tightly around mine, "we go to the Oracle."

CHAPTER 27
SOMEWHERE UNKNOWN, APRIL 1692

What can we expect from the Oracle?

I imagine an old woman with a scarf tied to her head and a crystal ball because, from what I understand, she sounds a bit like a psychic. I don't have time to ask many questions. There is no other way to see the Oracle but to use our traveling abilities, and no time to wait before we set out to do so. It's a blink, a fall through the black, and we're where we need to be. I have no idea where *that* is...but I guess that's the point.

I brace myself against one of the stone walls to stop my feet from sliding on the wet slate beneath us. Thick tree roots have broken through the rock, and the muted whistle of wind in the trees outside echoes softly through the cave's entrance, the cold breeze spitting dead leaves at our shins and ankles.

William squeezes my hand. "Are you ready?"

"How did you get here without knowing where it was?"

"We don't just have the ability to travel to places. Some of us— like Tess—can travel to people, too. But no one can travel to the Oracle who hasn't seen her before."

I purse my lips. "Then how do you travel to her the first time?"

"Either she calls for you or someone who has met with her

before brings you to her. Tess and I were called here when she was to come under my guidance."

"Wait—what?"

Tess is a few feet ahead of us already, standing where the last rays of moonlight reach as they filter in from the entrance. She nods toward the darkness that is deeper within the cave. "This way."

"The Oracle brought us together," William whispers. He starts to walk, but I'm glued to where I stand. He stares back at me. "Come on, Cord."

I shake my head. "I can't see."

He chuckles. "It's fine. Unless you're scared of the dark?"

I tug my hand out of his. "I'm not scared. I just thought we—the Ankou—could always see, even in the dark."

"Ah," he says, nodding. "Not so here. The Oracle's magic disables many abilities of visiting elementals. Cruor's fangs cannot descend, not that they are welcome here often. Ankou do not have the power of sight nor can they move spirits here. Strigoi cannot shift and do not have their usual strength. None of us have our usual speed."

"And other Chibold?" I ask.

"Other Chibold cannot come here. What point would there be? They can communicate with the Universe for themselves."

"What about the Oracle?" I ask. "She's a Chibold, too, but they cannot live without a host family, isn't that right?"

William nods. "That's true of the Chibold, but...she's the Oracle. She was the first. She's different."

"I see..." I sigh deeply and shuffle behind him as we continue deeper into the cave. "How do Cruor and Strigoi come here, since the Oracle does not allow visitors to travel to her on foot."

"They need an Ankou guide," he says. "Like me. Everything for a reason. These checks and balances. Trust me, the politics of this world are not what you need to concern yourself with."

The chill that has hung in the air between us for the last few days dissipates. Things feel comfortable again.

Tess cups her hands around her mouth. "Stop babying her. We need to move."

William grins at me and raises his eyebrows in a way that's almost flirty. He is without a doubt the most beautiful man I've ever known, even in the darkness where I can barely see him. There's some kind of perfect within this man, between us together.

"Do you trust me?" he asks.

My heart is flying. Absolutely. In this moment, I trust him with every fiber of my being—trust him to take everything I have and fix all my broken parts and make me whole again. I trust him with my life, and I trust him with my soul.

I've either lost my mind or I've gained heart, but if I've gained heart, how long before it's broken?

Surely if anyone knew how I felt right now, they would tell me to stop. That there is no room in this world for such feelings, that nothing good can come of it. That, as right as it feels, it's utterly wrong. And yet, for once, I don't care. Feelings don't have to make sense; you either accept them or you don't, and it's a personal thing. And personally, I'm ready for these feelings, and I'm ready to fight—for this world and for my life and for my heart.

"Do you trust me?" he asks once more.

I nod, unable to put a voice to my thoughts.

"Then let's go," he says, taking my hand.

And with that, he leads me into the dark.

"STAY CLOSE TO THE WALL," TESS ORDERS.

William walks in front of me, but he's reaching behind him to hold my hand as we trek deeper into the dark. Crumbling rock crunches beneath our footsteps, rattles over the ground when kicked away, and splashes through puddles. Water soaks through my thin leather boots and chills my feet. I shiver.

"Shame we couldn't have landed just a little closer to the Oracle," I say, half-joking.

I can nearly hear Tess roll her eyes, or maybe I can just hear that eye-rolling tone in her voice: "You think she wants someone plunking themselves into her existence just like that? Have a little respect."

I bite my lip. Tess is colder toward me than ever before. Does she blame me for what happened with Adrian? She doesn't seem to be taking it out on William at all . . .

The stagnant air feels thick in my lungs, and my hand brushes over sticky, itchy spider webs. I startle, jumping back and nearly lose my balance, my foot slipping down a steep incline that scrapes my thigh.

William yanks my hand, pulling me hard and fast against his body, and I gasp. He presses me against the wall, the fist of a stone poking in my back a welcome relief from my near tumble to my death.

"Jesus, Cord," he breathes.

My heart pounds, and I can't stop shaking. I cling to William's shirt, my other hand still grasping his tightly. My lips brush his sweaty shoulder, and I squeeze my eyes tight, wishing we were anywhere but here.

"Sorry," I mumble.

"You all right?" he asks, steadying me at arm's length.

"Yes...I'm—I'm okay." I wish I could see his face right now, take comfort in those dark eyes of his.

"Don't scare me like that."

Tess clears her throat. "She's fine. Let's go; we're almost there."

After a few more yards, light glows from a cavern ahead. The rush of moving water grows louder, until it's nearly a roar. Finally, our thin trail widens and deposits us beside the dancing light of flames from the wall sconces. A large river scores the ground of the cavern and rushes over the edge to our right.

I look down. I can't see where the fall ends. I don't want to think what would have happened if William hadn't caught me. If the Oracle is as harsh as the road to meet her, I am not sure I am prepared for this. What if she doesn't like me?

The fires on the wall sconces die down until diminishing completely, but the room fills with a cold light that seems to come from nowhere, as though the crystal clear water of the river reflects not only everything in the room, but even the memory of light itself.

Three large stones rise from the river, just close enough for us to reach, and across from there a granite throne juts from the water. Tess steps onto one of the stones and sits on it cross-legged. William does the same beside her, leaving one stone for me. I'm hesitant to sit there, amidst the water that gallops toward the great fall, but I take a deep breath and join them anyway.

"Do you think she's here?" I ask.

"Of course," Tess says. "The Oracle always moves, but those who know her always know where to find her."

William stretches his arms up, cracking his back. "Remember, we travel to her, not to her location."

The room brims with an ominous sense of a danger. A glow of warning. The rushing waterfall stops. The water stills, then trembles lightly. Steam rises from the water, taking the form of a child.

I can't take my eyes off what I'm seeing. "Is that—"

"Shhh..." Tess whispers.

The child materializes into the large granite throne. Her skin is so white it's almost blue, and her eyes glaze over in clouds. Her hair, pale as snow, falls in ribbons over her shoulders and down to her waist. The tips of her hair wisp in flames that quickly extinguish, turn black, then turn ashen to white again. It's almost scary, if not for how otherwise ethereally beautiful she is.

I had expected someone older, but now that I see her, I remember the Chibold have always traditionally taken the form of children. I suppose that applies to even the oldest of Chibold as it's true of her as well. Aside from her strange eyes and hair and skin, she has the body and features of a child, and there's an innocence about her presence.

Her lips shimmer, glistening blue, and her smile is comforting. She looks at me as though she can see me, but her eyes are so empty that I wonder if it's my breathing that has drawn her attention.

"I've been expecting you three," she says, her voice lilting melodically.

Flames rise at her feet. No. No, her feet are turning to flames.

"Don't look so frightened," she says to me, the stone lowering until her feet rest on the surface of the water, turning her skin that pale-blue again. "We Chibold have always had a gift over fire, but as I age, I fear it is more of a curse."

"How do you...I thought that..."

Tess clears her throat, and when I look at her, she's glowering, shaking her head.

The Oracle laughs. "It's all right, Tess." She returns her attention to me. "I am the oldest, and as such, I do not need to live with a host family. But," she says, her tone dropping, "one day I will die, and a new Oracle will replace me. You see, we all die, eventually. True immortality—" She giggles. "—could such a thing exist? Is immortality in life, or in what we create...what we leave behind?"

As she says this, images of Anna ripple across the surface of the river—I'm cradling her in my arms, I'm running my finger over the slope of her nose, I'm nuzzling my face against hers.

Tears pinch in my throat. But the Oracle does not wait for my reply.

"You do not have much time to ponder such questions," she says, and with a wave of her arm, the images of Anna are erased from the water, but not from my heart. "The Maltorim has created an army of possessed, yes, but you've been misled. Be careful from here forward whom you trust."

Though she is every bit as firm and confident as I imagined, she's certainly more pleasant and tranquil than I had expected. It's her *message* that troubles me.

I steal a glance at William. He's scowling. Just past him, Tess shakes her head.

The Oracle raises a tiny pale finger, closing her eyes for a long moment before speaking. "Ah, but there is hope, for a spirit elemental has indeed arrived." Her eyes spring back open. "She is the most valuable life source on this planet. Adrian was right in one thing: you must save her, for it is her blood that one Ankou is using to perform his magic for the Maltorim."

So Adrian had been a good enough liar to base his stories in truth. But can we trust the Oracle? I sense we can, but the last time we tried to save this elusive spiritual elemental, things didn't work out so well.

The Oracle, however, has helped many people before. Why would she mislead us now?

In the end, I come to one realization: if we don't try, we may be leaving an innocent woman's life hanging in the balance while allowing the Maltorim to have an upper hand we can't afford.

"Where do we find her?" I ask, determination so infused in my voice that it surprises even me.

The Oracle poises her arm beside her, palm up, and a flame rises above her hand. A vision of the Malleus Maleficarum flickers in the fire. "Your answers are here, in the very book the Maltorim is circulating in their efforts to stop you. The Malleus Maleficarum, the Hammer of the Witches."

The fire dissipates, but the book remains, now firmly in her grasp. She hands it to Tess, and Tess stares down at the cover, gripping the book firmly in both hands.

"She's being transported as we speak. You must find her before they reach their final destination. What they have done with her blood until now is only the beginning, but if she dies where they are taking her, it will break her spirit and unleash her abilities to them. You cannot let them have that power."

She smiles thinly at us. "Now go. Fight." Her focus centers on me. "You are our last hope." She vaporizes before our eyes, but her voice lingers. "I see a gift for you on this journey, Cord."

"A gift?" I ask meekly.

"From a stranger."

The rush of the waterfall returns, nearly drowning her out.

"It could be the end of your life or the beginning of your future," she says. "Trust your heart."

And, with that, she is gone.

CHAPTER 28
SOMEWHERE UNKNOWN,
APRIL 1692

BY THE TIME WE ARRIVE ONCE AGAIN AT THE MOUTH OF THE
cave, it's daylight. That might not mean much if we knew where
we were going, but then again it might mean everything.

"Can't we just travel to her?" I ask. "Like we traveled to the
Oracle?"

Tess chews her pouty bottom lip. "I know the Oracle, but not
the spirit elemental," she says. "I can't travel to someone I've never
met before."

"Of course..." I say bitterly. *Of course.*

We sit down in the silence, just out of reach of the sun's rays
that are slivering past the leaves of bushes and trees that block the
entrance to the cave. The Malleus Maleficarum presses into my
lap, but it's the darkness emanating from the book that weighs the
most.

Here are the answers we need, as well as a list of mistruths that
would have been better left undiscovered by mankind. The
questions we ponder are not the ones this book addresses, and I
resent that we need it to save the girl.

But we can't go anywhere until we know where we're going, so
I take a deep breath and break the book open to the first pages.
Tess takes to sitting on the other side of the cavern, sharpening

her sword, while William sidles in at my side, his hand on the ground behind me and the front of his shoulder against the back of mine. He peers down at the pages, his breath warm against my neck.

I breathe in deeply, taking in his scent of an ocean breeze, and it brings me back, back to Georgia beaches, back to my mom sitting in the sand, a big floppy sunhat shading her face as she watches me splash through waves.

I shake my head, refocusing on the book. I have to re-read the sentence I just read. Right now I need to stay connected to my spirit—to Cordovae—because without that piece of me, these words are gibberish. But my spirit knows German. When Thornhart had read from this book to us in jail, I had thought it was written in English, and now I wonder how much of what he said was his own perverted translations, or if this text was really so dark and vile as he made it sound.

As the darkness of these pages consumes me, I make some mindless efforts to channel my Ferrum nature. One passage on detailing the torture of a woman accused of being a witch gives me chills, and for a fleeting moment, my razor-tipped teeth emerge. I can feel the dark energy of the book, and if I allow myself to absorb it, I get the energy I need to control my 'gift'. But each time it happens, I'm startled, and they snap away again.

I continue reading, and it doesn't take me long to realize the Malleus Maleficarum is a possession of its own. What need was there for Morts to inhabit the living with a writing like this in circulation? You could scare people into believing anything—doing anything—even the unthinkable.

From the start, the Malleus Maleficarum sets out to convince any good Christian that they must believe in witches, and further they must never sympathize with them, that these are beings whom the devil uses for extraordinary works. That a witch cannot perform magic without intimate cooperation from the devil.

It quotes the bible, Leviticus, chapter nineteen: *The soul which goeth to wizards and soothsayers to commit fornication with them, I will set my face against that soul, and destroy it out of the midst of my people.*

I close my eyes a moment, anger boiling inside at the way this book uses the beliefs of others to manipulate them toward justified hatred. It sickens me that the Maltorim would go to such lengths to manipulate humankind.

William puts his forehead to my shoulder. "You all right, Cord?"

I swallow around the tight knot in my throat.

William lifts his head, and I turn to him, his face so close to mine that our noses brush.

"Fine," I whisper, and quickly turn back to the book. What's gotten into him? I want to melt into his arms and disappear from this world, but I know I can't. I point to the open pages instead. "What do you think of this?"

The page declares witches are a problem now more than ever.

William frowns and gives a non-committal shrug. "To give reason to those who aren't possessed why these witch hunts are suddenly growing in necessity?"

I smile sadly. "It says women are the ones most commonly addicted to the devil's superstitions, but the chapter seems to go more with its own superstitions: a woman who makes you weary may be a witch; a woman, should she be lazy or make you feel lazy, may be a witch. If she's tempted or makes you tempted, if she has what you have lost, if your cows produce no milk, if she's of old age —these are signs of a woman being a witch?"

William raises his eyebrows. "It's an easy idea for mankind to believe. God has not forsaken them. They have not failed. Someone else, someone evil or influenced by darkness, is to blame."

"But it's all a lie...isn't it?"

"The people reading this don't know that. These people are terrified, and the Maltorim knows that. A little fear can go a long way; a lot of fear can create an epidemic."

Indeed, the book has left no stone unturned in its efforts to instill fear in others. The Malleus Maleficarum implies that if you allow a witch to live, they make you ill or go as far as to kill and dismember men. Witch midwives will stop at nothing to kill your child in your womb or offer your newborn to devils. Allowing a witch to live not only puts your life in danger, but your soul as well. And forgiving them their actions makes you sympathetic to their darkness, and should you feel that way, you may as well be a witch yourself.

"I don't want to read any more," I say, flopping the book lower in my lap. "I can't grasp half of what it's trying to say. Look"—I skip back a few pages—"it says if a woman seems good, she may especially be a witch, as the devil is most keen to tempt the good than the wicked." I flip forward another page. "Except for when he tempts the wicked more than the good because they are easier to stray from their righteous path? It's contradictory."

"You're thinking about it too much, Cord," he says. "The devil's in the details."

His use of the phrase pushes a smile from me. "You're right. This isn't what we're reading this for."

"No," he says. "It's not."

Still, I have to trudge through page after page, considering anything that might be a clue to where they would take the girl. The overall message remains the same: if you are good, you will get rid of these witches before you become wicked yourself.

I skim through the remedies for how to cure any ill will cast on you by a witch, and I can barely stomach the last third of the book as it details who can try a witch—not just the Court of the Inquisition; bishops and their representatives can rid their parishes of these soothesayers, and the ecclesiastic and civil court can both pass judgment as well.

Chapter after chapter delves into the process of examining the witnesses—with four witnesses—and questioning the accused in two ways.

Should the accused be imprisoned? If so, how shall she be taken? Will the accused be told who her witnesses are? Will defense be allowed, and how will the witnesses be announced? After all, you would not want the witnesses to fall ill by the spell of a bitter witch.

How will the witch be questioned on the first day? Will the witch be promised her life? How can the judge protect himself from the witch's spells? How do you shave the parts of a witch so that they cannot conceal the devil's masks and tokens?

What tortures shall the witch endure?

This is to ultimately lead to a definite and just sentence, which will consider what kinds of magic the accused is convicted of, whether they confess, whether they renounce the devil, whether they were accused upon light or strong or grave suspicion. And each of these—and more—have their own dedicated chapter.

It is all written to sound so very fair, so very right, so thoroughly considered and concise. But everything about it screams how wrong it all is.

"That's it," I say, closing the book. "Did anything stand out to you?"

William shakes his head. He leans back against the cave's wall and stretches his legs out in front of him. "You?"

"A few things, perhaps."

He sits up straighter, raising his eyebrows. His interest gives me a fresh burst of energy.

"Okay," I say, "well there was the part about the trolls in Norway. Remember the part about how witches transport?"

William nods. "That was about levitation, though."

I shake my head. "But it was also about how a witch can and cannot travel. About how God will or will not permit it. I realize the Maltorim is making up these stories, but if this is also a guide for their men, then in a way isn't God a metaphor for the Maltorim? What 'God' permits is what the Matorim permits, you see?"

His whole face lights up. "You could be on to something."

Tess' sword clangs to the ground, and she rolls her eyes. "That doesn't tell us where we need to go."

I open the book and translate a passage to her: *"Did not the devil take up Our Saviour, and carry Him up to a high place?"*

"Are we looking for a spirit elemental or are we looking for the son of God?" Tess intones snarkily.

William glares at her. "At least let her finish. We have nothing else to go on."

I don't wait for Tess' permission, nor her interest, to continue. "The chapter was talking about levitation but said when the spirit is removed from the body, then it can rise up in the air. That is what the Maltorim wants, yes? They want to retrieve the spirit elemental's spirit.

"It says here witches have been transported on animals, which are not true animals but devils in animal form."

William's hand slides down to mine and gives a gentle squeeze. My cheeks heat and it spreads down my neck. My heart is racing so fast I can't feel it beat...or maybe it's stopped beating altogether. I swallow and break away from William's stare. We have to stay focused.

I clear my throat, and the trance is broken. "Sounds a bit like how most of the Cruor view the Strigoi, doesn't it?"

"Sure," he says. "That's one way to look at it."

Tess crosses her arm and offers a reluctant, "Yeah. Maybe."

"There's a story in this book on transportation that took place during the daytime in the diocese of Constance. A woman, detested by the town, was not invited to a wedding celebration that the rest of the town was attending. She sought revenge by summoning a devil and asking him to raise a hailstorm. The devil agreed, raised her up, and carried her through the air to a hill near the town, as witnessed by nearby shepherds. But she had no water to pour into the trench to raise the hailstorm, so she filled it with her urine instead and stirred it with her finger. The devil, standing nearby, raised that liquid and sent a violent storm of hailstones to rain down on the townsfolk."

"We already know what they want to do, Cord!" Tess glares at me. "WHERE? *Where* is this supposedly going to happen?" she demands. "That is what we need to find out."

"The book named a few places in passing. It spoke of the Bishop of Brixen, the Count in the ward of Westerich, and the Diocese of Strasburg is mentioned several times. There's also the priest in Oberdorf, and the transport of Habacuc in a moment from Judaea to Caldaea. The diocese of Freising is mentioned in the 'transportation of witches' chapter."

Tess shakes her head. "Can you narrow it down *at all*?"

"I'm getting there. We know these things: they need to transport the witch in a way the 'God' of this book would allow. The only witnessed transport mentioned here was in the diocese of Constance."

"So that's where we go?" William asks.

"If it's not there, I still think it will be in Germany. Freising, maybe." My blood is pumping so rapidly I feel like I'm buzzing. "It won't be under the stars," I say, "because the book said the stars are governed by the good angels, and also for the general order and common good of the Universe that evil spirits cannot alter the influence of the stars."

Tess goes back to sharpening her knife. "You think daytime, then? The Maltorim won't want to be out during the day, but sounds like they can't do it at night."

"Unless that is to throw people off," I say. "They are doing this to bring forth a change, correct? Well...they want to walk in the day, right? Isn't that the purpose all of this serves?"

"I think you're right," William says. "It's what they've always wanted. To walk during the day; to govern the stars."

CHAPTER 29
APRIL 1692, DIOCESE OF CONSTANCE

WHEN WE ARRIVE AT THE GOTTHARD PASS, NIGHT HAS ALREADY fallen. That narrows down the Oracle's current location to somewhere on the other side of the world . . .

We stick to land as much as possible; our bodies cannot handle much more *traveling*. Even Tess is vomiting blood after some of our skips through space. But time is not on our side, and the diocese of Constance stretches for miles.

We cover the ground of the Upper Rhine and scour the German land near Lake Constance, but there is nothing in any of these places to set us on a clear path. Tess' apparent irritation grows with each travel that leaves us no better off than where we began. If we don't find something soon, I fear she'll give up.

But we're close. I can feel it.

When our travels east to Freising prove fruitless, Tess tucks her hands on her hips and turns to me. "This isn't working. I told you we need to narrow it down."

I shrug one shoulder, wishing I could stop her from speaking. I can't deal with the stress. "There was nothing else in the Malleus Maleficarum to give any indication where the Maltorim would be taking the woman. How else are we to narrow it down? If there are any other hints on where to go, we're going to find them here."

William stands at Tess' side, and I feel the wall being built between us already. "Tess may be right, Cordovae. Our bodies can't handle much more, and the night is already half through. We should consider going over the book a second time and trying again tomorrow night."

I push out my bottom lip. "We'll be stuck inside all day tomorrow anyway. We can look at the book again then, if we don't find anything tonight. We don't have enough time to waste the night."

"No," Tess says, stepping nearly toe-to-toe with me, "what we don't have time for is prancing around Germany with no clue where we intend to go."

I scowl, then turn away from her, glaring at William with a challenge on my tongue. "Then you two go rest. I'm not giving up now."

With that, I head north to Frankfurt.

And that is where I find the destruction.

⁂

AT FIRST, I'M NOT CERTAIN WHAT I'M LOOKING AT. THERE'S A lot of blood and a lot of commotion. Grown men weeping over women, clutching those lifeless bodies to their chests, rocking back and forth, the blood staining their own clothing. Abandoned horse-driven carts turned over, their contents scattering the blood-moistened soil. Children crying in doorways and windows. Old women wailing beside their lost husbands.

At my feet lies the freshly murdered body of a young woman, her dress ripped away to reveal a naked bosom, her head rolled to the side, revealing the all-too-telling pierce marks on her neck. No one sheds a tear for this woman. No one but me. Gently I cover her exposed breast with the loose flap of fabric from her dress then step over her body to assess more of the town.

Those that aren't wailing or weeping stand with blank stares. At first I think it's the haunting effect of witnessing such unexplainable brutality, but then I see the darkness in their eyes. They are possessed. I spin back, looking to the woods behind me, and that is when I notice the hordes of Morts sweeping through the shadows.

A tall, pale, blond man with a golden sheen to his skin appears before me, touching my shoulder. He stares deep into my eyes and speaks to me with severity in his voice.

"We have this under control," he says. "Go on to your next destination. Good luck."

I know he is like me—Ankou. I grab his wrist before he can leave. "What about all these people?" I ask. "What about all they've seen?"

He nods solemnly. "They won't remember this day." His sad tone is foreboding. "It's for the best; not just for us, but for them as well."

I don't ask him the next question. I don't ask how he will make them forget. Instead, I release his wrist, and in an instant, he joins the blur of the forest. He's not alone; there are more like us, also weaving between the trees, and every so often a burst of black particles from killing a Mort glitters in the moonlight beneath the forest canopy.

The weight of how big this is hits me, knocking the wind from my chest. I'm just a piece of a much larger puzzle. A part of this *huge* mess.

"Will this war ever end?" I ask myself aloud.

"No." William's voice.

I spin around, the weight from my chest lifting to see him standing there. I'm so thrilled to see him that I can even ignore Tess' glare from two feet behind him, her arms crossed and a scowl set firmly in place.

"You came," I whispered.

"We couldn't let you go alone," he says.

Tess huffs, dropping her arms to her side. "I could have," she says. "William insisted we follow you. What happened here?"

I turn back to the nightmare behind us then stare at the blur of movement in the forest. "Guess."

She lifts her hand, indicating the Ankou and Mort activity surrounding us. "Should we help?"

I shake my head. "One of the Ankou said they have this under control. We should move on. Things will only get worse if we don't find that spirit elemental."

I can't hide the defeat in my voice. It's seems hopeless. I'll never get back to Anna this way, but I refuse to accept that this will always be my life.

William steps closer to me, takes both my hands in his, and stares down into my eyes. "We only have to get things under control, Cord. The Morts will always exist, but you will get to..." I see the lump in his throat bob. "...go home."

His last words come out strained, and my eyes sting with tears. "Right," I say, choking out the only thing I can manage to say. "Home."

Will I ever know home after this? There is no home without Anna...but what is home without William now? I wish we'd never met; I wish he'd been anyone else. Even leaving Tess behind may break whatever is left of me after all this is over.

Tess stomps past us, her shoulder bumping into mine and knocking William and I from our moment. "Come on. If we're going to find this woman in Germany, I think I have an idea where she might be."

⚜

WE FINISH OUR TREK AT THE BEGINNING OF A BRIDGE. Moonlight shines golden on the pale stone. There's a woman standing at the edge, leaning against the winter wind as though that is all that holds her up. I gasp and dart forward, but Tess grabs my arm and yanks me back.

The woman looks at me with empty eyes, then looks forward again and steps over the edge, plunging down and out of sight.

I pull free from Tess, but William grips my shoulder. "She's already gone, Cord. Has been for a long time."

"I don't understand."

He moves behind me and rests both hands on my shoulders and whispers in my ear, "Look again."

So I do.

And there's the woman once more, and this time I see that she's not the solid matter she appeared to be before. She's not Mort—there's nothing shadowy about her—but I can just barely see right through her. She lifts her empty gaze to me again, then looks ahead and jumps to her a death again.

Chills prickle the hairs on my arms, and again my razor teeth snap down. I can only surmise now that somehow it is my heart, not my mind, that controls my Ferrum nature.

I turn back to William and Tess. "What is this place?"

"Devil's bridge," Tess says. "The legend is that a man had begun to build this bridge, but could not build it fast enough, so he called on the devil for help. The devil agreed to finish building the bridge, in exchange for the soul of the first living being that crossed it. The builder agreed, but once the bridge was built, he sent a rooster across the bridge first."

"Then what?" I asked, both horrified and fascinated.

Tess shrugs. "Supposedly the devil tore the rooster apart, and the blood tainted this bridge so much so that people claimed crossing it too many times could drive a person mad."

"And that woman?"

"But one of the many afflicted," Tess says, twisting her lips to one side. "It's just a legend, Cord."

"The woman is real, though. Or was," I say.

Tess nods. "She's an imprint. No way to know really who she was or why she's here."

William takes my hand. "Crossing this bridge may be our only hope. It may be the only way to get closer to the spirit elemental we need to save."

"We could just travel there?"

William shakes his head. "Tess thinks they are around this bridge, but we don't know exactly where. Obviously not on this side of it, though. We don't want to arrive in their midst. We need to assess the situation first."

Tess reaches into her pouch and pulls out a small handful of nightshade. "This is the last of it. Here—" She hands me half. "Eat up. We'll need to find more along the way."

I stare at the poisonous plant in the palm of my hand. It's little more than a bite. My own pouch is empty of such herbs; I'm grateful Tess would share.

"What about William?"

William nods toward the woods on the other side of the bridge. "I'll find some small animal on the other side, before we continue our trek."

I stare at the darkness between the trees. "So this is it?"

William slides his hand to mine and gives my fingers a gentle squeeze. "We can only hope."

I drop my focus back to the bridge. I don't know why it terrifies me, but it does.

I tell myself it's just a bridge. But the ghost woman staring at me, jumping to her death—she's telling me it's something more. Something worse.

❦

THE REAL DANGER OF THE BRIDGE ISN'T THE LEGEND. IT'S BEING out in the open, an easy mark for our enemies. About a quarter of way across the bridge, Morts start to spring up. First only one here or there, edging as far away from us as the bridge will allow, but then further along, more and more, until they've formed a small crowd.

"Why don't they move?" I whisper to William.

He leans down to whisper back. "Because they belong here. Now's not the time for us to move them. Stay close."

Soon we are so crowded we have to push through, and I can

feel their cold souls pressing against mine. But now is not the time to deal with them. Instinctively, I reach behind me and grab for Tess' hand. She allows me to take it, and I hold tight, not letting us get separated.

We are nearly halfway across the bridge when the Morts begin to disperse, and now they are lined up like soldiers on either side of the bridge. Many of them are fanged, but a few I can see were once Marked Ones. The bridge abruptly ends, and I stop so quickly that I nearly fall forward.

William stiffens. "What is it, Cord?"

"The bridge," I say, frantically looking at him, then back to the broken stone.

His brow furrows. "We're almost there. It would take longer to go back."

"Look," I say, pointing just a few feet ahead.

His attention trails to where I point. "What?"

Tess laughs. "Oh, no, Cord. Are you falling for another one of their illusions? I would have thought you knew better by now!"

"Illusions?" I ask. Almost immediately after I say the word, I remember when I first arrived here—the truck in the field. But when I try to push the illusion away, it doesn't budge. "What if it's you and William being affected?"

Tess rolls her eyes. "Not likely."

William gives my hand a gentle squeeze. "If we *must*, we can travel," he says, "but let's not jump to that now. I sense we're close, and we want to remain untraceable and save what energy we have left to get the woman out of this place...if we ever find her."

I stare at the gaping hole in the bridge once more, unable to shake my unease. Panic rises in my chest. I'm still new to traveling. What if one of these days I try and it doesn't work? If Tess is right —that I am being illusioned—then I am obviously growing weak. I have gone so long since my last illusion, that I'd forgotten it was even something I need to worry about.

"You're all right," William says. His lips brush against my

temple, warming my chilled skin. "You're with me. Just close your eyes and try not to think about it."

I take a deep breath, trying to get the nerve to step where my eyes tell me there is nothing to step on. Sweat dribbles like pebbles of ice down the back of my neck and spine.

"Come," he urges softly. "Trust me."

The words open up a new bravery in me. If I am strong enough to trust him, I am strong to overcome this. To overcome anything.

I step out into the air, still grasping his hand. My foot slides on a patch of stone I can't see, and William tightens his grip on me, holding my body tight against his.

"I got you," he says. "Come on."

Solid stone presses into the sole of my foot. Each step is less terrifying than the last, and it becomes easier to trust the ground is really there, even though I cannot see it. And the more I trust William, the more I trust myself, the more the illusion breaks away. I start to see the stone beneath me—ahead of me and behind me as it has always been.

When the bridge once again looks as solid as it feels, I run. I run hard and fast for the last quarter of the bridge, William and Tess running behind me until we reach the shelter of the forest canopy on the other side. The skeletal trees and their early-spring branches are a welcome change, and I marvel in the almost musical sound brought on by spring. There's the whisper-snap of bird wings, the yip and howl of wild dogs in the distance, and the rasp of our own breaths.

We made it.

I turn to William, a big grin breaking across my face and a smile lighting his own. Even Tess is smiling.

But our joy fades when a branch cracks in the not-so-far distance.

CHAPTER 30

APRIL 1692, JUST ACROSS DEVIL'S BRIDGE

WILLIAM HUNCHES ON A BED OF PINE NEEDLES AND LIFTS A finger to his lips. Tess and I squat quietly beside him, peering over the underbrush. It's only then I notice the shrunken heads hanging from the trees branches above. My stomach churns. Their grayish skin reminds me of melted wax, their eyes disproportionately large to the rest of the face and sunken in like small boulders in quicksand, their expressions twisted with anguish and mutilated by horror.

I imagine they might be Ankou that had been affected by the sunlight, and then later beheaded. Where are the rest of their bodies? Why were these heads hung here? Shuddering, I force my gaze past the tiny heads that dangle by their hair and to the campsite beyond.

About twenty-five feet away, obscured by the spruce, pine, and beech trees, a campfire blazes, surrounded by four men so large I can only assume they are Maltorim soldiers. Except for one. His skin has a golden glow not unlike our own.

Laughter echoes on the wind. I squint, and the simple action seems to enhance and sharpen my vision until it's as though the men are only a few feet away. Two of them have the Ansuz marking on their neck—Marked Strigoi. Instinctively, I hold my breath at the feeling of sudden closeness.

A breeze sweeping through their clearing kicks up the debris of crushed dead leaves, and the branches above us creak. The smoke of damp wood wafts toward us, and my skin starts to itch.

And that itch sends my mind back to my life as Rose. Camping with Pa for the first time...before the abuse began. I broke out in hives. An allergic reaction to burning cedar, the doctor later said. Back when my Pa still let me go to a doctor when I needed one.

I swallow hard, pushing away the memories that want to follow, knowing that I will have to face those memories one day soon enough, face them to return to Anna. But I don't need to face them today.

In my weakened allergic state, the world around me dims, the way one would expect of a darkness only punctured by moonlight. I scratch at the rash forming on my neck gently, trying not to make noise as I focus on the men in the clearing.

We're out of nightshade. I scour the ground, hoping to find something. Anything. On the other side of the path, I think I can just make out some rotted Daphne berries on the ground. I crawl toward them, but someone grabs my shoulder. I think it's Tess. I swat her away. I'm almost there.

The voices from the campsite grow louder, and I freeze, tensing. I try to breathe soundlessly. The voices quiet down again, and I continue forward, quickly but silently, until I reach the berries. The moment I lift them, they heal to near perfect ripeness, and I pop the sweet berries in my mouth and chew quickly, my rash almost instantly disappearing and the world around me brightening to my usual Ankou-gifted night vision. My eyes sting at the sudden shift.

Tess is looking at me with her eyebrows all twisted up. She jerks her head to the side, signalling for me to come back across. I wait until all the men in the clearing have their backs turned, then hurry back to William and Tess' side.

"Look," she whispers, and I cringe, hoping those men can't hear us. "Do you see that?"

She points to the Far East corner of the clearing that the Maltorim soldiers occupy. My vision steadies and clears. There's an eroded dirt path, uneven with embedded stones, and a horse-driven cart is tied to a nearby tree, its wheels cracked. The wooden cage it carries is covered with so many shrunken heads hanging from the bars that the person inside is nearly obscured.

But I see what Tess sees. A woman. Shackled.

"That must be her," Tess says quietly. "Sorry I doubted you."

"You did it, Cord," William whispers. "This is it!"

He's grinning, all the way up to his shining maple-syrup eyes. But there's something more there, too. A sense of awe, maybe? Is he...is he admiring me? For finding her?

"We couldn't have done it without Tess," I remind them.

She starts to stand, but William reaches out and gently touches her arm, and she settles back again.

"We risked a lot to make it this far." He sweeps his oaky-brown hair away from his eyes. "We can't just go rushing in."

"There's only four of them," she says. I count the same—one Cruor, two Strigoi, and one Ankou. They are bantering loudly by the fire.

"That we can see," William counters. "Not to mention one of them is Ankou."

"So?" she asks, shifting her long dark braid away from her face, over the back of her shoulder. "That's never been a problem before."

William glares. "Stop and think for a minute. An Ankou could have transported her by traveling. But they didn't."

My mind grinds the idea, trying to make sense of what it could mean. "Why didn't they, then?"

William rubs his hand over his face, shaking his head. "I don't know. They must not have been able to travel her. And if they couldn't, then we might not be able to either. Which means we can't draw attention to ourselves."

Tess snorts. "Kidnap the Maltorim's most valued possession without drawing attention to ourselves?"

I close my eyes and take a deep breath. William is right, but at the same time, we need to act fast.

"I can distract them," I whisper. "It would draw attention to me, but it would also draw attention away from both of you."

William presses his hands against his thighs. "I don't think that's a good idea, Cord."

"Would it work?" I ask.

"Yes, but you can't—"

Before he can finish his thought, I dart into the woods, ducking beneath low-hanging limbs, leaping over fallen trees, and hopping between large stones embedded in the forest ground. I have to do this. We don't have time to spare thinking up the impossible; we need to get this girl and get out of here.

I curve to the right, sweeping around their campsite close enough to be both seen and heard. As I peek over my shoulder to ensure I've captured their attention, the red bands of my hair whip into my face.

"Hey!" shouts the heavy-set Cruor, stumbling to his feet from a log beside the campfire.

He pushes the shoulder of one of his comrades and points in my direction. The two pursue me with inhuman speed, a little faster than me but not nearly as agile. The Strigoi falls upon me first, and I pounce upward and twist, grab a tree branch, and swing toward him. My feet knock into his chests, sending him to the ground in a heap, before I pull myself the rest of the way on top of the tree.

One of the men—a broad-shouldered Cruor—catches up, only slightly slower than his comrade, and rushes at the tree trunk. He hits it with such force that the roots are ripped from the ground, leaning the tree into another larger tree nearby. I hadn't accounted for the strength of the Cruor, the strongest of the elementals. I leap from one branch to the next, and although this agility and strength is new to me, it feels natural.

For a fleeting moment, as I am suspended in the air between two branches, I want this life. I want to be here, where I am strong instead of vulnerable. Where I fight back instead of cower away. Where there are bad men, but there are good men, too. Where I don't have to hate myself.

But then my body is thumping into another tree, and Anna's presence in my heart reminds me where this strength came from and what I'm really fighting for. I will return to her, and I will bring this strength with me.

I flip backward from the tree and land solidly behind the two men. The auburn-haired Strigoi is up now, and he swings around and lands a blow to my face. But the impact only serves to anger me. Motivate me. I duck as he swings again, and in one swift movement, I crouch down, retrieve the stakes I keep tied to my ankles, and plunge the splintered wood into their hearts.

The result on the Marked One is very different from the Cruor. The Strigoi takes an animal form, lying as a dead mountain lion, where the skin on the Cruor braches out in black veins and ultimately decomposes to a pile of black ash.

The moment hits me like a cool wind in the midst of a Georgia heat wave, and all of a sudden, I feel like myself again. Like Rose instead of Abigail's imposter. It's invigorating! Allowing my Ferrum nature to guide me, I snap my teeth to their razor points. I can do this. I can conquer this world. I just have to stop fighting who I am and what I'm meant to do here.

The stakes, now covered in blood, *squick* as I tug them from the bodies, and my heart pounds in my chest as I watch their spirits lift. I snap my arms in front of me, through them, bringing their spirits to a final puff of black death.

Three sets of footsteps pound behind me, and I spin around. Tess and William are barreling toward me with a young, raven-haired child in tow.

"Go!" William shouts.

But I'm frozen. Staring.

The spirit elemental is a child?

I'm shocked all over again, just like I had been with the Oracle, but there's no time to process the thought. William and Tess and the child are storming closer.

Behind them, one of the Maltorim soldiers—the other Marked Strigoi—chases us, and I turn hard and run. When William and Tess catch up, I see the bleeding wound in William's side and the deep gash on Tess' thigh that peeks through a rip in her dress. I dip back just long enough to hook my arm around the raven-haired girl to help her so that William and Tess can focus on their own escape.

A waterfall roars up ahead. I keep checking back over my shoulder, my alarm growing as one of the soldiers comes up close on Tess' right side. She doesn't seem to notice.

"Tess!" I scream, but the thunder of the waterfall drowns out my cry.

She squints at me, and there's such innocence there, in those long, dark, fine eyelashes. I can't let her die.

"Beside you!" I scream louder.

This time she stoops down mid run and spins, sweeping out her leg to trip the soldier, then she's up and darting toward me again. But this only momentarily slows the soldier, who is already nearly closing in on us again. He shoots several arrows through the air.

At first, I think all three shots have missed. But as Tess spins around and raises her sword to the man, the spirit elemental beside me grunts.

One of the arrows is sticking out of her chest, just left of center, having impaled her though her back. Tess decapitates the man as I crumble to the ground with a dying child in my arms. For the first time, I get a good look at her. Her haunting eyes, shining with fear; her smooth, milky skin; her bright red lips; her large, deep brown eyes. Her tiny nose and thick, dark eyelashes, and her hair a river of black streaming along her cheeks and down to her chest.

William leans back against a tree, gripping his side, and slumps to the ground. Tess falls beside him, wincing as she reaches into her pack to retrieve some herbs.

"That was the last one," she says, and then she stares into the forest.

Her face and chest is covered in blood. I watch as the Marked Strigoi transforms to a beheaded hawk, wondering what passerby would make of it. What they would make of any of what we leave behind today. William kills the Strigoi's spirit and turns to us with closed eyes.

"We need to move," he says, opening his eyes. "The Ankou that's helping the Maltorim ran off. If won't be long now before more soldiers are after us."

I shake my head, looking at the girl in my arms. We can't lose her. Not now. Not after we've come all this way, risked so much.

"We'll get you help," I promise her, but even as I say the words I know it's too late.

Her hand grasps a locket around her neck. She smiles up at me. "Thank you for saving me."

The doubt of that statement must be clear on my face.

"I know I shan't live," she whispers, "but you did save me. You saved me from doing something I didn't want to do. This death is a kindness."

Maybe that would be enough for William or Tess. Enough that we at least stopped the Maltorim from using her to do harm. But it's not enough for me. I wanted to save her. I *needed* to save her. But I failed. And if I failed her, I fear I may fail Anna.

"Stay with me," I plead with her. "What's your name? Tell me your name?"

The girl's eyes flutter closed. She's still smiling. She is the peace I wish I felt within myself. Particles of light swirl up from her body, glimmering like gold dust in the moonlight. A cool mist escapes her lips and billows toward me, and I can feel her presence —no longer in my arms, with her body, but instead in the air between us. It presses into my skin with a weightlessness, a tingling energy, and I know it's her spirit. She's giving it to me.

It scares me at first, though it's nothing at all the way it felt when one of the Morts tried to possess me back in Salem. The Oracle's words come rushing back.

I see a gift for you on this journey, she says. *It could be the end of your life or the beginning of your future...Trust your heart.*

This must be that gift. And somehow, I know exactly what this gift is. Her spirits speaks to me not with words but with a sense of knowing. I can allow her spirit to become one with mine, or I can allow it to pass through me. Keeping it could give me the power to put an end to this war, but it could also mean never returning to Anna. I can't risk never making it back to Anna, and I might never make it back to Anna without the power to end this war. My heart tells me I only have one hope, one risky hope.

I must accept this gift.

HAVING TAKEN COVER, WE REST. WILLIAM AND TESS HAVE assumed that somehow the spirit elemental had no spirit for us to move, and I haven't told them otherwise. Not yet. Not until I understand what it all means.

William leans back against the stone of our cavern, sleeping, and I rest with my head against his shoulder. I sense his comfort and know my own, but I tell myself we are just both too tired to move. That's why we are snuggled close. Not because we simply want to enjoy these forbidden moments that we know can't last forever.

Tess pokes at a dish full of herbs. She's the only one who hasn't taken any real action to heal her wounds.

"What happened back there?" I ask.

She coughs. "Hmm?"

"It was as though you didn't see that soldier coming up beside you."

"Oh?" she says, raising her eyebrows. "Huh."

"Huh?" I pull away from William, tucking up my legs and leaning on my knees. "That's it? 'Huh.' He was practically right beside you."

"Yeah...so what?" she says. "You're upset that I didn't notice every last detail while trying to *run for my life?*"

I press my lips together, assessing her carefully. "There's something you aren't telling me."

"Fine," she says, pushing her disk of herbs aside and leveling her gaze at me. "I'm blind in my left eye, okay? It was as though I didn't see him because I *didn't*. And I couldn't hear him over the waterfall. That's it. No big deal."

Seems like a big deal to me. "Why didn't you say something sooner?"

"What difference would it have made?" Her face twists in anger. "Can you change it? Will you be here when everything is said and done? No, Cord. I don't owe you anything. No explanations, no heartfelt confessions. *Nothing.*"

With that, she stands, steps over her pack, and storms out of the cavern.

❧

WHILE TESS IS GONE AND WILLIAM IS SLEEPING, I AM LEFT with a lot of time to think. It used to be that my thoughts would always go to what few memories I have of Anna. Now, though, my heart is divided, and I feel like the worst mother ever. I've left my daughter behind and allowed myself to care about someone other than her—someone that isn't a part of her world. I know mothers do this all the time, but it's different for me. Anna is the only one I should care about, because in the end, it's her world or this one, and I will choose hers, even if it means leaving William and Tess behind. We all know this. And perhaps we all hurt over this.

I open my pack and pull out the doll William gave me for her. I run my fingers over her ragdoll hair. It makes my heart ache to reunite with Anna, but once I'm with her, seeing this doll will make my heart ache to reunite with William. As I smooth out the skirt of the doll's dress, a vision rockets across my mind.

I'm looking down at a baby girl in wooden cradle, but she's not my own.

I reach out and place something beside her. It's the doll. My hands, resting on the doll as I secure its place beside the infant, are so small. Childish. Nails bitten short and dirt packed underneath. The baby smiles up at me with razor-sharp teeth, and I startle, stepping back, thudding into something behind me. A strong hand comes down on my shoulder.

"Nothing to fear, my son," comes the deep voice behind me. "It is a gift. Our family has been blessed."

"Is she...is she...all right?" I look back over my shoulder and up to the man above me. He has kind eyes. I trust him. "Does it hurt?"

The man smiles and rubs his hands roughly on my shoulders. "It doesn't hurt her," he says, "and it won't hurt you. But it will hurt any Mort that comes near our family."

I turn back to the baby and gently caress the back of my finger along her cheek. She giggles a squealy, high-pitched giggle, and her whole body twists with excitement. "I won't let anything happen to you," I tell her, my little-boy voice maturing a decade's worth in that sentence alone. "Nothing ever. I promise."

❦

As William tumbles out of his sleep, I'm jarred from the vision. I gasp, sucking in air as though I'd been drowning in those memories that aren't my own.

William goes from sleepy-eyed to panicked and alert in mere moments. He grabs my shoulders. "Are you all right? What happened?"

I stare into his eyes with searching gravity. "You had a...sister?"

The last word comes out in a whisper, and William's Adam's apple bobs. I can't read his expression. Hurt? Anger?

"Who told you that?" he asks coldly, jaw tensing.

I look down at the doll in my hands and flop her back. I stare into the doll's eyes and struggle to get out the words. "She did."

Silence hangs like a thick fog in the room: heavy, pressuring, suffocating.

I return my attention to William, but his face is still twisted in that same heartbreaking expression. "Say something. Please."

He shakes his head and stands. "Why would you lie to me, Cord? Why? About this of all things?"

I clamber to my feet as well, letting the doll drop to the floor between us. He crouches down slowly and lifts the doll, eyes never leaving it.

I reach out to touch his arm, but he yanks away.

"Please, William. I'm not lying. I saw it through your eyes, as a child, looking down on her. I just did. I'm not making this up!"

He steps closer to me. Threateningly close. And though I feel his anger radiating off of him, I'm not afraid. He's the one person I just *know* I never have to fear, no matter how angry he might get. I stare up at him boldly.

"I'm not lying," I repeat.

His gaze is boring into mine with such intensity—such determination to make me crumble and confess who really told me about his sister. But I have no other answer to offer. He has to see that. He *has* to.

"Just take it," he says, shoving the doll back into my arms. "And don't ever lie to me again, or I swear I'll...I'll..."

I raise my eyebrow, but he's stuck stammering. I tilt my head. "What, William? *What* will you do?"

He steps back. "Nothing," he mumbles. "I'll do *nothing*."

I sense what he means by that. He won't help me anymore. I would be on my own getting back to Anna.

Why is he so upset about me knowing about his sister? Why didn't he just tell me about her himself? She was Ferrum, like me— he could have been helping me all this time. It's not like I don't already know what happened to his family. What could be so much worse?

He moves to where Tess had rested earlier, his eyes shooting daggers at me from across the room. His anger makes me feel small. Alone. I slink back to the floor and tuck my knees to my chest.

I haven't done anything wrong. I don't know what he thinks, but right now, I need his help, not his disapproval. I touch the tree pendant on the necklace he gave me and think of all the moments before this one. It was leading somewhere. Not to this, never to this. I wish I could say it would make leaving easier, but it won't. My finger slips over the tree engraving on the wood chip, and my mind buzzes and tunnels and another vision starts with William's father looking down at me, hand outstretched, dropping the tree medallion on a leather string into my awaiting palm.

"This talisman..."

I'm shaking and William is in front of me.

"Stop! Cord, let it go, please."

I shake my head, the vision clearing away, and I drop the talisman.

"Right," I mumble, "you probably want this back."

I remove the necklace from over my head and hand it to him.

He looks down at it and shakes his head. "No, that's not it." His eyes shift back to mine. "I'm sorry, Cord. I hadn't even considered...has this...happened before?"

"The visions?" I ask.

He nods.

"The one about your...sister...that was the first."

He grips the talisman tighter in his hand. "You're reading memories from objects," he says. "Psychometry. But you had to get that from somewhere. Do you have an idea where? What happened when you were in jail? No, never mind. It had to be after that."

He's not looking right at me, brow furrowed.

I gently touch his arm. "Could it be the girl we tried to save?"

"The spirit elemental? Do you have reason to think it has something to do with her? Is there something you didn't tell us?"

I shrug. "I felt something happen when she died." My heart clenches as my memories relive the scene, focus me on my failure. "It reminded me of what the Oracle said, about someone giving me a gift."

"We don't know much about spirit elementals. Could they transfer over their abilities? I guess it's possible...but I don't know."

"Don't sound so sure," I say bitterly. "Is it so bad to think this girl didn't' die for nothing?"

"I never said she died for nothing," he says sharply. "We stopped them from using her to hurt others. Isn't that something enough?"

I scowl at him. "No, it's not enough."

"I know," he says, shaking his head. I'm relieved to see some grief in his eyes. "Just please, give me one moment. I think I know something that might make sense of this." William strides away, still holding the talisman in one hand, then retrieves a book from his pack. He slides rapidly through the pages, freezes at one and, after a long moment, joins me once more. "Look at this."

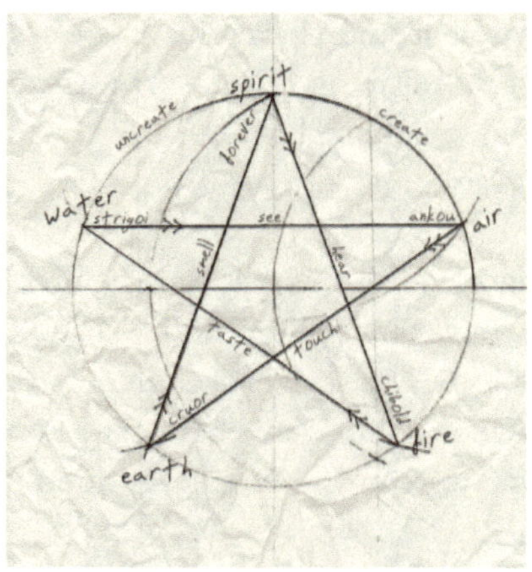

"Hmmm..." I try to make sense of it, but fail. "What does it mean?" I point to a few of the words. "These are the different elementals?"

William rubs the heels of his hands into his eyes, then settles next to me with the open book. "It's an explanation of sorts. More of a theory, really, because we can't confirm anything about the Forever Girls, but the rest of it holds up. My father created it."

"An explanation?"

"Yes. Look at the arrows." He points to them. "Spirit rules over fire; fire over water; water over air; air over earth; earth over spirit."

"But water puts out a fire."

"This isn't science, Cord," William says darkly. "It's talking about what elements we can control. See, as Ankou, we are *of* the air. But many Ankou have extra abilities relating to the earth, such as our ability to heal it."

I point to a few other words. "What do these senses indicate then?"

"What connects us," he says. "Now here's the other part. They rumored only one Forever Girl would be solely in the spirit. The rest are also grounded in other elements. This means most likely the girl we tried to save was another element. I don't think the only gift you would have gotten would be psychometry."

"How do we know which one then?"

"We test it." He leaves my side and returns moments later with a dish of water and a candle. "You can tap into your Ferrum nature now, right?"

"A little."

He pushes the candle over. "Channel whatever emotion does that, and try creating a wind to put it out or encourage the flame to grow."

I try. Nothing happens.

"We already know you have control over the earth from your Ankou nature," he says. That's how we heal things. So let's try the water." He slides over the small dish. "Touch it and see if anything happens."

I do as I'm told. All that happens is my finger gets wet. "Maybe all she gave me was that one gift."

William presses his fist to his mouth and stares at the two items. "No, I'm sure it's something else. It has to be."

"Why, William? Why does it have to be?"

As I avert my attention to the page William is looking at now, I regret my words. Scribbled next the image is a letter addressed to William and signed *Your Loving Father*.

These were his father's theories. This is the only way his father lives on.

"I could try harder," I suggest.

William's face contorts in disgust as he slams the book shut. "No, forget it." He returns the book to his pack and sits with his back against the wall. "I don't know what I was thinking."

I scoot closer. "I know what you were thinking," I say. "Maybe you're right. It makes sense. I'm just new to this. Give me some time. Or maybe she was also Ankou, so it just didn't change things for me."

He nods, but he won't look at me. "Do me a favor, Cord?"

"Sure," I say hesitantly. "What do you need?"

"I want you to keep the talisman, but my memories of my father—they're personal. There's something you can do to severe yourself from your psychometry with an object, but it cannot be undone. Will you do it?" He swivels his head toward me. "For me?"

I shrug one shoulder. "Yeah," I say. "Yeah, I could do that."

William explains what I must do, and the magic is simple. A small incantation while I hold the object and pass it over fire. It only works, he tells me, if I do it myself. I have to willingly surrender my ability to read this object.

I pass the object over the fire. "Deditionem. Oblitus. Dele."
Surrender. Forget. Erase.

Then, as William explains I must, I prick my finger and squeeze a drop of blood onto the object and then use another drop of blood to extinguish the candle's flame.

And just like that, it is done.

William takes the talisman and runs his fingers over it once more. He presses it into my hands and grasps his hands over mine. He looks down into my eyes. "Promise me, Cord. Promise you will keep this forever."

"I will." I stare at it a long while before slipping the necklace around my neck. "Can I control what I see as easily as what I don't?"

William shakes his head. "Maybe eventually, but many with the gift never get that far. The visions come when they come. You can block them from coming, as I taught you, but you cannot make them come. That relies on your compatibility with the object."

"I see," I say, even though I really don't see at all. I suppose it's like most things; not really important unless it gets me back to Anna. I'll figure out the psychometry as it becomes necessary to do so. I bite my lip, trying to work up the courage to say what I need to say. "I want you to do something for me now."

"Anything I can do for you, I will."

"I want to stop ignoring this." I wave my finger back and forth between him and me. "Us. You are the only thing in this world that doesn't terrify me."

"Cord—"

"No excuses. I'm not asking for forever, William. But I need us to be what we are without letting lifetimes stand between us. I need it to be all right, just for now, or I will go home from this place with a part of me left behind."

"That had to be the one thing you ask for?" His eyes droop in the corners. His mouth sags into a frown. "I can't pretend I don't care about you—can't pretend you don't fill that void in my life, bring back to life the essence of the family I have lost—but it complicates things."

I shake my head slowly. "It's already complicated, William. I'm the one who has to leave this behind."

"I know," he says sadly. "But if you think it would hurt you to leave a part of yourself behind, imagine how it would hurt me if you took all I had in me with you."

He says the words—words that should rebuild that wall between us—but instead it all comes crashing down. The longer he stares into my eyes, the closer his body comes to mine. My heart skips so fast in my chest I think I have forgotten what it feels like to breathe.

"Damn it, Cordovae," he says.

And then, his lips meet mine, and rain tumbles from the sky like marbles falling from the heavens.

I get lost in the kiss. The way his mouth presses to mine, the way his tongue prods gently at my own and slides over my teeth. I sink into his arms and wrap mine over his shoulders and around his neck. His hands trail up my sides but hesitate and ultimately freeze just below my breasts. My breathing hitches, and the kiss slows. He breaks away.

"You all right, Cordovae?"

I nod. His kiss proves things can be right between a man and a woman. It proves that I can be aroused instead of repulsed by a man's touch. But at the same time, I am all at once shy. I'm not sure what happens now. I stare out the cavern's mouth and watch the rain. For now, this is all right, and that's all that matters.

William points to the sky. "No clouds."

The words sit between us another moment. Forming something.

"No clouds!" he says again, louder this time, and he picks me up and swings me around, then gets his father's book and opens it to the diagram again. "I knew it! Cordovae—look!"

I stare down at the pages. The spirit elemental—she must have been Chibold. Ruling over water.

What that means for me, I don't know, but William is smiling, and that makes me happy.

CHAPTER 32
APRIL 1692

WE SETTLE BY THE FIRE, AND I CAN'T STOP LOOKING OUT THE cavern. Yes, the rain was magical, but I'm more concerned by what—or rather who—I hadn't seen.

"I hope Tess is okay."

William takes my hand in his. "She just doesn't want to be seen as weak," he says. "What happened, anyway?"

I tell him about the conversation.

"She doesn't like anyone knowing, that's all."

"But if I had known—"

He places his finger to my lips, silencing me. "Then you would look out for her better?" he asks. He doesn't wait for me reply. "That's exactly what she *doesn't* want."

"And you?" I ask. "What's your weakness?"

"You," he says, his tone only half-joking, his lopsided smile curling up a little more on one side. "Cord, I know you will leave me to return to Anna. I understand it, but I am still angry for the cards we've been dealt."

"Sorry," I whisper. I swallow around the lump in my throat. "I wish I could stay...that Anna was here."

"Don't be sorry. Just don't make this harder for me. I've seen enough people come and go."

"Can't we enjoy what time we do have?" I ask, but already I know the answer. We don't have the time to enjoy whatever is happening between us. Our moment has passed.

He smiles at me sadly, offering a certain kindness in his silence. He sits up and wraps his strong arms around me, pulling my back into his chest, and I rest my hand on the forearm he has draped over my shoulder.

"You're a strong woman," he says. "Strong enough to break a man like me."

WHEN TESS RETURNS, I TELL HER ABOUT THE GIFT THE SPIRIT elemental gave me. The gift of her spirit joining with mine, the psychometry, the chibold abilities.

Tess chews on her thumbnail. "What does it mean?" Her hand drops away from her face. "Does this mean you are a spirit elemental now? Are you still Ankou?"

William sips at a canteen filled with animal blood that Tess has brought back for him. "She's still Ankou."

"I don't feel any different," I admit. "Not now, not like I felt while it was happening. I don't have much control over it, either."

"Then it doesn't really change much," Tess says, "does it?"

William stands and helps me to my feet. "We don't know," he says. "Maybe it changes nothing, maybe it changes everything. But right now we have nothing to rely on. It won't be long now before the Maltorim find us, and we can't risk *traveling* right now or we might have a collapse."

My brow tightens, and I frown. "I thought we only sleep every decade?"

"Normally, yes. But excessive traveling can cause an early collapse. You might be all right as you had one not long ago, when you were reborn as Ankou. But Tess and I have already gone nearly eight years since our last."

"Then where do we go?" I ask. "We still have a lot of Morts to move."

William tosses his items into his pack and slings it over his shoulder. "We'll have to find other Ankou. Help them for a while until things settle down in Salem. Then we can return there. Hopefully the damage won't be too far done by then."

"We can't do that," I say. "We don't have the time. *I* don't have time!"

He reaches out to gently touch my arm, but I snap myself away. His expression falls, but he doesn't say anything. He turns and heads into the forest. Tess stares at me as though I just killed a kitten and follows him outside.

My whole self is shutting down. I don't know where to go, and I know my best hope is to stay with them until I figure out what I'm going to do. Fear twists knots in my stomach. What if I never figure out what to do? What if I never get back from here...get back to Anna?

I grab my pack and take a shaky breath, then start after William and Tess. As soon as I step out into the woods, I'm grabbed from behind and yanked behind a large berry bush, a hand pressed firmly over my mouth.

"Shhh." It's William. Slowly he releases me and lifts a finger to his lips.

Tess elbows me and points into the shadows draping between the trees. Fresh young flowers are springing up along the deer paths, giving the false appearance of a beautiful world in bloom. Weaving between the trees are Morts and Maltorim soldiers. We can't even risk going back into our shelter, as stepping out into the open again only further risks us being discovered.

The darkness of the night sky pales, and I know we don't have much time to relocate. But nor do the Cruor following us have much time before they need to seek shelter themselves.

Tess tugs my sleeve and tilts her head to indicate a small passage in the trees behind us. I glance back to William, who gives a reaffirming nod and nudges me to follow Tess.

We walk a few yards before Tess spins back to face us. "They have Marked Strigoi with them," she says in a warning tone. "That's the last thing we need. We'll have to find a new shelter, but first we need to lose them."

She crouches down and digs her hands into the soil, then starts to rub it over her dress and skin. William does the same, and I follow suit. The soil is sticky from pollen and rain.

"This is to cover to our scent?" I ask.

Tess rolls her eyes. "No, I just like playing with dirt."

William stands. "Let's go."

But we don't make it another two feet before we nearly walk into a large wolf blocking our path, growling.

William yanks me to the side and starts running, nearly dragging me along, Tess right ahead of us. "Faster!" he yells. "Go, go, go."

The first rays of sunlight are already starting to peek over the tree tops in the distance. I don't care what William and Tess think, we're going to have to *travel*. I just don't know where we're going to go. I don't know where we could ever be safe now.

The wolf is joined by a leopard, both barreling behind us, and then a hawk dipping overhead. It seems to only be the three of them. The Cruor must have already taken shelter nearby.

Our feet shuffle over the deer path. William and Tess' heavy breaths are like thunder in my ears. The legs of the Strigoi in our pursuit whip through tall grass.

They're everywhere.

The world around me turns gray and black, the ground and trees turning to crumbling decay. Panic races through my chest. The forest is dying right before my eyes. Everything falls away to barren, cold, black desert of cracked earth.

"*Illusions*, Cord!" Tess screams from somewhere ahead of me.

But I can't see her. I can't see William. I can't see anything real, and suddenly it's like I'm running blind, feeling my way through the forest, branches whipping at my stomach. I am nearly winded as I crash into a tree and push my way around it, feeling the cold rough bark, trying to envision what is really ahead of me.

There's not a hint of life anywhere in sight, but the scent of wildflowers brings me back. The aroma of spring breaking through winter, the taste of honey on the air. Slick leaves slide under my feet, twigs snag at my hair, and hanging moss tickles coolly against my face and neck.

Slowly, my vision forces its way back, and I can see Tess and William ahead of me, looking back at me over their shoulders, and I can hear the animalistic growls of the wolf and leopard behind us.

I run harder, my legs burning, my skin tingling, almost itching. Smoke blooms up ahead, but forward is the only clear path for us to take. The smoke is so thick I'm choking now, even as I run, and the itching is intensifying—must be cedar smoke. But the lack of oxygen sends thoughts flooding into my mind.

There was a way for Adrian, a Cruor, to walk in a field of dandelions. The Maltorim has already used the magic of the Ankou and the blood of a spirit elemental to control the Morts. Now they plan to use the magic of a spirit elemental and the blood of the Ankou to walk in the sun.

If only we *could walk in the sun . . .*

As we break out into an open field, the pressure of the sun tingles my skin, but the real heat is from the fire surrounding us. A forest fire. How did all that wet wood catch fire?

I cough on the smoke and resist the urge to scratch the hives welting on my arms and neck. Through the billows of gray, I can't see very far in any direction, but William comes up beside me and takes my hand. Patterns of light shift behind him, and I can't tell if it's the daylight through the forest canopy or the dance of the fire.

"Where are they?" I whisper between my coughing fits.

But as soon as the words leave my lips, I sense them behind me. William and I spin around and back further into the clearing. William feels heavier next to me, holding my hand, and I know the sunlight torches him, though it is not bothering me in the same way it had before. With the impending completion of sunrise, my bones do little more than ache.

I can't see Tess, and my heart beats out of my chest. Where is she? Where's Tess? My mind screams her name, but I can't do anything other than stare at the glowing eyes of the Strigoi—only the leopard and wolf visible now—as they prowl closer.

The hawk falls to a patch of wild mushrooms on the ground in front of us, dead.

"Got him," Tess says from somewhere behind us.

I'm trembling with the urge to turn around and look at her, to get the visual confirmation that she is all right, but I can't take my eyes off our attackers. I ball my hands into tight fists as the smoke burns my lungs and makes my throat itch.

My wings tingle along my spine, and that is my only real indication that the sun has taken full effect in the clearing. The wolf and the leopard back away, whimpering, and it's only then I dare a glance over my shoulder.

The fires have smoldered. The smoke is dissipating. And Tess and William are staring at me wide-eyed from the shade of my veined, amniotic wings.

"*Your wings*," she whispers.

I turn toward her. "What?"

Tess grabs my wrist. "Come on," she says. "We have to get out of here."

❦

NOT FAR FROM THE BURNT-DOWN CLEARING IS A LARGE waterfall, and we take shelter just behind the wall of rushing water. When we are sure we haven't been followed, we sit on the moist stone and catch our breath. Already my hives are clearing. Tess passes over the nightshade for me to replenish myself, and William sips at what is left in his canteen.

"How did you do that?" she asks. "Your wings...their shade completely blocked the sunlight."

I press my lips together. "I had been thinking a little before that, if we could walk in the sun...this would be so much easier. There aren't as many Strigoi as Cruor with the Maltorim. We could do more work during the day."

William nods, but he's frowning. "That would be great, but if you don't know how you did it, you can't replicate the effect. Unless your wings are just that way now—from joining with the spirit elemental."

I chew quietly on the nightshade, inspecting each small berry before popping it into my mouth. A beetle crawls across one of the twigs. There's an answer here, somewhere. "There's always an exception, a way around the rule. Adrian and the dandelion field, for example."

"Sure, if you know what to do."

"The Maltorim were going to use our blood with the magic of the spirit elemental to walk in the sun. So there's a way, and it has to do with our essence and the spirit elemental's."

Tess bites her lip and tilts her head slowly side to side. "The Ankou were once trapped by daylight and not moonlight. It could have something to do with that. But that can only be reversed at the change of the century."

William presses on his knuckles until they crack. "We need to find out more about what the Maltorim are trying to do," he says. "If we had more answers—"

"No," I say, then I turn toward him and Tess. "All we've been doing since I arrived is running and hiding and trying to find answers. There's been no progress—only avoiding an inevitable defeat. We are still outnumbered and that will never change, will it?"

William frowns. "We just need time to—"

"No more sneaking around," I say. "No more running, no more hiding. Remember what you told me? *Whatever you do, fight.* I was brought here to fight, and fighting is the only way I am getting out of here."

"We're only trying to keep you safe," he says.

Tess rolls her eyes. "*You* are only trying to keep her safe," she snaps. "And that is not what we are supposed to do."

William's eyes are steady on mine, as though Tess has not even spoken, and my heart flutters. He takes my hand in both of his. "I admire your willingness to fight. I've let my feelings get in the way while at the same time trying to keep you at a distance. But I got it backwards, didn't I? I should have let you in while staying true to my calling. But I can't help how I feel, and I can't risk our lives without you knowing how I feel."

I smile at him sadly. "You don't need to tell me how you feel. I already know. And you know how I feel...about you, *and* about my daughter. Fighting is my only way back to her."

"And that is all you want," he says, dropping my hand, his eyes begging me to tell him otherwise.

I want to tell him that I want it all. I want Anna...and I want him. But that's not what I say.

"It's what I want *most*."

I know it means leaving him behind, and that thought stabs in my chest. I can't live with the pain of losing them both, but I have to be willing to lose one of them. Without William, my heart will ache indefinitely, but without my daughter, I cannot live.

"You're both so horribly lovely," Tess says, standing between us. "I'm with Cord. We should fight. Worry about the rest later. I say we test Cord's new ability and lure the Morts and Cruor out during the day."

William opens his mouth, but I can't let him speak. We need to stay focused. I lock eyes with Tess. "So we bait them. Can they sense I'm a spirit elemental or only that I'm Ankou?"

"Use you as bait?" William shakes his head. "Is that what you're suggesting?"

"You two can stay close by."

"They'd be happy to capture any of us," William counters. "Let me do it."

"I'm clearly better bait," I say. "They'll know I have less experience as an Ankou."

Tess chews her lip, avoiding eye contract. I stare at her, waiting for her to take my side.

"What do you think?" I press.

She's twitching her foot in an irritated way, but not saying anything, until finally she looks up to glare at William. "Are you going to tell her?"

"We still have other options," he says.

She raises her eyebrows, and now I'm the one glaring at him. "I think I should be able to decide, whatever it is."

"Not now," he says more firmly.

"I will do this alone if I have to," I say, anger building in my chest. "If you want to help, you need to be honest with me. Stop trying to protect me!"

"Stop needing me to," he says, his eyebrows pulling lower of his eyes. He immediately shakes his head as though that can erase his words. "That's wrong," he says. "You're strong, Cord. *You* don't need me to protect you, but *I* need to."

I understand now that his anger is his only defense; it both worries and endears me to him that he cares so much to protect me that he would rather me be cross with him. But I can't let it go. Not now. I swallow, trying to keep my emotions at bay. "This isn't about what you need."

"Nor is it about what you need," he says smoothly. "I've stood by while many people fighting this same battle have died. I blame myself for not putting an end to it, but there was always someone new...someone else who could fight this war."

"Then fight with me," I challenge him.

He looks away. "Not everyone can be replaced. Sometimes there are people...sometimes...Cord—" He breathes out slow. "—I can't stop you if you want to fight, so of course I will fight beside you. But is that what you really want? To risk your *life*?"

I steel myself against his words, trying to keep my expression unreadable. He is the first man I've ever felt I could trust with my heart. But can I trust him to allow me to decide my own fate, to allow me to face the Maltorim, whatever the consequences may be, so that I can take the only chance I have to get back to Anna?

When I don't respond, William lifts my hand with his fingers. "We could try something else first. Something with less risk."

"We don't have time to try other things first," I plead. "If we are going to take a risk, now is the time to take it."

"If you fail, you will never have the chance to return to Anna."

"And if I don't try, the same will still be true. *You* told me that. At least if we try, I have a chance."

He presses his lips together and stares past Tess. Determination sets his expression, replacing all his previous hesitation. "We will have to get rid of the Morts, too, and that includes the ones already possessing human flesh," he says. "We won't be able to attempt any healing until after the fight is over. Be prepared that some innocent people may die waiting."

"So we work fast," I say optimistically. "Just tell me what we need to do."

CHAPTER 33
APRIL 1692

WE DO NOT WAIT FOR NIGHTFALL. WILLIAM DRINKS SOME OF Tess' blood to help counteract the Cruor side of his nature. He can only drink so much without weakening her, but it should buy us a few hours. We set up an altar in a large clearing near the ocean, in the place where it all began, where I first met William and Tess. I know it's the same field because the tree stump in the middle of the clearing is unmistakable, seemingly made of many thinner tree trunks woven together.

I have everything I need—even the witch's ladder is still in the pocket of my dress, available to me in the event I ever need it again.

I act under the direction of William and Tess, while they hide beneath the shade of my wings. The sunlight is uncomfortable, but there is a distinct difference from how I feel now to how I've felt in my history as an Ankou when touched by the sun's rays.

Now that I've got a handle on my Ferrum nature, I'm counting the minutes in clicks of my teeth. Snap out. Snap in. Snap out. Snap in. The Cruor's fangs seem like child's play by comparison.

Since we're performing moon magic, and the moon has such a pull on the tides, we've chosen a ritual connected to the element of water. My command of this element has been strongest since I've joined spirits with the spirit elemental, and I sense my connection with her is our only hope.

Our altar, a flat-surfaced rock, faces west, encircled by large white oval stones. On it is a silver flask filled with water and a moonstone engraved with the raiðo rune—the rune of journey. William has made dragon's blood by mixing water with a red powder he derived from the stem of a dragon's tree found on the little-known island of Socotra—one of the few travels we have *had* to make. Floating in the dragon's blood is a white lotus flower.

William steps up behind me, takes my wrists, and crosses them over my chest. "Close your eyes," he whispers. "Imagine the full moon. Imagine her beauty, imagine her as a reflection of yourself."

My heart flutters. I allow my body to relax against his, my head leaning back into his chest. "You are universal and constant," I say aloud, and I try to envision the moon, not William, as I say this. "In the dark of night, you shine down upon us and bathe us in your light."

"Stay steady," William instructs. "I'm going to share my energy with you now."

His fingers intertwine with mine, his palms cool against the backs of my hands. This magic has nothing to do with being Ankou; it's a ritual his father wrote based on Pagan traditions. Together, we raise our arms up, and a surge of energy—a palpable tingle—travels down my arms, covers my breasts, and spreads to my stomach.

"I am the wind in the sky," I say, recalling the words Tess had me memorize, "the spark in the fire, the seedling in the earth, the water in the river."

As William's energy continues to course through me, it's as though a magnetic force is weaving itself around our bodies, and there is both comfort and fear in that—the comfort of having him, the fear of losing him—but I don't let it deter me.

"I am the sun and the moon, together on this day," I say.

Speaking the words aloud, I start to believe them. That somehow, with William at my side, I see the beauty and perfection within myself. And I want more now. I want more than my life with Anna back. I want to share my gift with William. With the world.

After a deep breath, William releases my hands, and I pluck the lotus flower from the dragon's blood and eat it.

William breathes in deeply again, and my lungs act with his. He whispers close to my ear, sending shivers down my spine. "Feel the power within you," he says. "When you are ready, you can conclude."

The energy is welling within me like a chattering in my soul. My own. William's. The spirit elemental's. My passion. My love. My pain. My joy. Until finally the emotions are on the brink, ready to overflow.

"Now," I whisper to William and Tess.

My eyes are closed, but I hear the tinkling as they put their chimes back on. I feel William's large hands slide over my hips and stomach as he ties my own chimes around my waist.

It's time.

"Come, moon," the words leave me like a mist of warm air on a cold river. "Come black the sky, come allude the night."

I breathe in one last slow, deep breath, trying to find confidence in my words. Trying to trust that what I say will somehow truly impact the physical world around us. Trying to trust that what I feel goes beyond my connection with William.

At least, I brave the final words.

"Come, the dark."

I don't open my eyes right away. I just *feel*. And I feel the moon; I feel his glow, feel the soothing airiness he brings to the world.

"You're doing it, Cord," William says low in my ear, awe floating from his voice.

I lower my arms and blink my eyes open, and what I see sends a rush to my chest. The moon has eclipsed the sun, has swallowed her whole, so that only an orange ring of light glows around his edges.

Cruor know to avoid an eclipse—know when they are coming. But this one is a surprise. We might actually be able to trick them into believing it's night.

I peek over my shoulder, meeting William's intense gaze with my own. I can't speak, can't tell him what's on my mind, but I know now that I must find a way to bring William back with me when I return to Anna. I am strong enough to love him and to love her. My love has not been divided all this time, as I had imagined; instead, it has multiplied.

My guilt melts away, but a new weight replaces the emotion. I can't lose him.

There is no time to dwell on this discovery, though. As Tess weaves between the trees enclosing the clearing, her chimes call out the Morts. They know it's us, and the Cruor and Marked Strigoi will soon follow. The creak of trees on a quiet day is soon replaced with the loud thunder of footsteps. The moon is out, the moon is full, and already Maltorim soldiers are whipping from between the trees and into the clearing.

I focus my energy on holding the moon and allow the battle to take place, only hoping that William and Tess are prepared for what lies ahead—to keep the Maltorim's Cruor soldiers at bay until enough of them have entered the clearing to demolish them all in one fell swoop. We only get one shot at this.

William and Tess pounce in front of me, standing half crouched with swords drawn. Cruor infiltrate our clearing, and hundreds of humans possessed by Morts stalk into the battle as well.

But nothing is worse than the dead. The dead the Maltorim have risen. The soldiers with no life left to lose. Their expressions empty and their movements unnatural. A truly terrifying, mindless army.

Along the edges of our battleground, water sweeps in, lapping up to my feet. The waves cast the field in a blue ambience—sterile, cold reflections of light in the dark clearing. I need to keep the water at bay. Our chimes cannot get wet, yet the water is what will lend me strength enough to complete this task.

Sticks and weeds float along the surface. The peaty smell of algae, dirty water, and wet animal accost my senses, and the presence of ocean water is so heavy I taste the salt on the air. Soon, the seawater is rushing over the dead grass, rising until we are ankle deep. Flooding the clearing in a way that only magic can, drawing water from distances so great I wonder if all of Salem has been washed away.

The water moves with cold fluidity around my ankles and splashes onto my shins, and I step onto the altar. The water splashes up against the rock, as though drawn to me, and I know that, although I am an element of air, I am a ruler of water. I can control it. I *need* to control it.

William and Tess have taken out half a dozen of the Maltorim soldiers already, but the field is crowding. They will not survive much longer, but a little longer is all we need. I twist my wrist, and the water below me trickles upward, defying gravity, pledging its allegiance to my command.

I can do this.

I sweep my hand upward and forward, directing a wave of water to crash into a crowd of Maltorim soldiers. The water glitters with my inner ability, a force beyond itself, knocking the Cruor men to the ground. It's enough to allow William and Tess to regain superiority long enough to move several Mort spirits from the dead bodies they possess. My heart pangs as the human shells fall with a splash. The humans that are still alive—I will need my Ferrum nature to save them, to remove the Morts without harming or possibly killing their human bodies.

Almost there. Hang on.

There are at least a hundred Maltorim soldiers now and even

more humans possessed by Morts. I hadn't realized so many had been working against us. Tess and William drop the Cruor and Marked Strigoi one by one while trying to fend off the possessed humans a little longer. The fur of slain animals peek out of the water's surface, and the black tar of the eliminated Cruor oils the water's surface.

On the opposite side of the clearing stands a man, his black shirt unbuttoned and chest open to the wind that the sea I have conjured has brought with it. His charcoal hair is slicked back, and his dark stare is intent on mine. The golden sheen to his skin gives him away for the traitor he is: the Ankou that has betrayed us to help the Maltorim.

I can't concentrate on holding the moon while the battle is going on around me. Tess and William need me to stay strong in my purpose, but they also need help fighting. In the end, we can't run forever. Right here and now is our best shot.

Tess warned me we could not afford to travel anymore, but William had managed it to get the supplies we needed for the ritual. I need to risk it now, too. I cannot cross this field any other way, not with the hordes of the mindless and possessed and walking dead. I can only hope my decision to fight does not mean abandoning my call on the moon too early.

I take a running step off of the altar and directly into time and space, coming out on the other side of the clearing with my sword drawn and swinging to decapitate the traitorous Ankou. But he grabs my wrist, stopping my blow, and stares into my eyes with burning intensity.

"*Cordovae*," he says, as though my name is a disease.

Something stabs into my lower back, just to the side, and a burning spreads into my bloodstream and scorches my skin. My arm drops to my side, sword still in my grasp, but my world grows dark around me. I cling with everything I can to the moon, to keep her there for William and Tess a little longer. More than half of the possessed dead bodies have dropped into the waters now.

"I loved you once," he says to me, grabbing my arm, and I feel my face twisting with my mind as I try to figure out what he means. "You were too good for me. Too pure. Too *weak*."

His nails dig into my bicep. "*I led you to the stakes*," he whispers loud in my ear, his voice like a snake. "*I set the fire myself.*" He shakes me now, and the look in his eyes—it's pure insanity. He thinks I *am* Cordovae? Not with her spirit, but herself in the flesh? His eyes are nearly black. "*How* dare *you come back*? You were meant to die in Logroño! I *saw* you die! Tell me how you did it." He shakes me again. "Tell me how you came back!"

He's becoming increasingly frantic, and I realize then he doesn't want me to die. Not again, not yet—not until he knows how Cordovae is still alive.

I turn my nose up at him. "Does it matter? You'll die here today. You will die with this pathetic army."

He laughs, staring over my shoulder. "And so will your friends."

I twist to look behind me, my heart sinking at the sight: A Mort, possessing a large, dead human man, stalks up behind William, holding a large rock over his head.

Even as it's starting to come down, I force my way through the pain to swing once more at the Ankou before me. This time, my sword slices into his neck, decapitating him, dropping the rest of his body first to his knees and then to the torrents below.

"She never loved you," I say to his corpse.

I spin back to William. He's staring at me, a stunned look in his eyes as the remaining possessed dead bodies in the field drop into the crystal blue water. The body of the one holding the boulder is instantly crushed. Those bodies were nothing without their spiritual puppet master.

"Now, Cord!" William yells, and I release the moon.

It moves slower than I hope. If it doesn't lurk away from the sun fast enough, it could mean the death of any or all of us. I close my eyes, drawing more energy from water that floods the clearing and embracing the spirit of the moon, both working together, empowering me as I use my willpower to control the elements.

Finally, the moon creeps away from the sun, and light bursts out, slanting onto our battleground and incinerating the remaining Cruor...sending them up in flames until all that remains is their charred ashes falling like snowflakes into the water.

In that one moment, the majority of the Maltorim's Cruor delegated to preventing us from our goal are eliminated, and with the Maltorim's lone Ankou dead and unable to control the Morts, they are more disorganized. But we still have a lot of work to do before a new army is forged.

The Marked Ones—the Strigoi that work alongside the Maltorim—still remain. A hand thuds on my shoulder, and I turn around. Adrian and his comrade, Charles, stand behind me.

"Now we make amends," Adrian says, and with that, he and Charles charge into the clearing, engaging the remaining Maltorim warriors.

Their alliance stuns me, but does not move me as much as the two other presences that glide into the battleground. On the other side of the field, closest to my altar, stand Vanessa—the postpartum woman I helped escape Salem—and Grace, the woman who saved me and yet who I abandoned.

Relief that Grace was, after all, someone I could trust, floods through me. I run across the soggy clearing to where most of the Strigoi have gathered and fight alongside my comrades—all of them—for once feeling like we have a chance of survival. A chance to put an end to the darkness.

That is until I remember that William and Tess are fighting under a blanket of sunlight, one that surely suffocates their Ankou bloodline. Their weariness reflects in my own, as I'm weaker than I realized from forcing one final travel to put an end to the miserable Ankou who was controlling the army of the dead.

My adrenaline subsides to make way for reality. The pain in my back and blood from the injury drop me to the ground. I crawl to a tree, my vision darkening.

"Hang on," a voice calls out, but I don't know who it is—only that it's female.

Through the shadows and blur, Verity's face fills the frame of my vision. "You're hurt!" she cries. "What happened?"

"I don't—I don't—" *Know.*

What had happened? I want to tell her how glad I am to see her. To thank God she's all right. But I can't speak.

"I have you," she says. "Don't worry. Hang on. Stay will me, you'll be all right."

Verity's voice soothes me like a mother's lullaby soothes a child, and my own mother fills my vision. The woman she had been once, before the darkness arrived. Memories of being little and her grasping my wrists and spinning me over the tall grass in our back yard, until we were both dizzy and fell back to stare at a pale blue sky full of white cotton fluff, the only sound aside from our laughter the snapping of crisp linen hung to dry in the cool, early autumn breeze.

"You're going to be fine," Verity's voice cuts in again, and my vision clears. "Here, take this," she says, pressing some Daphne berries to my mouth. "Chew. Come on."

Are those tears in her eyes?

I swallow the berries and grasp her hand. "How did you know?"

"Vanessa found me in the woods, shortly after you disappeared. I convinced her I was a friend and trying to help you, but by then, you were already gone. She said you might need my help one day and told me what to do. Then I saw all the townsfolk marching to the woods...and...I just knew you would be here. Oh, Abigail. You should have told me. Thank heavens you're all right."

Somehow, Vanessa had known to trust Verity more than I had. I wouldn't make that mistake again.

"Verity, I—"

"Not now, please. Your friends still need you."

She's right. This battle isn't over yet. Though the sun has killed all the Cruor on the field, we still have the Marked Ones and the remaining Morts to finish off. But we're outnumbered, and William and Tess won't make it long enough to finish this battle without my help.

I shake my head, willing her to leave my side. "Go. Please, Verity, don't worry about me. If you're going to . . ." I can't say it. Can't admit she's risking her life because of me. But she is, and I need her to. "Help *them*."

She bites her lip, nods her head sadly, and then pops more Daphne berries into my mouth before running into the fray.

I GRASP AT THE UNDERBRUSH BEHIND ME, HOPELESSLY HOPING I'll find more nightshade or Daphne berries or anything to help me recover, instead of leaving me incapacitated on the side of the battlefield.

But there's nothing but branches with their first few leaves of spring waiting to break free.

Water laps against my back like waves on a beach at low tide. I shiver involuntarily against the chill, my body aching from the cold, but soon the water is soothing. My head sways as though I sit atop an iceberg on a choppy sea, and the pain of the cold is like needles pressing into my skin. But each time the tide pulls back, the poison seeps from my wound.

I feel the water healing me. Making me stronger than before. But it's not helping quickly enough. Something black and pooling is in the water, swirling like smoke in the sea. I see my chime bob in the current, and my heart sinks.

Never let the chimes get wet.

The blackness snakes out toward the Morts, and soon I see their spirits growing and twisting. Their eyes glow red, and their increased strength is apparent by the way they begin to overtake our group. Their spirit-forms had at least resembled humanity;

these morphed beings are less deceptive and more terrifying. They are monstrous, disfigured, and vibrating with a thudding evil.

One of the Morts grabs William by the neck and lifts him up onto his toes, and then further until his legs dangle.

They can touch us now—without the need for a human host.

The Mort uses his other hand to grab William's chime necklace, and holds it up to inspect it as it reflects the sun's rays. A grin twists his face, and he drops the chime, letting it plunk into the water to create its own smoky pool.

"No!" Tess yells, but she can't get to him with all the other Morts and Marked Ones still between them. They need me.

I grab the root of the tree behind me and use my healing abilities in a new way. Not only for regrowth of what has died, but to force as much new growth as possible. The tree sprouts new branches. Old ones twist and extend, poking out further into the clearing. My energy is draining rapidly, but I won't let go. I can't.

Soon one of the branches is pressing so hard into another tree that the tree is leaning into the clearing. Its roots are lifting. The Mort who has William opens its new monstrous red eyes wide as the smaller tree begins to fall. He releases William to duck out of the way, and William twists his body in the other direction. Everyone in the tree's path parts like the red sea. Bodies dive away to save themselves.

This won't be enough, but it bought us a little time. I slump back against the tree, nearly unable to keep my eyes open. The water tingles my wounds and laps against me, rolling over me, soothing me.

Then, suddenly, I'm weightless.

The water pushes me up, until I am levitating above the clearing, the waves an uplifting swirl beneath me. Peace floods through me. Perhaps I was always meant to die in the water. Maybe that's where my life went wrong—when my father saved me from drowning, only to later make me wish I were dead.

If I die today, will the water carry me back to Anna, or will my soul be lost forever?

Below, Adrian, Charles, and Vanessa have taken over fighting the Strigoi. Grace, though she can no longer move the Mort spirits, assists William and Tess by tossing any possessed humans out of the way, keeping them at bay as my friends do the work I should be doing alongside them.

The spirits crouch together like a pack of wolves, except their dark forms are so varied in shape and size that they resemble trees incised with human faces. All of them—even the children among them—are bereft of beauty and innocence.

In the horde of spirits, one captures my attention. His eyes hide in shadows, but his thick aquiline nose casts an elongated shadow that cuts through his lips and graduates to a point on his cleft chin.

Rage boils within me, my ears burning hot, my body trembling so fiercely I am surely hurting the air around me.

That particular Mort was the first.

He stole my family in Georgia.

My mind fixates on the moment before the accident. The moment before Pa lost control of the car. A man standing in the road. But it wasn't a man. No, it was *him*: this Mort in front of me now. Pa jerked the car sideways to avoid what he *thought* was a man. The truck squealed as it angled on two wheels, and then it tumbled.

Anger cuts my peripheral vision, and I focus on him as though through a tunnel. The spirit of the Forever Girl swells within me and lends me the strength and energy I need. My muscles jerk with a surge of unexpected power. The Mort's translucent body shimmers around a face as resolved as a dead-skin mask.

I reach out, squeeze my hand, and then pull my fist to my stomach, willing the Mort forward. Even in his spirit form, he stumbles. As though he's opened his eyelids, the shadows peel back from his forehead, showing tiny green vortexes that seem to absorb the air around him. His middle teeth, as long and craggy as stalagmites, gleam with feigned moonlight.

I lift my arm, and his spirit rises, joining me in my levitation.

When he closes in on me, I thrust my hand forward, my elongated nails slashing into his forehead, but before I can send him to an eternal non-existence, he thrusts his spirit hand forward and plunges it into my chest. Filaments of burning pain coil around my organs and constrict.

My lungs seize, and pain pulses through my chest as though I've swallowed a gulp of boiling water.

I gasp for breath. My vision blurs.

His blurry face grins, and he pulls me closer, yanking my body as if I'm his puppet.

"You," he whispers with a voice like a rattlesnake.

His face stops inches from mine. I dig my nails deeper, and his smile turns into an angry grimace.

But he doesn't stop. He presses so close against me that I can feel his spirit entering my body.

"*No*," I try to say, but the word leaves me like a dying breath.

This is what I have spent a lifetime trying to avoid. This is the spirit that forces itself on you. The spirit that violates you. Now he's taking everything that is left of me. Making my body his own.

I can't surrender. I can't be like Pa. My head feels thick and fuzzy. He's pushing my body forward, down. My face plunges into the water, and I hold my breath. I can't breathe. I open my eyes, but all I see is debris floating by, obscuring dozens of pairs of feet. I flail my arms, push against the ground, try to pull my head back up, but he makes me resist every effort. My arms are not my own. My spirit is breaking.

Finally he pulls me out of the water and throws my body back. The water surrounding us parts, as though running away. My emotions spill, and my tears soak my face. My mind flashes back to my Pa, and my body shuts down completely.

Get off me. Leave me alone.

His voice rattles: "*You're mine.*"

Not yet. There's still a part of me left. I can't let him take me.

My body struggles to fight back, but I can't overcome him. He's stronger than most other Morts I've encountered. I went about this the wrong way. I should have hidden myself with my wings on my approach. Too late now.

He is inside of me, and his form wreaths around my spine. I fall back, twisting in agony.

Tess straddles me, pinning my shoulders down. "Let her go!" she screams. She pounds my chest. Tears gleam in her eyes and fury twists her face. "Get out! GET OUT!"

Through the haze of my vision, I see black veins branching on my shoulders where Tess touches me. The skin starts to gray, and my heart throttles into a panic. My mouth twists open and my neck bends to one side, and vertebrae pop between my shoulder blades. My eyes roll back. Then laughter that is not my own bubbles from my throat.

"Kill me," he says, mocking her. "Kill...me."

Killing the host is the only way an Ankou without Ferrum nature can end a Mort spirit that has possessed human flesh. But Tess is driven by her sense of justice. She wouldn't kill me to kill him.

Would she?

Tess' long dark braid falls in front of her shoulder, and loose strands of hair stick to her face. Water drips from her nose. "You won't take her from me," she says through her teeth. She slams her hand into my chest again. "You won't take her!"

In my blurred vision, she reaches into her pack at her side and removes the Malleus Maleficarum. She grabs my hand—his hand?—and presses it again the book. "Cord, please. We need you. *Anna needs you.*"

Images flash into my mind. My gift of psychometry sends visions flying by as it searches for a memory I can use imprinted on the book. Anything. All I see is destruction. Burnings. Beheadings. Hangings. Slaughter. Lies. Deceit. A world in which women are the sexual playmates of Satan. I want to break away from this—the idea that witchcraft sprang from carnal lust. That in women, lust is insatiable.

The image freezes. Clears on a girl in a white flowing gown, standing still in a sea of commotion, her dress fluttering gently in the breeze. She's reaching toward me. She's saying something . . .

Regna terrae, cantata Omne, psallite Cernunnos.

The spirit tenses within me, bends my body painfully sideways. It coils my organs, and it squeezes. I hear myself scream—my own voice. The Mort is deep within me, harboring in my body, recoiling. Growling.

Regna terrae, cantata Omne, psallite Aradia.

It grips at my gut and twists my body so hard that Tess is thrown from me, but she doesn't let the book leave my hand. I pull my face out of the mud, and there is a moment of solace before the spirit twists around my belly again. I scream again, this time in the spirit's voice—a cougar's voice.

In my vision, a dark storm surrounds the girl in white.

Caeli Omne, terrae, Humiliter majestati gloriae tuae tu a nobis, Ut ab omni infernalium spirituum potestate.

The Mort shrieks. He lifts one of my hands and plunges my fingernails into my own face. I try to press out my Ferrum nature, in hopes of biting myself, but he won't let me. It's too late.

Laqueo, and deception nequitia. Omnis fallaciae libera nos, dominates. Exorcizamus you omnis spiritus malus.

My body jerks backwards until I'm up straight, and then slams backward again, hitting a rock and opening my scalp. My vision clouds, but the girl is still in my mind. Fading and returning, fading and returning, her voice somewhere in the distance . . .

Omnis malus potestas, omnis incursion, infernalis adversarri, omnis legio. Omnis and congretatio secta diabolica!

The roar in my head is so loud it feels as though my brain is bleeding. My body convulses. Pure evil pours from my mouth, a raspy voice that is not my own. "No one wants you, Tess! Go away. Go away, little girl! You're dead, you're dead!"

I feel Tess' trembling, but I cannot comfort her.

I hate myself. I want to die. I want my life to end before this Mort makes me do anything unforgivable. Is this what it had been like for my father? Was he as much as victim as me?

The girl from the book's memories continues, a fire catching behind her, blazing in the background. *Ab insidiis mali, lobera nos, dominates, ut coven tuam secura tibi libertate servire facias, te rogamus, audi nos!*

My whole body is convulsing. Something wet drops from the corner of my lips, and I taste it on my tongue. Blood. My blood.

Terribilus Omni Sanctuario cernunnos virtutem plebe. Aradai ipse fortitudinem plebe suae! Benedictus Omni, Gloria Patrie! Benedictus Dea, Matri Gloria!

And it's calm. Eerily calm.

I look up to see the flashing red in Tess' eyes, and I know exactly where's he's gone. And exactly how to end him once and for all.

I lunge toward her and sink my razor teeth into her shoulder.

Tess shrieks in the Mort's voice.

Desperately I bite at her again on her forearm and again on her neck, calling up shrieks that are progressively more intense. Her hand comes up firmly to my shoulder before I can bite again, and when I look in her eyes, I see it's her again. Really her.

She stumbles back, but catches herself. After a deep breath, she turns away from me, facing the destruction, then takes off to return to combat. Behind where she stood is Verity, smiling sadly at me, a pile of dead at her feet. She had protected Tess so Tess could help save me. I nod my thanks to her, but it's not long before my attention shifts to the clearing beyond.

The water lifts me back into my levitation, and my gaze cascades over the remaining enemy. I feel the power thrumming in me. I hear my call—hear the drum beat in the ground, a building crescendo inside of me.

One of the possessed is sneaking up on Tess' left. She won't be able to see it, not with the blindness in that eye. And she won't be able to hear me over the roar of the battle. I plunge toward the possessed and use my Ferrum nature to extract it from the human. The body thuds into the water, and the Mort tries to run. But it's too late. My fingers are already in its spirit skull, and soon it is nothing more than black particles on the breeze. Tess nods her thanks to me, then refocuses her attention on the Morts that have evolved from our wet chimes.

This ends now.

I zip around the clearing biting every possessed human I can before returning to neutral ground, then I reach out both my hands and pull all the Morts *toward* me. I pull them from the shadows, I pull them from their battles, I pull them from the human bodies they fight to keep possession of. The clearing is filled with the shrieking cries of Morts and the thudding slosh of host bodies falling into the ankle-deep water.

Now it's just me and the Morts. They claw at me, fighting back against my control over them. I clutch the witch's ladder I still keep in the folds of my dress and begin chanting. The spirit of the Forever Girl is with me, and the power of the triple goddess swirls through me, making her presence known and giving me the strength and energy I need.

"Veni, tenebræ," my voice trembles low, the Latin words coming out with a guttural tenor. "Veni, tenebræ."

The Morts slog forward. Through the wall of their shadowy forms, I see William trying to break through.

"Cord! No!"

He's yanking Morts back. He's moving two of them at a time, reducing them to black particle that turns the water below a shimmering gray.

"Veni, tenebræ."

Come, darkness.

I repeat the chant until all the Morts have been extracted from the human bodies. Bodies that now lie drowning in inches of water, waiting to be reborn.

William is low now; the crowd of Morts have swallowed him.

They hover closer and closer, until I can feel their deadly chill, until it's like ice melting over a Georgia sunburn. I hold tight to this world, not allowing the fragment to push forward.

"No!" William yells again, but his voice is drowned by a sea of moaning spirits.

Soon, they are on top of me, suffocating me, too many for me to fight back, wrapping their fingers around my arms and legs, pulling my levitating body from the sky to the ground below. The water surges away, clearing a circle around me as I land.

If I let my friends fight this battle without me, they could die. Do I sacrifice the lives of some of the people I love in order to save Anna? That was never possible. I had to save them all to save her anyway.

If I die here today, maybe I still would make it back to Anna. Just so long as I do what needs to be done. Maybe that would be enough.

Maybe.

And if not, I can only hope William or Tess would return for me to make sure she is safe.

My heart is weak—a slave to my emotions. Fighting is perhaps the only strength I have left. But deep down, I know why I've been hiding behind my reasoning. I've been hiding from what I've always known: the only way to win this battle is to fight it myself. This war has always been mine, and finally I realize that it won't end until I own it. Embrace it. The power of the very moon is on my side. I am stronger than I ever could have imagined.

It has to be enough.

It has to.

The resolved energy swells within my chest, and I will the waves around us to rise in great walls, the crystal blue water sparkling in the sunlight. As the waves coalesce around and above us, shadows turn the waves black, and soon I'm trapped under a dome of water. Everything goes dark.

My friends can't help me now, and I have no idea what I am doing. I can only act out my instincts, my urges. I can only trust the magic given to me by the Forever Girl.

Two walls form, blocking out my friends and encasing me inside with my attackers.

My prisoners.

I try to use the pull of my power to bring the Morts together, to pit them against one another, but it's useless. They pass through each other, swirls of shadows that deepen the darkness around us. They press up against me, and my stomach lurches. They want to take me, to be part of me, and I have to fight images of Pa's body over my own.

I crouch to the ground, and my chest tightens in panic as they hover over me. I can feel their cold energy on every inch of my skin. I close my eyes in the dark and try to focus on the ground beneath me. The earth's drumbeat thuds against my fingertips.

I squeeze my eyes shut tighter, focusing harder, soaking in the energy. Darkness consuming me. Is this what it will take? Inviting the dark into myself in order to destroy it?

Beneath the shrieks and moans of the Morts, my body trembles with the earth. My fear is gone. It's the energy alone that shakes me to my core. Finally, I let go. I stop pulling. I stop pulling the Morts, stop pulling the energy from the earth, stop pulling my strength from the water, and I...let go.

I let go of every emotion, every dream, every hope.

And the energy bursts from me in bright rays of echoing light, bright and blinding and turning my world white. But as this light temporarily destroys the color of my world, it permanently destroys the Morts in the clearing. Each and every one—vaporized. Sucked from this existence almost as though they never existed at all. A Chibold gift I hadn't even known I possessed.

Icy salt water crashes down around me and slaps into my face, stinging my skin, and I can taste the ocean on my tongue.

When I open my eyes, the clearing is silent. The air around me is ruined by the scent of wet ashes as the sky snows in shades of black and gray. I rise, looking at each of my comrades in turn. Charles and Adrian stare at me in surprise; Grace and Vanessa, in awe. Tess, in apology, and William in...admiration? They don't move, even as I walk toward them.

What we've accomplished here is nothing great. It is only the end of something horrible. Anyone can murder. Anyone can silence the life of another. Be they evil or pure, their blood is on our hands now.

I spread my arms out to the piles of humans around us.

"They need us now."

❧

I didn't know I was this person, but on this day, I became myself. Became who I always have been but have never known.

I learned I was a fighter, that I am strong enough to overcome evil. And I realized that my ability to do so comes from a darkness within myself...a darkness that was born in me back in Georgia, a darkness shaped by all I have been through and all I am yet to do. Because this isn't over yet.

It's not over, but my time in this place, with these people, ends here. And of them, I will miss William and Tess most of all. I will leave here knowing that they would risk themselves to save me. They would save me even knowing I would just as soon leave them to save my daughter.

That is what makes leaving so hard.

It's what makes me want to stay.

And I hate myself for even thinking it.

CHAPTER 35
APRIL 1692

It takes hours for William, Tess, and me to heal the once-possessed humans of their wounds. Each one we heal is then, in turn, addressed by Charles—Adrian's dual-breed friend—who whisks them swiftly back to where Adrian has taken cover from the sunlight. Adrian wipes their memories, Charles returns them to their home, and then he swiftly abandons them to return to us for the next.

Some of the Morts' victims don't make it.

Vanessa, Verity, and Grace assist us in putting them to rest. They carry them into the woods, almost ceremoniously, and with the way the sun slants golden in the clearing, it's almost beautiful. Beautiful, if not for the finality of it all.

That could be Anna if I don't return to her soon.

As I heal one of the humans, I stare across the clearing to where William is under a heavy shade, tending to a young man. My heart thumps in my chest. His eyes lift to mine, and my mouth goes dry. My very soul aches, knowing I will leave him soon.

Then my wings tingle again, and at first I think it's from the sunlight, but then I wonder if it's something more. But could being Ankou really run that deeply in me—so deeply that it has rooted itself to my emotions?

"Tess?" I ask as she heals a deep gash in the stomach of an older woman.

She doesn't look up. "Yeah?"

"When I go home, will I still be...this way?"

She shrugs. "How could I possibly know the answer to that?"

"Right," I say, defeat settling in, kicking its feet up and getting comfy. "Sorry I asked."

"Don't be," she mumbles. "But the people who leave here, we never see them again, get it? So how do we know what life is like for them once they leave?"

I don't say anything more. We work silently in the somber clearing, our clothes drying stiff in the early spring sun. The waves have swept back to the ocean. The only evidence of their recent presence is the way our knees and toes sink in the muddy, saturated ground as we kneel over one body after the next.

"Too late on this one," Tess says, and though at first her words seem matter of fact, when I look at her I can hear the sadness in her voice. She gently closes the eyes of a rosy-cheeked, blonde-haired little girl. "You can be at peace now."

Tess turns away. "This woman's next."

I slosh across the overwatered grass to join Tess' side. I want to look at her, to search her face for answers, for clues that will lead me through the passageways of her mind, but I don't. I allow her the privacy of feeling whatever she feels without me knowing, without me seeing.

Her hand finds my own; our fingers intertwine. I give a gentle squeeze.

"So much lost," she whispers. Then she shakes her head. "Her lungs are filled with fluid, Cord. You'll have to pull it out."

I nod, then place my hand inches above the young woman's mouth. Tess' energy flows through me, strengthening my energy, but it's my own gift—this control I have over the water—that will save this woman.

The sensation starts in my fingertips, then some outside pressure pulses against my palm. A droplet of water slides out of the woman's mouth, then rises into the air. A few droplets later, it's a small rivulet swirling up toward my hand, coalescing into a sphere of water.

The woman coughs, sputters, gasps. I flick my wrist to the side, sending the water to splash against the mud. Before I can say a word, Charles blurs past, and the woman is gone.

It was my gift that saved her, but it was also my gift that nearly took her life.

I had no other choice.

William calls us over to the next victim. When he looks at me, his mouth twitches on one side. Half smile, half apology. When he puts his arm around me and pulls me to his chest, I don't think about it. I don't analyze. I'm just *there*.

I'm alive.

❦

IT'S NOT UNTIL AFTER ALL THE SURVIVING HUMANS HAVE BEEN returned to their homes—memories wiped—and the dead buried or reburied, that we can tend to our own wounds. The pain has settled in, and it's made me too lightheaded and ill to eat. William rubs nightshade into the large wound in my back. I wince, and he lightens his pressure, his touch so tender than it's almost sensual. I close my eyes and try to ignore the feeling.

Suddenly, Adrian appears at our side.

"I can't say long," he says. I look up from where I sit to take him in. His dark skin is reddening and peeling.

"I thought—"

"Tess' blood is wearing off. I won't be able to stay in the sun now." He turns his attention toward her.

She shakes her head, arms crossed. "You—" She presses her lips together, and her eyebrows furrow and her fingernails dig into her arms. "No, Adrian. Never again."

This is all she says before she stalks off.

Charles strolls over, and I ease William's hand from my back, away from the wound that has mostly healed. William helps me stand, then gets up beside me.

"You okay?" he asks.

"Fine," I say. "Maybe you should gather some supplies for our travels?"

Charles places his hand between Adrian's shoulder blades. "Come, my friend. Time to go."

"Before you go..." I say, touching them both on the arm.

They both look me in the eyes, and this time I influence them. The spirit of the Forever Girl is with me, and she washes through their memories, crashing through the mind like rapids, carrying any trace of us away.

Erasing memories from a Cruor is something only a Forever Girl can do, as only Forever Girls are able to cross the mental planes to where the dead have their thoughts. I must work quickly if I am to succeed before they realize what I am up to.

Within moments, I am in their heads, my energy washing through their memories like the roar of a strong ocean wave.

Hodie viderunt memini. Forget all you have seen today.

Grant...in saecula saeculorum. Forget us. Forever.

Memoriam ablue. Memories wash away.

As I near the end, I feel them starting to fight back. But as their memories are sucked away, I also steal their energy, and within minutes, they crumple to the ground. It's best we don't leave a trace of our presence with *anyone*. Not even our allies. They can't remember this day, and they can't remember any of us. I leave them only with the memory of their friendship and the knowledge that the Maltorim cannot be trusted.

Tess runs over and pushes me to the ground. "What have you done? Cordovae, how could you?"

My hands slide into the mud, and she jumps on top of me before I can get back on my feet. "They aren't dead," I say defensively. "I just took their memories of us."

Her face contorts like this is somehow worse. She pounds her fist into my chest, and I grab her wrist and push her off of me.

I wipe the mud from my hands on my shredded dress and glare at her. "What the hell is wrong with you?"

She points her finger into my chest. "You just don't want anyone to have their life because you can't have yours!"

William rushes over. "Slow down, Tess. What happened?"

Tess shoulders past him. "Ask your stupid girlfriend," she says, and she storms off.

William's turns his puzzled expression my way. "What was that about?"

My face and ears are burning. "I'm not entirely sure. She's mad I wiped our presence from Adrian and Charles' memory."

His expression softens. "Oh," he says softly. "I better go talk to her. You will do the same with Grace, Verity, and Vanessa when they return from their last burial?"

I nod. Verity will be the hardest, but it must be done. Only William, Tess, the Maltorim, and myself will remember what happened on this day. It has to be this way; we cannot risk Adrian, or anyone else, turning on us ever again.

It's funny that the only people we can trust not to talk about this are the Maltorim, but that's only because they would never want to admit their defeat. And with their resources so rapidly depleted, it will be a long time before they can try something like this again.

Maybe next time, they'll think twice.

❧

TRUE NIGHT IS SOON APPROACHING, AND IT CAN'T COME SOON enough. William's skin is already starting to peel as Adrian's had. We need to act fast, so it is with haste that we move Adrian and Charles to a cave nearby, and Vanessa, Verity, and Grace to an abandoned cabin in the woods. They will be disoriented and confused when they wake, but they will be safe. I left them each with one memory from this all: that the Maltorim can never, never be trusted.

Tess still won't talk to me. I try to tell myself that I don't care, that I'm going home soon and how she feels about me means nothing. But I can't convince myself of the lie any more than I can understand why I feel this way.

William offers me some nightshade, but I can't consume anything right now. My stomach flutters are making me ill. Anxiety over finally being able to return to Anna bubbles in my chest. As soon as we get to safety—get to where the Maltorim can't send anyone to kill us—I can travel away from this time and place and back to my own. Back to Anna.

I wish I could be excited. But I'm afraid. I've been racing time since I arrived here, and only now can I learn if I was fast enough, or if I'm trapped here forever. I could find happiness here, I know, but it would be clouded with the sadness of losing my daughter and trampled by the guilt of finding love in a world where she doesn't exist.

Unwelcome tears trickle down my cheek and salt my lips. Some of joy, some of sorrow. And it's the latter that bring the tears of guilt flowing next.

I need to get away from William and Tess before this gets any harder. I need to get back to Anna before it's too late.

Finally, I am free to leave.

So why, in my heart, do I still feel like a prisoner?

CHAPTER 36
APRIL 1692

Night has returned. Truly and completely. And I hope what I have seen here is hell, for I can't stomach that there could be anything worse. The Morts are like the very demons Mama told me about as a child. They walk the earth, they possess the pure. If hell exists, its prisons must not be well guarded.

It's not that I've ever been a very religious person, as far as I know. I believe in God, I've said my prayers. After all of this, one might think any faith I held would be shaken. That the miracles of this world have been explained to me now, and I should no longer believe in some unknown deity. But if anything, I believe more.

I just don't know what it is I believe.

Is the Universe God? Or does the Universe render God irrelevant?

I've entertained that thought, too, in this new life...a life I am ready to leave.

The mysteries of this world may never be completely answered, and I don't care one way or another, so long as the great powers that be reunite me with my daughter.

But something still nags at me: Will I remember all of this? Will I remember Tess? William?

Right now, I can't bear the thought of losing them, even if it's only in my memories that I keep them, and yet I wonder if forgetting them would be a type of kindness.

We hike by foot, avoiding *travel* in fear of alerting the Maltorim to our location. This battle may be over, but that won't stop them from killing us if they can. The closer we get to our destination, the more my steps wobble. I'm anxious to return to Anna, and at the same time, I dread saying goodbye.

William must sense my distress, because he squeezes my shoulder and says, "Relax. You need to reserve your energy, especially as you don't know exactly what you're returning to."

Then he releases me and hikes a little further ahead, scanning the woods in every direction before pointing down the path we will take next. We need to be as far from any other elemental populace as possible before I attempt to *travel*.

My Ankou night vision is a blur around William. I'm breathing in this last moment as I stare up at his wide shoulders and the way the muscles in his neck move when he looks from side to side. The determination of his strong jaw and the purpose of his stride. The golden Ankou shimmer on his skin is more beautiful on him than any other Ankou I've seen. And yet, all of this beauty does not hold a candle to who this man is, and my heart aches because this is the last time I will watch him lead the way.

We reach a clearing on the other side of the mountains, far from where the Maltorim last spotted us. Fresh blooms of early spring sprout from the ground, and I avoid stepping on them; it's more of a distraction from the impending goodbye that awaits.

Why am I sad? I'm returning to Anna. I barely know William or Tess—I can't give good reason to the way I feel around them. How could I miss them? How can I be so heartbroken about leaving them behind?

How is it that I have fallen in love with William?

Deep down, I know the answer. I know that love cannot be explained. Though Mama would never agree, I know you can love someone at first sight; even before first sight, as was the crashing love I had for Anna—how I knew I would lie down and die for her, do anything to protect her.

But I never knew I could feel a fraction of that love for anyone else.

Until now.

At far end of the clearing, we stop. Tess walks over to a tree and leans her forearm against the bark. I can't stop staring at her—at her long dark braid, her smooth, pale skin, her juvenile wrists. She's still in a child in many ways.

I open my mouth to say something to her, to say goodbye, but I don't know what to tell her. Not while she's still mad at me for stealing Adrian's memories of her.

She picks at the fray near the waist of her medieval dress. The toe of her boot digs into the dirt, pressing up against a root that protrudes from the ground. Slowly, her focus slides to me, and she tugs on her earlobe.

She clears her throat and says something so fast and rushed that it takes a moment for my mind to make words of the sounds.

"Bye, Cordovae." This is what she'd said.

"Bye," I whisper.

The air thickens; it's harder to breathe. I want to say goodbye to William—I feel him staring at me—but I can't look away from Tess. Though Adrian had betrayed her, he'd also helped save us. And I'd taken him away from her.

"Tess—"

"Screw it," she says, turning toward me, tears in her eyes. She crosses the distance between us impossibly fast and wraps her arms around me, pulling me into her. "Fuck you, Cordovae. You're really leaving us."

Tears pinch my throat, and I'm suffocating. I wrap my arms tightly around her and bury my face in her shoulder. "I have to, Tess. Anna needs me."

She pulls back and wipes her eyes with the back of her wrist. "Yeah, I know. I'd hate you if you didn't leave, too."

I smile sadly, and a small smile breaks through her turmoil as well.

Tess tilts her head toward William. "The hardest part, huh?"

She walks away before I can answer, and I let my gaze fall into William's. This is the moment I have dreaded. The moment where I must acknowledge the decision I am about to make. I am forced to choose between the only man who has never betrayed me and a daughter I can't fully remember but will never forget.

But as hard as it is to leave, my decision is easy. Anna *needs* me. Her life depends on my return, while William and Tess will be fine without me. And if I don't return soon, there will be no undoing time, no undoing all that has happened and will happen to her in my absence. In the end, it comes down to one irrefutable fact: I can live with losing William, but I cannot live without my daughter.

The choice is not difficult to make, and yet, acting on it painfully cripples my heart.

"We never had a chance here," I say.

"No..." he says, and there's more hanging there, but his frown presses too tight for any more words to slip through.

My heart rate picks up in my chest as I try to find the bravery to ask him the scariest and most important request before I leave. "Come with me," I say. "You *and* Tess."

His head drops back, and he lets out the saddest bark of laughter. "God, Cord, you're killing me." He shakes his head and takes both my hands in his. "It's not that I don't want to. I hope you know that. But we can't go where we never belonged. Understand?"

"I know you've traveled outside of this time," I tell him. "things you have said, things that belong hundreds of years from now."

He nods. "I have—when the Universe has needed me to. I wish more than anything they needed me to go with you. But, Cord...they don't. I can't...leave here."

"Then I'll bring Anna back here," I say. "If I can. If I'm still Ankou when I get there."

I already feel defeated. What if once I travel home, I can never travel back again? What if I lose all of my abilities once this is really over?

"Will I be?" I ask meekly. "Will I be Ankou when I return?"

If I am—if it's possible—then I could save Mama and Pa. I would never be able to look at them again, but I could save them. I could make them whole again.

"I don't know," he says quietly. "Normally, no. Because it is Abigail's body that is Ankou, not Rose's. But things are different for you."

"So then maybe I might be able to come back." I don't feel the excitement I should. William's expression is so forlorn. If I could come back, wouldn't he be happier?

"Anna doesn't belong here, either," he says finally. "And even if you could bring her here, would you, really? Would you want this life for her?"

"It's not worse than where I come from," I say.

William presses his fist to his mouth and sighs deeply. "I'll never forget you." I shake my head, but he doesn't stop. The words just keep pouring from his mouth. "I fell in love with you even when I knew I shouldn't."

And for some reason, *that* is my breaking point.

All this time, I have wanted him to tell me how he feels, but now I desperately want to stuff those words back into his mouth, to undo them, to make them never happen so I can leave this place without knowing I am leaving someone who loved me back.

I can barely speak. Barely squeak out the whisper of words. But eventually, they come. *"No one falls on purpose."*

And I know this. I know this because I love him, too. I don't know when it happened, but I know it's been happening since the day I met him, since that first spark that eventually ignited to a fire that can't be ignored.

Except I need to ignore it. I need to leave.

"All this time," he says, "I thought I knew my greatest weakness. That my capacity to love was what endangered my obligations in this world. But I was wrong, Cord. It was my fear of losing. You showed me that when no one else could. And as much as it pains me to see you go, I would never, never ask you to stay. *Because* I love you. And because I know your daughter will bring you a happiness I cannot substitute."

My shoulders tremble, and I wipe tears from my eyes. "Why would you tell me this *now*, William? It's cruel. Couldn't you just—"

He presses his finger to my lips. "Shhh. Shhh." He pulls me into him and strokes my hair. "I would never ask you to stay here for me, but I couldn't let you leave without telling you how I felt. I'm sorry if it makes this more painful for you, but I know you are strong enough to still do what you need to do."

"Right," I whisper. It's all I can get out.

I feel his Adam's apple bob against the top of my head. "Please understand that I deserve to follow my heart, too," he says. "I had to tell you how I feel or those unspoken words would have haunted me forever."

His words only make my love for him burn deeper. Burying my face into his shoulder, I can still smell the wood smoke on his clothes from the campfire earlier. I can still smell his sweat. Still smell me on him.

"Don't fall apart now," he says soothingly, brushing an amber wave of hair from my eyes. "I was wrong about you, you know. I said you were selfish, but really, no selfish person would make the sacrifices you have. But now it's time for one more of those sacrifices." He holds me at arm's length. "Great love can both take hold and let go, Cord. And now it's time to let go."

I swallow and shake my head, but in my heart, I know he is right. I turn to face the open clearing. As badly as I want to get back to Anna, I don't know how I'm going to do this. I don't know how I'm going to run from the man I love. The guilt over feeling this way is only another weight holding me where I stand.

A butterfly floats by on the warm breeze and settles on a dandelion by my feet. It has waited all this time to make its flight, and now it's free. But I cannot relate. I am destined to never learn the feeling of freedom.

"Go," William says from behind me. When I don't move, he shouts. "Go!"

I tense, then take a deep breath, centering my thoughts on Anna. Remembering the way the earth felt between my bare feet as I ran to save her from Pa. I take another breath, breathing in the pain I felt that day. In my heart, in my lungs, in my womb.

I take the first step.

Though my stiff and achy body has begun to relax, tension is already returning as I fight the magnetic pull I feel toward William and Tess. I push through it and take another step.

Then another.

I'm scared. Terrified, really. I can't imagine going back. I can't imagine what awaits me there. Can't envision it at all. Salem has a magnetic pull on me that I can't explain. Leaving feels unnatural.

Shouldn't returning to my daughter feel like the most natural thing in the world?

I feel trapped, and each step I take I have to push through that feeling. I have to accept that part of my heart will always belong here, but it's not where I belong. With Anna is where I belong. Only her.

It's always been her.

I take two more steps.

And right now, she's alone with Pa. I can't leave her with him.

My steps turn quicker.

Five more steps.

I miss her, and I love her, and the love of a mother is stronger than any other kind of love. Finally, I'm returning to her. To my Anna.

Ten steps, then with my next breath, I am breaking across the clearing.

My hair whips back, out of my face, like flames on the wind behind me. Tears are streaming my face as I run, but my heart is soaring ever closer to her. I can feel it. Back to where I belong. Back to Anna.

I run harder, my legs burning, until I break through space. Through darkness and light.

And then . . .

I'm still here. I'm still with William and Tess. I'm still in this clearing with the chirr of crickets and the light thudding of deer running in the fields behind us and the soft roll of thunder that threatens a storm.

I crumble to my knees in the clearing, and my calf rubs against a fallen log with bark softened from an earlier storm. I press my forehead into the ground. Sobs heave from my body. I'm going to be sick.

William and Tess run over to me. I hear them shouting at me, but it's all a haze.

"Cord! Are you okay?"

"What happened?"

I don't even know which of them is talking. William puts his hand on my back, but I just feel numb where he touches me.

"I did everything I was supposed to," I mumble through my tears. "I need to get back. Anna needs me! I did what you said. Why am I still here?"

I grab fistfuls of the fresh spring grass and cry against the earth and hate the moon for casting her miserable light on my failure.

I'm angry and I'm upset and I'm ripped up inside and out and my heart and my soul and my mind all want to explode. I can't do this. I can't take anymore. I can't bear being alive. I can't stop crying, I'll never ever stop crying.

If hope is gone, I have nothing.

William and Tess are talking, but I can't make out anything they say. It's all muffled, drowning. The words are mushed and warbled.

I cry until I fall asleep. I wake up in the night again, crying. William and Tess help me to my feet. My mind is foggy and my vision blurs, but I stumble with their help toward wherever we are going.

To wherever we could possibly go from here.

The next day, I'm well enough to hear William and Tess speak, but I'm only willing to listen if they're trying to help me get home. I no longer care about leaving them. I hate myself for having ever felt that way. I hate them for existing.

Tess hands me a cup of tea made from nightshade that she brewed over a small campfire just outside the cave we've taken shelter in. I sip it gently, and my stomach gurgles its thanks as the tart, poisonous berries that flavor the water start to recoup my body. The heat of a nearby fire warms my face and ears, and I drop the blanket from around my shoulders—early spring and already I feel overheated, perhaps from all the crying.

"Maybe you're still torn about where you want to be," Tess says quietly. I can tell it wasn't easy for her to suggest this, but I glare at her just the same

Her words also pang my heart, feed my guilt. I may be torn, but I'm not unsure. Part of me may have wanted to stay with William, but all of me wanted to return to Anna.

"You might just need time to give it all more thought. Meditate for a little and try again."

This time, William glares at her.

"There is nowhere," I say, not attempting to hide the edge in my voice, "that I'd rather be...than with Anna. If it's too late to return, then what did I fight for? This world is dead to me without her."

Tess stares at me in pity, and I both love and hate her for it.

"You don't think..." I swallow around the painful lump in my throat. "You don't think it's too late, do you? It can't be, not now. Not after all that."

Tess makes a sound—the start of a word I'll never hear, because William lifts a hand, effectively silencing her. He stares down at where I lie, and I can't tell if he's angry or if he's hurt, but he's clearly not happy. And I don't care.

"We'll take you to the Chibold," he says. "They might help."

Tess scoffs. "Don't do this to her, William. Don't give her false hope."

I bolt upright, life returning to my body at these words. "It's better than no hope," I say. "When can we go to them? Can we go there now?"

Tess throws her arms up in the air and rolls her eyes. "You're an idiot, William. A real idiot."

He pulls her aside. I can't hear what he says, but I hear Tess' not-so-quiet whispered reply: "She needs to accept her fate, just as everyone else has. We can't risk taking her to them."

"She deserves any chance she can get," he says, loud enough that I know I'm meant to hear. "We can't deny her that."

❧

THE CHIBOLD WILLIAM KNOWS DON'T LIVE THE SAME ELUSIVE life of the Oracle, but William seems to think they will be equally wise in solving my problem. We find them not living hidden in some cave, not tucked away in some forest up in the mountains, nor any other inconspicuous location. Instead, they live in a small colony of ordinary Strigoi. We travel, even before nightfall, under the protection of my wings.

Under the shadow of the early evening, the small town is gloomy and eerily calm. The fog lends a muddy darkness to the atmosphere, and I beg the darkness to come early, to hide every feeling I have, to leave me be to feel it alone and unseen.

My body aches with every step. Even the fabric of my dress is like sandpaper on my skin. I'm freezing, but the cold comes from a feeling of loss instead of the lingering chill not yet overcome by the moist, early spring evenings.

"Can they really help?" I choke out quietly.

William wraps his arm around my shoulders. "If they don't have the answers, they can get them."

Tess clears her throat and gives William a sideways glare.

He twists toward her, never letting me go. "They've always been receptive to helping us in the past." He turns back to me. "I'm sure they will do their best."

"But there are no guarantees," Tess says daringly.

William growls beneath his breath. "There never are."

We cross a small creek over a rickety bridge and reach a small house with cracks in the window and jars of the elements on the sills. Jars of salt. Jars of stone. Jars of various herbs. And, oddly, even a jar of light, though I cannot see where this light originates from.

I could get lost staring into that jar, but William whisks me inside, through a thin wooden door to a cozy kitchen of a family I don't know. He hasn't knocked, and the family inside seems unconcerned. I'm instantly comforted by the familiar aroma of smoke and the taste of charred cold air wafting inside the walls of their small home.

"Cord, I'd like you to meet Jessup and Eleanor," William says.

I reach my hand out to the older woman, and she laughs, then points to the children beside her.

"This is Jessup and Eleanor," she says, before attending the whistle of a nearby kettle.

I freeze, unable to process her words. Jessup is a boy of perhaps seven years, and Eleanor about two years his elder. The boy is sandy-blond and pale and Eleanor brunette and freckled and a good half of a foot taller. Both have unsettling dark eyes.

William leans into me and whispers in my ear, "Chibold appear as children, remember?"

I nod slowly, staring at these poor children. I still can't get over the Chibold looking like children yet having such knowledge beyond their physical years.

I force a smile. "Hello, Jessup. Hello, Eleanor."

Eleanor grins mischievously. "You look like you've seen a ghost! You must come to take things as they are and not as they seem, yes?"

Jessup leads us into a small sitting area and sits awkwardly beside me, while Eleanor plops down close, as though we're old friends. She sweeps some hair from my face, and I half expect her to start braiding my hair, but instead she pinches my ear firmly and stares into my face.

"William says you are here to learn why you cannot return to where you belong."

"That's right," I say, resisting the urge to pull back from her and get her hand away from my face.

"Take Jessup's hand," she says. "I need him to complete the charge."

I don't bother to ask for an explanation. If all goes well, I will be leaving this world and leaving behind the need to understand the way all these things work. I try to ignore that this is my world, too, that the life I came from was only unaware of its existence. I want nothing more than to return to my ignorance.

I take Jessup's hand, and he closes his eyes My hand burns slightly, enough to cause to discomfort but not so badly that I can't tolerate it for a short while. Eleanor takes my other hand with one of hers and closes her eyes as well. The fingers that pinch my ear start to trace the edges of my earlobe, trickling down and stopping just behind my ear. Leaving her pointer finger there, her thumb slides across my jawline, and now it's as though she cradles my face in the most unnatural way possible.

My eyes find William's, and he offers a small smile and reassuring nod. My throat closes and my heart races and the moment hangs in the air like a dandelion weed in a light breeze, unable to reach ground and plant its seed.

Eleanor breathes deeply through her nose. "You're a Forever Girl?"

"My spirit joined with a Chibold who was. We weren't able to save her in time."

"No." Eleanor shakes her head. "You already were. This is why you so easily became one with Cordovae above your connection with Abigail. Abigail is but one of the many lives that descended from Cordovae—a Forever Girl spirit. There were so few of them then...it's not something I often have the opportunity to reveal!"

She sounds absolutely giddy. I cannot share her excitement. "You're wrong. I didn't have any abilities before this."

A smirk plays at her lips. "You did, though. You were a Seer before you became Ankou. Rose was a seer. Wasn't she?"

I nod. "Kind of."

"When you joined with that other spirit, you gained power over the water, which you would not otherwise have, being an air elemental normally."

My whole body tenses. "I really don't care if I already was or not. The Universe brought me here to help, and I did my part. I want to go back now. I have a daughter to return to. I don't need to be here anymore."

Eleanor's serene and almost happy face starts to fade to something confused...concerned, perhaps. Her brow furrows deeply and her lips purse. Finally she lets out a small gasp and snaps her hand away from my face. Quickly, she stands, and then she's smiling again, but it's too affected to be sincere.

"What is it?" I ask.

Eleanor looks to William with uncertainty clear on her face.

I grab her hand, forcing her attention back to me. "Whatever it is, Eleanor, you have to tell me."

"You can't go back," she says. "There is nothing to go back to. *That* is why you are here now."

"I have Anna—*that* is what I have to go back to."

"No, dear Cordovae. You cannot return. Rose's body is gone."

I shake my head, not wanting to believe it. "I'm...dead? That can't be. I was running and then I was here."

"This is what I'm seeing," she says gently.

I lean in close to her face. "You're seeing wrong, then."

Her face goes blank. "I'm never wrong."

I don't even care anymore. There has to be another way. There has to be. "I *need* to get back there. I don't care how."

I don't even care if it makes me as bad as the Morts.

"Abigail was your ancestor," Eleanor explains, "and she was murdered moments before you arrived by a townsman who believed her a witch. When he saw what he did, he panicked and ran from the town, later to meet his own brutal finality—mauled and eaten by a coterie of Cruor. But one good thing did come of Abigail's death. It gave your spirit a doorway back in time."

I swallow hard, trying to fight the tears stinging my eyes. I can barely choke out the words, "I don't want a way back in time, I want the way back *home*."

"Don't you see?" Eleanor looks at me with big, dark eyes. "This is the only way for you to continue on in life. Without this, you have no life at all. Once the lineage ends, the only way for a Forever Girl's spirit to continue is to be reincarnated *back* in time. Something that otherwise is not even possible. You are lucky that—"

"I'll find a way back," I say angrily, but even I don't believe myself.

"If you would just listen—"

I am on my feet now, though I hardly remember standing.

Eleanor reaches up and puts her hand calmly on my shoulder. "You don't need to go back, Cordovae. There's nothing left there for you." Her gaze is so intense it stops me in my tracks. "Cordovae...Anna died before you arrived in Salem."

CHAPTER 38

APRIL 1692

ANNA AND I BOTH DIED BEFORE I ARRIVED IN SALEM.

The conversation echoes dully in my mind. I can't go back. I can't save Anna. It's too late.

"You're lying," I say, half hopeful, half angry, and mostly numb from shock. "You just want me to stop trying to return. No one ever cared about me leaving here!"

Jessup grabs my shoulder firmly, and before I can resist, warmth spreads up my neck and into my skull, and a vision melts into my memory. Pa pressing a pillow over Anna's small body. Her legs kicking. Her arms flailing. Then, she's still. Pain stabs through my chest, and I can hardly breathe. I'm dying with her. My entire soul is being ripped in two. My legs are falling from beneath me, but Jessup holds me up. I try to pull away from the vision, but Jessup has strength that goes beyond that of the physical world. I'm stuck here to suffer these horrible visions.

"Don't do this," I whisper to him, but he doesn't stop.

There's a blur of things I remember. The pick-up truck, the forest, running. And then, there's a jolt. This time it's not the jolt that sent me flying to Salem. This time, it's the jolt of a bullet pelting into my stomach. Another jolt, into my heart. Footsteps. Loud. Another jolt, into my skull.

Pa killed me.

Killed *us*.

And now I know why—now I know the Mort spirit could not risk any evidence of what he had done, that he couldn't risk his host body being caught and hauled away to jail, trapped in a cell. He had to destroy the evidence. He killed Anna so no one would ever see the resemblance, and he killed me so that he could say I had just run off.

Why didn't he just let me run off, then? I was going to anyway.

Jessup plucks the thoughts right from my brain. "Even Morts have their obsessions. You were his. If he couldn't have you, no one could. Not even Anna."

I'm trembling with equal parts of disgust and anger. It's more than I ever wanted to know, and it destroys the little hope I had left.

Jessup releases me, then stares at me apologetically. "I had to, Cordovae, or you would never move on from that life."

I bite back my tears and stare him angrily in the face. "I still want to go back. I should be dead. I might as well be."

"It's fine," Jessup says. "All is not lost."

I turn my fiercest glare toward him, my whole body shaking. "You are wrong, Jessup. If I've lost Anna, I've lost all purpose in life. I've lost everything."

William eases me back into my seat, and I don't resist. Eleanor reclaims her place at my side and wraps her warm around my shoulder, her other hand pressed to my arm to give me a gentle squeeze.

"No, Jessup's right," she says. "There is good that has come of this."

I feel like I'm going to vomit. Tears blur my vision and my head pounds. I wish I would just lose consciousness.

"Cord, please, listen to us! Anna is still with you!"

My trembles turn to tremors. I can't control my body right now. I can't handle their platitudes. Of course Anna is still 'with me'. She will always be in my heart. But that's not the same. That's not enough.

"Look," Eleanor says pressingly. She grabs my chin and lifts my face, then points to Tess. "*Anna is still with you.*"

Tess is Anna?

I repeat my thought, aloud this time. Then: "How?"

Jessup's whole demeanor relaxes. "You brought her with you."

"No," I say, defeated. They can't help me after all. They're supposed to know everything, have all my answers, and yet they don't. "You're confused. Anna was just a baby when I left."

I turn, intending to leave, but Jessup's gentle touch on my arm stops me in my tracks. There's a part of me, deep down, that wants to believe him. Because if it's true, Anna is alive, even if it's through Tess.

"Please," Jessup pleads softly. "Just listen. If you want to leave after that, you can leave. If you still want to return to that time, we'll help you, somehow. But once you hear what I have to say, you won't want to go back."

I chew at my lip, slide my attention to him slowly. "I'm listening."

"You see, Forever Girls can only reincarnate to one person at a time. Cordovae was with you, but your daughter was still her descendent, and therefore a Seer as well."

"But only Forever Girls can reincarnate," I say defensively, "and you said that Anna and I both died. How could Anna be here if she died, too, if Cordovae's spirit could only be with one of us?"

Eleanor cuts in before Jessup can respond. "That's what Jessup is trying to tell you," she says. "Your spirit—Cordovae—came back here because you could no longer go forward, but your love also brought Anna with you, without you realizing it. The Universe knew Anna as an infant would not be safe here, where you were needed, so they placed her in another life years before your own. They could not give her to you as a daughter, but they gave her to you as an ally and a friend."

In the far corner of the room, Tess crosses her arms and rolls her eyes. Every so often, she shakes her head; I can see her almost literally biting her tongue. A part of me wants to tell them to stop talking, stop upsetting her, but I need to know more. Need to know if this is all true.

I hadn't noticed Jessup leave the room, but now he is standing beside me with a glass of water. I take it only to be polite, but holding it makes me realize how dry my mouth has gone. I take a tentative sip, unsure my stomach can keep anything down.

"Anna was reincarnated as Tess," Jessup continues. "A five-year-old girl who had died in her sleep due to complications from cholera. But when Tess arrived, with no memories of her own, she was unable to communicate. Her family ignored her. She taught herself how to speak and care for herself, and when she was ten, her guardian was instructed to call for her. After training, the Oracle united her with William. She's been with him for seven years—and then you showed up."

I want so badly to believe this. To hold Tess—my Anna—in a hug that lasts forever. Then I want to wrap my arms around William's neck and press my lips to his cheek and thank him for looking after my little girl. I also want to find the family that had her before and hurt them—badly—for ignoring her.

William's expression seems thoughtful. He steps in closer. "Is this why Tess doesn't have memories from her life before? We thought she had amnesia before arriving and that was why she couldn't remember."

Jessup and Eleanor nod in unison.

It's a beautiful story. A lovely idea. But I can see that Tess has as many doubts as I do. Her agitation is growing, and I know she's about to burst. No one seems to notice her but me, until she plows across the room and pokes Jessup in the chest like he's an annoying little brother who has been pestering her for hours.

"Bullshit!" she screams. "Sorry, Cord, but this can't be true! Think about it! How could you have fragments from your life as Rose if Rose died before you came here, if you are just a reincarnation of Cordovae, a woman from before Rose existed!"

Jessup doesn't flinch. He eases her finger away from his chest. "Cordovae carries memories of all her lifetimes, as do all Forever Girls, and what she remembers is at the discretion of the Universe or her ability to uncover such memories through magic."

"And what good would those memories serve?" Tess challenges him.

Jessup tilts his head. "Cordovae was a part of Rose, and therefore her love for you was just as strong."

"Her love for *Anna*," Tess corrects.

There's a moment where all Jessup does is press his lips together. Composing himself, perhaps. Thinking up another explanation, perhaps. "You don't believe anyone can love you."

Tess scoffs, but then her mouth hangs open, her words stuck in throat.

"You were a carrot on a stick," Jessup says. "Other spirits are only moved, not truly reincarnated. They have memories of the life they will return to in order to keep them connected. Cordovae was...different. There was no life for her to return to this time, and she did not want to fight this war. So she was given her memories from her life as Rose to motivate her, and her memories as her life as Abigail to keep her grounded in the time she was thrown into. But I assure you, Rose and Abigail are both gone, and you, Tess, are Anna."

Tess keeps shaking her head, anger writ on her face. "You are unbelievable."

She shakes her head again and leaves for the kitchen.

Eleanor looks at me with raised eyebrows. "Well?"

"Well, what? I'm not convinced, either. Why can't I remember my life as Cordovae if that is who I really am? I just want to go *home*."

"You *are* home, Cord," Jessup says. "This is your home now. If the Universe gave Forever Girls fragments from all of their precious lives, they would go insane. You remembered what you needed to, and now your life can start anew."

"But Rose knew Cordovae," I argue. "How could she know that then, before all of this? And why didn't the Morts try to possess me as they did my family. Or Rose's family, or whatever it is you are implying."

"Roses family, yes," Eleanor says. She spreads her skirt and sits in a large, winged chair. Her feet don't reach the ground, and her cheeks are rosy pink. I still can't piece together the way they talk with the way they look. "And the Morts of your time didn't take you because they are afraid of Seers, most of them. And that's because of what happened here, in Salem. As for Rose, you—Cordovae—protected her. You came forth to shade her from the abuse. Most girls would have fallen apart at the seams. Killed themselves. Killed the baby. *You* gave her strength."

They have an answer for everything, it seems. A 'logical' explanation, if ever there was any. I have no reason to doubt them any more than I have reason to believe them, but in the end, none of it matters. All that matters is whether Anna is with me. Really and truly. That's all that has ever mattered.

I stare at Tess. Could it be true? Could Tess be...could she *be* Anna?

"I don't remember anything about that life," Tess says angrily from the living room doorway. "Wouldn't I remember now that you're telling me? Something, anything!"

Eleanor perks her eyebrow. "How could you have fragments of a life you were too young to imprint upon? You died as an infant, after all."

Though my belief in this story is increasing—be it because it's true or because I wanted it to be—I still can't help but grieve Anna's loss. At the same time, I understand now the bond I have always felt with Tess, even if she hasn't always felt the same about me.

If all this is true, I haven't stolen Abigail's life as I had feared. And if this is true, my daughter is safe. And with me. Really, truly with me. But what if they've got it all wrong? What if they're lying?

Tess doesn't remember me. She'll never remember me. She's been robbed of her mother, and even if she is here now, I have still been robbed of my daughter. We can never get that life back.

The Universe had been misleading. They said I would get Anna back if I finished this war, but they never told me *this* would be how I got her back. But if this is all true...we can have each other now, and that would keep me alive.

William puts her arm around Tess. "Come on, *say something*."

"Say something?" she asks, pulling away. "What could I possibly say to *this*? It's ridiculous! You can't be buying into this, William, please! Just make them tell her how to go back!"

I shake my head, confused. Why is she so angry about this?

Eleanor's expression goes stony, and she stares at Tess. "We are *not* liars. I'll prove it. Cordovae, sing the song."

My heart tightens. I can't do that. That song was for Anna. Only for Anna.

Eleanor grabs my arm. "You will find no peace if you don't."

I feel the urge stirring in my stomach. Perhaps it is confidence lent to me from Eleanor. Strength. Like a fire in my pit.

The words leave my lips unsteady and unsure, though my heart knows this song inside and out. I mumble the tune.

Better days...ahead, my love...
better days, rest your head, my love.

Better days, when you awake,
we're moving on, moving on, moving along,
and I'll take you there
to better days.
For better days
With you.

Tess' expression falls. She looks disgusted. Does she know the song? Could she remember, somehow? There's only one way to know for sure if she's Anna. I cross the room with such urgency that Tess meets my advance by stepping back.

"Sorry," I whisper, freezing just inches away from her.

She swallows. "Yeah."

"If you are my daughter," I say carefully, "you have a birthmark on your left shoulder. It looks like this—"

I hold my hand out and pull off the fingerless glove that covers my wrist, showing her the pale brown patch of a misshapen heart on the skin above my thumb and forefinger. She stares at it, but says nothing.

"Do you?" I ask.

She gives a non-committal shrug. "Even if Anna did, would I?"

She is looking at me when she asks the question, but then turns her focus to Eleanor and Jessup, as though it is them she is really asking.

Jessup purses his lips. "This is new, even to us," he says, "but in theory, it's possible."

"What does that mean," Tess asks.

"It means," Eleanor says, speaking softly, "that Anna's birthmark could very well be your own, just as Abigail's body carries the mark from Rose."

Everyone in the room is staring at Tess. Nearly crowding her. She's glaring at us, backing away, inching toward the door. William stands in her way.

"No," I say. "Let her go."

He steps aside, and she storms outside.

Jessup touches my arm. "Want us to talk to her?"

I shake my head. "I'll talk to her. Alone."

I stand on the other side of the door, trying to work up the courage to follow her out there. Would me being her mother be such a horrible thing? Does she really hate me that much?

I feel a room full of eyes on my back, and my breath is tight in my chest. Finally I reach for the doorknob, open the door, and step outside. Tess is sitting on the porch, hunched over something.

I sit carefully beside her. She won't look at me, but now I can see what she is holding. Her music box. Slowly, she lifts the lid. Her hands are shaking. The tune begins. My lullaby to Anna. To her. A tear splashes to the small wooden box. I place my hand on her shoulder, but she twists away, and I drop my hand back to my side.

Her gaze slides to mine, her eyes puffy and red. She turns her back to me and slowly pulls her braid over one shoulder. Then she slips a piece of her dress down. And there it is. Right where I remember it. Right on the back of her left shoulder, nearly a carbon copy of my own.

My hand covers my mouth as my jaw drops open.

Tess tugs the shoulder of her dress back up, then glares up at me. "Happy?"

Tears sting my eyes. "Of course I am. I'm just...so glad you're okay."

"Of course I'm okay," she says. "But I'm not Anna, okay?"

But she *is* Anna. In my heart, she always will be. At the same time, we are not who we once were. I can't ask that of her. I don't expect her to call me Mama. Not now, maybe not ever. Having her with me is enough.

"I...know that. I'm—I'm just sorry it turned out this way." I try to summon some kind of motherly wisdom. Try to give her a piece of something I was never able to offer before. "I don't deserve any credit for the woman you've become, but I'm glad you're alive."

It kills me not to just wrap her up in my arms and pull her

against my chest and...be her mother. Like I was supposed to be. But I have to do what is best for her. Which means respecting that she is Tess now. In my heart, she is Anna, but in this life—in the only life she has ever known—she is Tess. I can't take that away from her.

"Disappointed?" she asks, narrowing her eyes at me.

I smile. "Not at all. Are you?"

She doesn't answer, and my heart twists. I am the cause of all of her pain. I am the cause of her deep-seated feelings of abandonment. But I never wanted it that way. Never.

Tess finally shakes her head. "I've been...awful to you."

I want to grab her and hug her, but instead I tentatively reach out and grasp her hand. "Not all the time," I say lightly. "I suppose it's what all good daughters do."

This sparks a smirk from her, and if I'm not mistaken, a breath of a laugh, too. I've never seen her laugh before.

Will Tess be more forgiving of my failures now, or more critical? Or will she ignore our familial connection altogether?

I know this new information changes everything in my heart and in her mind, but it will never change our reality. She will always be Tess. To her, I will always be Cordovae. But she's here. And I know it's her. And if that's all I get in this life, well, I'll take it and breathe it in all the way down to my toes and shut my eyes and say *Thank You* to the powers that be for this small kindness.

Every time I had tried to return to Anna, I had, after all. I'd been with her all along. This stirs up new doubts and fears in my heart. Was I so broken that I hadn't known? That I did not know my own daughter as she stood right by my side? Finally I have succeeded in returning to Anna, and yet, I still fear failure.

Perhaps some part of me had known. I'd felt drawn to William and Tess since I'd first met them: what if it was Tess that I felt the connection to? What if my connection with William was only secondary? Had my love for him sparked independently of the odd magnetic connection that has always tugged me closer to them?

More words choke in the back of my throat. I am seeing Tess

for the first time. I should have seen it sooner. We have the same large, round, pear-green eyes. She's outgrown those gray-blue eyes of infancy after all. And we have the same sleepy eyelids and long lashes. She'd been spared my sinful, fiery hair and my overly-fair skin, but she hasn't escaped me completely.

I haven't lost her, but still I might never truly have her back.

IT HURTS TO CALL TESS BY HER PREFERRED NAME—TO KNOW I will never get to speak Anna's name aloud again, that the name will no longer have any purpose in my life outside of my mind. But I do it. For Tess. Hoping that, someday, this strange feeling leaves my stomach, that the moments with her will one day feel natural again and not strained.

Back in the house, Tess and I sit side by side, stealing glances at one another as the Chibold explain more. Such as that Tess and I are rather close in age. I am only a few years older than I had been prior to being moved here, but she is nearly two decades older than she had been at Anna's birth—*her* birth.

It's the merging of lives, the Chibold explain. Our lives are our own, but we share the memories of the ancestors we have become —of the spirits we share.

William hasn't left where he stands in the corner of the room. He is silent, but his presence comforts me. He is not a river, not an ocean. He is not moving, not going anywhere. He's steady, he's present, he's the mountains, and he's my shelter.

I have Anna, in a way, *and* I have William. So why does sadness still plague me? Am I wrong to grieve the loss of Anna as I knew her, of the dreams I had for her, for us? Dreams of Seaside and cookie-cutter cottages and a small girl running through the yard with ribbons of curly hair trailing behind her on the golden light of an early summer day? Should I not love my daughter for who she has become and not on who I had hoped she should be?

When the sun sets, William, Tess, and I return to the

mountains. There was no ground beneath me the day I fell into this world, but now I am ready to plant my roots, to become a part of this new life. Right here in these mountains.

We stop at a plateau, staring out over a clearing below covered in fresh blooming flowers and scarred by the rushing water of a small river cutting across the heart of the land. The air is thin, fresh, and energizing. Even the family of otters below seem rejuvenated by the arrival of spring.

In the great distance—a distance not so hard to see with my Ankou abilities—Salem's hangings continue. It seems the humans never needed the Maltorim to guide them toward destruction. They have their own morbid reality without any influence from the elemental races. Or, perhaps, the brainwashing of the Malleus Maleficarum has done its job too well.

There is little we can do to save them now—we were never designed to protect humans from themselves. Finally, the time has come to save ourselves. To reclaim who we are outside of the elemental world. In time, I will come to terms with being a Forever Girl. I will acclimate to my new life as an immortal, and I'll build some semblance of a relationship with Tess.

And, one day, so I'm told, I will assist other Forever Girls in a final battle that will once and for all put an end to the treachery of the Maltorim.

For now, though, I have family.

Hundreds of fireflies have taken possession of the clearing, blinking lights of hope ahead of us, each flickering a promise, a dream, a spark of life.

I take Tess' hand, and she gently wraps her fingers around mine. Moments later, William's warm, rough hand comes palm to palm with my own. I lean my head into his bicep. My connection with them is stronger than ever. This is my world, and it's worth saving after all. But this is just the beginning for us.

I take in a deep breath through my nose, allowing myself to fall completely into this new paradigm. Standing here, with William and Tess at my side, I'm weightless, and I finally understand how life is *supposed* to feel. How it feels to be safe, to be loved, to be...*free*.

Join my newsletter for special deals, freebies, and giveaways!
http://www.rebeccahamilton.com/free-books

ABOUT THE AUTHOR

New York Times bestselling author Rebecca Hamilton writes urban fantasy and paranormal romance for Harlequin, Baste Lübbe, and Evershade. A book addict, registered bone marrow donor, and indian food enthusiast, she often takes to fictional worlds to see what perilous situations her characters will find themselves in next.

Represented by Rossano Trentin of TZLA, Rebecca has been published internationally, in three languages: English, German, and Hungarian.

Read More from Rebecca

www.rebeccahamilton.com